Chasing Mayflies

VINCENT DONOVAN

Black Rose Writing | Texas

First printing

ISBN: 978-1-68433-804-7
PUBLISHED BY BLACK ROSE WRITING
www.blackrosewriting.com

Printed in the United States of America
Suggested Retail Price (SRP) $20.95

Chasing Mayflies is printed in Georgia

*As a planet-friendly publisher, Black Rose Writing does its best to eliminate unnecessary waste to reduce paper usage and energy costs, while never compromising the reading experience. As a result, the final word count vs. page count may not meet common expectations.

Cover design by Michael Beaudoin

To my dad, who modeled with humility and courage the purpose and promise of a Christ-filled life. And to my wife, Robin, and daughters, Heather and Taylor, for their constant love and support which sustains me and nourishes dreams no matter how old.

Chasing Mayflies

CHAPTER ONE

The first thing I noticed was the large white ceiling fan. It was one of those nostalgic types, like something straight out of *Casablanca*. "Here's looking at you, kid," I whispered, remembering how my mother recited the line from her favorite movie whenever we said goodbye.

I'm not sure why the fan caught my attention since my best friend of sixty years lay dying in a bed underneath it. But it did, and the distraction irritated me. Its five blades were long and moved in a counterclockwise direction. I watched them pedal backwards for a while and detected a low grinding noise every third revolution. A worn ball bearing was my diagnosis and it provided a momentary distraction in this sorry place.

I sighed and looked down at my lifeless friend and lightly stroked his bony right hand, which felt as cold as Boston Harbor in January. With little effort I could make myself believe this man was an imposter since the Jack Nagle I knew embraced perpetual motion and kept life's accelerator pegged to the floor. Everything he did was fast: enlisted in the Army the day after we graduated in '66, married his high school sweetheart that summer, and came home a decorated Vietnam vet two years later. Yet too much sprinting can also make one prone to muscle tears, and the same held true with Jack. He separated from Sarah a half dozen times before it became permanent due to his love for the ponies. The break with his daughter, Kate, bordered on tragic. Little wonder my friend's favorite song was "I Can't Get No Satisfaction."

The fan blew another cold kiss my way and I hoped when my number was called, I would simply drop dead and avoid death's waiting room. I turned and scanned the well-appointed room decked out with glossy hardwood floors, tray ceiling, cherry nightstands, and even a tan leather recliner in the corner. Absent were the usual medical devices with their beeping and whirring noises. Except for the standard-issue hospital bed, the room looked more like a furniture showroom than a hospice and even had the lemony smell of an air freshener hidden somewhere nearby. I picked up a brass table lamp from the nightstand to see if there were any price tags hanging inside the herringbone lamp shade or attached to the green felt base, wishing I could just slap a FedEx label on Jack and ship him home. But good ol' Stuart, Jack's brother, made these final arrangements. Knowing him, I questioned if his motivation was out of love or fear he might lose a few nights' sleep keeping watch.

"I hear her coming."

I almost dropped the lamp. Jack opened one eye and looked toward the door behind me.

"Who?"

"Nurse Nancy. She's the drug queen for death row."

"What?" There were steps behind me.

"Hurry up and get rid of her." Jack went back to playing dead.

A plump middle-aged nurse in white garb entered studying a small disposable syringe.

"Oh, I didn't know he had company," she said without looking up.

"His name is Jack," I replied quickly. Like my aging body, the muscles were getting lax in my tongue too. Being a senior meant I could say almost anything and get away with it. I studied her black punk haircut and wondered how she defined a bad hair day.

"Are you going to be here long?" She continued inspecting Jack and began taking his pulse.

"And my name is Dennis Sullivan," I said loudly and looked down at Jack. It surprised me when Stu called last night with the sad news, although it hurt to know he'd been terminal for the past six months and never called. I figured Jack was probably too embarrassed to contact me after he went AWOL when my wife, Merriam, got ill. But I decided to be the bigger man today and take a break from packing and stop in to say my goodbyes, knowing heaven would never grant the time required to put things right between us. At least I would be able to attend his funeral before moving west to live with my son Mark.

"Well, he's due for morphine," she said to the plastic syringe. "But it will make him sleepy if you're going to stay awhile."

"Sleepy? He looks comatose to me." I studied his boulder-sized head and the few patches of turf cropped short and white as snow; the decades of dyeing it black had finally succumbed to all the chemo. His face had a yellowish tinge and the ruddy complexion I first met in grammar school belonged to some other kid now. I wondered if I imagined the previous apparition.

The nurse checked her digital watch attached to a thick leather band strangling a pasty plump wrist. My eyes continued down to her extended fingers with visible dirt under three bitten nails.

"Okay, I'll come back in an hour. And it's nice he has some happy company for a change." She turned to leave and I noticed the hem of her pants was much too long and swept the floor.

I began to follow her, wanting to ask more questions, but lost the motivation and counted off a dozen steps to French doors leading from the bedroom onto a small patio and a good-sized yard lined with tall pine trees. Dark clouds continued their three-day siege with a barrage of pelting rain attempting to reclaim the region for spring. The campaign thus far proved successful. Less than a week ago, the region remained buried under half a foot of snow. But today's rain combined with temperatures in the forties produced a fog above the remaining snow warriors as they slowly expired. However, the cost of the three-month occupation proved significant. A half dozen pine branches littered the ground and the color of the grass resembled a patchwork of old guacamole and cornmeal.

I took a new pack of Juicy Fruit gum out of my pocket and focused on its happy yellow and blue packaging for a moment, hungry for color after weeks of staring at a monochromatic landscape. Carefully unwrapping a piece, I savored Wrigley's mystery flavor, which was an interesting cross between peach, pineapple, and banana.

"Is she gone?" a raspy voice suddenly called out.

I swung around and the terminal cancer patient had one eye open and glaring at me in obvious discomfort. Guilt welled up and made me panic.

"The nurse was just here with your morphine," I said, bolting for the door. "I'll run and get her."

My buddy sprang up in bed like a true jack-in-the-box. "Shhhh!" he hissed, holding up a bony finger. His large meatball eyes were open wide and looking past me. "Quick, close the door."

My friend had always been a bit melodramatic, but given his condition, I gave him a pass. My stomach ached and I knew I should have tracked down my best friend even though the estrangement was all his fault. I prepared for a final tongue lashing and decided to resist the urge to blow the accusations right back at him. After all, where was he when I lost Merriam a year ago? All I received was a crummy sympathy card with a Tampa postmark and the standard *sorry for your loss* condolence scribbled in blue ink probably between races. The envelope contained no return address, probably because it originated from some run-down hotel as he barnstormed through the south. God forgive him, I thought, knowing that prayer was a substantial plea. Even so, I would gladly trade my Judgment Day with his in a second, but now wasn't the time to dwell on that.

I obeyed his command and quietly closed the large oak door. Returning to his side, I thought it best to be preemptive in order to clear the air.

"Look, I'm sorry I haven't been here for you," I said to the nightstand. When I had the courage to look at him again, a bony digit was pointed at my chest.

"What do you think you're doing? Going to confession? Yeah, I'm mad about a lot of things, but we don't have time for that now." He looked toward the door again. "Did you see anyone out there?"

"No, the hall is empty. Actually, this whole wing looks like a morgue." My cheeks turned hot. Did I really say that?

Jack didn't notice the gaffe. "That's good," he sighed, sinking back in the bed and finally taking full stock of me. "Dennis, we have been the best of friends our entire life."

I nodded and looked around for a box of tissues and of course there wasn't any in this fake furniture store. Maybe that was on purpose too. That way they never had to wash the floors. They just mopped up the tears. I reached in my pocket to lend Jack my starched white handkerchief in case he broke down. It would be weird to see him cry now, since the last time was in third grade when he took one hell of a punch from a neighborhood bully three years older.

"I have a favor to ask."

"Sure, buddy, anything at all," I replied. Jack knew I hated animals, but if he asked, I would adopt his black feral cat named Lucky. I would never let the dirty little hairball sleep with me, but I'd take her in until I moved. Then maybe one of the neighborhood kids would adopt her.

My best friend smiled liked he did whenever I became Silly Putty in his hands, which was nearly always, and he took great glee in deciding whether to stretch or bounce me.

"I knew I could count on you." His hand reached up and pulled me in close and his breath smelled like rotten eggs. "Denny, you gotta break me out of here!"

CHAPTER TWO

"I can't imagine what you're going through," I whispered. "But I'm here now."

My friend let out a hoarse laugh that sounded like an old car trying to start on a frigid morning and slapped his barrel-sized chest, which mysteriously still looked immune to the lung cancer wasting everything else on him. "Easy for you to say; you're not the one lying here dying," he said, then paused to catch his breath while giving me a once-over. "Denny, you've always been like a chameleon blending in with your surroundings. Since you're in a perfectly ironed white shirt, black dress pants, and wingtip shoes, I'm guessing you're interviewing for a position here. Kudos for having their lingo down too. Maybe I can put in a good word and get you assigned bedpan duty, though I know how easy you turn green when you smell something nasty. He shot a quick smile, apparently pleased with his wit. "But if you're still determined, take some advice from me and lose the tie in case something splatters."

"If you didn't enjoy using that fat head of yours to ram into my stomach whenever we were supposed to be playing touch football, you'd remember clothes say a lot about a man. I guess that explains why you lived in flannel shirts and frayed dungarees," I replied in machine-gun fashion, amazed how you don't see someone for years and still pick up where you left off. I wanted to remind him I quit being called Denny in the fifth grade too. Instead, I kept my hands busy stroking my spotless red silk tie.

Jack scanned the closed door and listened for a long moment. "I need you to get me out of here," he whispered real fast. "I have to take care of a few things."

I figured the pain killers were doing the talking.

A scrawny hand rich with liver spots motioned for me to lean in close. "There's a camera directly behind you mounted in the ceiling. That's how they monitor me day and night."

I rubbed my chin, unsure whether to play along or try to explain the hallucination. Unable to decide, I smiled and slowly backed away and scanned the ceiling. Yes, there was a small black box in the ceiling panel with what looked like a tiny aperture, but it resembled a fire alarm more than a snooping device. Poor guy. Paranoia must be a side effect of the powerful meds.

"Look in the closet," Jack said and began flashing signs like a catcher calling for a fastball low and inside. "My clothes are in there. If we hurry, we can escape before Nurse Nancy comes back with another dose of happiness."

So what if it was a camera? After all, the nurses had to know if a patient experienced distress, as most were too sick to call or push a button. If that was the case, they would see my buddy pretty agitated at the moment and would be down any second with the syringe.

Jack suddenly frowned. "Are you still driving that living room on wheels?"

I leaned in and braced for the coming attack. "I never understood why you didn't like my Cadillac. Its suspension system makes you feel like you're riding on a magic carpet."

"Don't give me that marketing mumbo jumbo. You only bought it for the prestige so people would think you were someone important like a doctor or lawyer and fawn all over you. When they found out you sold vacuum cleaners at Wayne's Appliance Store, probably not so much."

"I sold washing machines too."

"Vacuums, washers, they both deal with dirt, don't they? And such a noble profession, I might add," he said with a wink. "I know you had to do something easier after getting fired from that awful car dealership and then having a meltdown of sorts. But I never expected you to stay for a lifetime."

"Thirty-six years," I said happily and glanced up at the ceiling fan again. It was the third Monday in March and in New Hampshire, the blades should be warming the room instead of producing a wind chill. Then I realized the fan might be set on reverse for a reason. After all, why would anyone on their death bed want to watch those blades go round and round to mark each passing hour as the countdown for the big reveal ahead? No, it was much better to have the fan subliminally encourage the dying to look back on a lifetime of memories even if it included reminiscing about all my troubles.

I glanced over at a black-faced clock hanging on the wall opposite the recliner in the corner, which allowed family members to rest and keep track of the vigil. "Selling cars never appealed to me, but I needed a job to put food on the table. My father was a selectman in town and the owner of Henley Dodge owed him a huge favor for approving a variance." I tugged on my right ear lobe but couldn't stop my father's booming voice even after all these years. *"Now, you have the ball, son. Don't let me down."*

I faked a cough to silence my father. "All I can say is it's nearly impossible to sell muscle cars when the price of gas doubles overnight if you can find any at all. Lucky for me I left Henley's during that recession because they went under after the next energy crisis five years later. Ironically, there's a gas station on the site now and they sell toy cars and trucks. My only wish is they sold little plastic dolls that looked like my old sales manager at Henley's, Frank Riley. I'd place a standing order just to begin every day by running over that little bald man with his big eyes and little nose."

"Glad you don't hold a grudge."

I laughed. "Okay, so pistons, wheel bearings, and disc brakes were over my head, but at least I know what a nice car feels like. You, on the other hand, wasted whatever money you made and could only afford *Flintstones* cars."

"At least I didn't need air conditioning in the summer. All I had to do was drive through a puddle to cool my feet."

I glared at him, and he back at me. I could still hear the laughter which regularly overflowed its banks in our youth. Too bad we didn't store any in canteens for when the silence came.

I was the first one to crack a smile. "It's been too long, buddy."

"Yes, much too long." Jack reached out to shake my hand.

I grabbed it and held on tight, enjoying a few seconds in the warm sun. Jack always lived in the moment and had a very short fuse. He would sometimes blow at the smallest annoyance, but just as quickly the clouds would depart and all would be forgotten. And if you tried to reminisce with Jack about one of his little hissy fits, he punched you hard enough in the arm to make you drop it.

I shook my head and studied the man in the bed. With trees, you could cut them open and study their growth rings and identify seasons of want and plenty. No axe was needed to read my buddy. The deep furrow across his forehead reminded me of the no-fly zone from the first Gulf War. Combined with the puffy pillows under his eyes, they were tell-tale signs of some hard living. Not that I would ever follow in Jack LaLanne's footsteps and become a fitness superhero and live to ninety-six. Strip off the dress shirt and pants and my middle looked like a bicycle tire losing air fast.

"Here's some late breaking news. Mark finally convinced me to sell the house and move out west to be near him. He's arriving this week to help me pack so I'll have a California tan soon and spend my days humming Beach Boys tunes."

"You're lucky I'm incarcerated here because I'm two inches taller than you and the girls always said my eyes looked like chocolate cake. Crayola should have named a crayon color after me," he said matter of fact then yawned. "Okay, enough small talk. Are you going to get me my clothes or what?"

I turned and mouthed "Help me" at the small eye in the ceiling. Standing there, I resolved when my time expired, I'd sit in a lawn chair in Napa Valley and enjoy a nice bottle of wine. Too bad I couldn't bring the maple tree I planted the year my son was born. Both grew fast like bamboo and Mark turned thirty-five three weeks ago.

"So what are you standing there for?"

"Don't you think we should call your brother first?" I asked, hoping if I stalled he might forget the absurd request. I was feeling disgusted Stu should even be consulted. After all, it was Stu who had campaigned hard to have his brother admitted into Restful Waters even though the facility targeted a "high turnover rate" with the average stay lasting three days. The fact Jack might not expire for a week gave the hospice pause and made his brother frantic. He had few choices. Sarah hadn't talked to him since the Berlin Wall fell, and the last time his daughter said she loved him was when the Y2K panic gripped the planet. As it stood, Stu and I were the only ones who gave a hoot; or at least I didn't pretend to.

Jack scratched his left arm dotted with small purple contusions. Minus the bruises, the skin looked encased in a thin layer of plastic wrap. He pointed at the closet again. "Bet you'd like to tuck me in right now and wave goodbye and get back to packing for the move, but that's not happening."

I whipped out my black iPhone and noticed two missed calls from Mark. Three thousand miles away and my son insisted on checking in every day. In the beginning it was sweet; now it felt like long-distance babysitting. "I'm going to dial your brother."

My friend cut the air hard and accidentally launched the lamp from the nightstand. When it landed it skated across the shiny hardwood floor. The light bulb shattered and left a trail of glass slivers.

But flying objects and crashing noises could not distract the veteran soldier and teacher. "Stu has been MIA for the last day." The angry look quickly turned desperate. He reached under the white sheet and pulled out a beat up silver flip phone. "And I leave message after message and still no call back."

Suddenly, the frail man swung himself out of bed and tried to stand up. His legs were the color of dirty chalk and hairless. The pastel green hospital gown reminded me of the ugly wallpaper my mother had in her bathroom for twenty-five years.

I jumped forward and caught him just before he hit the floor. He weighed only a hundred forty pounds at most, but his unsteadiness was catchy. I began to sway trying to hold him up.

"Too dizzy," he whispered to himself as I helped him back into bed.

"It's all the meds they pump into me. Nurses here have the easiest job in the world. They juice you up good and plenty after lunch so they can watch their shows all afternoon."

"C'mon, buddy, that's not fair," I said. "Look. They're just trying to make you comfortable."

"Yeah, like a dead man."

I undid the top button of my shirt and loosened the tie. "You can be such a pain in the butt that if I did work here, I'd have you on automatic refill." I slapped the metal bed railing like a drum and enjoyed the low hum.

The joke was dead on arrival and he looked past me.

"When you came in how many rooms did you walk by?" he asked, changing the subject.

"I don't know; maybe twenty or so. Why?"

"I never hear anyone."

"You said you need to take care of a few things?" I asked, steering the conversation back on course.

He bit his lip but didn't answer.

"Okay, I won't push if you don't want to talk about it. But if you change your mind, just tell me and I promise to take care of it for you." I looked down and listened for the sound of a click to confirm I'd stepped on a booby trap.

Another laugh followed; this one longer than the one before and only stopped by a coughing spell. "I wish I could, Dennis, I really do. Unfortunately, this task is all on me. But you can help me though."

"How?"

He pointed toward the closed door. "If you won't help me escape, the least you can do is cause some sort of distraction in the hall while I sneak out the back. Maybe you can show the staff your webbed toes. They used to gross out all the girls when we went to the beach."

I laughed and stroked his bony shoulder. "Why don't we just stay here and reminisce about all the good times we had together. There's no need to dwell on things left undone. Everything will be okay."

I expected resignation to finally set in. My friend never admitted when I was right and would simply change the topic like a toy kaleidoscope changing scenes.

"Now, listen to me really good, Denny," he said as his face suddenly reddened. "I'm not done living, so don't go writing my obituary just yet. I'm going to be dead a long time and I can't leave until certain things are taken care of." He pounded on the bed rail hard and the entire bed shook. "That's why I asked Stu to call you after he deposited me here. Not that I would expect you to understand because you were always the guy with a plan. You wouldn't buy a house, a car, or heck, a six pack of beer unless it fit within your budget and all those stupid little manila envelopes your wife fed every payday. And how did all that incessant counting work out for you, Denny?" he asked. "Your wife is dead, your son's out west, and your best friend is hours away from being plowed under." He paused to catch his breath. "Me? I planned for zero, zip, zilch, nada. And I never looked back because the disappointment would have consumed me like the maggots plan to do soon. It didn't matter whether it was saying goodbye to my shop class every June or when the missus left me for the last time. Same held true when Kate disowned me." He shook his head slowly. "We took separate roads, but I never would have bet we'd end up in the same sorry place."

I looked around the room, suddenly happy with my lot in life. "Hey, it's all a crap shoot once you get to be our age. The average lifespan might be eighty years, but you know what Yogi Berra said: 'It's tough to make predictions, especially about the future.' I realize I'm the lucky one standing here."

"Yeah, but we're both alone."

The wave broke over me and I forgot to close my mouth and coughed. "I disagree with every syllable," I whispered. "You never reached for the pity pot before, so why start now?" I searched for my gum and found it parked as always between my second molar and cheek and gave a long chew. "What do you want me to say?"

"I don't want you to say anything. Instead of all this yakking about accepting the status quo, I want you to get mad like me," and pointed toward the door.

"What do you mean?"

His face relaxed a bit as he drank in the rain. "When we were kids we would start planning our spring camping trip in March. Remember?"

"Sure," I replied, hoping for some easier conversation.

"Besides the weather, do you remember the mayflies?"

I ducked and started swatting the air with both hands. "Every spring those tiny black flies were like the birds from the Hitchcock movie. We used to pull our T-shirts over our heads to hide from the beasts and when that didn't work, tried to outrun them."

Jack smiled. The picket fence teeth were crooked and looked too large for the gaunt face. "Yeah, I've been thinking about them a lot. Their life span is only a few weeks at most and they're at the mercy of the wind. But they're like tiny kamikazes attacking your eyes, taking a bite out of your scalp and almost making you wish for winter again," he said, suddenly animated. "They live for today, but make you remember them forever."

He pointed at the eye in the ceiling as his face became red. "Chasing mayflies, that's my new mantra. I want to be just like them and you should too."

I was astonished at the sudden performance and didn't know what to say.

Jack took a deep breath and his eyes became moist. "Like the mayflies, I have to fly now before the wind picks up. You owe me that much, Denny. You know you do."

I nodded and looked outside. The rain knocked hard on the French doors. Winter was dying and so was my best friend.

"Hey, the real storm is in here. Are you going to help me or what?"

CHAPTER THREE

I ignored Jack's pleading and backed away. He punched his pancake pillow and rolled onto his side so I could converse with his bony butt. There was a glossy booklet on the nightstand and I picked it up. Its cover featured a peaceful river meandering through a lush green valley with a complementary flowing caption in lemon yellow: "Welcome to Restful Waters." The only thing missing was the rainbow.

`The hospice was located on busy Route 28 in Salem, New Hampshire, not to be confused with the other namesake where they burned witches. Salem, New Hampshire, was a town of about thirty thousand and located right over the Massachusetts border, a half hour north of Boston. The town was the gateway to Live Free or Die New Hampshire and a shopping mecca with no sales tax and cheap cigarettes and booze. I imagined the Grim Reaper in a beat up rowboat peddling spare ribs, sweet tea, and durian stinky fruit—cash only—to the newly departed as they drifted down the dark waters of Spicket River out back. Intrigued, I put on my reading glasses and scanned the first page to find reality. *"Your guide to end of life care,"* it promised. A sweet thirty-something blonde that could turn a head even at my age graced the opposite page. I noticed the photo was cropped so you couldn't see the six-pack of morphine she was holding.

It was pretty late before the pain reached a threshold that humbled a proud soldier. Nurse Nancy finally reappeared and dispensed the contents from a small syringe under his tongue. In short order, Jack began drifting in and out of consciousness before settling into a troubled state, not to be confused with sleep.

The nurse suggested I go home and get some rest and I begged her to call me if his condition worsened. She lectured me in a tired and rehearsed manner that my best friend might remain like this for a few days—then in the next breath, said things could change as suddenly as New England weather. Spoken like a meteorologist trying to hedge her bets. I watched her shuffle away with the soiled hem of her pants dragging behind.

"Goodnight, Pigpen," I whispered.

***

The ride home to Windham was only ten miles up Route 111, a fifty-mile east-west highway which weaved through southeastern New Hampshire. In the summer it wasn't unusual to have a motorcycle on your butt because some kid thought he was invincible and wanted to feel the wind in his hair as no helmets were required in the Granite State. Unfortunately, you needed a head of rock to survive an accident too. But tonight the road shivered alone. The rain finally stopped and the gauge on the dashboard indicated the temperature had plunged to twenty-five degrees so I crawled along on the watch for black ice—the real bogeyman in these parts. The radio didn't help in distracting my thoughts as some talking head ranted about an upcoming election my friend would never live to see. I scanned the FM stations for a favorite tune. The time capsule of my generation was limited to a couple of oldies stations and they were honoring the Beatles again. Any other day and I would have surrendered to the silence, but I continued to listen anyway, needing to drown out Jack's desperate plea.

When I finally made it home, the stench of fried haddock from lunch permeated the kitchen. It got me thinking about rotting fish and the mores we have in place to delay decomposition by embalming loved ones. I didn't know if Jack wanted to be buried or cremated and wondered if Stu had cared enough to ask.

If Merriam were alive she would have lit a vanilla candle to chase away the nasty smell and my repugnant thoughts. Regrettably, the only candles I owned were small votive types in case a storm knocked out the power. So I struggled with the kitchen window with the blown seal, and let the cold March air rush by me while I listened for the first cricket. How I longed for the return of that evening symphony which had sustained me through the first months after Merriam died. It wasn't until the frost came last October that I finally understood how deafening silence could really be. At Christmas, Mark and his new girlfriend gave me some newfangled recordings of outside noises: wind, rain, and frogs croaking.

It was like watering plastic flowers and just as useless.

The cold air felt good after baking for hours in the hospice. "A few more weeks yet," I said, closing the window and realizing Jack would never hear crickets again.

The blinking red light on the outdated answering machine suddenly caught my attention. Either Mark was aggravated I didn't answer the phone or Jack passed away before I made it home. I retrieved the message, listening to Stuart urging me to call him back.

The phone rang and rang and I recalled Jack complaining he could never reach his brother. I was about to hang up when it finally clicked.

"How is he?" Stu asked in a high-pitched voice that for some reason had never graduated from puberty.

Even if you had caller identification, wasn't it courtesy to say hello first? "Jack is having a pretty rough time," I replied. "And he says he's been trying to reach you." I leaned against the side of the maple china cabinet, expecting a long conversation.

"Guess they have him so drugged up he doesn't remember we checked him in yesterday and I visited early this morning. Then again, my brother never minded a clock unless running to place a bet."

Jack did chase the ponies. And in this vice, he embraced the philosophy of "fail forward fast," even before it became a cool management cliché. I always thought maybe you need that type of outlook to forget about the beating you took yesterday in order to have the courage to double down on today's trifecta. "What time were you there today?"

Jack's brother sighed. "Check the sign-in register if you don't believe me. You should also swing by the Salem police station. Seems my brother visited a couple of banks last week trying to secure a ten-thousand-dollar loan. When he was denied he made some nasty

16

threats. Good thing he's on his way out or he'd have some additional company to while away the hours."

Jack had the same relationship with money he had with women: both were troubled. Nonetheless, begging for a loan while terminally ill? "Why did he need the money?"

"C'mon, Dennis, you know him better than that. He probably wanted one final day at the track with his bookie." Stu sounded bored by it all. "Do you know how many people I had to call to get him into RW?"

"RW?"

"Restful Waters is the only hospice within fifty miles. And if you haven't noticed from the obituary page, a lot of people are dying."

I wanted to laugh imagining Stu doing a statistical analysis on the death rate in New Hampshire. What did he do, look for an opportunity to place his brother at the hospice when there was a dip in the death futures? The only other outlandish explanation was that he forced some other poor slob to postpone an upcoming stroke so Jack could get admitted. "You can't be serious," I replied, fighting to contain a chuckle. A dust kitty clinging to the leg of the pine coffee table caught my attention and I made a mental note to vacuum tomorrow.

"You might think I'm nuts, but it's true," he continued. "There's nothing sinister involved here, just pure demographics really. Up until a few years ago, a lot of folks retired and moved south into retirement communities designed to handle end of life logistics. That was fine since the remaining Yankee stock around here expired at a fairly constant rate, with the exception of a severe flu season every now and then. Now the baby boomers are aging and many too broke to stop working, never mind retire someplace else. Unfortunately, the system is becoming overloaded because we don't have the necessary infrastructure. Ten years younger and I'd open a combo hospice and funeral home and make a bundle advertising the efficiency."

I rubbed the back of my neck and it occurred to me again why I never liked Jack's older brother. Besides being a know-it-all, he was a caustic human being. Luckily, a career in sales trained me how to redirect the conversation. I began pacing around the living room and frowned as I passed the dark brown bonded leather couch and matching recliner. Mark grew up on that couch watching the Red Sox, Patriots, Bruins, and Celtics pursue championships. Now he dismissed his favorite perch as fake vinyl and destined for the dump.

"Jack says he wants to leave hospice."

A brief silence followed by a shorter laugh. "And go where, may I ask?"

I took a deep breath because closing this sale would be hard, but I had mulled over the options on the ride home. "You have a good-sized colonial and could make him pretty comfortable in the family room. I would be happy to stay and help if you like. The way I see it, maybe if Jack's in familiar surroundings it might help him let go. I know how much it would mean to him to be with family when he passes."

"Are you sure we're talking about the same man? My brother is so cold they wouldn't need any liquid nitrogen if he wanted to be cryopreserved. Come to think of it, I'm surprised he didn't ask. A few millenniums in limbo would give him enough time to develop some fail-safe gambling schemes."

"Stu, that's not fair—"

"Look," he said, cutting me off. "Jack has never shown any appreciation for anything I've ever done for him. God forgive me, but it will be a relief when he finally croaks. When he showed up at my door last year after losing what little he had left, I called in a favor to get him into a low-income rental. When he couldn't ignore the painful cough any longer and was diagnosed with lung cancer, it was me who carted him back and forth to Lahey Clinic in Burlington every week for chemo." Stuart breathed into the phone like an overheated dragon. "I'm supposed to be enjoying retirement, you know."

I stopped pacing.

"Did he put you up to this?" Stuart said.

"No," I replied, scanning the worn wall-to-wall gray carpeting. When it was first installed, Merriam and I would hold hands and flex our toes in the thick pile and laugh. Now she was gone and the carpeting had the cushiness of a worn out pair of sneakers. I toyed with selling the house after she died and Mark used that small opening to push, plead, and cajole me to join him out west. If he hadn't decided on pursuing law, he would have had a superb career in sales. As much as I valued independence, he simply wore me down with his incessant comments on how the yard was too big, the heating bill enormous, and how I needed protection like some endangered creature.

I sat down on the couch and a worn spring groaned. My next suggestion would really anger my son because it might delay his detailed plans of packing up the house this week. "Listen, Stu. My place is small, but I'd be happy to have Jack come here if you like. I could put a hospital bed in the living room and make it work for a few days." I bit my lip, remembering how belligerent my buddy acted earlier today.

"Okay, that's quite enough." Stuart said with a rising voice. "You two haven't spoken in years and now you want to fly in and play hero? No way."

If I could have reached through the phone, the police would have arrested me for attempted murder as I pulled off his fast talking lips. "This 'ghost' spent his time taking care of his dying wife and dealing with the aftermath. So stop playing the prima donna for once and think about your brother."

"My brother is through calling the shots, Dennis. I had to prepay for a week at the hospice and it's non-refundable if he checks himself out. I'll talk to his doctor tomorrow and request they up his meds to deal with the anxiety."

Now I knew where Jack learned to never apologize and just move on. Nice family trait and probably what cost both of them their marriages. I had pretty harsh words lined up on my tongue, but decided to save them for after the funeral.

Stu read my silence. "Look, there's no reason to make this difficult between us. Actually, if there's anyone I'm ticked off at, it's his daughter. As with everything else, I'm the one footing the bill and it's costing me three grand a day. And Kate won't contribute one red cent. She's just as irresponsible as her old man." He let out a short cough and it reminded me of Jack minus the cancer. "With my luck, he'll hang on and live for another month just to bankrupt me."

A woman in the background called his name. No doubt, some new girl he met on the internet.

"Look, I have to go. I have steak on the grill and my honey hates it well done."

"Then her stomach will really turn when she discovers you're rotting from the inside out." I hung up and walked down the short hall to the bathroom. After splashing cold water on my face, I looked in the oval mirror. Gray hair surfed the top of my ears and I resembled an aging Chia Pet gone wild. If I didn't get a haircut before Mark arrived on Friday, he would use it as another example of how I couldn't take care of myself. And if I told Merriam what I decided to do tomorrow, she would remind me I had flashes of brilliance between long bouts of stupidity. I wasn't sure which category this decision belonged in, but knew Mark would be angry. He could never understand the debt I owed my best friend.

Jack said mayflies bite and Stu would feel the first sting.

CHAPTER FOUR

A petite middle-aged woman with shoulder-length auburn hair eyed me up and down. She wore sunglasses on the top of her head, which made me wonder if it was a fashion statement or intermittent sensitivity to the bright fluorescent lighting. Twenty years ago, I might have thought the receptionist was checking me out and my cheeks would have turned red. But at my age and this address, I wanted to simply assure her I had a few more good years left before being measured for a wooden box. Age might relax lips and stomachs, but this time I managed to keep the comment in. However, if she called me "sweetie" or "honey," all bets were off. Given my mood this morning, I would be tempted to take out my front partial and gum her to death if she did. I felt good and ornery after trying to psych myself up all night for what I was going to attempt, knowing the roaring lion at midnight is sometimes nothing more than a cowering kitten at sunrise. Was I really prepared to become "Dennis, Senior Action Hero"?

I got a whiff of her lilac perfume and fought off a cough. I signed the visitor register for Tuesday and felt the receptionist watching me. A simple smile or a throwaway comment on the weather would have put me at ease. But her lips remained horizontal and I decided she was either a joyless soul, or saved her pearly whites for the inmates. I felt up to the challenge and returned a blank look. Her hazel eyes were caked with too much mascara and didn't blink.

"How long has it been since your last vacation?" I asked, which usually worked to get a reaction.

She glanced down at my signature, which I scribbled on purpose. A digital clock beside her on a cherry credenza read 10:02 a.m. and she filled in the exact time. I had skipped it on purpose and almost signed in as John Doe, but it was senseless to hide behind an alias. Once we escaped, I would have my picture hung on their wall of infamy for sure.

"Are you immediate family?" she asked, bored.

"I like to think so," I replied matter of fact. "He's been like a brother to me most of my life." Soft elevator music radiated from the ceiling and began an instrumental version of "Fire and Rain."

She turned the book to read who I was visiting and finally cracked a smile. Her reaction surprised me. It had been decades since Jack had been the catalyst for joy.

"Oh, you're here to see Mr. Nagle. I'm glad."

I knew better than to leave a trail, but couldn't help myself. "Why do you say that?"

"Well, for starters, he thinks he knows everybody. When he first arrived, he took one look at me and yelled out: Hey, I know you! Jack had me guessing all afternoon until I heard he said the same thing to the janitor. He's quite a character," she said with a chuckle. "At first, I thought it was his shtick to make friends quick, until a nurse told me the cancer spread to his brain and that's how it's manifesting itself. How sad, yet so endearing."

It seemed unbelievable a stranger would know more about his condition than me and actually sit there and blab about it. I looked at the register and scanned the entries. "Was his brother, Stuart, here yesterday?"

The overcast look returned and she adjusted the sunglasses. "Sorry, I can't answer that. Patient confidentiality, you know."

"Seriously?" I shook my head and started to walk away.

"It's Ruth," she called after me. From her tone, I figured she wanted me to remember her name when I received a customer satisfaction survey after Jack died.

When I reached his room, a new nurse was examining his sorry-looking legs. She looked about sixty-five with high bouffant white hair. Jack, never one to be shy, stared off into space like he wanted to be anywhere else than here. He didn't acknowledge me and I had a

VINCENT DONOVAN

flashback to Merriam's last days. For all we knew, his gaze found a landscape only the dying could see.

"How is he?" I whispered.

She looked bored and quickly covered his legs with a thin blue blanket. "Well, he's not done yet."

"He's not some turkey you're stuffing," I replied quickly before realizing today was not the time to get into an argument.

Thankfully, she had the same bad manners as Nurse Nancy and ignored me. "How's the pain, honey?" she asked Jack.

Jack nodded slightly and I winced. If he was feeling himself, he would have picked up from yesterday and launched a scud missile.

The nurse checked her diamond-studded watch. "I'll bring your meds in another hour when I come back from running some errands. In the meantime, Nurse Nancy is down the hall if you need anything." She gave me the same blank stare as the receptionist and turned to leave. At least this one had hemmed pants and clean nails.

I looked around at the immaculate surroundings. The sun streamed in through the French doors and highlighted the sterile container. Sure, the walls were painted a pretty light yellow but they had no pictures or religious markings whatsoever to provide comfort. I looked at the empty nightstand. There wasn't even a pitcher or glass.

"What did my friend have for breakfast?"

"Eat?" Nurse Big-Hair-Betty pointed toward the nightstand. "If you read the guide, you'll learn most don't want to."

I bit my tongue, wanting to tell her how my Merriam enjoyed a bowl of fish chowder and Italian bread the night before she died. I wasn't so naïve to think patients expected three meals a day, but this place was looking more like a pretty concentration camp. My friend's lips looked dry and chapped. Ice chips would sure help.

The nurse left and I returned to my mission. We had a short time window to work in, but I had expected to find the same man I left yesterday. I recalled the conversation with Stu and how he planned to call the doctor and up his meds. As usual procrastination erased my best laid plans.

"Jack," I whispered urgently, wondering if the angst I felt all night might have been needless.

The big head remained fixed on the white pancake pillow but he opened his eyes and gave me a scowl. "I'm exhausted and they won't let me get any real sleep. Whenever I do start to drift off, another nurse comes in and launches me to Jupiter. When I finally make it back to earth, my mouth is a desert and guess who's waiting with another syringe?" Jack picked at the piece of loose skin on his bottom lip. "And to make matters worse, the morphine tastes as bitter as baker's chocolate. They shoot it under my tongue and when I ask for a chaser to wash it down they just smile and walk away. The least they could do is give me a glass of Tang if I'm going to be an astronaut."

I glanced at the open door. "I thought about what you said yesterday."

He nodded. "Hoped you would."

The camera caught my attention again. I learned the hard way that once you make up your mind, quick execution is critical before second-guessing sets in. The best example was stopping on multiple occasions to assist a painted or snapping turtle crossing the street. No matter how many times I attempted to be the hero, they all ended up like smashed pumpkins when I hesitated stepping into the traffic. I never saved one. It got to the point where I wouldn't stop anymore, knowing I was despised throughout turtle land. Jack's Achilles' heel might be rashness; mine had always been overthinking things.

I quickly closed the door, then spit out the Juicy Fruit gum I worked on all morning and stretched it carefully cover the camera's eye. The chewing gum refused to stick at first and I moistened my index finger with some additional spit to use as cement. The wet compress finally worked.

Jack watched me play a scene out of *MacGyver* and smirked. It was a welcome change from the expressionless stare I first encountered.

"If you want a bed in here you know you have to be dying, right?" he said with a short laugh. "Fortunately for you, all the mental hospitals have closed."

"Yeah, I'm nuts, all right." Opening the closet, I found my friend still traveled light: one red tartan plaid shirt, tan chinos, black belt, and an old pair of white bulbous sneakers. On the top shelf sat a lonely white bottle of Old Spice cologne. "Where's your coat?"

"Didn't really think I would need one again," he replied with a smirk. "When you leave here, it's in a nice black plastic body bag that keeps out the weather just like an expensive raincoat, but at a tenth of the price."

He had a point, so I didn't push the issue. Turning around, I found him still lying in bed watching me taking inventory.

"Good grief, man, you're killing me. Do you want to get out of here or what?"

Jack didn't move. "Why did you change your mind?" he asked. "Did you get religion last night or something? Last time I saw a conversion like this was when you voted for McGovern in seventy-two and we know how that turned out." His brown eyes drilled into me. "I thought your better half was the one with faith."

This was not the time to explain my motivation so I pulled the sheet off him and threw it on the floor, afraid I underestimated the effort needed. Even though I'd doubled the project plan estimates on the ride over, I quickly realized I should have tripled the time to get my buddy dressed.

My friend suddenly grabbed my shoulder. "Are you okay?" he asked.

"What are you talking about?"

"Your forehead has red welts all over it and I've been watching them grow since you arrived."

I pulled out my handkerchief and gently dabbed the itching daggers. "When I get really stressed out nowadays I break out in hives."

"Poor Denny, always the nervous Nellie."

I watched him put on his shirt and noticed a six-inch tattoo of an upside down cross on his right forearm and I swallowed hard.

"Don't tell me you're a Satanist now?"

Jack chuckled. "No, dummy. It's the cross of St. Peter. I thought a Catholic boy would know that."

I made a mental note to ask about it later. "So are we good to go now?"

Jack stuffed the bottle of Old Spice in his pants pocket. "Not yet, I need my lucky hat. Look in the top of the closet."

I obeyed and found a beat up brown corduroy cap at the back of the shelf. It reeked of stale beer. "Aces" was embroidered in cursive font on the front panel in letters once white, but now dingy yellow.

"You mean this old thing?" I asked incredulously. "It looks like it belongs to some derelict on skid row."

He motioned for it and I handed to him. "Ah, be careful with this one, lad. I won it in a poker game twenty years ago and it's been with me ever since." He stroked the aged logo. "It made me remember what it felt like to win when things got tough. It's brought me more luck than I had a right to expect."

"Okay, are we all set now?"

Jack frowned as he slipped his cell phone into his back pants pocket. "Almost. The pain meds are my life line and I can't leave without them."

"What do you mean? Can't we just stop at a drug store?"

"Sometimes you're so clueless," he replied. "We need to rip off the pharmacy on the way out. Maybe we can find something to fix those hives of yours too."

CHAPTER FIVE

The February temperatures hovered near zero along with my sales at Henley Dodge. Surveying the frozen tundra from the toasty comfort of the showroom, I watched a woman with a small child in tow walk along a rusting chain-link fence half buried in the snow which separated the back of the dealership from a cat food processing plant. By the time I made it to another window for a better look, the pair were looking at a horribly worn, cream-colored '66 Dodge Polara. The car had so many problems that if it were a horse even the glue factory would reject it.

I sized up the pair in their ratty white wool coats and filed them under "C." My sales colleagues called these penniless prospects "chaff" and taught me early on to let them blow right on through, because they had little means and would suck you dry with their endless requests. Even if you persevered, the net commission would barely feed the snack machine.

When mother and child began slowly trudging toward the showroom in their matching olive rubber boots, I scurried back to my desk far from the front lines. However, my colleagues had also concluded this fish wasn't worth the small bones and everyone ignored her. I watched her do laps around a new mango-colored Dodge Charger, checking us all out until she smelled my inexperience.

"Big mistake," I whispered and put my head down to feign interest in some technical report that might as well have been written in hieroglyphics and thinking "timing is everything." In the final gasp of the sales month last week, I would have moved heaven and earth to

even earn beer money and show my boss some initiative to keep my job. Now it was a new month and I needed to focus on building a pipeline of sales leads for the upcoming Presidents' Day sale and didn't need this distraction.

The little girl must have inherited her mother's sense for sniffing out weakness too, because she suddenly tugged on my arm and giggled.

My resolve broke and I looked up.

She was a sweet little thing; no more than four years old with dark hair like her mother's but in a ponytail. Her big chestnut brown eyes danced even before she flashed an innocent smile into my life. She smelled like Play-Doh.

"Hello, sweetheart," I said.

"I'm interested in one of your cars," the mother replied.

I bit my lip as the adult world intervened and moved to study the mother's face, which looked about thirty and was pretty enough. She had matching brown eyes too though they looked like they needed a long rest. The only makeup she wore came from the cold which colored her cheeks and the end of her nose red. With the exception of thick dark bangs, the rest remained hidden under a red woolen hat.

I glanced back at the little girl and noticed a dainty silver cross around her neck. Maybe they had money and dressed cheap to be unpretentious. "Hi, I'm Dennis. And what's your name?"

"This is Maggie." The woman stroked the little girl's hair and extended her free hand toward me. "I'm Jean Bradley."

You can tell a lot from a handshake and this one felt cold and limp.

Jean eyed the new cars in the showroom and wore the same expression my mother did whenever window shopping for things she could never afford. "I've been watching the Polara at the end of the lot for a while now. How much do you want for it?"

Her voice bounced off all the new aluminum, stainless steel, and chrome surrounding us and I decided to practice my pitch. "It may sound like a cliché, but that car had one owner and she only drove it around town and to church on Sundays," I said while looking at the little girl fiddling with her necklace because I couldn't tell a lie face on yet. Frank Riley, the bellicose sales manager, defined it as a weakness to overcome ASAP or be gone. My sales colleagues could pass a polygraph, no matter the whopper they told, and bragged about it.

"A thousand dollars and you can drive her home today," I said.

A knowing smirk appeared at the corners of her mouth. "Are you pulling my leg? I know that car belonged to Hank the plumber and he put a hundred thousand miles on it before trading it in for a Challenger last month. I told him he should have bought a Datsun. But he didn't listen and now spends his days sitting in gas lines."

Frank had instructed me to never give tactical advantage to the buyer. Denial came in various forms ranging from shock to outright indignation. "You must be mistaken." My cheeks grew hot and I flexed my toes in my salt-stained black loafers.

Jean crossed her arms and studied my sparse desk. "I think you better check your records. I also know that car has a serious oil leak and bled all over our street for years. Fix the leak and I'll give you three hundred to take it off your hands." She looked down at the glossy tile floor. "It would sure make a mess if anyone tracked little tar balls inside here on the tile or heaven forbid inside one of those beautiful cars."

The little girl reached up for my hand and I ignored her.

"Three hundred? You can't be serious." I let out a snooty laugh I learned from my colleagues and shook my head with vigor. "And how much are you planning to put down anyways?" The financing angle always provided a surefire way to extract more.

"No, this is a cash deal," she replied, though it was her turn to look at the floor.

Frank watched me from his perch high above the battlefield with his arms crossed. "Then I think you better go home and start rolling more coins. We're open until nine if you finish."

Jean's face fell and she picked Maggie up and headed for the door.

"Chaff," I whispered.

CHAPTER SIX

Merriam called me a typical man because I loved action flicks, where the hero is challenged to overcome a cunning villain. Given my past, it was easy to understand why I avoided dramas. That said, I still wondered with all the pain and suffering in real life, why would anyone want to dedicate their free time to absorb more? In contrast, watching men break rocks and jaws felt liberating given all the compromises we make every day.

I discovered a new crop of hives on my left wrist and gave in to the urge to lightly scratch them while considering our escape route. Granted, this was no Alcatraz, but we still had to get past a few women that could easily kick my arthritic butt. At first, I thought about simply escorting Jack out the front door. It was such an audacious move, who would stop us? However, after my conversation with Stu last night, I knew the hospice would certainly delay us until they checked with Jack's legal guardian, health proxy, and most importantly, payer. Stuart would raise holy blazes for sure and call the police to escort me out. And no matter how many police brotherhood stickers I displayed on the bumper of my car, they would side with Cain.

Since Charlton Heston passed away years ago, I no longer had the motivation to lead a grand escape that he might someday reenact on the big screen. The easiest and most direct route remained sneaking out through the French doors twelve steps away. We would then make a beeline across the soggy lawn to a long row of pine trees lining the yard. Evergreens are one of the few reminders in winter that nature has not abandoned the region forever and their open arms would easily conceal us as we made our way parallel to the death camp. The Caddy was gassed up and waiting in the front parking lot ready to transport us to life on the lam.

As usual, Jack didn't like any plans that weren't his.

"Didn't you hear me yesterday? I want to be like biting mayflies, not cowering chickens." Jack raised his arm like he was brandishing an imaginary sword and slashed the air ready to behead me. "We should be like Custer making our last stand."

I rubbed my forehead to make the ache stop. "And how did that work out for the good general?" I asked. "Even though you taught shop for thirty years, I'm surprised you didn't pick up a little history along the way. Sorry to be blunt, but I have a different time horizon. You may want to go down in some comic blaze of glory. I'm just looking forward to planting a new vegetable garden out in California."

The dying man folded his thin arms and put on the angriest face he could muster, though it was hard to take him seriously in that ugly hat with the "Aces" logo.

"Look, I learned some tough lessons in 'Nam and I'm not running from anyone. We're going out the front door and that's all there is to it. And like I told you, I need to stock up on meds."

"Well, it's your funeral," I said, letting it sting on purpose then checked the hall.

Minutes later, Jack threw the thin blue hospital blanket over his street clothes and I pushed him down the hall in a wheelchair. Even that small concession proved hard won, until I referenced a Trojan horse strategy. On the way to the nurses' station, I decided to let him take the lead on this final mission. While Jack had dedicated a lifetime to convincing young minds, I had a sinking feeling he was ill prepared to pull off this caper and gain access to the medicine cabinet. Maybe with some luck he would only tick off the nurse slightly and we could retreat back to his room and sneak out the back like I first suggested. Then we would figure out the drug situation after we escaped. But if things didn't go well, at least my conscience would be clear and Jack could sing "I Did It My Way" as the light faded.

Nurse Nancy didn't see our approach, which I found surprising and gave me the inspiration to head straight for the lobby instead. Perhaps with some luck we could just walk out before anyone noticed.

But Jack stuck to the plan and used one foot to stop his Trojan horse at the oak desk. Studying our nemesis, I noted we had interrupted an early lunch date with a deep dish pepperoni and pineapple pizza and the reason for our cloak of invisibility. Nurse Nancy sported cheese on her chin and I would have laughed, except it smelled delicious and reminded me I skipped breakfast. Even facing possible catastrophe, my mouth watered.

The nurse gingerly laid her Italian lover on a paper plate. "Glad to see you're up, honey," she cooed through tomato-stained lips. Then she glanced coldly at me and her half smile looked as fake as the movie set fan over my friend's bed.

"Faux," I said without thinking.

She shot me a puzzled look. "Foe?"

Touché, I thought and couldn't resist the urge to tweak her a bit and pointed to my chin to indicate her next date should be with a napkin. She quickly complied and I was disappointed to sense no embarrassment. It grossed me out to think she ate with dirty nails too. I took my microbiology seriously.

"Isn't it time for my meds?" Jack asked rather harshly.

"In another half hour, dear," she replied in a tone reminiscent of the wolf from *Little Red Riding Hood*. I noticed she had a long nose too.

Our eyes locked; two healthy bodies sizing each other up.

She looked down at Jack. "Since you're up why don't you watch some TV in the Douglas Room? We have quite a library of old movies in there," she said, obviously trying to get rid of us. I wondered what she had for dessert and scanned her desk. If I discovered a double fudge chocolate brownie, my buddy would be on his own.

"How do you know I don't like new movies?"

"Where is the room?" I said, hoping to motivate my friend to retreat.

"It's down there," Jack answered for her, pointing down a dark hall to my right. "Douglas Funeral Home donated all the furnishings. Good marketing plan to seed their pipeline, don't you think?"

He reached up and grabbed the nurse's hand. "Nancy, I'm in a lot of pain and didn't want to buzz and disturb your lunch. So I asked Dennis to wheel me down here," he said, stroking her hand. "Please give me a little morphine so I can get through this rough patch. I don't think we need to be afraid of addiction now, do we?" He smiled weakly and let out a dry cough. "And I promise not to bother you again until you make rounds."

The nurse glanced quickly at the pizza box and the three remaining slices growing colder by the second. "We have to be careful in administering too much pain medication since it could compromise your breathing," she recited verbatim then glanced at her watch. "I can give you half a dose now and the balance in another hour." She felt the top of her hair like she wanted to make sure all the spikes were still standing at attention. "Wait here," she said before disappearing into a small adjacent room.

Jack eyed me and I shrugged. "Now what?" I mouthed.

"Can't you ever stop with all the analysis paralysis and just do what needs to be done?" he whispered.

When I didn't move, he waved me off and pulled down on the brim of his corduroy hat as if preparing for a strong gale. "You can be such a wimp sometimes." In one motion, the terminally ill man pushed his wheelchair around the counter toward the closet-sized dispensary. I hesitated for another moment before following him, uncertain what would happen next.

Jack was always a bull in a china shop and caught the door molding with the armrest of the chair as he entered. The noise startled the nurse and she almost dropped the syringe she worked on filling.

"You can't be in here," she said sharply.

In a flash, Jack catapulted out of the wheelchair and tackled her. She let out a small whimper and I lost sight of the nurse for a second behind the long blue blanket. When she reappeared, Jack had her pinned on the floor with one hand over her mouth.

"What are you doing?" I moved too fast in pushing the wheelchair aside, and in the process caught my foot and toppled onto Jack before landing next to him. Nurse Nancy saw her opportunity and crushed my ear with an intense head butt and yelled for help as Jack scrambled to regain control. I spit one of her hair spikes out of my mouth then struggled to my feet and cupped my throbbing ear. I kicked the door closed to contain the bedlam and tapped Jack on the back with my free hand. "C'mon, buddy. This madness wasn't in the plan."

My friend turned and shot me a look that could reverse global warming. "Did you forget whose side you're supposed to be on?" Jack motioned with his head toward the open medicine cabinet. "I'm sure there's some tape in there. Throw me a roll so I can put her on mute. And find something quick to tie her up. In my condition I can't hold her much longer."

The poor painted and snapping turtles came to mind. They were determined to cross the two-lane road and lay their eggs. And I stood on the side of the road, paralyzed by the oncoming traffic, lacking the testicular fortitude to run out and prevent the splatter. Now, I stood watching something even more dangerous. Even in my action film fantasy world, this escape appeared doomed and likely to end with me spending the rest of my days in some dark cellblock with a much younger boyfriend, while Jack whooped it up in heaven. The alternative was not pretty either. How could I desert him now?

"Ouch!" Jack suddenly cried. Nurse Nancy bit his palm.

"Help!" she yelled. Jack grabbed the end of the blue blanket and wrapped it around his injured hand as a shield before attempting to cover the lion's mouth again. She tried to roll left and Jack kicked out one leg to stop her momentum. From my view, he might have won the early rounds but she was quickly wearing him down like a skilled prizefighter.

"C'mon, Denny! I'm down to hours and don't want to spend any more of it wrestling a lady with a loaded syringe," he said, struggling to control the large-boned woman.

Suddenly Nurse Nancy rolled right and Jack held on for dear life. "Earth to Dennis! Hurry up before someone comes."

I stepped over the wrestling alligators, opened the medicine cabinet, and pulled out some gauze and medical tape. I quickly rolled the gauze into a tight ball and cut three pieces of tape.

I knelt down beside my buddy ready to assist and avoided the nurse's eyes. "Do you want the gauze first so we can tape her mouth?"

"Hey, I have a better idea," he said, shooting me a sour look. "Why don't we just hand her all the stuff and she can tie herself up while we finish her pizza? Think, Denny! Tape her legs and hands and make sure it's extra tight. She's liable to kill me if she gets loose."

"You mean both of us." I grabbed her feet and made wide circles around her ankles with the tape. She kicked at me with worn white sneakers, but I was able to avoid the deadly strikes and got pretty good timing each wave. I considered whether to take a few seconds and tape up the hem of her pants so they wouldn't drag on the floor anymore. Maybe she would appreciate the kindness when she testified against me in court. A muffled sound came from under Jack's hand.

"Hurry up, Denny. I'm losing my grip and can't hold on much longer." Sweat glistened on his sallow forehead as he continued to hold the drug queen. I grabbed one hand, then the other, and crisscrossed the tape ten times to make a nice pair of white handcuffs for our nemesis.

"Now, I'm going to take my hand off your mouth, but I want you to promise me you won't scream," Jack said to the nurse. "If you do, I'm going to have to tape your mouth shut tight and I don't want to do that as I know it makes me feel claustrophobic when I have to breathe through my nose. We're not going to hurt you. I just need some medicine so I can function on the outside for a couple days at most. I know you're mad as a hornet and I'm sorry for the upset. The good news is I'll be dead soon and you can scream at me all you want and it won't bother me none." Then he pointed my way. "But Dennis will be around if you feel the need to have something a bit more interactive. Maybe he can buy you dinner to make up for the lunch we ruined."

Jack slowly lifted his hand off her mouth.

Nurse Nancy let out a loud belch and the smell of digested pepperoni filled the small space and made me turn my head away. "You betta hurry up and kick the bucket then, because you're going to wish you were dead when I get out of here." She turned and looked at me and if looks could kill, I'd be on my way to the morgue. "And I promise you'll get your payback in spades. All I need is a pair of nail clippers to make you cry for your mommy."

A shiver ran across my chest.

"Well, that's a farewell I won't soon forget," Jack replied and glanced my way. "And good luck to you."

Thirty seconds later we had the nurse all tied up and tucked comfy under a prep counter.

When I stood up, my buddy continued surveying the shelves and reading labels. "What are you doing now? Just grab what you need and let's get out of here."

Jack gave me a sharp look. "Take it easy, Denny, will you? We'll need to rob every drug store in town if we don't take the right provisions," he said, inspecting another bottle. "It's not like I'm preparing a Thanksgiving dinner. I just need some Roxanol and Atropine. Liquid morphine will take care of the pain and the other med dries up the secretions so I don't sound like a coffee grinder when I breathe."

He spoke like it was a Sunday afternoon and we were strolling through the produce market squeezing melons and avocados to find the best lot. "Plus you'll never get any sleep if I don't have the right stuff."

"That's the least of my worries," I said, watching him stuff a handful of bottles into a small paper bag and straining to listen for paratroopers on the roof. "After this ruckus, I don't know where we will go. The police will have an APB out for us."

Suddenly a bottle flew toward my head and I caught it. "What's this for?"

"A little something for your nerves. It should help with the hives too."

I looked under the counter at Nurse Nancy struggling to free herself and mumbling something in Spanish. I left the bottle next to her as she would need it more than me. If we had the time I would have left some antacids too. "See any antidiarrheal medicine up there?"

"Why?"

"Because I think my stomach wants to make a great escape too."

My friend shook his head. "Well, you better grab the rest of Nancy's pizza to keep it busy. I don't think they provide any box lunches to go."

Strangely, it was the best idea he had all day even if I had a new revulsion for pepperoni.

CHAPTER SEVEN

Jack motioned to a side door with the bright sun streaming in like an illuminated path to paradise. "There's a sidewalk heading to the parking lot. Let's take it."

I wanted to say something smart about canceling our grand exit through the lobby, but the pizza tasted too good to bother. Now I understood why Nurse Nancy was so enamored with it and why she had another reason to seek revenge. The pineapple had a real tangy taste and I appreciated her leaving me the largest piece in the pie. At least now if we were arrested, I would be through the booking process and in my cell come supper time. I imagined a diet of TV dinners with all those tiny compartments where everything smells like aluminum and with portions that wouldn't satisfy a ten-year-old boy. The thought made me take another large bite as I pointed at the large sign in red which screamed A-L-A-R-M.

Without missing a beat, Jack noticed. "Well, we can't go out that way, the alarm will go off."

I rolled my eyes. "You don't say."

At the far end of the hall, I caught sight of a young nurse entering another patient's room. There was no time to double back to Jack's room and sneak out the back. Chances were good one of the staff would discover Nurse Nancy. I checked my watch and winced. Nurse Big-Hair-Betty would be returning any minute from running errands and then all hell would break loose.

The front door was the only option now. We walked down the hall, around the corner, and into the lobby.

"Leaving already?" Ruth the receptionist said, looking up from a magazine. Then she eyed the pizza crust in my hand and looked disappointed like she missed the invite to a party.

I gnawed quickly on the remaining piece and studied the visitor register, wanting to erase my name so this whole sad episode didn't look premeditated.

I coughed loudly like I was choking and watched Jack stagger up from behind and overtake our next victim. His eyes had a drugged look and I figured he must have taken a good swig of the morphine.

"Don't move, either one of you," he said in a low mean voice while sticking something in Ruth's side and cupping his other hand over her mouth.

I hadn't been in a play since seventh grade but fear provided the right motivation. "Jack, please don't shoot me," I said, holding up my hands. "I told you I can't take you out of here."

"I'm leaving this prison."

"I don't know how you were able to smuggle a gun in here, but please don't do anything silly."

Ruth's hazel eyes got so big it reminded me of putting a bag of popcorn in the microwave and watching it expand. I was afraid they might explode any second and ruin her nice cream-colored silk blouse. Tears began flowing down both cheeks. When the April showers came next month, I would think of her.

"Shut up," Jack said, shooting me a dirty look. "Now, give me your handkerchief."

Merriam said a handkerchief could tell a lot about a man, so she always ironed mine. Somehow, she sensed whenever I was going through a difficult period and would spray her jasmine perfume on one and slip it into the pocket of my overcoat. I wished I had one right now to give me courage.

"I know tissues are more sanitary, but don't worry none because I haven't used this today," I said, handing it to him.

Jack looked like he wanted to bop me good. He always had to orchestrate everything.

"Okay, Mister Hygiene, now give me your tie so I can blindfold her so she doesn't see me beat the stuffing out of you."

I hesitated, as the yellow silk tie was a birthday gift from Merriam. "Can't we just ask her to put on her designer sunglasses?"

Jack looked like I lost my mind so I undid the Windsor knot and handed him my favorite tie. He used a roll of surgical tape he took from the dispensary to tie her hands and feet. We had Ruth neatly packaged and beside her desk in five minutes.

"Listen up, lady," Jack said in his tough voice. "I suggest you play dead unless you want to hear something so nasty you'll wish you were a resident here."

I scowled at Jack for playing it so heavy. He read my face and shrugged.

Ruth began shaking badly and whimpering. I took off my gray wool dress coat and laid it over her, hoping to provide comfort. I knelt down and pushed her auburn bangs away from the blindfold. "Don't worry, Ruth, everything will be okay. I promise." I put the magazine next to her head. "Have you read this article on new beauty tips for the summer? It looks interesting so I'll leave it right here along with your expensive sunglasses."

"You can get her number later. C'mon, man, let's go," Jack said, pulling me away.

We made our way across the well-appointed foyer and the front doors parted like the Red Sea. The bright sun made me squint as the cold air stung the sweat on my forehead. I grabbed a stick of Juicy Fruit gum out of my pants pocket and began speed chewing, looking back at the entrance of Restful Waters and thinking we had pretty much undone its moniker.

"What did you use for a weapon when you snuck up on the receptionist?" I asked, trying to take my mind off the chaos behind us as we headed down the cement sidewalk.

"Just two fingers. Jam them hard enough under a rib and it does the trick." A dry cough kicked in and he held on to me for support.

I wanted to tell him he watched too much television, but he suddenly stopped next to a small pea-green Renault. A strong cold wind kicked up three months of sand and salt from the parking lot and I lost hold of him as he stepped off the elevated cement sidewalk to street level.

"What are you doing?" I asked, pointing to my midnight blue Caddy sitting alone fifty feet away in the same row. If he had listened to me, we would have been gone by now and with a lot less hoopla.

"If we drive around in that living room of yours, we won't make it five miles." He unlocked the door of the foreign car. "We might as well drive to the Salem police station before they finish lunch. The way you inhaled that pizza you'll be happy to know they upgraded from serving only bread and water to the inmates. A couple of months behind bars and you'll really resemble the Pillsbury Doughboy."

"And you don't think we'll get caught in your car?" I said, sucking in my gut.

"This isn't my car."

"Then whose is it?"

"Nancy's," he replied, handing me the keys.

My mouth opened so wide I risked lockjaw. "Now we're going to steal a car? Do you realize how many laws we've broken in the past half hour?" I stammered. "We used to be model citizens." Then I remembered who I was talking to. "Well, at least I was."

Jack ignored me and held onto the car as he went around to the passenger side.

I jingled the set of keys. "Hey, we have her house key. Are we going to rob her place too?"

"Don't be ridiculous," Jack replied.

Getting into the driver's seat, I adjusted the worn blue cloth seat and noticed the Renault had a manual transmission. It had been a few years since I used a stick, actually twenty years. I pushed the clutch to the floor and the starter whined before finally catching. "I gotta say I feel jinxed stealing a car. You know what happened when I worked at Henley's and Jean Bradley stalked me and—"

"Put a sock in it and drive, will ya? We have no time for ancient history now."

My hands and feet began moving like a mad marionette working the clutch and shifter, but we remained fixed in place.

Jack punched the door. "Man, you never would have survived 'Nam. C'mon and hurry up."

I heard Jean Bradley laughing and knew the ghost must be messing with the shifter. "I can't find reverse." The pizza in my esophagus began to rebel and I fought the urge to belch like Nancy.

A car suddenly went by us and I watched Nurse Big-Hair-Betty park her silver Honda Civic on the other side of my Caddy. A moment later she came barreling down the sidewalk.

Jack reached up and put his sun visor down and I followed suit. "We can't tie her up too. If she sees us it's all over," I whispered.

"Have a little faith, Denny. Now turn the car off and don't move." Jack slid down low in the seat.

I obeyed and the nurse walked past our position and never looked in. She was talking on her cell phone and waving her other hand like she was conducting an orchestra.

I thought we were in the clear when she suddenly turned around and headed back our way. She looked right at me and I let out a terrific sounding burp.

Jack punched me hard in the leg.

CHAPTER EIGHT

They came back every day for three weeks. No matter the weather, mother and daughter would appear about mid-afternoon in a strange pilgrimage to an old rusting hulk. While Jean waved at me and pointed at the oil leak under the dented front bumper, the little girl would wipe the sad-looking headlights with a checkered blue handkerchief. It was a bizarre ritual and made me think about the personalities we imprint on automobiles. Muscle cars looked mean and spit testosterone out their tailpipes. Jean Bradley's strange object of desire looked nothing short of woeful. I wondered if the designers considered the wear and tear of middle age. A new Polara's eyes appeared big and round which, combined with the elongated chrome grille, projected a look of adventure. But as it aged and the chrome grille became pitted, the Polara turned melancholy looking.

On the last day of February, Jean arrived at the usual hour but without Maggie. I feared the little girl had finally caught pneumonia from this daily nonsense. The feeling spiked when Jean put her head on the hood of the car and began crying. My legs wanted to run out and ask about her daughter, but the rest of me felt too numb to move since she evidently had made it her life's mission to stalk me until I sold a lemon destined to be in the junkyard by the Fourth of July.

In the midst of another seventy-hour work week, I walked slowly to another window to watch this sad freak show. I expected February sales to be strong due to the "Presidents' Day Sell-abration," but this year proved to be a total bust with the deep recession. The oil embargo caused U.S. automakers' sales to plummet and suddenly fuel-efficient foreign brands were dominating the news. My stomach constantly ached from filling up on "yellow death" mac & cheese which Stop and Save pitched at five boxes for a dollar. Any day now I expected to wake up looking jaundiced. On the bright side it might help me win a sympathy sale.

When Jean began marching toward the front door, her strategy hit me. Like a sly fox, she'd waited until the end of the month to make a move.

I bolted for my metal desk and estimated I had just enough time to grab my coat and escape through the service entrance. Frank Riley, the general sales manager, made us park across the street in an empty dirt lot to make a prison break difficult, but not impossible. But I misjudged the tenacity of this lady and she called my name before I could disappear behind a wall of brochures.

"Tough month for sales?" she asked much too loudly. "You might be the sales professional here, but it seems to me if you put on your coat and actually came outside once in a while to talk with potential customers you might sell a car." She looked around and shrugged. "I'm just saying."

I walked toward her with my fists clenched and only stopped when I smelled Play-Doh and remembered she was a mother. "And if you actually had any money, I would escort you over to my desk and we would negotiate the purchase and sales agreement. You can cry all you want on the hood of that car, lady, but it won't follow you home because I have the keys."

She bit her lip like she wanted to cry again, but pulled herself together and whipped off the red wool hat. Dark hair fell to her shoulders except for a dozen strands in the back which took advantage of static electricity to defy gravity and make her look like a mad madam scientist. "Okay, I'll give you five hundred bucks, but that includes a new oil pan."

Frank heard the ruckus and called me up to his perch.

"She only offered me five hundred, but I know I can get much more," I said to preempt another sermon.

The bald sales manager with his little black eyes and fat nose looked like he stepped on dog mess and wanted to scrape me off his shoe. *"You've been way below quota every month since I brought you on. If it wasn't for your daddy knowing Mr. Henley, I would have cut you at Christmas."* He pointed at my midsection. *"Now go get me seven hundred or you're toast. Burnt toast."*

I nodded with too much gusto.

Frank glanced toward Jean as she made laps around my metal desk. *"She should have brought the little kid with her to win a little sympathy. She doesn't have anything else going for her."*

I walked slowly back to my nemesis, estimating seven hundred dollars would buy me maybe another week of employment, but eight hundred might secure a month and allow me to break my sales slump. Paper hats at McDonald's were waiting unless I did something bold.

"The best we can do is eight hundred," I said, knowing Frank lurked nearby. *"And we'll plug the oil leak and give you a free inspection sticker,"* I whispered quickly.

"Look, I really need that car." She studied her worn olive boots for a moment before returning to search my eyes. *"The very best I can do is seven hundred, Dennis. Please take it,"* she said much too loud.

Her plea reverberated around the showroom and landed at my feet. All I had to do was nod and she would be happy and Frank satisfied for today. I could see Merriam smiling weakly as she pushed her fork through a sea of yellow macaroni minus the steak I promised this morning.

I focused on the top of her head and addressed the crazy hair. "I just learned we have another interested party coming in tomorrow afternoon. I'm sure I can get eight fifty from him, but it's yours for eight hundred."

Jean burst into tears and ran for the door before I could react. She wasn't gone thirty seconds before Frank drilled his finger into my chest. "Are you an idiot? You had the sale. Now get her on the phone and make the deal or you're through."

CHAPTER NINE

Nurse Big-Hair-Betty reached the hood of our car and stopped. I trembled, fearing she would sniff the air and smell my belch pollution or hear Jack's rapid wheezing. The wind suddenly kicked up and blew the nurse's white hair across her face and into her mouth. She turned her back to us, no doubt to gag. I glanced quickly in the back seat hoping to find a piece of newspaper or a coat to prop against the windshield to hide behind, but only spotted three empty soda cans on the floor.

The nurse became animated again and pointed at the ground with her free hand as the heated phone call continued. I held my breath until she began walking vigorously toward the building.

I restarted the car, but still could not find reverse and thought it might be divine recompense for terrorizing the two women in the hospice. I chomped on my gum and repeated the sequence again and again.

"Do you know Albert Einstein's definition of insanity?" Jack asked, watching me.

I rolled my eyes. "You flunked American history a half hour ago and now you want to wow me with the theory of relativity?"

Jack took my hand off the worn shifter. "Einstein defined insanity as doing the same thing over and over again and expecting different results."

I sat back in the seat and rubbed my eyes until they hurt. "I don't get this Rubik's cube. My dad had a Pontiac and taught me how to drive a stick when I was only fourteen. I've never had a problem until today."

I grabbed the shifter and put my foot on the clutch and tried again. This time the car lurched forward and the undercarriage hit the elevated sidewalk and made a sickening scraping sound. I moaned. "The only possibility is the French manufacturer uses a different gear format and unfortunately there's no 'Rosetta Stone' kiosks nearby."

My passenger became restless and opened his door, which made an awful squeaking sound similar to when Dorothy's Tin Man needed oiling. "Well, we can't drive up on the sidewalk unless you want to lose the exhaust system. Then we will really have a *Flintstones* car." He smirked and patted my stomach. "Though I bet if we put you in some hospice pajamas with a blue tie you'd look an awful lot like Fred. Heaven knows you eat like him." He took a deep breath like he was about to go free-diving and push the limits of human endurance. "Just put it in neutral and I'll give you a push."

I grabbed my too long hair with both hands and pulled hard. "Are you kidding me? As much as this would make for a great story at your wake, I'm not asking a man with one foot in the grave to give me a push. No, I'm the one breaking you out of here and we're taking my car which moves seamlessly in every direction. Got it?"

My friend shook his head. "Okay, I'm too tired to argue but we may as well untie Nancy and Ruth then because we'll be caught within five miles." He let out a short laugh. "But at least you'll save three gallons of gas."

"Show a little faith," I said then froze.

Jack noticed. "What's the matter?"

I put my head down on the sweaty steering wheel and let out a deep cry like a baby seal. "My car keys are in my coat and I covered Ruth with it," I said barely above a whisper.

"Like I said, you're a chameleon. One second you're Fred Flintstone and in the next instant Larry from *The Three Stooges*. How lucky am I to have a buddy with so much comedic range?"

"Since you're always trying to play boss, I guess that makes you Moe then," I said, opening the door and trying to keep my voice steady. "Change places with me and let me push."

Suddenly an alarm went off like someone just broke into Fort Knox. A middle-aged man that I recognized as the janitor came running out of the hospice and began searching the parking lot. In the distance a siren began to wail. We were ruined.

In the next instant, Jack fell out of the car and disappeared.

"Are you okay?" I asked, leaning over the seat.

Jack moaned in pain as he pulled himself up with the help of the open door, then transferred his grip to the front fender and slowly made his way around to the hood. If the Grim Reaper viewed this scene, I reckoned he was laughing pretty hard at this point and might give us another few hours to see how it all played out. I put the car in neutral and watched Jack heave with all his might and ever so slowly, the car started rolling backwards.

"Stop!" the janitor yelled and began running our way.

My wingman noticed and shuffled quickly to the passenger door and jumped in.

I popped the clutch and left the first patch of rubber since I was nineteen. Granted it was only a short burst, but the burnt smell filled the cabin. As we reached the exit, two ambulance vans met us with lights flashing as they sped toward the scene of our crime.

"Well, looks like they found the ladies," Jack said dryly. "If I had to do it over again we would have brought them along for the ride and negotiated for their release. Who knows, maybe it would have paid for a few nights at a five-star hotel." He fiddled with the heater controls and the fan blew cold stale air as we made it through two sets of lights on Route 28 before the first cruiser went flying past us in the opposite direction with its siren howling. A mile later the scene repeated.

"Probably just a coincidence," I said more to myself than my passenger. "There's always an accident on this road." My hands were shaking badly.

When Jack didn't come back with a smart retort, I glanced over. He sat low in the seat, with that ridiculous brown corduroy hat of his shading his eyes. His complexion reminded me of the dead winter grass and filled me with guilt. A real friend would have listened and tried to provide comfort about the regrets we all have. Instead, I let Jack take control and now we were in the middle of a terrible mess. For years, Merriam tried to protect me from being sucked into the chaos of my friend's life whenever he called looking for help. As the years passed, the tension between them increased and I had to give up my role of being the dustpan and broom for Jack's antics. I never appreciated how right she was. Within twenty-four hours after reconnecting, I had a leading role in his nightmare. This had to end.

We were flying at twenty miles an hour over the speed limit when I finally came to my senses and pulled into a strip mall and stopped in an empty section of the parking lot. My left foot trembled and the clutch felt too heavy for the soles of my dress shoes. Looking in the rearview mirror, I gasped in fright at the multiple colonies of red welts populating my throat. I pushed on one lesion the size of a half dollar and watched it turn white.

My cell phone rang and I fully expected the police were calling to report they had us surrounded and to let me know what entrée they were serving in jail this evening and whether I preferred still or sparkling water. Instead, the screen read "Mark."

"Good morning, son. How's the 101 this morning?" I asked softly so not to wake my comatose passenger.

"You'd think after three years I'd be used to commuting from Novato into the city. Except for the blue and gold license plates, most mornings I think I'm still on Route 93 inching my way into Boston. I didn't get into the office until a few minutes ago."

"Well, Cambridge is the place to be these days. Kendall Square is exploding with biotech companies and they could use a corporate lawyer with your smarts."

"Yeah, but what's the weather back there today?"

I reached over and felt Jack's hand. "Cold and clammy," I said and shut off the car.

Mark let out a short snicker. "Well, I ran this morning in a T-shirt and shorts. If you ask me, New Hampshire has two seasons: Fourth of July and winter. Spring doesn't arrive until April if you're lucky and by late August a few eager maple trees begin to change color."

"Well, I like the change of seasons, though the winters are much too long." I watched everyday life play out in front of the store. A short man in a navy wool coat raced around the lot shagging carriages, a red van pulled out of its parking space too quickly and almost hit a silver truck in its path. I missed my usual diet of boring normalcy and everyday dramas. "So, how's my favorite bridge today?" I asked.

"It's playing hide and go seek in the fog. By the way, I tried calling you a few times yesterday. Where were you?"

"I'm still trying to figure out this iPhone," I replied quickly. "I saw a show on the History Channel the other night about the Golden Gate Bridge. They said it was painted international orange so it would stand out in the fog. So what gives?"

"Do you believe everything you see on TV? You can see for yourself when you move out here. Now let's get back to your phone. Christmas presents shouldn't be difficult to use, you know." He let out a sigh. "I don't know why you find some basic things so hard. Apple has sold an iPhone to almost everyone else on earth without a problem."

"I think you're exaggerating a bit. And you're talking like I was born before Alexander Graham Bell."

"Well, you used to have the same rotary phone they display now in the Smithsonian." He laughed. "About this weekend. I decided to take the red-eye on Thursday night. That way, I'll get into Logan early Friday morning and we can start the day looking at what you're shipping out here. You can donate the rest to charity if they'll take it."

"What do mean, if they'll take it? Your mother and I bought quality furniture."

"Maybe the bedroom set, but not the fake leather in the living room furniture. Linda ribs me constantly about it."

I rolled my eyes. "Is she coming with you too?"

"No, why?"

"It's just that we'll be going through a lot of private things of your mother's and I thought it was best if you and I—"

"Look, Dad. I know you two didn't hit it off when we visited at Christmas. Now every time I bring her up you act like she's a Yankees fan. I just wished you'd give her a chance."

I smelled something akin to dirty socks and leaned over and sniffed the air around Jack, trying to determine if it was him or the car. In the drama of the morning I couldn't remember if I used deodorant and cracked my window open.

"She's a real pretty girl, I'll give you that."

"I hear a 'but' coming."

"Okay, if you ask me, she's a bit stuck up."

"Why do you say that?" Mark asked, his voice growing loud.

I held the phone a little farther away from my ear. "Well, for starters she looked disgusted when I offered her a glass of wine Christmas Eve."

"Are you kidding me? I gave you thirty bucks to buy a nice bottle of Chardonnay and you had the nerve to show up with a box of wine and then flaunt it by displaying it on the dining room table and boasting about the built-in spigot. Really, Dad? You know Linda grew up in Napa. My guess is you wanted to tick her off because she made fun of your silly wine coolers last summer."

I looked over at Jack and he began to stir. "I thought your Mother and I brought you up to be humble and genuine. I bet if I transferred that boxed wine into some fancy bottle, Linda would have raved how bold it tasted and thrown in some cockamamie description of it having a buttery hint of coconut. Someday the wine snobs will have the courage to change their packaging. I mean how many glass bottles of soda do they sell nowadays? And by the way I saved you twenty-three dollars." I shook my head. "How do you think we were able to put you through college? There's nothing wrong with being a little frugal. You should tell your girlfriend that if you ever want to actually own something instead of leasing everything."

"So you're going to make Linda your poster child for wine snobs and big credit card bills?"

I glanced over at Jack and felt as exhausted as he looked. "Listen. I just think having her move in with you is a big step. Back in my day, there was a process everyone followed. You'd date and if you fell in love get engaged and then married. These days the steps are all mixed up if there are any at all. It's one thing to have a career but now—"

"There you go, Dad, living in grandma's world again. You grew up in the sixties, remember? Your generation questioned everything and is still proud of it. You can't put the genie back in the bottle now."

I watched Jack's chest rise and fall. "Well, I wish you hadn't broken up with Michelle. She's such a pretty girl and didn't make it look like penance whenever you were running late and hung around to watch a few innings of a Sox game with me. Now there's a girl I could love as a daughter."

"Why do you hold on to the past? We broke up five years ago, Dad. We wanted different things. Linda is ambitious and she's doing very well in pharmaceutical sales."

"Yeah, that's a real hoot. She makes a living pitching better living through chemistry but only eats organic. I'd like her to explain that contradiction."

"Look, I can't do this over the phone. Linda and I have been together for over a year now. It's time you accept her."

Jack opened one eye. "Why have we stopped?"

"Who's that?" Mark asked.

I took a deep breath. "Sorry, Mark, you're breaking up. I ate too many prunes for breakfast so have to literally run. Talk to you tomorrow." I quickly punched the screen with my index finger.

"You better figure out that gear box, Dennis," Jack said, rolling his head to look at me with bloodshot eyes. "I'm way too tired to give you another push."

"I must be some type of lunatic taking a dying—I mean, sick man out of the hospital."

"That was no hospital and you know it. And you can stop pussy footing around. I know I'm dying." He reached over and rubbed my arm. "I'm eternally grateful for what you did back there and I know that wasn't easy for you. You have a nice sedate life and I live like a sailor on leave. All I know is over the course of a life you make many acquaintances, but you're a rich man if you find one true friend."

"To an untrained ear, this would be touching, but I know you too well. I need you to level with me, Jack. What do you need to take care of that I can't do for you when you're gone?"

Jack inhaled and shook his head. "I'll explain tomorrow," he said in a raspy voice. "Right now I need some sleep."

I gently tapped his shoulder. "You'll be sleeping for eternity soon enough and I'll be left to clean up after you. What's this all about?" I asked again.

Before Jack could look away, I noticed the frightened look and it suddenly hit me. I should have figured it out when Stu first called me.

"Look, I know you're scared about what comes next and I understand because I'm no spring chicken either. But really, Jack, do you think all this upset will win you some sort of get out of hell pass?" I whispered with as much sensitivity as I could muster. "If you won't take my word for it, maybe you'd find peace by hearing it from a priest instead." I offered my iPhone to him. "If you want, I can call Father McGowan at St. Joseph's. He was a godsend when Merriam was dying. I can get him on the phone and stand outside to give you some privacy."

The message found its mark and Jack took off his lucky hat and rubbed his scalp hard like something inside wanted to escape. "I never thought much about dying until I got sick. At first, I thought I could be like the good thief and sneak into heaven at the last minute. In comparison with what I read in the papers every day, I wasn't really that bad a guy. I studied one verse for months: *'Jesus, remember me when you come into your kingdom.'* Nine words secured paradise for a criminal but it would never work for me."

"Why not?" I asked, surprised to see a spiritual side I never knew existed. Yes, we were both raised Catholic and made our First Communion and Confirmation together, but faith remained on the fringes of our relationship. We followed the stereotypical guy track and talked about girls, sports, cars, politics—anything and everything except our innermost thoughts and beliefs.

Jack sighed and I could tell the pain wasn't physical this time. "The thief gained heaven because he was heartfelt and spontaneous. Sure, I'm sorry for all my mistakes and as you can see this morning, I'm going to make a few more before I check out. But a deathbed conversion feels too premeditated and convenient," he said, holding up clenched fists. "A wonderful lady I met at chemo believed in the end we're judged by how often we were the hands of Christ in the world." He opened his and they looked sallow and were trembling. "I'm afraid God wouldn't recognize mine, but the Devil sure will." Jack studied his outstretched hands. "I need to undo some of the hurt I caused and win forgiveness even if it's very late."

I opened my mouth but didn't know what to say to give comfort. We lived in a broken world but his had many missing parts.

He closed his eyes and groaned. "I'm not used to baring my soul to anyone like this. All I know is if the path to hell is paved with good intentions, the stairs to heaven are built with good works. You'd think for a shop teacher they would be easy to construct, but I don't have all the tools or the energy and need your help."

He let out a short cough and sat up straight. "So, what's the plan?"

I took a deep breath, knowing hell would have an extra special place for me if I betrayed Jack's noble quest and drove him back to the hospice.

"Well, originally I hoped we could stay at my house, but your brother nixed the plan last night. We can head up to Manchester or down to Boston and check into a hotel. Your choice."

"I know someplace better we can stay."

"Okay, but first I need to swing by my house for a minute."

"Why?" he asked, exhausted.

"It's no big deal, really. I packed some things in case we're gone for a while."

Jack opened the pharmacy bag and looked in. "In case you haven't noticed, Denny, you're not going to find me featured on the AARP website next month. My expiration date is about the same as a pot of coffee. I'm traveling pretty light so what on earth could you really need?"

The sour smell hit my nose again and I pinched my nostrils. "Well, for starters some deodorant for you."

Jack laughed and fished for the white bottle of cologne out of his pants pocket. "I'm surprised that dreadful hospice didn't have a little sign in my room with the same cliché all the hotels use about not replacing towels because they're trying to be green. In my case they calculated by the time anyone saw me again the undertaker would have given me a nice sponge bath." He opened up his shirt and applied the cologne like it was a salt shaker."

"You're right, I do turn green easily." I pinched my nose and started the car.

Jack laughed. "Don't worry none because I applied enough for us both. But let me guess, you packed flannel pajamas, slippers, and of course a fresh dress shirt and tie for tomorrow."

I was embarrassed because close friends sometimes know too much. My folks used to brag they were "green" before sustainability became fashionable. Truth be told, they lived paycheck to paycheck and shunned the oil deliveryman like a leper. So to me, flannel pj's were comparable to a space suit designed to maintain one's core temperature even if your ear lobes were numb when you woke up.

"Well, neither one of us has a coat," I replied quickly and turned the radio on to stop the embarrassing interrogation.

"You've always been such a control freak. Haven't you learned anything today?" Jack sighed.

"Yeah," I said. "Hanging around you has always been dangerous and French cars don't have reverse."

"And the lesson for this afternoon is it's dangerous to go home when you're a wanted man."

CHAPTER TEN

On the way back to Windham, I carefully obeyed every rule of the road to not draw attention. Two miles from Birch Street my senses went on high alert as another cruiser passed us. Jack sank low in the seat and surveyed the landscape. I almost convinced myself not to stop home and buy our necessities at the store. But everything I needed was nicely packed and waiting, so why throw away good money? Plus, there was a certain prayer card I especially wanted which would never be found in any card aisle or church on earth.

My obsessions might be peculiar, but did not make me reckless. I did a quick drive by to make sure my white ranch house wasn't wrapped in police tape. The only sentry was a sorry-looking forty-gallon trash barrel.

I pulled around the corner and stopped in front of the Meissners' milk chocolate–colored Cape with white shutters. They wintered in Florida and no one would hassle us parked here.

"Be back in a flash," I said quickly, not wanting another argument.

"Leave the keys in the ignition because if you're not back in fifteen minutes, I'm leaving without you. You're not going to mess up my plans."

I sniffed the air. "I thought short-timers were supposed to be nice."

"Nice gets you thrown under the bus most of the time," Jack said. "Want to bet fifty bucks you won't make it back in fifteen minutes?" He sat back and pulled the hat down to cover his eyes.

I scratched my cheek and opened the door, which squeaked just like its twin. "Are you really going to gamble right up to the end?"

Jumping out of the car, I immediately missed my coat. The temperature remained only a smidgeon above freezing and my T-shirt and white button down oxford didn't offer much warmth. I rubbed my hands together while quickly walking toward my ugly brown trash barrel two houses away. It had a series of holes in the bottom and would be prime real estate for flies to lay their eggs in a couple months. I had planned to buy a new one today and leave it for whoever bought the house. Errands like these were minutiae to most, but they provided me with a sense of purpose. Would I ever enjoy such mundane tasks again?

"Oh, Dennis," a high-pitched voice suddenly called out.

I caught sight of Mrs. Werner's tan flat shoes quickly approaching from ten o'clock. She was a sweet and attractive German woman with platinum hair pinned up in a tight bun and today she wore a burgundy turtleneck sweater and light jeans. The last time she cornered me I received an hour dissertation on how much chicken manure to put in my garden. I nicknamed her husband "Silent Cal"; he passed away eight years ago. Through the years I wondered if his sparse communication style, which consisted primarily of nods and short sentences, forced his wife to overcompensate.

And to make matters worse, Mrs. Werner had taken a liking to me. No doubt Merriam looked down from heaven enjoying a good belly laugh watching this pursuit. At first, I considered the extra attention to her being neighborly after my loss. But after six months of crock-pot dinners highlighting gastro-feats from multiple cultures and a never-ending supply of Swedish jelly cookies, she must have concluded I was either a thick-headed Irishman or just plain stupid. I knew I had to tell her I was moving out west to be close to my son, but I kept delaying the conversation until the Realtor put the "For Sale" sign on the lawn sometime next week.

Mrs. Werner grabbed my right hand and stopped my forward progress. "Dennis, where is your coat?" she asked in alarm.

Her hand felt warm and it made me think back to New Year's Eve when she invited me over for a mug of Glühwein. The hot spiced wine made for a wonderful distraction to break up an otherwise lonely day and helped to ready myself for another year of the same. I enjoyed the wine and chuckled to myself as the widow's cheeks blushed the more she imbibed. She finally asked why I called her Mrs. Werner instead of using her first name. Kirsten was a lovely name indeed, but I hesitated using it in fear of leading her on. Thankfully, I looked up in the nick of time to find myself strategically positioned under a sprig of mistletoe. My lonely neighbor became startled when, after a hearty guzzle of wine, I leapt up and pulled out my new iPhone.

"I didn't hear the phone ring," she said, stating the obvious.

I put my hand over the receiver and whispered that I had it on vibrate. Walking into her dining room, I carried on a spirited monologue. Within five minutes I had extricated myself to address an imaginary emergency with my son. Looking back, I shuddered to think what might have happened with another glass of hot wine.

Mrs. Werner still held my hand. "And why is your face so red? Are you allergic to something again?"

I remembered getting hives on New Year's Eve too. "I'm fine, but just upset over an old friend of mine dying in hospice." I backed up two steps to regain my personal space. "I'm rushing so much today I forgot my coat back at the hospice."

Her expression told me she wasn't buying the truth this time.

"Anyone I know?"

No harm, no foul, and she had every right to be upset after the New Year's Eve episode. "I'm sure you remember Jack."

Her face soured and the sudden transformation alarmed me. "Merriam told me all about that man," she said, shaking her head. "If he's such a good friend he would have been here for both of you." She stroked my arm and her floral perfume, which made Merriam sneeze, enveloped me. "I didn't see him at the funeral. Am I right?"

I gave her a half smile, afraid if she kept talking, I might be tempted to let Jack expire in Nurse Nancy's French contraption. I glanced toward my trash barrel. It was leaning badly and I questioned whether it was just my perspective.

"Well, that's just like you. Helping a friend through his last days; teaching him how friendship means never having to say you're sorry."

I tried to resist, but couldn't help myself. "No, the line from the movie is, 'Love means never having to say you're sorry.'"

"Movie?"

"Yeah, *Love Story.*"

"Can we rent it?" She moved a step closer.

I could see that wanting expression. I couldn't tell her it was rated as one of the most romantic films of all time.

I shook my head slowly. "It's a really sad movie from 1970 about someone losing his wife after a terrible illness. I'm afraid it would be difficult for me to watch it after losing Merriam last year." I avoided her cat green eyes altogether and checked my watch. "Wow, I have to get a move on."

She did her best to hold a smile, even though disappointment weighed down the corners of her mouth like she asked me to the prom and I turned her down. As a kid, I used to imagine being someone different when I became an adult. Truth is you're the same in your late sixties as you were at nine or seventeen years old, except for the aches and pains and a bunch of experiences many confuse with wisdom.

I had no more to add to the chitchat, so I smiled and hoped to be dismissed.

"Okay, but when things settle down you'll have to come over for some tea," she said, hoping to establish a new beachhead. "I just received the new Burpee seed catalogue and I found some varietals which are absolutely incredible." Her eyes danced and looked skyward. "It won't be long now. They used to say no planting before Memorial Day to be safe, but I think there's something to all this talk of global warming. The last two years I planted tomatoes in early May with no problem."

"May also brings swarms of mayflies around here which discourages people from standing around and shooting the breeze," I said by accident. Nodding politely, I began moving again. My driveway was only another hundred steps away. I imagined slipping through the kitchen and down the short hall to my bedroom. The small black suitcase was nestled next to my bureau with the memorial card sitting on top. On the way out, I would grab two down jackets out of the hall closet. With focus I could be dashing past Mrs. Werner's house again in under three minutes. My stomach suddenly growled and I remembered the plump green seedless grapes I had in the fridge and decided to grab the bag on the way out too. Maybe their coolness would be good for poor Jack. Maybe he would accept them as a peace offering for this detour and maybe even turn nice for a while.

Suddenly I caught sight of a dark green SUV police cruiser with a black battering ram attached to its front bumper, coming down the street. The vehicle looked like it belonged in a SWAT movie and could easily trample through my house. My lungs seized and prevented me from running back to Jack.

Closing a sale always hung on proper delivery. The next sentence I uttered would seal our fate.

"Oh, Kirsten," I called out and spun around.

Mrs. Werner was halfway up the short asphalt driveway and stopped dead in her tracks. The way she turned and looked at me made me think she heard a heavenly choir.

"Come to think of it, may I borrow your seed catalogue for a day?"

She almost skipped toward me, her smile as wide as I had ever seen. She had nice white teeth which made me admire the pink lipstick even more.

"Sure, but why?"

In a flash, I grabbed her arm and escorted her up the sidewalk to block the view of the approaching cruiser. She readily obliged, no doubt startled by my sudden advance.

"Jack and I have relived the same tired stories ten times to Sunday," I said as we made our way toward her front door. "I need something new to interest him. Talking about gardens would get his mind off his illness for a bit. It's probably no surprise he likes wildflowers."

"But I already have all the pages marked." A frown interrupted her smile and we hesitated at the front steps.

I remembered the line from the movie *Glengarry Glen Ross* which every salesman knows by heart: "Always be closing." "I promise to return it," I said and raised my right hand to make the scouts honor symbol.

The possibility of me owing her a favor was not lost on the good woman. I could sense an invite to watch *Love Story*.

Mrs. Werner bolted up the three red brick stairs and held the white storm door open. "The catalogue is yours. Come inside and I'll make us some tea."

I preferred a quart of Glühwein to wash down a handful of aspirin.

CHAPTER ELEVEN

My finger was becoming numb from dialing the rotary phone but ten minutes before closing time, Jean finally answered and I offered to sell her the car for seven hundred dollars, explaining the "extra courtesy discount" from my considerate sales manager.

There was a long delay on the other end and then a faint sniffle. I wanted to tell her I should be the one bawling my eyes out, but bit my tongue as I'd said too much already. I fingered the worn coiled cord, ready to hang myself if this didn't go well.

"Things have changed," she finally managed to get out. "You gotta meet me tonight."

My radar went up; I didn't want to go anywhere near this desperate woman outside work. "Look, it's late. Come in tomorrow morning and we'll do the deal, I promise."

"No, it has to be tonight or not at all." The tone was urgent.

I checked with Frank Riley and his dark counsel demanded I meet this crazy lady anywhere this side of hell as my botched sale trumped any safety concerns. So an hour later I found myself across town at the 400 Club. Jean sat alone at a small dark wooden table in the corner nervously caressing a bottle of Schlitz. When she saw me she unzipped her shabby-looking coat.

I bought a gin and tonic at the bar before taking a chair across from her. The legs were not square and I rocked side to side. We sat in silence for an awkward moment seeking solace in our drinks. Her beer bottle shook whenever she raised it to her mouth. I felt bad but not that bad.

"Okay. Let's get this over with so I can spend the rest of my life trying to forget you," I said to her black turtleneck sweater before I could stop my mouth.

She took a long swig of beer and frowned.

"And you should tell your face you're happy. You're stealing the Polara at that price."

Jean smirked and began searching her coat pocket and I half expected a gun to appear. Instead, she slid an automobile key across the dark and sticky wooden table. The head of the silver key bore the familiar Chrysler insignia of a five-pointed star. My throat tightened like it did whenever Frank turned soulless and gave one of my hard fought leads to someone else to close. "So let me get this straight. You wanted to meet so you could tell me you bought a car from someone else? That's wicked, but I guess we're even now." I began to stand.

She grabbed my arm. "You have it all wrong as usual. This is the key to the Polara."

I sat back in the chair. "What are you talking about? All the keys are locked in the cabinet. I should know because I have to move every car before a snowstorm arrives then afterwards brush off a hundred frozen M&Ms before moving them all back." I took a drink. "Lot duty is miserable."

"This is the spare key. Hank gave it to me when he promised me the car."

I guzzled the remainder of my drink and immediately wanted another. "That's a nice memento, lady, but the key won't do you much good without owning the other ninety-nine percent."

She began peeling the label off the beer bottle with enthusiasm. "How much did you make this month?"

My jaw dropped open. I held up my hand to get the bartender's attention and ordered another drink before returning to Jean. "That's none of your business."

Jean leaned in close and her tired brown eyes came alive. "I've been watching you for weeks now and you haven't sold a single car. Rent must be getting pretty tough to make." She pointed at my empty glass. "Want me to buy the next round?"

I sat back too fast in the unsteady chair and almost lost my balance. "I'd quit drinking first. What do you want?"

The skinned beer bottle slid my way. "I don't have enough money to buy the car."

The words got stuck on the dark sticky table and I wanted to get sick all over them. The chain reaction would now be set in motion. Frank would fire me, causing my father to be embarrassed and Merriam left crying unable to pay the bills. I looked toward the bar and noticed a hippie-looking guy with three shot glasses in front of him. He would be my new best buddy after this meeting.

"But don't fret none, Dennis," Jean continued. "You're going to sell me the car but this one will be off the books."

I refocused. "What do you mean?"

She leaned forward and produced a white business-size envelope from her back pocket and put it on the table in front of us. "Here's three hundred. All you have to do is unlock the front gate at midnight."

My eyes were fixated on the bulging envelope. "I don't understand."

"The less you know the better. My daughter and I have to leave Salem tonight."

The reality hit me. "So you're planning on stealing the car?"

She picked up the key. "Possession is nine-tenths the law."

"And you think I'm going to help you? You're nuts." I glanced back at the bar looking for my drink.

"Help me?" She laughed. "Only in planting the idea. When I was making a fool of myself this afternoon in front of your desk you said the car wouldn't follow me home because you had the keys. Then I remembered I had one too."

"Why would I risk my job and do that?"

"Because you're broke and you need this money to tide you over until you find another job. But my advice is stay away from selling cars." She shrugged. "I'm just sayin', it's not you."

I stroked my jaw and felt my five o'clock shadow. The three hundred would cover next month's rent. The bartender came over and placed the drink on the table.

"This is the best commission any lot boy will ever make. And if you're nervous, beat up the lock with a hammer so it doesn't look like an inside job."

Who was in sales now? Frank couldn't blame me for a stolen car.

"If you're caught, how do I know you won't blab?"

"Because I never fink on anyone." She searched my face. "Promise me you'll unlock the gate at midnight."

I nodded and picked up the envelope and in one gulp swallowed the drink and my pride.

CHAPTER TWELVE

Peeking through the white sheer curtains, I spied the dark green police cruiser in my driveway. The suitcase and prayer card were now hopelessly beyond reach and my stomach hurt. I wished I could sneak through the cellar and get my stuff without being noticed like they did on TV.

"Make yourself comfortable, Dennis," Mrs. Werner sang from the kitchen.

I moved away from the window and caught a faint scent of bacon and wondered if it originated from breakfast or perhaps something creative for lunch. My gaze fell on the small blue velvet couch which my neighbor always referred to as a love seat. "Good grief," I whispered and quickly surveyed the ceiling to make sure the mistletoe wasn't still hanging there from Christmas, rotting but still lethal. Could my life get any more complicated?

The seed catalogue sat alone on the oak coffee table. A generous population of pink Post-it Notes peeked out from multiple pages. Evidently, my neighbor prepared well in advance for the short planting season. I remembered reading if the Pilgrims had settled on the west coast first, New England would be sparsely populated today.

I looked around for a television and planned to mute the sound and quickly scan the local channels for reports on our shenanigans. However, my neighbor bucked the trend and didn't have a TV or computer in the living room. A tall pile of books sat next to a healthy Bella palm. Judging from the titles, Mrs. Werner liked romance and murder mysteries. I shivered.

The tall walnut grandfather clock in the corner ticked off the passing seconds. Ten minutes had elapsed since I left the Renault. My buddy was a stickler on time and would abandon me on principle.

I took out my cell phone and held it up to my ear, wishing I was more than a one-trick pony.

"Hi, Tom," I said loudly then silently counted out ten Mississippi's. "Well, you've put me in a tough spot and I don't appreciate it one bit." I heard the floor in the kitchen chirp and waited another few seconds to make sure Mrs. Werner found the best position to eavesdrop.

"Look here. I don't care if the transmission is shot. I need my car back this afternoon. Do you understand? My best friend is dying and he'll be six feet under by next week." I paused for a long moment. "Well, I think in this type of emergency you should provide a loaner vehicle. That you don't is very disappointing."

Plopping down on the love seat, I let out a loud moan and right on cue, the sweet lady entered with a dessert plate full of her famous Swedish jelly cookies. She knew I had a weakness for them and I usually let the lonely woman talk for an hour so I could get my fill. However, I decided to rethink my cravings moving forward given her taste in novels. If things went badly after today, I could envision a future episode of *CSI* where the victim is pelted with kisses then poisoned with tea and dessert.

Mrs. Werner ignored my one-act play and smiled. "I have the kettle on and the tea will be ready soon."

Given the situation it wasn't hard to scowl and I grabbed a cookie off the plate and impolitely stuffed the whole thing in my mouth and chewed vigorously.

"What is it, Dennis?"

I glanced over her shoulder and could make out a mean-looking forest green Dodge Charger pulling into my driveway. The chevron belonged to the New Hampshire State Police and I stopped chewing. State Police were formidable lawmen and wore crisp uniforms with broad-brimmed high hats that commanded respect. My house hadn't seen this much activity since Merriam died. Although the police couldn't enter my house without a search warrant, they would certainly trample all the flower beds lining the house and track mud all over the place in the process. Given my luck, I expected another cruiser to arrive any moment and unleash a police dog that would smell his way over here as I waited for tea.

Mrs. Werner watched me intently and nibbled on a cookie.

"I just hung up with my mechanic," I said in a squeaky voice. "I had car problems when I drove to the hospice this morning so I dropped it off at the shop and took a cab home."

Mrs. Werner dabbed her mouth with a napkin. "Yes, I saw you leave. But why didn't the taxi drop you off at your house?"

I took a deep breath to consider possible alibis. "Well, the silly driver typed the wrong address into his GPS and brought me to the Meissners' instead of mine. After being cooped up in the hospice, I welcomed the fresh air even without a coat."

She nodded slowly, weighing my white lie, and I reached down to grab another cookie. "His mistake was my good fortune as I'm clearly addicted to your baking."

Her warm smile returned.

I gently rubbed the tiny bumps on my forehead as they began to itch in protest to this continuing charade. "This morning my mechanic promised to have my car back by tonight, but I found out he can't get the parts until the middle of next week." I shook my head slowly. "Now I need to find a rental and don't know when I can make it back to the hospice today." I picked up the seed catalogue. "Jack would have loved looking at all this beauty in his final hours." I bit my lip and held my breath.

Mrs. Werner took another small bite of her cookie and chewed slowly while studying me. "Nonsense, take my car," she finally replied. "I've already been to the market today."

I blew out a long breath. "Bless you." I wished I could tell her the truth, but didn't think she would take kindly to aiding a couple of fugitives even if I promised a candlelight dinner and dancing. No, better to leave her in the dark and hope she would bring me cookies when I landed in prison. I was sure my cellmate Bubba would enjoy them too.

"Is he at Restful Waters?"

I nodded slowly, afraid of the question.

"Would you like me to drive you over? I don't want to see that terrible man, but I would make an exception given the circumstances."

"No," I said much too quickly. "Jack is very particular about who sees him right now. I'm sure you can understand why. He looks frightful in a johnnie and he hallucinates about people watching him from the ceiling."

Five minutes later I said a prayer of thanksgiving as the garage door opened on the gray split-level house with black shutters. Mrs. Werner owned a 3 Series silver BMW, or as her late husband used to boast, "the ultimate driving machine." I knew from my brief days of selling cars it was all about marketing spin no matter how many engineers advanced the technology. In this case, the allure of owning a premium brand had succeeded in extracting forty grand from an old guy who drove like he lived in a school zone and too introverted to brag.

After I hunkered down in the driver's seat, I grinned to find this car came equipped with automatic transmission and with German engineering, eagerly agreed to go into reverse. I backed slowly out of the driveway, using the side mirrors so I wouldn't be profiled by the men in blue next door.

When I backed into the street I looked up at the house. Mrs. Werner stood in the front door enthusiastically waving goodbye, no doubt too occupied plotting my repayment schedule to notice the gathering next door. I waved back and then patted my bulging shirt pocket, which contained four pilfered jelly cookies. If I survived this odyssey, I decided to take her out for one of those early bird specials around town before I moved out west. Based on the spicy crock-pot dinners she sent over I knew she would enjoy Mexican. I glanced in my rearview mirror and caught sight of a policeman looking in my neglected trash barrel. Was I really that interesting?

My luck held when I rounded the corner and found the Renault still sitting where I left it twenty-five minutes ago. I parked in front of our getaway car and looked in the rearview mirror. The Renault looked empty. At first, I thought Jack must be napping before realizing he might be lying dead across the front seats. "That would be just like him," I said. "Throw me like a lobster in boiling water and then listen to me scream."

The street was deserted. I stuffed a cookie in my mouth and jumped out of the car and rushed to the driver's side of the Renault. I checked the back seat twice before concluding with certainty the car was empty. Spinning around, I surveyed the sickly-looking yellow lawns of the surrounding houses. There were few bushes to hide behind. "Are you kidding me?" I yelled and ran my hand through my hair. A piece of the cookie got stuck in my throat and I bent over coughing.

I considered rummaging through the yards, but where to begin? The last thing I needed was a neighbor calling the police about some old guy with no coat munching on Swedish jelly cookies and wandering yard to yard calling out Jack's name. It occurred to me that maybe my dying friend left a note in the car, so I jumped into the driver's seat and looked around. Finding nothing, I opened the glove compartment and noticed a small white envelope with something scribbled across its face. I grabbed for it and it acted like a fisherman's net and caught a bunch of other stuff and deposited everything on the floor.

I grabbed the paper and read an alphabetized grocery list written horizontally: cereal, cheese, crackers, mayonnaise, milk. That's when the sandwich bag on the floor mat caught my attention. It looked like catnip, but I remembered the '60s enough to recognize marijuana. Now I knew why Nurse Nancy ordered a whole pizza. She had the munchies.

A severe cramp bolted across my stomach and I closed my eyes to think. No one could ever deny I went to the mat for my best friend. I decided to return the BMW to Mrs. Werner, grab another handful of cookies for courage, and walk next door and turn myself in. I mean how much would they punish an old guy trying to be there for his dying friend? Any lawyer worth his salt would have fun with this case, especially if the jury had a majority of veterans.

I opened my eyes and sat up. That's when I found Jack. He strolled out of the Meissners' front door like he lived there, peeling an orange.

A flash of blue lights in the rearview mirror caught my attention as a cruiser pulled in behind me.

CHAPTER THIRTEEN

"Just another smashed turtle," I said as the hives around my throat pulsated in unison to scream "way to go, big guy." Once again my rescue mission failed because I hesitated instead of running. God's green earth covers almost two hundred million square miles. Remaining undetected for a couple of days should have been relatively easy in the busy Merrimack Valley where we had so many choices. Boston was only thirty minutes south, or we could have headed east to Route 1 and threaded our way along the Atlantic coastline into Maine. Alternatively, a tank of gas would carry us north to the White Mountains or west to the Berkshires, unless an idiot like me decided to return home to retrieve pajamas and a prayer card. I imagined sitting on the love seat right now with my German neighbor and concluding the rescue operation was "kaput." I looked forward to landing a spot on *America's Most Stupid Criminals.*

I glanced at Jack expecting fury, but he was leaning against the black lamppost on the sidewalk with half the buttons on his plaid shirt undone looking like some mad lawn ornament. Every few seconds he would spit out a seed, as he calmly took in the drama unfolding in front of him. Another quick look in my side mirror confirmed the worse. I was tightly wedged between the silver Beamer and the cruiser. The blond policeman remained in the cruiser talking into a hand piece, no doubt summoning the other cops at my house. Tomorrow, he would be the talk of the town as the arresting officer and his mug would be on the front page of the *Eagle-Tribune* explaining how he handily apprehended two geezers before their crime wave spread. In typical police jargon, he would boast how he discovered the "perps" and made the arrests before back-up arrived. But at the station, he would be teased by the brotherhood for arresting "one and a half men."

Anger welled up and I almost threw up a half dozen cookies. Fear produced an offspring of smashed turtles and a laminated prayer card which demanded nightly penance. Unable to escape the past or move forward pretty much summed up my life. What no one knew—not my wife, son, or best friend—was the burden I shouldered alone. All they saw was a husband, father, and friend made of brittle stone. They didn't understand stone and stoic have the same number of letters and share the first three.

I beat the steering wheel with both hands and vowed not to let failure end with a whimper this time.

The cop kept talking on his radio, like he assumed I was some sort of arthritic invalid who wouldn't dare make a run for it. I decided it was time to teach this youngster how much hesitation costs.

In a flash, I buckled myself in and started up the Renault. Revving the engine until the tachometer redlined, I held onto the steering wheel with a death grip and popped the clutch.

The car leaped forward into the back of Mrs. Werner's beautiful silver BMW. Clearly, I was now deep into deficit spending and would have to make it up to her, even if it meant sitting on the love seat and dabbing myself with calamine lotion to control the hives. Luckily, mistletoe is hard to find in March.

Unfortunately, the "ultimate driving machine" lived up to its billing and the car barely moved. I pushed the accelerator to the floor, but the only thing moving were my rear tires as they spun and smoked and the smell of burnt rubber filled the car. Looking in the rearview mirror, I could see the policeman had finally decided to take me seriously. The cruiser door flew open.

Panic engulfed me and pain shot across my chest. While I wasn't ready to greet my Maker, I preferred the odds because the cop looked so angry. Granted, he would have to write up an additional accident report now before his cameo appearance on TV, but did he have to look so irate?

Instinctively, I grabbed for the shifter, trying to find reverse knowing it was a futile effort and wishing Jack possessed magical powers to push the car sideways. My right hand shook badly and I grabbed the shaft rather than the top of the stick. Suddenly, I was being catapulted backwards and plowed hard into the mouth of the cruiser. My head hit the headrest pretty hard before I remembered to let up on the gas.

Seconds later, Jack appeared and helped me out of the car. He still held the half-eaten orange.

"I see you finally found reverse," he said matter of fact like we were at the batting cages at Hampton Beach and I found my groove. "While you were gone, I read the owner's manual and found out we missed seeing the stupid ring below the shift knob. You just have to pull up on it to shift into reverse."

My head ached and I looked at the police car. I had pushed the Crown Victoria back a good two feet. Its front end was steaming with a green puddle collecting underneath and the sweet smell of antifreeze filled the air. Jack stood next to me carrying on about the manual transmission while stuffing another piece of fruit in his mouth. It looked so good and I felt my shirt pocket. Two cookies were still comfortably nestled in my pocket and I considered trading him one for a piece of fruit. I looked at the Renault, expecting to see myself still strapped in the driver's seat, which would explain this out of body feeling.

"You're under arrest," the policeman said, swaggering toward me.

I envied his warm blue down coat. When my gaze moved north, I read contempt in his graphite eyes.

"You stupid old man! Get down on your knees before I beat twenty years out of you."

The boasting that belonged to him moments ago now would be laced with ridicule. I remembered Jack telling me that nice gets you thrown under the bus most of the time and this cop considered me nothing more than a worn out trash can where common houseflies and other filth reside. So I didn't hesitate a moment before reaching back and hitting him as hard as I could, catching him above the right eye. It was the first punch I'd thrown since high school and amazingly he collapsed on the ground. My hand hurt like hell and I shook it hard.

Jack dropped the remainder of the orange which I thought was a shame and pulled me away. "Easy now, big guy. You better hope he doesn't remember this when he wakes up."

The back of my head felt funny, like the blood looked frantically for an escape hatch. I tried to think what we should do next, but my thoughts ran as thick as molasses. Seemed Jack had somehow found a way into the Meissners' and they left oranges. One would taste so good right now. I never did get my green grapes in the fridge and I fantasized hiding in their basement and eating oranges while the police searched the neighborhood. It sounded farfetched but given everything else up to now not out of the realm of possibility.

There was a hard tug on my arm. "What are you waiting for, Denny?" Jack asked, bringing me back to the present. It was good to see color in his face again and he pointed at the policeman beginning to stir.

"You didn't knock the cop into the middle of next week. We have to get out of here and quick."

"Well, the Renault is no good." I surveyed the back of the car. The trunk was smashed in and the rear bumper lodged behind the right rear tire.

"But didn't I see you drive up in the BMW?" Jack asked.

Yes, of course. The trunk had a good-sized dent, but the "ultimate driving machine" was still sitting there, inviting, just like its owner.

Seconds later the black leather seat felt good and reminded me of my recliner back home even if Mark called it vinyl.

Jack turned and looked out the back window. "C'mon, let's go!"

I started to panic as I couldn't find the keys. I checked both pant pockets. Had I left them in the Renault?

"Denny, your new buddy is coming."

My finger felt the oblong widget in my shirt pocket under the cookies as my eyes located the start button on the console. My mind cleared enough to remember the keyless entry.

I pushed the start button, the car roared to life, and I threw it in drive.

A hard slap on the trunk made me jump. In my rearview mirror I caught sight of the cop. He bled above one eyebrow and the look on his face would haunt me for some time. I pushed the accelerator to the floor, hoping I would never see that face again.

CHAPTER FOURTEEN

*Frank Riley waited at the front gate. This was the same guy known
for never venturing outside the showroom unless pursuing a prospect
attempting to flee his evil closing tricks. Gloves were foreign to him
and I took notice of his clenched fists as my headache worsened. I had
successfully blocked him out of my sleep last night after a pint of
Seagram's. Merriam sensed my sour mood and went to bed early
without kissing me goodnight. By eleven o'clock I felt medicated
enough to dial Jean's number to tell her I changed my mind about
being an accessory to grand theft auto. I planned on returning the
three hundred less fifty bucks for the aggravation she put me through.*

*The phone rang until my ears were ringing too. "Well, she can do
the penguin shuffle all night if she's waiting for me," I said to the
empty whiskey bottle. "And my finger is still numb from dialing her a
hundred times earlier, so she will be sorely disappointed if she thinks
I'm going to try all night."*

*The bald sales manager with the big head and little eyes watched
me approach. Even from twenty feet away, I could read the question
on his face. Did I get the sale? I decided to tell him the truth and try to
convince him we were both taken for a ride.*

*"Hello," I called out with all the bravado my pounding head could
stand. Frank had made it clear early on that "Good morning" was
reserved for those that made target. Everyone else could just go to
hell until they moved some metal boxes with wheels.*

Frank exhaled and white smoke danced around his nostrils like the dragon he didn't have to pretend to be. "That crazy client of yours really lit up the town last night." He pointed behind him.

I followed his stubby finger to a ten-foot section of fence that apparently King Kong tore up in the darkness. Bent aluminum posts stood as injured sentries on each side of a gaping hole but still married to the torn fencing. Broken glass and cream-colored plastic pieces littered the street. The smell of gasoline hung in the air.

"I don't understand," I mumbled, trying to rationalize what happened and knowing the answer would somehow include Jean.

Frank blew into one of his fists hard and his cheeks puffed up like a trumpet player. "You not only fail at selling cars but current affairs too," he said, eyeing me in amazement. "Why, it's been all over the news this morning. That lady you decided to play hardball with came back and stole the car."

I strained to survey the far end of the lot, looking for where the old Polara used to stand bleeding from under its chest and blocking the dingy blue cat food plant. "Did she get caught?"

"Stopped cold when she tried to outrun a cruiser. The news said she tried to take the interstate but missed the on-ramp," he said dryly. "If you had let her take the car out on a test drive, she would have known the front end was shot and didn't corner well over forty."

Frank looked down at his black penny loafers and frowned before wiping some dirt off one toe with his bare hand. "Dodge may build cars for safety, but not for head-butting bridge abutments at eighty miles an hour. It's a miracle her daughter only suffered cuts and bruises. That piece of chaff should have buckled herself in too."

I wanted to hold my breath, but couldn't until I asked, "How bad did she get hurt?"

Frank didn't nod or flinch a muscle and just stared at me, like I was some interesting sort of bug that needed to be squished with his cold nubby thumb.

An awkward moment passed as the sweat on my forehead turned cold. "Promise me you'll unlock the gate at midnight," she'd pleaded. The bribe was still in my breast pocket and I feared it would explode any second. I decided if I could make it to my desk and get lost in studying the lead sheets, maybe I could delay processing all of this.

I took a step past Frank before his icy fingers dug through my wool coat and into my right arm. "Where do you think you're going?"

I pointed past the broken fence and all the madness. "To work."

He shoved me backwards. "If you followed my directions, you would have closed the deal with that head case. But no, you wanted to pin all your inadequacies on her. Then I told you to go and meet her last night and get it done and you choked again. Now the car is totaled and instead of seven hundred bucks, maybe I'll see two hundred from the insurance company. Add in the expense to fix the fence, not to mention our reputation, and you've created an unbelievable mess for me."

There was no soul in this talking head of his. I looked at the bent aluminum poles and knew how they felt.

Frank extended his arms wide. "You can tell your daddy you've got a killer instinct all right. A young woman is dead because of you."

Chills ran through me and my ears started to ring. My head pounded and I wanted to throw up and struggled to keep it to a gag.

I stumbled backwards two more steps. "What?"

"Get out of here before I have you arrested for trespassing." He came toward me fast and I expected to be pummeled with brass knuckles and braced myself. Instead, he slapped a worn silver key in the palm of my hand and I remembered Jean holding its twin at the bar last night. "Here's a parting gift from me so you never forget how big a failure you are."

Jean was dead and a little girl had no mother because of me. Who was chaff now?

CHAPTER FIFTEEN

"How much cash do you have?"

That question should have been emblazoned on a T-shirt years ago for Jack. He claimed he didn't carry much scratch because he would blow it if readily accessible. In truth he was broke thanks to the perpetual financial tsunami which laid waste to everything in his life: cars, homes, and relationships. While most people's largest expense each month is housing or child support, for Jack it came down to paying his bookie. And as bank after bank deserted him over the years, he came to rely on cash for all transactions.

After one painful period ten years ago, Jack moved into a studio apartment above Ned's Variety Store, a renovated hundred-year-old white farm house only a stone's throw from Rockingham Park Race Track and afflicted with a gaudy neon sign advertising a carton of Camel cigarettes for $39.99. The arrangement turned out to be a model of efficiency. Jack could simply walk downstairs, cash his pension check at the register, and pay Paco the bookie. With whatever funds he had left to live on, he could pick up a few groceries within a twenty-foot radius along with a scratch ticket or two. It was pathetic to see someone with a monthly income many would envy, having to scrounge for a meal by the end of the month. On the rare occasion his horse came in, he lived like a soldier about to be sent to the front and showed all his adopted new buddies a good time. The binge and his friends would last until the money ran out, which at his burn rate never meant more than a few weeks.

"I have around twenty bucks," I finally replied.

"Wow, aren't you afraid of being rolled carrying so much?"

I was tired of randomly trolling through residential neighborhoods for cover and pulled over. I tilted my head back to look through the sunroof and there wasn't a cloud to mar the denim blue sky. "Well, I didn't think I would need more than a few quarters for the vending machine with the way you've been carrying on. Yet, here you are still jive talking. And if you didn't look so bad, I'd agree with Stu this was nothing more than a chance for one more fling." I threw a fresh piece of Juicy Fruit in my mouth.

His laughter filled the car. "You're on to me, Denny. I thought if I lost a hundred pounds and coughed my insides out, I could make it look like lung cancer and really soak my friends." He turned around and inspected the back seat. "But you're the only one here so I guess my plan failed. Now I'm left here with you and you're so tight with money I'd have to break into Fort Knox to get a dime. Man, you won't even share your gum with me."

I reached in my pocket and offered him a stick.

Jack shoved my hand away. "I have mouth sores from the chemo and never understood your addiction to that brand. And by the way you should keep your mouth shut when you're chewing. It's gross."

"But you said you wanted a piece."

"Just making a point, Denny. Just making a point."

I moaned and chomped extra loud with my mouth open and studied a small snow pile across the street in the shadow of a large red brick colonial. Salt, sand, and exhaust made it look like rocky road ice cream and these last vestiges of winter sometimes lasted well into June, no matter the temperature. I couldn't wait to trade this in for Napa mustard blossoms next winter.

"It always comes back to money, doesn't it?" Jack said barely above a whisper. "That's why you had a lousy job selling vacuum cleaners and I visited every race track on the east coast." He let out a long sigh. "And here I am at the end of my life still chasing dead presidents. They're such a finicky bunch and none ever took a liking to me."

I figured the meds must be doing their job, as his rant wasn't short circuited by a coughing fit this time. Even so, he remained the color of a manila envelope and I wondered what kept him going. Stu told me

Jack got angry when he was denied a ten-thousand-dollar loan. I wondered why he needed such a large purse. And I didn't see how throwing ten grand around, even for charity, would motivate St. Peter to unlock the pearly gates.

"So now what?" I asked. "We can't sit here all day." I played with the windshield wipers and they came alive and waved once.

Jack sat up in his seat. "You always get crabby when you miss a meal. McDonald's is just down the street and we can have a late lunch." He slapped the dashboard and I heard a dinner bell. "Sure hope they can break a twenty."

Five minutes later I scanned the parking lot surrounding the golden arches for any police presence. Happily, there were none and the lot was half full which provided good cover.

A short string of vehicles lined up for the drive-up window and we pulled in behind a burgundy minivan. The air was heavy with the smell of French fries and I felt a kindred spirit with the small convention of pigeons milling about three pine picnic tables on a small cement slab. Yesterday's rain had finally removed the frozen tarp and the birds were searching for any leftovers from Thanksgiving when the first snow of the season buried everything.

The queue remained stalled and I watched the takeout window attendant pass two huge white bags of food to a red Camry. Weren't the kids in school? My stomach accused me again of neglect. "Want to treat that lucky hat of yours to a Happy Meal?" I asked my frowning wingman.

The joke missed. "We need cash, Denny."

"Have you forgotten what this country runs on?" I said, holding up my black leather wallet. "Plastic."

Jack pointed to his temple. "Think again, will ya? Use your card and they'll trace us by dinner time."

He had a point, although I couldn't imagine being on the lam for more than a couple days at most. Maybe if we were terrorists they would have FBI helicopters up in the sky looking for us, but this bordered on hubris. "All right, I'll use my debit card then."

"They'll still trace us, Hansel."

I chewed my gum faster.

Jack rolled down his window and stuck out his arm and waved. "Hey, buddy!" he called after a man half our age. Given the multiple white paint stains on his blue jeans and sports visor, it wasn't hard to guess his vocation. He carried a good-sized bag of delicious food.

"You talking to me?" he asked, looking over his shoulder.

"Don't you recognize me? It's me, Jack."

The painter made a U-turn and strutted over and bent down to study us. His thin face looked about twenty-five with at least three days of stubble. "I think you have me mistaken for someone else." He began to back away.

Jack looked disappointed. "How's that pretty wife of yours?"

The question stopped the man in his tracks and his gray eyes narrowed.

"How do you know my Debra?"

Jack hesitated and before I could intercede, he decided to wing it. "She used to come around and hang out with us at the track, but I haven't seen her in a while."

The painter came back and leaned in the open window. I could smell the Big Mac and if my hand wasn't still stinging from hitting the cop, I would have wrestled him for it.

"Well, if you see Debra again, please tell her to come home soon. And you might want to remind her she has three kids asking where Mommy is."

The painter suddenly backed away and karate kicked the passenger door with his paint-covered leather work boots. "And don't be flirting with my wife or I'll plant this steel toe in your face," he yelled. "I don't care how old you are."

He jogged fifty feet and hopped in a white box van with rust outlining the wheel wells and three long aluminum ladders tied to the roof.

I didn't have to get out of the car to know Mrs. Werner would need some serious bodywork to take care of the new dent. I figured they could repair the door at the same time they were repairing the trunk. The words were lined up on my tongue to spray all over Jack, when I remembered what the receptionist told me. *"He thinks he knows everyone."* It wasn't enough the cancer was killing him, it wanted to humiliate him too. "You just can't make this stuff up," I said instead. A shadow on the dashboard caught my eye and I looked up and noticed a large white bag sitting on the closed sunroof. It was the painter's food. He must have placed the Mc-treasure on the roof while he beat up the car.

Ever so slowly, I opened the sunroof and snagged the treasure, feeling like King Pigeon.

Jack watched and laughed. "Keep the twenty, lunch is my treat."

I looked in the bag and smiled. Big Mac, two cheeseburgers, and a large fry. Wow, for a thin guy he must have a hollow leg." The delicious smell filled the car and erased the last of Mrs. Werner's floral perfume. I looked through the sunroof again and smirked. "What no Coke?" I laughed and threw a French fry at the picnic table and three birds raced for the greasy treasure.

Suddenly, there was a flash of white and the cargo van pulled alongside us. For the second time today, we were pinned with a minivan in front and truck behind. The painter jumped out and began kicking Jack's door again with gusto.

"So you steal my wife and now my lunch?"

Jack began to open the door.

"What are you doing?" I asked.

"I'm going to buy him lunch. Give me your twenty."

The minivan in front moved forward and I used the opportunity to dart out of the service lane and almost hit the painter. Jack bounced around in the seat looking like a flying trapeze artist in trouble with the door half open. If it hadn't been for the seat belt, he would have fallen out of the car.

I bolted for the exit straight ahead.

Jack opened the food bag and extracted a three-inch-long golden French fry. "I've only had an orange today and it tasted pretty dry. I don't know why they even sell fruit with seeds. They're such a pain to deal with, especially when you have no place to spit them out."

I was too busy watching the rearview mirror to answer. Jack read my face. "Hey, I did know him, though I can't remember Debra. It's not my fault he's having a tiff with his girl."

"Listen. You didn't know that guy." I watched the van speeding toward us in the rearview mirror.

Exiting the lot, the van gained on us and odds were good we would be victims of road rage over a missing wife, burgers, and fries. I flew through the next intersection even though the light was red. The oncoming traffic stopped the madman.

"Twenty bucks won't even buy us a double bed at some fleabag motel and I'm not spending my last night listening to you snore and hogging the covers," Jack complained. "And besides, you don't have your flannel pajamas. So what are we going to do now?"

"And what's your contribution to this road adventure?" I asked, checking the rearview mirror for the hundredth time. "It sure feels like I'm doing all the heavy lifting here."

"I have money, but it's tied up."

It was my turn to have a belly laugh. "I forgot your millions are in a Swiss bank account. Don't you just hate the inconvenience?" I spit my gum out the window and reached over and grabbed a handful of fries. "But back here on earth, we need money you can take out of a wallet. If we don't figure out something soon we may as well dump the car and ride the rails like a couple of hobos. Since we have no money and no coats we should fit right in. All we need now is a harmonica and we should be able to buy a toy one for a couple of bucks." I shoved the food in my mouth.

My friend looked out the window.

I knew how futile it was to pry anything out of Jack, but given the circumstances I pressed ahead anyway. "Your brother told me you were trying to get a loan. After all I've done for you, I want to know why."

Jack began rummaging around in the hospice paper bag. "You make it sound like I owe you."

"And you don't?"

"Friends don't keep ledgers," he said matter of fact.

I didn't either, until Merriam got sick and he was nowhere to be found. According to my accounting rules, that's when he bankrupted our friendship. I bit my tongue to keep it in.

"I would do the same for you, Denny. Keep talking like that and you can bring me back to the hospice."

"If it was only that simple." I pulled into a convenience store advertising two hot dogs for a buck and decided if that was our next meal, I would rather starve than eat something that had probably been logrolling since Carter was president.

Jack must have come to the same conclusion. "Well, I guess I'll have to make a withdrawal."

The offer made me momentarily forget my anger. "And how are you going to do that?"

"Why, the old-fashioned way," he began with some hesitation. "I'll take out the rest of my savings, which will carry us for a while. Since I'm an eternal optimist, I hope a month from now we'll be looking for another revenue stream."

I studied his face, looking for a lie.

"I have enough pain meds, but I can't stand watching you scratch every other minute. You're making my skin crawl. We need to get you an antihistamine."

I looked at my complexion in the rearview mirror and my face looked blotchy enough to get me on the no-fly list. "Yeah, we'll need buy some toiletries too."

"Toiletries? I don't think I've ever heard a man use that word before."

"Well, they were all packed in my bag and by tomorrow I'll be smelling almost as ripe as you," I said in self-defense and trying to steer clear of the flannel discussion for good. "Plus we need to buy some cheap coats."

"Okay. I think a thousand should cover it."

It surprised me to find him willing to open his tiny wallet. I feared an anorexic-looking moth would appear when he did.

He looked across the street at a small strip mall populated by a grocery store, dry cleaner, and sandwich shop. "Is that Republic Bank over there at the end?"

I squinted to see and frowned. "Why? Is that where you got denied?"

"No. By the way, let me see your iPhone for a second."

85

Puzzled, I handed it to him.

He opened the car door wide then slammed it shut on the device, making a terrible crunching noise and sending a few plastic pieces flying across the dashboard.

"Are you crazy?" I yelled. "That phone cost over six hundred bucks and was a Christmas present from my son. I don't have insurance for it and now Mark is going to worry when he can't reach me."

Jack giggled. "Calm down, man, will you? It's just a fancy phone, not the crown jewels. We need to go off the grid so they can't track us." He reached in his pocket and handed me his beat-up silver cell phone. "This is one of those prepaid jobbers. If you want to call your son and tell him you're okay go ahead and use it, although I wouldn't because he won't understand." He pointed toward the store. "Buy me some sort of sports drink to wash down the morphine, will you? Just a small bottle, though, in case I don't make it past dinner."

I sat back in the seat and got lost in the Big Mac and its special sauce to prevent myself from telling him I hoped so.

"What are you going to do?" I asked when I finished.

"I'm going to make a small withdrawal from that bank across the street."

CHAPTER SIXTEEN

"Are you sure you don't want me to come in with you?" I asked for the third time, feeling like a jerk for being so hard on a dying man, even if he was a terrific pain in my butt.

Jack had an anxious look on his face and it made me wonder if it was caused by the cancer devouring his insides or by wounded pride. He always had been a hard read. You think you know someone after a lifetime, but you never really do.

He shook his head vehemently as if to rally himself. "I don't need you knowing all my business. And while I'm at it, how many more times do I have to tell you I'm okay? You'll know when I'm not. It's called dead and it's pretty unmistakable," he said, closing his eyes tight and opening his mouth wide and sticking out his pale tongue. "At this stage I should be conserving energy, instead of spending most of it explaining myself to a half-wit like you."

"Ah, there's the soft-spoken friend I know and love."

A finger suddenly appeared an inch from my nose. "Now listen to me good, Dennis. I don't want you planning a quick field trip while I'm in the bank. Promise me you won't slip down the road to Dunkin' Donuts so you can snag a honey-glazed doughnut and coffee. The way I watch you inhale pizza, burgers, fries, and cookies it's a wonder you're not three hundred pounds."

I looked down at my poor belly. "Since Merriam died, I've lost five pounds. I'm a lousy cook and eat takeout a lot."

"Well, I used to entertain folks at chemo about your addiction to hot dogs and they would ask how many years have you been gone? I would laugh and say you were still kicking and must be related to Keith Richards because you both defy nature. Go figure. You consume all those nitrates and I'm the one that gets cancer." He worked to catch his breath. "You never learned to cook because you have a problem following directions, so let me say it again." He pointed at the red brick–faced bank. "I'll be furious if I come out and you're not sitting in this exact parking space. Do you understand?"

How ironic that Jack remained a mystery to me but he easily read my intentions. "What's the big deal if I went for coffee anyhow?"

"Because knowing our luck, you'll run into some cop on his break and get busted. Meanwhile, I'll be standing here hacking up my insides all over the sidewalk."

He grabbed my arm. "Give me your word you'll stay here with the windows up and the heater running. This no coat thing isn't working for me. I'll be warmer when I'm six feet down."

"I remember you wearing a fringed deerskin jacket even in the dead of winter after you came home from Vietnam. You strutted around like a rock star, especially with those long cool-looking sideburns."

Jack smiled. "Flattery will get you nowhere. Now promise me."

This felt over the top, but I nodded quickly. "Okay, as long as you don't ask anyone if they remember you."

"That's an odd request. What if I see someone I know? I would hate to be rude since I won't have another chance to correct my mistake."

I watched him struggle with the thought and gently rubbed his shoulder. "Listen, Jack. The doctor said part of your illness is you think you know everybody," I said slowly so it would sink in, not wanting to remind him how the cancer had traveled to his brain. "Given our encounter back at McDonald's, it's probably best to let the other person say hello first. Okay? And if someone does say hello, listen to what they say so you're not confused with someone just being nice." The confused look on his face confirmed I was making things too complex. "If you're unsure, just smile and leave it at that." I played with the seat controls to find a more comfortable position. "My mother used to quote Lincoln all the time: 'Better to remain silent and thought to be a fool than speak out and remove all doubt.'"

"And to think my best friend is a vacuum salesman and a philosopher too. What a strange brew." Jack glanced at the bank and the anxious look returned. "It's a weird experience. It started about a month ago. I would recognize a face, but couldn't dial in the name. Granted, that's not unusual given all the students I've taught." He opened the car door. "On the flip side, I'm sure there are quite a few who wish they could forget me."

"Tuck in your shirt and pull up your pants, please."

"Okay, Mom," he replied and slammed the door shut.

The heater began to give me a headache and I turned the blower down to low. It was almost four in the afternoon and all but a dozen of the hundred parking spaces were orphans. Before the advent of the internet, this bank would have been buzzing, especially Thursday through Saturday with six full-time tellers required to cash paychecks. I used to wait in line every Thursday marking time by chewing my gum for a small handful of twenties that Merriam would feed her insatiable budget envelopes.

"Who died and made him king?" I said to the dashboard and rolled down the window to get a good shot of March air. A large Dunkin' Donuts coffee with cream and two sugars would taste wonderful right now and provide the octane boost I needed. Throw in a honey-dipped or chocolate-covered doughnut—or maybe both—and I could forget our troubles for a while. The nearest coffee shop was just up the street and would be our next stop whether Jack liked it or not.

Restless, I felt my guilt spike knowing I should have been insistent on accompanying Jack into the bank after the lunch fiasco. Clearly, my buddy could get himself into a lot of trouble very quickly. Watching the glass front doors, I thought it strange he would pick a big bank instead of a small community one. Then again, maybe he empathized with the losing bets the big banks made which triggered the Great Recession.

My stomach grumbled. Patience and I were mostly strangers, even if it was the secret to success in sales or almost anything that mattered in life. Still curious as to whether our crime spree had made the news, I fiddled with the radio and got lost in exploring satellite radio and its offering of one hundred fifty stations. As a kid, AM radio used to be enough.

The passenger door opened suddenly and startled me. Jack quickly slid in, panting hard and holding a small cloth bag.

"Did you take it all out in rolled coins just to spite me?" I asked, remembering our earlier argument. "I hope you know I didn't mean it about the vending machines. Once we check in, I'll get you some nice chicken soup. That will warm you up good."

He ignored me and placed the bag on the floor. "Let's go!"

I thought maybe he got sick in the bag and was too embarrassed to tell me. I pointed to the radio and talked above a guitar riff. "You have to check out this radio and all the channels. It even has one dedicated to traffic reports in Philly. I'm sure we can find out how the Red Sox made out today in Fort Myers if you give me a minute."

Jack grabbed my hand and put it on the steering wheel. "Denny, I'm not joking. Hurry up and drive!"

The alarm in his voice made me nervous, though I scanned the lot and didn't detect any threat. But the look on his face made me delay asking about coffee. No sooner were we out of the parking lot headed north on Route 28 than two Salem police cruisers with sirens wailing flew by us going the other way. I watched in the rearview mirror as they made a sharp turn into the strip mall.

I let out a soft whistle. "Wow, what's going on? Must be something huge." I shot Jack a look. "Please tell me nothing went wrong at the bank."

"Well, I met some real characters in that operation," Jack said like a news anchorman back from the front. "You always hear them boast about customer service on television. Well, I wasn't impressed at all when I handed the young teller my note. She studied my shaky penmanship for a moment then looked up and asked if I was joking. She was a pretty young thing even with all the makeup, but her smirk really irritated me."

He cupped his hands over the heater. "I read her badge and told Ms. Miller if I had the time and knew more about computers, I'd post my dissatisfaction online, but no, I was very serious about the withdrawal." He turned halfway in his seat to look out the back window. "All I can say is it's good we got out of there quick. Just imagine if you had wandered off to buy a doughnut. I would be in handcuffs and asking Ms. Miller how I sign up for overdraft protection so you don't have to rob a bank when your account is overdrawn."

The realization of what he just confessed suddenly hit me and I pulled into a gas station and parked in front of the air pump.

"I don't think you should stop here. It's too close," he said. "Keep driving."

I turned the car off. "What did you do?"

Jack didn't answer for a long minute and concentrated on dosing the morphine then taking a long swig of the orange sports drink. "Well, I took out a small withdrawal just like I'm doing now with the meds. I could have asked for a lot more when I think of all the fees I've paid over a lifetime. But I only asked for a thousand so I wouldn't appear greedy." He picked up the bag from the floor and looked in. "And I asked for small bills as it's such a hassle trying to break a hundred nowadays. Most want to see identification and then make you wait while they scan it under a fluorescent light." He reached in the bag and took out a handful of twenties and stuffed them in his left pants pocket.

I found the gum parked in my cheek and chewed for a moment so I wouldn't stutter. "So, you're telling me you robbed the bank?"

"You always put things in a negative light. I merely requested an expedited bridge loan and told Ms. Miller on the way out my best friend would reimburse them shortly."

"You did what?" I pointed at the air station. "Do you have three quarters so I can pump some air into your brain? Apparently it isn't getting any."

"Calm down, will ya? We needed money and I took care of it like you asked."

I cupped my hands over my ears, not wanting to hear any of more of this twisted logic. The right side of my neck began pulsating and I looked in the rearview mirror. It came as no surprise to find a new welt in the shape of Italy forming and imagined playing hive geography in the prison yard soon with my new gang. Even the warden might watch.

The creases on Jack's forehead rippled. "Stop acting so naïve, Denny. You know very well that I'm broke and you embarrassed me into doing this. But don't worry none. I'll make a couple calls and my associates can take up a collection to repay the bank if you don't want to cover it for me."

"I'm one big fool," I said, looking at him in disbelief. "You tell me you don't want to follow the example of the good thief because it would be too premeditated, so you go and rob a bank? You think becoming the bad thief will give you more opportunity to be saved? What part of *Thou shalt not steal* don't you get?" I asked in amazement. "I want no more of this. Take the car and check yourself into a fancy hotel and live it up. I'm done."

"And what will you do?"

"I'll turn myself in and ask for mercy."

"You might have been able to cop a plea before you robbed the bank, but not now."

This is why I sometimes despised this man. He would turn purple if his coffee wasn't right, but when a hurricane threatened to rip the roof off his house, he would get cocky and calm.

"What are you talking about?" I yelled loud enough to make my throat hurt. "I stayed in the car like you ordered. And by the way, I won't miss you bossing me around like some tin-pot dictator."

Jack opened his mouth then quickly closed it again. "Is that what you think, Denny? Fact is I tried to protect you."

"It's ironic the cancer makes you think you know everyone else in the world except me. What are you talking about?"

"Well, with everything up to this point, you could say you were being forced by your mad and dying friend to go along. Sure, the judge might threaten you with some jail time for punching that cop, but that's your gig. Even so, given your boring life up until today, you'd probably only get probation for that too." He rubbed his face hard. "I think it'll do you good to have you volunteer at the parish food pantry or thrift store a couple times a week. At least it would get you out of the house. I know you've been cooped up way too much since Merriam died last year."

"And where were you when she got sick or after she passed? Nowhere to be found when I needed you the most."

A pained look crossed his face. "I'm sorry you feel that way; I truly am. But getting back to our current situation, everything's changed. You've participated in a robbery."

"Why do you keep saying that?"

Jack's cheeks suddenly flushed deeply, which combined with the jaundice made his complexion match the bottle of orange drink at his feet. "I made you promise to stay in the car and keep the windows up with the heater running. And why did I do that?" He breathed on the side window and it fogged up. "Because I didn't want the car windows to steam up and prevent our escape. And what did you do? As usual, you're bent on improvising, so you rolled your window down. How do I know this, you ask? Because I saw it on the bank's TV monitors as Ms. Miller prepared my little package. Now they have my accomplice on film raking his face with his nails, so it doesn't matter if you were in the getaway car or standing beside me passing the note to the teller. They will have a heck of time trying to collect their pound of flesh from me, so you owe two pounds now." Jack rubbed his eyes. "You should give thanks every day you were never sent to 'Nam. Over there you followed orders or got yourself or your buddies killed. You would have surely come home in a bag or ended up in the Hanoi Hilton."

It's funny how one second you feel so hungry you could eat an elephant and the next moment you could throw up one. I hesitated to get sick all over Mrs. Werner's beautiful German leather seats. I needed time to think through what to do with my renegade friend.

I started the car and threw it in drive and left a six-foot patch of rubber as we blew out of the gas station and banged a right on two wheels intending to jump on Route 111 and flee west to Nashua, the second largest city in New Hampshire and only a half hour away. Wanting to become like mayflies sounded romantic yesterday, but besides a short life span most are swatted dead by irritated folks.

Unfortunately, our delayed getaway proved to be a mistake. A Salem police cruiser barreled past us headed toward the bank then made a U-turn with lights flashing.

I nixed Nashua and cut east through Salem. The speedometer clocked us doing seventy in a school zone. Being wanted had taken on a whole new meaning late in life.

"Speeding through here will cost you plenty," Jack said. "Besides losing your safe driver's credit, you'll be assessed a surcharge which will haunt you for six years. You really should have taken another route."

I glanced over at my partner in crime and he looked genuinely upset, which really ticked me off. "This is so like you. You don't care one iota if we tie up two women, steal a car, and rob a bank. But speed through a school zone and then you're concerned?"

"You forgot to mention assaulting a police officer," he added, "but like I keep saying, that one is totally on you." He looked in his side mirror and frowned. "Dennis, I know this car is a pocket rocket, so now that we're past the school zone I suggest you put that reputation to the test or you'll be a really ripe prune before they let you out of jail."

The white lines in the middle of the road were flying by so fast they looked like they were touching one another. The speedometer approached eighty when Jack reached over and pushed down on my right knee and began surfing the radio with his free hand. "If I remember right you only let your hair down when Creedence Clearwater is playing. The Beatles made you mellow."

Pins and needles shot across my chest. The idea I might drop dead right now and let Jack deal with the ugly aftermath made me almost hope for a coronary.

We crossed into Massachusetts at ninety miles an hour and I clawed at my neck whenever the road straightened. Jack didn't find any Creedence but Aerosmith filled the car with "Dream On." The ballad came out just after Merriam and I were married in 1973 and saw me through many dark days after Jean Bradley's death. Now I hoped it would still serve as life preserver. The on-ramp for Route 495 loomed straight ahead. As one of the longest interstate highways in the country, it provided many options. We could run north to the coast or head west and link up with Route 93 or the Mass Pike. The highway would be better than playing cat-and-mouse on side streets.

"Okay, Einstein, what should we do?"

"You're the one driving," he replied, watching the blue lights a quarter mile back while pouring another generous shot of cologne in his open shirt.

There was no time to shoot him a dirty look, or ask if he hoped to be frisked by a pretty female prison guard as I passed three more cars and dodged an old lady crossing the street with her mail.

"But if I were driving, I would stay off the highway."

"Why?"

"You have a fast car, but cops in Massachusetts drive souped-up Crown Victoria's and Chargers. And I'm sure your friends behind you already radioed ahead to have the exits blocked. Remember O.J. in the white Bronco?"

I had already committed to the entrance ramp before processing his logic. Braking hard, I turned sharply to the left. The front end of the car proved responsive and clung to the road. Unfortunately, the rear tires weren't as committed and the car began to drift and I realized in that awful moment I might die the same way Jean Bradley did. Talk about poetic justice. A flash of gray metal appeared as our front left fender kissed a Ford truck in the next lane. There was an awful grating noise and a puff of white smoke as we catapulted down Broadway.

"Yeah, that's what I'm talking about!" Jack squealed and punched me in the arm much too hard for a dying man. "Tell me that doesn't make you feel alive. We're both going to be dead an awfully long time, and that, my friend, we can reminisce about when we meet in the clouds for a beer."

"Forget the beer. How about a swig of your morphine?" I asked. We still had a quarter-mile lead and I intended to use it to our advantage. I took the next right, then a quick left and repeated the maneuver a half dozen times through a meandering neighborhood of tightly packed single-family homes.

Jack sat up and looked around. "Lucky for us this route is working out perfectly."

"What do you mean? I'm making this up as we go. I have no idea where we are."

"Relax." He scanned the white and green street signs. "Okay, take the next left and follow the Merrimack River into Haverhill. There's an underground parking garage we can hide in."

"Is it safe?" I asked as the street gradually turned commercial with a long row of red brick buildings.

Jack smirked. "Cheer up, big guy. We're the ones folks are scared of now." We took two more rights and then a sharp left.

He pointed ahead. "The entrance is right after the fire hydrant. Roll down your window quick and take a ticket."

I followed orders and went down the ramp and wheeled into a spot next to a beat-up blue Audi.

The garage was deserted. "Okay, now what?"

Jack pulled his hat down and closed his eyes. "Be quiet, I need a minute to recharge."

"You can't be serious."

I rolled the window down and heard police sirens but with the echo couldn't make out if they were coming closer or moving away.

Jack started snoring and I pinched myself, hoping to wake up from this nightmare.

CHAPTER SEVENTEEN

Many people keep memory boxes to cradle special mementos: the pay stub from a first job, a withered carnation from prom, perhaps a watch that stopped telling time years ago but belonged to your grandfather.

Mine included an autograph from Carl Yastrzemski after the Red Sox's impossible dream of '67. But three related items in my collection trumped everything else, even Carl. The first was a simple memorial prayer card. On its face was the image of a Damian cross and on the reverse side a bold inscription: "Jean Bradley, who passed into eternal life on March 1st, 1974." It resided inside an envelope containing a fistful of dirty twenties totaling three hundred dollars. These two items were invisibly tethered to a Polara car key I kept hidden in my wallet as a daily reminder of the consequences from broken promises.

In the first few weeks after Jean's death, I handled the prayer card so often her name began to fade from the glossy paper stock and I entombed the prayer card in a plastic sheet to preserve her identity and my agony. True to my secret nightly ritual, I studied the back of the prayer card aware I remained imprisoned behind the laminate too. Included under Jean's name was the Lord's Prayer and I whispered each word fervently, intent not to miss one word and hoping for relief. When none came I discovered Canadian whiskey is comparable to rock salt. It doesn't work in a deep freeze and can be just as corrosive.

"Clearly, that young woman desperately wanted to escape her troubles," Merriam said over and over again, hoping to get through to me. "Even so, that didn't give her the license to put her daughter in danger like she did." Her Caribbean blue eyes searched my face for a flicker of hope. "I don't understand why you think any of this is your fault. She only wanted to use you to steal the car."

When logic failed Merriam tried another tactic, hoping I would get lost in her instead of some dead woman. But whenever I peered out from our jasmine-perfumed sheets, Jean Bradley waited for me in the corner of the bedroom peeling a label off a bottle of Schlitz.

"Promise me you'll unlock the gate at midnight," she would repeat and no amount of whiskey from my secret stash in the cellar would silence her.

"Why don't you talk to Father Houle?" Merriam finally asked, clearly exasperated with the whole situation. "He can provide a fresh perspective and absolve the guilt you feel."

If the roles were reversed, I knew she would find peace through the confessional, but I recoiled from the suggestion. How could I seek God's forgiveness when I could never forgive myself? Jean nodded in agreement.

May came; the lilacs bloomed and so did my drinking.

"I need a husband who will support his family instead of obsessing over a stranger," she said after finding me passed out on the couch again. "Get out!"

Packing my things, I knew when I arrived at hell's gate, the cover charge would be three hundred bucks.

CHAPTER EIGHTEEN

In our great escape, it seemed poetic to seek refuge in an underground garage called Double-Down Parking. Unfortunately, I soon discovered the facility also proved to be the Haverhill office of Murphy's Law. We'd no sooner ditched Mrs. Werner's Beamer when we discovered the lone elevator out of service.

The sirens grew louder and even Jack couldn't ignore them anymore. Our only option meant hoofing it up the stairs, but Jack suddenly had trouble walking. This significantly slowed our mad dash to a crawl. I had lost any patience hours ago and tried to help my friend along but he pushed me away. Instead, Jack willed himself forward one half step at a time, which would have been admirable any other occasion except this one. It appeared his muscles were only receiving intermittent signals from the brain. As we slowly shuffled forward, I kept my eyes peeled for any peripheral dangers between the parked cars. Given all the dark corners and the musty smell, no wonder so many suspense movies had a parking garage scene.

When we finally reached the stairwell, I watched for blue flashing lights to fill the cavern. The hairs on the back of my neck stood at attention and I knew they would quickly locate our car and then us. At best, it would only be a few minutes more before the garage would be crawling with police and maybe even dogs. We were done.

Jack knew it looked grim as he surveyed a mountain of stairs he could not climb. He sat down stiffly on the bottom stair and hung his head in resignation. What little color he had left quickly drained from his face.

"Like you always lectured, my planning needs work," he said, breathing hard. "Isn't this ironic though? I wanted to build my staircase to heaven and here I sit too exhausted to begin. I would have lived large if they had purses for horses that came up lame." He took off his lucky hat and sighed. "Just give me the car keys and get out of here."

I bent over. "What do you mean?"

"Because it's stupid to continue this sorry quest of mine, so I'll tell the cops you had no idea about the bank robbery and left me when you found out. That should make things a bit easier for you in court." He looked up and smiled weakly. "And don't you worry none. I'll tell them the truth and how you only tried to help your old pal take care of a few things. Come to think of it, maybe I'll kick the bucket when they interrogate me down at the station. Hopefully it will haunt them for a while. If not, at least I'll make them do some extra paperwork." He chuckled. "I feel like I'm back in the sixties when so many wanted to 'stick it to the Man.'"

I took a quick look behind; no sign of the cops yet. "You keep talking about taking care of a few things. Tell me what they are and I promise to do what I can. The way I see it, you'll still get credit upstairs because you had good intentions."

Jack shook his head. "Didn't we go over this already? No pinch runners are allowed."

He slowly traced the logo on his hat with his index finger.

"Forget it, Dennis. It's too late."

An acrid odor filled my nostrils and I discovered a dark urine stain next to me beginning waist high and running down to the cement floor. Men could be pigs, relieving themselves anywhere convenient and moving on. Yet, I wanted to move on too.

Jack's head hung low like it was too heavy for his body and might snap off any moment. Death sat beside him and taunted me for losing the tug of war. Any moment now, I expected Jack to snap to attention; to give me one of his legendary tough looks and dismiss me. I realized this would be my last memory of him alive.

"And what will you do now?"

Jack looked up and smirked. "What will I do?" he repeated. "I'd like to take a nap but will have plenty of time to sleep once I'm below the frost line. I'll stall them long enough so you can make it out of here." He unbuttoned his shirt and took out the small prescription bag and handed me a fistful of twenties. "You must be famished. A-1 Deli is just down the street and serves wonderful home-cooked meals. I recommend the meat loaf as it comes with a heap of garlic mashed potatoes and carrots glazed with brown sugar. For dessert get the apple pie." He winked and looked in the bag. "Luckily for me, I still have enough money to buy all the cops dinner and plenty of morphine left to drown out Stu when he arrives."

Looking at him, I wanted to confess my selfishness. When I decided to spring Jack from the hospice, I wanted to reconnect and hopefully share one last sunrise together. But I also imagined as the darkness faded and the first light revealed zeppelin-shaped clouds floating across the pink morning sky, I would extract a promise from my best friend. I wanted Jack to remind Merriam she wasn't supposed to leave me alone like this. If anyone could get a message to her, Jack could.

He let out a painful cough. "I read somewhere when you die you lose your bowels. Maybe I'll die right here so they'll have a huge mess to clean up. Wouldn't the Sanitation Department be pleased?"

The sound of squealing tires filled the air.

"For the love of heaven, stop with your constant hesitation and get out of here while you still can."

I looked away, embarrassed. No one could blame me for leaving. I did my best and despite the circumstances, the end of this story was never in doubt. Even if we succeeded in eluding the cops, there were no guarantees we would have ticked off anything on that wish list of his, whatever it contained.

While I was preparing to run, the urine stain caught my attention again. The pungent odor reminded me of caring for Merriam in her final days and how I changed and bathed my dying wife and did it with love. I remembered looking in her half open eyes, promising never to leave, no matter how difficult things became. And they did, but we saw it through together and that made me love her more than I ever could imagine. My stomach felt hollow realizing I couldn't leave my best friend alone in a foxhole.

I knelt down.

"What are you doing?" he asked. "The time for words and hugs is past. If you ever cared for me just go."

"Don't you remember? Back in grammar school, we were the champion chicken fighters and our reputation grew because we fought on land instead of in the pool. I hit puberty first and had the height, so you rode on my shoulders. Teachers were forever trying to stop us, but we compared ourselves to King Arthur's knights, triumphing over the enemies of Gaul. We were undefeatable," I said quickly.

"Don't be ridiculous," he wheezed.

"That's a funny thing to say coming from a man who dedicated some of his last thoughts to making things difficult for the Sanitation Department." I grabbed one of his arms and put it around my neck. To my surprise, he didn't fight me.

While I would love to brag and say it took a herculean effort to carry Jack up those dozen steps it would be a lie. Whether out of sheer terror or the fact Jack weighed less than my trash barrel, I couldn't say.

We stumbled out a metal door and onto the street. The cold breeze felt refreshing after being entombed. The traffic was heavy at rush hour on River Street and I caught a few rubberneckers checking out this strange sight, but no good Samaritans appeared to whisk us away.

"Okay, Denny, you can put me down now," Jack whispered.

He began to get heavy, but we had no time for his slow shuffle. "Once we find a place to hide," I said and spun around looking for a restaurant or a movie theatre for cover. The options were few. There was a used car lot across the street that was closed and we'd quickly freeze without coats. A long line of tenement buildings sat on a high hill a quarter mile away but might as well have been the City of Oz. And even if we made it, what ruse would we use to gain entry?

"Head downtown," Jack said firmly.

A siren pierced the air and I decided not to argue. Panting harder than my dying friend, I hugged a guardrail and covered two blocks faster than I ever imagined. Jack's grip weakened as we progressed.

"Cross the street," he said, pointing. "We'll be safe in the Dawg House."

"Really?" The building resembled one of those stereotypical watering holes that caters specifically to neighborhood clientele and doesn't take kindly to outsiders. Consequently, the back of the building bordered the river and disposal of strangers would be easy, especially this time of year with the winter melt. It was a one-story building with a flat metal roof and light yellow vinyl siding that may have been white once. Not surprisingly, it had no windows.

I didn't want to know how the bar got its name, or how my friend knew about this joint, but I bolted across the street.

"Hurry, Denny. A cruiser is coming."

I almost decapitated Jack before realizing the door wasn't tall enough to accommodate a man strapped across my back. A frantic moment followed before I could demount and throw him inside the wooden door.

My eyes were still trying to adjust to the dim light when I heard a voice that sounded like it came from the three-headed guard dog in hell.

"What are you two geezers doing in here?"

CHAPTER NINETEEN

I felt like a guy on death row about to be cheated out of his gluttonous last meal. Forget lobster tails, filet mignon, and baked Alaska. At this point, I would settle for a quick peanut butter and jelly sandwich, as I expected the tattooed executioner wearing a Grateful Dead T-shirt to produce something very sharp as he barreled toward us. Entering eternity hungry would be unfortunate and I wanted to tell the six-and-a-half-foot giant he didn't have to stab me in the stomach because I already had a hole there.

"Hey, I know you," Jack said with far more enthusiasm than a man in his condition usually showed.

The big guy quickly pushed us aside and locked the heavy wooden door with no windows before turning to hover over Jack in the dim light. Tobacco reeked from the behemoth with greasy shoulder-length brown hair and goatee. I bet he smoked Lucky Strikes, because filtered cigarettes would be much too mild for him.

"Well, I don't know you none and that's all that matters." He turned and looked me up and down. "You look like you have measles or chicken pox," and took one step back to study me from a safer distance. "Ain't you got a tongue or are you a mute?"

I thought about a number of responses and crazy thoughts flooded my mind. My tongue wanted to correct his grammar and also offer him a breath mint even though I didn't have any. Certain death made me swallow the irrational thought and in the process I discovered the gum in my cheek missing. I scanned the dark wood-planked floor, certain there were bodies buried underneath, and then at the monster's black work boots, hoping I hadn't spit it out in fright. If so, there would be serious consequences. Not finding it, I looked toward the bar area where two beefy men with crew cuts and wearing white T-shirts were playing pool and drinking beer from long-neck bottles.

"We thought we would stop in for a beer," I finally said in a small voice.

The hulk laughed. "And I bet you drink ultra-light too cause you're counting calories." He gave us both the once-over again. "You're not from around here, are you?" He spit in a nearby metal trash can. "I suggest you and gramps leave before I think you're from the IRS."

I searched the guy's face for a smirk but found none. "Just unlock the door and we'll be happy to leave." I wanted to add, *into the waiting arms of the police.*

"But I know you!" Jack repeated, stepping forward.

My eyes pleaded with Jack to be quiet and I pulled him toward the door.

"You're Mad Dawg, right?" Jack asked in a half question tone like he wasn't sure now either.

I thought back to McDonald's and how we were wrapped in a steel vessel when the painter went crazy. Now we might join the other stains on the garage wall too or go for a swim in the Merrimack River out back. I couldn't swim and would need to hop aboard an ice floe.

"What's it to ya?"

"Because we're here to see M.B."

The Mad Dawg studied Jack, and I watched his expression change and shoulders relax. It felt like we had cracked a safe and the last tumbler fell in place.

"Well, this better be on the up and up, old man, because if you're playing me I'll whip you good." Then he glared at me. "And after I'm done with Mr. Pasty White, I'll work on curing that speech problem of yours." He took another step back. "Though I'll wear gloves not to catch whatever disease you're carrying." He put two fingers up to his mouth and let out an ear-piercing whistle. "M.B., you got some sad-looking company out here."

The men in the back room were either deaf or didn't give a hoot, as they continued playing pool.

"Who is it?" a throaty voice yelled back.

"A couple of old geezers that I'm sure are posers."

Given the sound of the approaching footsteps, I expected some Amazon to come strutting out of the shadows. Instead, a middle-aged woman sucking on a long skinny cigarette appeared. Her shirt and pants were faded denim and hung so loosely either she recently lost a lot of weight or liked to wear clothes two sizes too big. The only things that fit right were the knee-high black boots with three inch heels. Her long dark hair was tied in a ponytail and revealed a pretty face. I sensed M.B. must have been a real looker twenty years ago, but the heavy bags under those piercing brown eyes gave her a worn expression which she didn't attempt to hide with makeup. The silver cross she wore around her neck caught my attention and I hoped she didn't just wear it for show.

"Hey, M.B.," Jack said in a tone much too friendly.

I swallowed hard. This wasn't going to end well.

She squinted and took a long drag on her cigarette. Her fingernails were long and painted black. When she exhaled, the smoke just hung in front of her face like it didn't know how to escape either. "Is that you, Jack?" she finally asked in a husky voice.

My friend glanced my way and flashed his "I told you" look.

"It's only been a couple months, but I would never have recognized you." she said softly. "How are you doing?"

"He's dying," I blurted out before I could catch myself. The courage I displayed back in the stairwell was ancient history now. The three of them looked at me like I belonged in some freak sideshow.

"Aren't we all," Jack said to break the tension. "But I've been living large at Restful Waters until recently."

"Figures," said Mad Dawg, pointing at us. "Old codgers like you two don't give a hoot about what happens to us average folks. Haverhill used to be a good town for working stiffs and now we're being forced out by the likes of these types," he said, twirling his finger in the air. "And they're enjoying it all with fat social security and pension checks and scream bloody murder if the city wants to raise taxes to build a school." Mad Dawg shot M.B. a disgusted look. "I'll bet you a six pack of Bud Restful Waters is one of those subsidized housing for old folks where they have happy hour every afternoon by the inside pool. It makes me sick."

M.B. rushed forward and pushed the big man into a dark paneled wall that looked like it could use a deep cleaning with a fire hose. "Norman, stupid doesn't begin to describe you sometimes. Restful Waters is a hospice, you idiot."

I don't know if Mad Dawg felt more embarrassed about being pushed around by a woman not much taller than five foot two minus the boots, or being called by his real name.

Suddenly, the door shook.

"Police! Open up."

A sudden scuffle in the back room competed for my attention. I didn't want to guess what type of contraband they might be hiding back there.

Jack spoke before I could find my voice. "I'm sorry, M.B. This is all my fault. The cops have been chasing us since Dennis rescued me from the death squad."

M.B. nodded and looked over at me. "Is that how he got wounded?" She pointed to my chest and looked impressed by my stamina.

I looked down at the pulverized cookie in my shirt pocket. In our mad dash, Jack had ruined the last of Mrs. Werner's cookies. The strawberry jelly had bled through my white oxford shirt and it looked like I had been either shot or stabbed. Just to be sure, I licked my index finger and went fishing in my pocket and transported the last of the goodness to my mouth.

She looked puzzled and I smiled sheepishly.

Big Dawg took a step toward the door. "Maybe there's a reward for being a good citizen. Plus, we have enough trouble already."

M.B. stopped him mid-stride and grabbed his wrist. "Hide them in the backroom closet, while I take care of this. And when they come in, keep that big trap of yours shut."

Norman hesitated and his hands remained on his hips. "We'll see what Mr. Leonard says about this."

"Do what I say or I'll tell the men on the other side of that door about the two outstanding warrants out on you," M.B. said sharply.

Another loud bang on the door followed. Norman pointed to a short corridor and we followed him past a long oak saloon-type bar to a six-panel solid pine door. The big man opened the door, revealing a closet filled halfway to the top with cases of Bud and Bud Light. "Get in," he ordered.

I stood there trying to determine how best to position myself when Norman suddenly hoisted me up and deposited me sideways across a stack of beer cases. A second later Jack landed on top of me.

"Your elbow is killing my ribs," I said.

"Too bad. Remember I'm the one dying," Jack whispered, imitating my crazy comment. The elbow stayed put so I rubbed my bare red arm across his cheek.

"What are you doing?"

"Hoping hives are contagious."

Jack pinched my ear and we began to wrestle and only stopped when the murmurs grew louder on the other side of the closet. I could hear M.B.'s heavy footsteps scrape against the wooden floor and hoped I never came back as a pair of her boots.

"So, Sergeant Duncan, what can we do for you today?" M.B. asked.

"You can cut out the sweet talk, lady, and tell us where they are," an authoritative voice replied.

"Look, I'm going to tell you what I told the detective last night. We don't hire any illegals. I know Norman looks like one, but he's originally from Maine."

"Do you take us for fools?" the voice returned. "We want the two men you're hiding in here. The way I see it, you have two choices. You can hand them over right now, or I can have a team take this dump apart piece by piece. And when we do find them, we'll charge you both as accessories."

I held my breath, knowing M.B. might hold her ground, but Norman would certainly cave. I anticipated when the closet door opened the cops might crack a smile seeing their two "perps" stacked like firewood.

"I don't know what you're talking about, Sergeant. People are always knocking on the door trying to get in but we don't open until eight p.m.," M.B. replied in a rising voice. "Either you produce a search warrant right now or get out of here because we're not open yet. Give me any more grief and I'll call my lawyer friend. You know the one. He shares the same last name with the mayor. I can have harassment charges filed by tomorrow."

I hadn't kissed a woman since Merriam died, but I blushed in the dark.

"Stall all you want. We'll have men posted outside until we come back with a warrant. And the mayor doesn't scare me none. I voted for the other guy."

CHAPTER TWENTY

Jack stood in the doorway of the brightly lit hospital room, looking tan and fit. "Denny, you look like you got hit by a bus. What happened?"

"Well, when you took Merriam's side, I asked a couple of new drinking buddies I met at some dive for a place to stay. Come to find out the address was a nearby alley. They beat me up pretty good to get my last ten bucks."

Jack pulled a celery-colored cushioned chair next to the bed and we sat in silence listening to the traffic in the hall. The high point came when some lady started yelling for the tapioca pudding she ordered for a snack and two nurses had to intervene.

"Remember that awful hike we took one Saturday afternoon in seventh grade?" he asked when the hubbub died down. "We were determined to go into the woods and get lost. We thought it would be a good challenge to make it home by nightfall."

"It was the only time I ever saw you cry," I replied, happy to keep the focus off my swollen bruised eyes and the dozen stitches underneath my chin.

He let out a short laugh and touched my bandaged right hand. "Denny, you're like an elephant with that memory of yours. I'll tell you this—I never cried in 'Nam, but I was scared to death in those deep woods. We thought we knew it all and left without a compass, a canteen, or bug spray."

"Yeah, that was your idea. Survival of the fittest, you said."

"It seemed like a great adventure at the time. I thought if we followed the sun's path, eventually we'd hit the highway. But that spring the mud turned epic and we had to zigzag this way and that looking for a better route. When the sun went down we were in trouble."

"And without the moon it was so dark you couldn't see two feet ahead," I added. "And the pricker bushes kept cutting us in the face, never mind the welts from all the mosquito bites." I fingered the sharp edge of a stitch under my chin.

"Then it started to rain."

"And I thought coyotes might attack us at any moment." I started to laugh but it hurt too much.

"We might still be out there if you hadn't found an ancient-looking stone wall and talked me into following it," he whispered.

We sat in silence reliving the memory. I wanted to be thirteen again even if it meant being cold, wet, and in the dark. It was far better than wandering in this never-ending barren desert with Jean.

The pain meds kicked in and I fell asleep and dreamed of a mother in a long black woolen coat holding a little girl with long brown hair and wearing only a white party dress in the winter cold. They stood in front of an old Dodge automobile the color of wet beach sand. The mother put the shivering little girl down on the frozen pavement and bent over and put her ear to the hood of the car as if receiving some great secret. The sky drew dark with pregnant purple clouds which began to spit sharp pellets of ice that cut the little girl's face and arms. The wind began to howl and the little girl screamed for her mother, but the woman paid no attention and kept her head on the hood of the car. I called out and the woman slowly stood up and faced me and I recognized Jean Bradley. Her eyes were as dark as the bottom of a cistern and they drew me into the black abyss.

I woke up gagging and discovered a typed note on my chest.

Your Spring

It's been winter for too long.
Months marked by heavy snows;
Driven by lonesome winds,
Where unwelcome memories
Are buried outside your door.

But Dennis, look around
And recognize your spring!
The receding snow unmasks
A cluttered landscape of guilt,
But the field begs to be sowed.

I feel your apprehension,
As you grip the plow in trepidation.
Your hands are uncalloused and raw;
Your legs tremble at the terrible task;
Your soul marinates in self-doubt.

But call on that persevering heart,
Which has always sustained you.
Recall the boy that did not run
From the neighborhood bullies,
But took them on one by one.

So take a deep breath, my friend,
And move the plow forward one step;
Confident you will never be alone.
For I will remain by your side,
To ensure your rows are straight.

Winter will no doubt come again,
Unannounced and uninvited,
As it does for each of us.
But with His help you will endure,
And rejoice in each new spring.

CHAPTER TWENTY-ONE

Somehow Jack managed to fall asleep in our closet prison, but the beer case mattress proved too hard for me to follow suit. A half hour later, I was tired of breathing through my mouth so I wouldn't smell Jack's rotten egg breath or the manly cologne he had been showering in, and decided to crack the door open as the police were gone. To my horror the handle would not turn and oddly brought Edgar Allan Poe's "The Cask of Amontillado" to mind. Being buried alive had given me the heebie-jeebies since childhood.

I heard something heavy hit the floor on the other side of the door and figured the bricks must have arrived. Since Mad Dawg thought we were milking the system he would be a motivated mason to wall us in.

I moved too fast and elbowed Jack in the ribs. "Hey, let us out!" I banged on the thick pine door.

Jack moaned and rubbed his side. "What's all the fuss about?"

"They locked us in." I banged on the door again. "And I thought this lady was your friend." I began to hyperventilate.

Suddenly, there were footsteps and the door knob turned. I didn't wait for the warden and jumped out.

M.B. stumbled backwards and almost did a back flip over several additional cases of beer piled alongside the closet. "What's the matter with you?" she asked with a puzzled look.

I looked at the floor, remembering how M.B. had been our hero with the cops. I deserved to be buried alive.

She rushed past me and helped Jack as he moved stiffly. "The way your buddy screamed I thought you were in trouble."

Jack shot me a sour look. "I think Dennis has a good chance to get into the *Guinness World Records* book someday as being the world's biggest scaredy-cat."

"So what now?" I asked.

M.B. ignored me and ushered Jack over to an orphaned wooden stool in the corner.

"Sorry for getting you in this mess," Jack said.

She straightened the silver cross on her necklace. "Well, we got ourselves a real challenge here. No doubt you heard the tussle with Sergeant Duncan. He hates the guy who owns this place and is just itching to close us down. Duncan posted two cops outside until he gets a search warrant."

"So how do we get out of here without getting you in trouble?" I asked.

M.B. finally acknowledged me. "That's the first intelligent thing you've said since you arrived." She frowned. "I could hide you both down in the cellar until I figure something out, but it's cold and musty down there and the last thing Jack needs in his condition." M.B. looked at my friend and pointed my way. "Unless you want me to ship him downstairs so you can get some rest up here."

Jack smiled. "Don't tempt me."

"Okay, then, I'll have Norman take some of the beer cases out of the closet to make it a bit more comfortable. But you have to stay hidden until I figure something out. I can't have you two roaming around the bar in case there's a raid."

We retired to the closet again after extracting a promise not to be locked in. Jack took a dose of pain meds and quickly fell back asleep. I helped myself to a couple of beers, making sure I drank full-bodied Bud and not the light stuff and nursed them slowly.

The beer relaxed me and I no sooner shut my eyes than I heard a loud rumbling noise in the distance and wondered if the police had sent their SUV with the battering ram to ferret us out. But as the sound grew into a loud symphony of high-pitched whines mixed with low throaty rumbles, the building began to shake. I couldn't imagine how many motorcycles were outside in the cold March evening air.

The noise woke Jack up and he looked surprisingly refreshed. "Something tells me our ride is here."

The motorcycles went quiet and I heard a stampede of boots scraping against the wooden floor.

"How about some music?" a baritone voice yelled. A second later heavy metal music filled the air. Jack said something but I couldn't hear him.

I leaned over and opened the closet door a hair and let out a soft whistle.

"We're not in Kansas anymore," I reported back to Jack. "It looks like the bar scene in *Star Wars*." There was a hodgepodge of bikers bathed in a cloud of cigarette smoke drinking beer out of large mason jars. Some of the men had shaved heads, others sported ponytails halfway down their backs, and the majority had multiple silver piercings on their face and ears. All wore faded blue jeans, black leather jackets, and leather boots with silver clips. I counted thirty in the gang before another ten women suddenly joined. Half the ladies had ponytails like the men and the remainder wore spiked hairdos dyed wild red. They wore leather jackets too and their leather boots had three-inch spike heels like M.B.'s. I noticed a white emblem of some sort stitched on the upper back of all the coats and I strained to read it.

Jack became restless because he couldn't see and tapped me urgently on the shoulder. "Who are they?"

One short bald man with a goatee backed up to allow another gang member access to the oak bar and a dim fluorescent light above highlighted the back of his coat. I made out the image of a skull and crossbones with the logo "Bad to the Bone." I swallowed hard. That sounded a lot meaner than Hells Angels.

"Bad to the Bone?" Jack said, excited. "I know them." He pushed me and the door swung open wide and I fell out of the closet.

"Stop fooling around," Jack said, continuing on. I scrambled to my feet and followed.

The short bald guy with the goatee saw Jack and opened his arms wide and gave him a bear hug.

"My man, how are you?"

Jack nodded and brought me alongside and up close so I could hear above the music.

"Dennis, I want you to meet my good buddy Ink."

"Linc?" I asked, surprised. I hadn't heard that name since Clarence Williams played Linc in *Mod Squad*. Now there was a dude with a lot of hair.

"No, it's Ink," Jack said, correcting me.

I shook his hand and tried not to stare at the steel ball piercings lining both eyebrows although I wanted to ask how many aspirin he took a day.

"Ink is one hell of an artist." Jack pointed to his arm. "He did my tattoo."

Ink smiled and grabbed my arm and began undoing the button on my right sleeve. I felt violated but I didn't want to offend anyone that was bad to the bone.

Ink rolled up my shirt sleeve to my elbow and smiled. "Ah, a nice blank canvas," he said, sounding inspired. "Come see me and we will do something special." He leaned toward my ear. "Since you're a friend of Jack's, I'll give you a discount."

I nodded and bit my tongue before asking if I could get an AARP discount on top of that.

With the loud music, I never heard M.B. approach. She pulled me and Jack away from the tattoo artist and back toward the open closet. Her eyes kept darting around the room.

"I called in a favor and asked my friends to come down and help me get you two out of here. Initially, I was planning on waiting until closing time, but found out Duncan intends to send his entire night shift here when we close so they can ID everyone leaving."

"Again, I apologize," Jack said.

M.B. waved him off. "There's only two cops out there so we have to leave now before the others arrive."

Jack and I nodded in unison.

"So will the gang cause some sort of ruckus so we can sneak out some other way?" I asked.

M.B. shook her head. "That won't work and you'd be sitting ducks when they call for backup. No, you're going to ride out."

"Say what?" I asked.

M.B. called over two tattooed hulks. If the New England Patriots needed to bulk up on defense to secure another Super Bowl ring, I had their guys. They were six foot four with long blond ponytails. They looked like twin brothers but who knew?

"These are your rides and we don't have time for introductions," M.B. said quickly.

I noticed both had glassy eyes and I couldn't help myself. "How many beers have you boys had tonight? Are you fit to drive?"

They glared at me. M.B. motioned to one of the ladies with red spiked hair and she came over carrying two dirty blond ponytail wigs and black leather coats.

"Why the wigs?" Jack asked.

"Because if we throw you in a helmet the cops will catch on right away. The trick is to blend in."

The biker chick handed me the wig and I tried to nonchalantly examine it for lice.

One of the behemoths noticed and grabbed my arm. "That's my spare, man. Do you think it's dirty or something?"

I shook my head no with vigor and tried not to giggle thinking of him combing the wig before he put it on. "Just admiring the weave." I put it on and immediately my scalp began to itch.

Another woman came by and handed us mirrored sunglasses and then smeared bright red lipstick on our lips. It tasted like strawberry bubblegum and reminded me of the first girl I kissed. I looked at Jack and he winked and blew me a kiss.

M.B. shut the music off and stood on a white plastic chair. I noticed she was wearing a Bad to the Bone jacket now too. "I'm so grateful for friends like you. Beer is on me next week."

They clapped and howled. I caught sight of a bowl of pretzels on the edge of the bar and hurried over and took a handful to munch on as M.B. lined everyone up behind the locked door.

"Now remember, play it cool but don't dilly-dally out there."

I stuffed the remaining pretzels in my mouth. They tasted salty and I wished I had time for another beer. I looked at my watch and noted the time: 10:15 p.m. The next five minutes as a biker chick would prove mighty interesting.

The door opened and the parade proceeded quickly. I pulled my sunglasses down on my nose so I could see and spotted the two young cops straight ahead. One spoke into a two-way radio, no doubt calling for backup as M.B. expected. They began walking through the bikers watching everyone put on helmets. I followed my partner and he handed me a black helmet, which I struggled to put on over the wig. I watched Jack do the same three bikes down.

"Hurry up," my partner said.

I looked at the mean black brawler Harley-Davidson with wide chrome exhaust and a long leather seat. I didn't know how to get on.

Monster man grabbed my right arm and pushed me upwards. "If I get busted, you're dead. Now move!"

I swung my leg over the frame and positioned myself in the seat just as one cop walked past us. My driver started the motorcycle and I looked up and down the line of bikes and felt a sudden pang in my stomach. The popular song from the *Sesame Street* game which I played with Mark years ago filled my ears. "One of these things is not like the others." In our case it was two. Everyone else had their own bike with no riders. In our haste to leave, M.B. forgot to assign decoy riders so we wouldn't stick out. Then I looked down at my dress pants and winced. Instead of a wig, I should have borrowed a pair of dungarees.

The cop that just passed us put it together too and started moving toward me. I yanked on my driver's fake ponytail. Lucky for him he strapped his helmet on tight. "We're busted!"

Suddenly, the front of our bike went airborne as Mr. Bad to the Bone popped a wheelie. I lost my balance and desperately threw my arms around his waist and held him closer than I would ever admit.

When we hit the ground the motorcycle was screaming and we catapulted down the street. I looked back for one instant and lost sight of Jack in the chaos.

We took a hard left and almost collided with a cruiser responding to the call. The police car slammed on its brakes and impressively the squeal of its tires almost drowned out the motorcycle as it turned around to pursue us.

I closed my eyes as we screamed down Emerson Street with "Born to Run" playing in my head, and I debated which was worse—being buried alive behind a brick wall or hugging a head-liced horseman.

CHAPTER TWENTY-TWO

I never predicted I would get so close and personal with shag carpeting like I did spending a night sleeping on something that felt akin to artificial turf except it was bright orange. After the hellacious ride through Haverhill, we hid out at some deserted mechanic's garage on the outskirts of the city and rendezvoused with Jack and his escort after midnight. Then we were transferred into Mad Dawg's truck and didn't stumble into M.B.'s apartment until 2 a.m. By then, I would have welcomed a cement slab to sleep on after the long day of terror. But sleeping on shag wasn't easy. I couldn't lie on my stomach like I preferred, because the ancient fibers tickled my face and the scent of fossilized nacho cheese tortilla chips from the last century filled my nostrils. So I ended up sleeping on my back like a dead man, thinking Jack would be locked in this same position soon and wishing Wednesday morning would move along a little faster.

At eight o'clock, I felt a crick in my neck starting and stood up and wiped Jack's burner phone with my T-shirt, afraid where it might have previously toured. It rang seven times before it finally clicked.

"Hello?" a sleepy voice answered.

I winced. "Mark, it's me."

"Dad? What's wrong and why are you calling me from this number?"

"Nothing," I replied as usual, no matter the circumstances. I looked down at the orange shag as it replayed Jack smashing my iPhone. "My phone broke up pretty bad yesterday then died, so I borrowed this one from a friend."

"Does your father know what time it is?" a frustrated woman's voice said in the background.

"Go back to sleep," Mark whispered. The phone went silent for ten long seconds. "Okay, Dad, I'm downstairs now. I hope you're not calling at this hour to complain about your phone. Like I told you, we'll go over it this weekend, and by the way, I didn't like how you hung up on me yesterday. You know how I worry."

Mark always covered himself, although it sounded like he had no trouble sleeping. "I'm sorry to call so early but wanted to catch you before you went out for a run and left for work. You need to cancel your trip out here for a couple of weeks," I said quickly then held my breath.

"C'mon, Dad, let's not start this now," he replied, clearly awake. "We've planned this trip since you finally came to your senses at Christmas. Everything's in motion and your procrastination drives me nuts. If Mom never got sick she would have taken the road trip out here with me and hung the curtains in my apartment. Then she would have dragged your butt out here every year to visit whether it fit in your budget or not. I still can't believe you've never seen where I live. You should be embarrassed."

"You don't have to get huffy about it. I'm moving out sight unseen, aren't I?"

"Yeah, but only after of a year of hounding you. Talk about a tough jury. I don't know what you're scared of either. You'll have your own room and private bath and I'll set you up with your own television so you don't have to wrestle Linda for the remote." He let out a long yawn. "If you think she's a wine snob, you'd go bonkers with her love of foreign films."

"You mean the ones with the subtitles?" I asked, rubbing the back of my neck and hoping I wouldn't have to spend another night on the floor. "How can you enjoy reading a movie?"

"I didn't say I like them, did I? Sometimes you have to go along to get along. I know Mom said the same thing about you and how you had to watch the *Rocky* movies over and over again like you expected a different ending. If it makes you feel better, Linda and I don't want you living with us forever as the condo is small. I've done some checking with a Realtor friend out here and there's a half dozen apartments for rent within ten minutes of our house."

I bit my lip and imagined two empty soup cans and a long string between our houses. Mark would install it to keep tabs on me because he didn't think his father could handle technology. Another chink in my independence.

"Dad are you still there?"

"Yup."

"I hate when you go silent on me like that. It's been almost a year since Mom passed and I'll ask again. What do you have back there?"

"My life," I replied as the orange shag projected a close-up of me dining on hot dogs and baked beans most nights. I closed my eyes to turn it off.

"How long were you planning to keep the house before I talked some sense into you? You don't need it. The market has come back nicely since the crash and you'll make a nice profit now."

"I know, but your mother is here."

"No, she's not and why are you always so morbid? We have the same conversation over and over and today you woke me up super early so we could fit in a doubleheader. Like I've told you, you're not getting any younger. I see it all the time when I talk with my friends. Their folks wait too long to make the necessary adjustments. It's time, Dad."

I inspected the hair on my left arm. The red welts had faded a bit with the morning light and now just looked like a werewolf with a bad case of psoriasis. If only I could get my hands on some talcum powder maybe it would act like crabgrass killer before a new crop germinated. "Mark, I can't do this now. Jack is dying."

There was a three-second delay followed by a yawn. "I'm sorry to hear that. Tell you what. We'll go out for breakfast on Sunday and after you stuff yourself on blueberry French toast and sausages and wash it down with a pot of coffee, we'll swing by St. Joe's and light a candle for him. Then we can begin tackling that basement of yours."

"But I can't leave him."

"After everything he put you through? You're by far the better man to feel that way. If it will make you feel any better, go and visit him today at the hospital, hospice, or wherever else they have him plugged in and say goodbye. If it were up to Mom, she'd bring him an arrangement of dead dandelions for what he put you through. Do what you have to do, but don't spend too much time because you have to sort through what you want to bring out here. Just remember it has to fit in my single-car garage, so if in doubt get rid of it."

I took a deep breath and looked toward the couch in the corner of the room twenty feet away. "You don't understand, Mark. I'm helping him take care of his affairs."

"So you're calling from the race track?"

"I don't have time for this. I have to go."

"Don't hang up on me again, Dad," he said, sounding very much like a lawyer.

"I never have until now, but you're testing me. We'll talk later but please postpone your trip. Bye for now."

Looking down, I surveyed the matted shag. "Now that's what I call Orange Crush."

I heard a giggle and turned around and found little Rosa waiting with a steaming mug of coffee. I met M.B.'s daughter briefly when we arrived and all the commotion in the small apartment woke her up. She looked about nine years old and inherited her mother's chestnut eyes and hair, but the easy smile must have come from her father. Winning the lottery couldn't have made me happier when she offered the purple ceramic mug.

"Go ahead and laugh. I talk to myself all the time," I said, admiring her black pants and brightly flowered top. "Off to school?"

"Soon," she replied quickly. "So, mister, are you going to drink your coffee?"

Direct just like her mother too. I preferred my coffee with milk and sugar, but beggars—or should I say robbers—couldn't be choosers. I took a quick sip and tried to appear like I enjoyed it.

"Did you make it yourself?" I asked, hoping she said yes to confirm M.B. wasn't poisoning me.

Rosa nodded and I felt compelled to take another drink. Dark and bitter was my favorite pairing.

The little girl looked toward the corner of the room where Jack slept on a straw-colored couch. If I felt this strung out from our ordeal yesterday, what did he run on?

"Does he eat?"

It was the same question posed by Nurse Big-Hair-Betty, but its intent worlds apart.

"Yes, and maybe we can make him some cereal or toast?" I asked, hoping she would invite me into the kitchen so I could find something for breakfast too.

She took two steps closer and went on tippy-toes to get a better look. "Mom says he's real sick. What's wrong with him?" she whispered.

I'd asked myself the same question for years, though after yesterday wondered what was wrong with me. I had multiple chances to take an exit and missed them all. Now I slept on itchy and smelly shag in some strange safe house which served battery acid roast for breakfast. I took another gulp of the coffee and let the bitterness roll down my throat. Perfect.

"Does he have cancer like my Uncle Bob?"

"Where's your mother?" I asked, not wanting to go there.

"She went down the street for a few minutes."

"To see who?" I bent over to talk at her level, intent on finding out why we were here. Why would M.B. go out on a limb to rescue us from the police dragnet then sneak us into her home in the same town? Talk about risky business. Jack had remained vague when I pressed the question last night.

"I don't know."

"Tell me about your family."

"I don't have brothers or sisters, but that's okay. I have my mom and that's enough. Someday, we're going to move to Orlando. Mom is going to get an office job, instead of working at the bar. She told me she'll get dressed up pretty for work and be home every night with me. We'll go to Disney on weekends."

I smiled. "Sounds like a great plan."

"Until then, we rent from Mr. Leonard and Tina babysits me when Mom works."

Loud footsteps sounded in the hall and sure enough M.B. appeared. This morning she wore a different pair of dungarees with a navy blue sweater and they looked oversized too. I wondered if she had a stiff neck like me the way she held her head downwards, her shoulder-length hair concealing half her face.

"How's Jack?" she asked, motioning toward the couch.

Rosa stopped fidgeting and stared at me to see if I would finally give it up.

"Well, he had some trouble breathing in the middle of the night so I gave him some more Atropine," I answered quickly, intending to also thank her for the hospitality before noticing the leading edge of a red mark on her left cheek. Her hair hid its length and intensity.

"Rosa, would you be a sweetheart and go and make another cup of coffee? I think Jack will be waking up very soon and he'll be upset if he thinks you only treat me special."

The little girl giggled and ran to the kitchen.

"Get your backpack ready too. We have to leave for school in ten minutes," her mother called after her. M.B. gave me a forced smile and turned to follow her daughter.

I cut her off. "Who hit you?" I whispered. Anyone else and I would have probed around the edges first, hoping the abuse would come out on its own. But yesterday I learned this woman only respected straight talk.

The Bad to the Bones mom glared at me. "Do you always butt into other people's business?"

"I learned a long time ago not to as it has consequences," I replied, wishing I had kept my mouth shut. "Is there anything I can do?"

She moved toward the couch so I couldn't study the bruise. "Yeah, go wake Jack up. He called last weekend and promised me five hundred bucks if the both of you could stay here a few nights."

"He called you last week about us staying here?"

"Look. I need the money to pay someone who isn't very patient," she said as her husky voice turned hoarse and she pointed at her cheek then the couch. "Ask him yourself when he wakes up. But if he doesn't, you're still on the hook. Try and stiff me and I'll have Norman take care of it." She shot me a dirty look. "I should charge you an extra five hundred after last night's circus."

I looked over at Jack and froze. He was the color of a cotton swab and twice as rigid. I raced over and bent down, waiting for his chest to rise and fall.

"I think he's dead," M.B. said over my shoulder.

CHAPTER TWENTY-THREE

The ice dam suddenly burst and I buried my face in my hands as hot tears poured from my bruised eyes. The flood could not be stopped no matter how much it stung and I gasped with each new wave. When the tears finally stopped, I lay back on the hard mattress drenched in sweat.

Samantha breezed into the room. She reminded me of my mother with gray hair, rosy cheeks, and warm green eyes and I expected her to begin reciting lines from Casablanca *at any moment. I looked out the window, hoping to hide my regret and shame in the branches of a birch tree that caressed the window. Its leaves shimmered in the afternoon sun and were hypnotic.*

Just like my mother, nothing got by this committed caregiver and she went over to the sink and wet a white facecloth and draped the cool piece of heaven across my forehead.

She looked at the empty hospital tray. "Can I get you something to drink, Dennis? Maybe some ginger ale?"

I tried to smile but my face refused to go along. "No thanks."

The nurse smiled like she had seen cases like mine a thousand times before where the real wounds can't be stitched or bandaged. She reached into the side pocket of her flowered scrubs. "Then I insist you have a chew," she said and offered me a piece of Juicy Fruit gum. "It tastes great and it gets your mouth working to digest whatever ails you. Take it from me, it will do wonders."

CHAPTER TWENTY-FOUR

Rosa came bounding into the room with her pink backpack flapping against her back. "Mom, I'm ready to go." She stopped and looked at Jack and her eyes opened wide.

"Is he dead?"

M.B. quickly turned the little girl around and patted her on the head. "No, honey, he's just sleeping really deep. Now be a good girl and get my coat and I'll walk you to school."

"Okay. Hope you enjoy the rest of your coffee, mister." She skipped out of the room.

I began searching for a pulse on Jack's wrist when M.B. pulled me away. "Give it up. He's gone." She stuck her index finger into the jelly stain on my shirt, which had picked up some orange fuzz from the long night on the rug. "Like I said, don't try and stiff me out of my money or there will be serious consequences." She looked over at the corpse and threw her head back and sighed. "I would do anything for your buddy, but he's left me in a fine mess now. I can't have the undertaker show up here or the cops will arrest me for sure." She started pacing back and forth in front of the couch and rubbed the back of her neck deep in thought.

A minute later, she threw her hands in the air. "Okay, don't touch anything until I get back. After I walk Rosa to school, I'll talk with Norman and see where he can move him."

"Well, it better be back to the hospice or a funeral home," I said strongly. The cold Merrimack River flashed across my mind and I could envision Norman putting Jack in a pair of swim trunks. At this time of year between the snow melt and the heavy rain, Jack would cover the fourteen miles to the Atlantic in record time.

M.B. didn't acknowledge me and I stood paralyzed until mother and child left.

When the door closed, I shuffled slowly to the kitchen, trying to get comfortable with the reality that Jack was dead and my new address would soon be the State Prison for Men in Concord. Simple as that. I sat at a small butcher block kitchen table and began working diligently on a sleeve of stale saltines and a two-pound tub of no-name peanut butter. The saltines were not designed for the brown glue and cracked every time I tried to spread the peanut butter. Now I knew how sailors and soldiers felt eating hardtack. I wondered how Rosa ate this cardboard for breakfast and still smiled like she did.

I kept my mouth busy for a good fifteen minutes looking out the large kitchen window and watching a pair of sparrows perch on the power lines, enjoying electric foot warmers in the bright sun. It was cathartic to watch the birds and concentrate on swallowing, instead of turning the air blue wondering why Jack set me up. Chewing on the last cracker, I considered spending my next Social Security check to buy new carpeting for M.B.'s apartment. That way, I could roll up my conniving buddy in the ancient shag and let him smell nacho cheese for eternity. Would serve him right.

After a long drink of tap water to liquefy the cement lining my esophagus, I strolled into the living room to weigh my next move.

Jack was lying on his side, eyeing me warily.

"Where's Merriam?" he asked.

I blinked hard at the dead man talking and quickly came to his side and watched his chest rise and fall a few times to make sure I wasn't conversing with a ghost or suffering a hallucination from drug-spiked peanut butter.

Jack grabbed my arm. "I said, where's your wife?"

"What? She's dead."

His confusion confounded me and I stared at his questioning eyes. No one had referred to my wife in the present tense for so long I wanted him to ask me again.

Jack remained silent and drifted off to sleep again and I monitored his breathing. A minute later he woke up terrified.

"This isn't my house," he shouted. His eyes were darting about wildly and I couldn't tell if he recognized me.

He reached up and grabbed my hand. "I thirst."

I bent over and offered him a sip of water. "It's alright, buddy," I said as soothingly as I could muster. "We're at your friend's house. Remember M.B.? She brought us here last night after all our troubles."

Jack held the water in his mouth for some time and I thought he might spit it back at me. When he finally swallowed, his face relaxed and I sensed he was back.

"M.B. and I thought you were gone. How are you feeling?"

He nodded and took another long drink and I helped him hold the glass. I kept my tongue busy freeing the remnants of a cracker cemented to a back tooth.

Finished, Jack leaned back on the pillow.

"M.B. said you called her last week," I said, wanting to spit out something too and it sure wouldn't be water.

Jack rubbed the back of his head with one hand and closed his eyes. I was competing with the pain meds and rubbed his arm to keep him focused. "How do you know M.B.?"

"Poor girl, she got dealt a tough hand," he replied, no doubt keeping his eyes closed afraid I could read them. "She's been a good friend."

My chest felt heavy with the lava flow of peanut butter. "So tell me why you called her last weekend."

"Why ask if you already know?"

I rubbed his arm again, careful not to injure the paper thin skin. "Because I can't believe you set up this whole sorry adventure down to the smallest detail. How could you tell M.B. we would be staying here before I even visited you in hospice?"

Jack opened his eyes and looked toward the popcorn ceiling.

"Talk about conceited. Were you that confident you could guilt me into helping you escape then accompany you on this wild senseless escapade? Well, it's good to know you have M.B. as your new best friend because your old one feels betrayed."

Jack turned his head and stared at me with a blank expression, as if watching a movie and deeply engrossed in the plot. He wore the same look yesterday, when he was eating an orange and watching me become unglued. "Don't you have anything to say?"

"The problem is I don't have enough time to say all the things I should or explain why I did what I did," he whispered. "Yeah, I called a few people that mattered to me. Not to ask forgiveness, mind you, or give anyone a piece of my mind. What would that have accomplished? They would think the cancer was doing all the talking. Like I told you, deathbed confessions are too convenient. Living that way, you can walk all over people through life and apologize just before the sandman catches the last grain. No, I wanted to have a few pleasant conversations with people I cared about so they would smile when they recalled our last exchange. I thought it would be nice to seed a few smiles to offset all the frowns at my wake."

I opened my mouth to launch a scud missile, but stopped when I heard the cry of a siren. I rushed to the side window and watched a police car go flying by.

"Okay, there were a few people I didn't call, because I didn't have the right after hurting them the way I did," Jack continued. "You're one of them. So all I could do was pray you would come visit me in hospice after I told Stu to call you. I knew the odds were in my favor because you've always been a true friend, unlike the way I behaved. I would have waited for your arrival until I closed my eyes for good. That's the God honest truth."

I ignored him and started for the kitchen and another sampling of crackers and peanut butter to glue my tongue shut.

"Look. I'm sorry I wasn't there when Merriam got sick," he called after me. "I should have been and it was selfish of me. Okay? I hope someday you can forgive me."

The sudden apology dismantled the bomb I'd kept with me for the past year that contained so much shrapnel. There was so much I planned to say given the opportunity, each word designed to burn and pierce the skin. I turned back around and Jack motioned me to come closer.

"Like I keep saying—and you're tired of hearing—I need to take care of a few things and need your help, Denny." Jack locked eyes with me. "But you should leave right now if you're going to be a whiny old man that pities himself whenever things get difficult. It's little wonder you're willing to sacrifice your independence to live in some sterile box your son is designing out west. I bet you won't be out there two years before Mark talks you into moving into an assisted living facility. And his siren song will sound so tempting, because everything will be taken care of and life will look so easy. Then one morning you'll wake up in a nursing home sharing a room with some character named Bradley who frightens you with his sleepwalking, steals the chocolate chip cookies you hoard in your dresser, and regularly uses your toothbrush, which is how the doctors think you contracted mono. 'Hotel California' will be your new theme song. The lyrics will really resonate with you."

I drilled the air with my index finger. "How can you say that after everything we went through yesterday? The laws we broke; the chances we took. And what do you know about the life I will lead in California? Mark said he has a nice apartment nearby for me to check out. He thinks I will be like the pioneers when they headed west in covered wagons seeking a new start. It will be a grand adventure."

"Mark thinks, Mark says, Mark does. Listen to yourself!" Jack staggered to his feet and wrapped his arms around me and we both began to sway. "I appreciate everything you've done, Denny. I really do. But to finish this race, I need to run hard through whatever obstacles remain and I can't have you holding the back of my shirt trying to slow me down and complaining about the risks. I don't have time for that and whether you believe it or not, neither do you. Now, I don't know if you have to eat a pound of prunes and wash it down with a quart of strong laxatives, but you need to flush whatever poison you digested years ago. Whatever it is, it's wrapped so tightly around your innards I can barely recognize the kid I wanted as my best friend in grammar school. Get rid of it, Denny. And next time you think of taking Mark's advice, I want you to remember changing his dirty, smelly diapers when he was a baby. He's not some grand oracle who wears sandals, he's your snotty, pimple-faced kid now old enough to shave."

The words were like a knife that quickly sliced me to the core. Jack collapsed on the couch and I lost my legs and sat down on the floor. "Am I that hopeless?" I asked in barely a whisper.

Jack winced as he tried to find a comfortable position. "Look, I'm a simple guy that taught kids how to build birdhouses and sheds. But my dad had one saying that stuck with me all these years. He said 'the man who thinks he can and the man who thinks he can't are both right.'"

"Your father said that? If I remember right, you only quoted the wisdom you found in fortune cookies."

"Actually, the quote is from Henry Ford and would have served you well during your sorry stint at Henley's. Maybe it would have made a difference."

I let the words marinate in my brain for a long minute and then crawled over to the couch and grabbed Jack's bony hand. "Okay, I'll give the move out west some more thought." I looked him straight in the eye. "But right now, I promise to see this adventure through to the end no matter what happens."

"How do I know you're serious?" he asked.

With my spare hand I felt for my black bifold wallet, thinking about the hidden Polara key deep inside one pocket. "Because I learned you're only as good as your word." I took a deep breath and smiled. "Even though I don't know what I'm signing up for. We'll strive to be the new dynamic duo."

"Yeah, just like Batman." Jack let out small laugh then groaned. "Terrible pity that it hurts to laugh. I'm thinking Batman and Robin may have dueled with the Riddler and the Joker, but never saw the likes of us."

I laughed and missed the feeling. "Yeah, I can see Robin getting a load of your escapades and exclaiming 'Holy Headache, Batman!'"

Another siren sang out in the distance and we looked at each other and smiled.

"So where does M.B. figure into your grand plan?" I finally asked.

Jack licked his cracked lips. "You're going to have to trust me on this one, Denny, which is your first big test. M.B. is a good friend and that's all I can say at the moment."

I shrugged in resignation. "Well, she will be very relieved to find you still alive. I hate to say it, but you had an ugly date with Norman later. Chances were good you might have hit Salisbury Beach early this year or been the first planting this spring."

Jack laughed. "That might be fun if I could come up like tulips each year and have people smile at me for a change. Now, help me get dressed because we have to be at the cemetery by ten o'clock."

"Why, is there some new layaway plan?" I asked, my mouth running crazy again.

Jack smiled like he did whenever he was up to no good. "You might want to look into one, because yesterday was just a dress rehearsal for today."

"Are you trying to scare me now that I pledged?"

"Perhaps. Grab the car keys on the table as we're leasing M.B.'s car. I also secured us some coats last night."

CHAPTER TWENTY-FIVE

Pine Grove Cemetery was no doubt an apt description when founded on the edge of a deep forest three hundred years ago. Now only a few scrappy pines remained and are rapidly losing a popularity contest to newly planted maples.

The first inhabitants were interred on a hill facing east. White marble markers greeted the sun and were embossed with funny names like Letitia, Matilda, and Cuthbert. New England weather had little regard for posterity and slowly worked to erase these odd entries.

Modern graves were arranged on a large rolling plain fifty yards away. Row after row of handsome multi-colored stones competed to be noticed. The most dramatic gravestones were those containing a portrait of the deceased, etched into its smooth black marble.

When Merriam's time got near, she became intent on walking the cemetery as if relocating to a new neighborhood. One hot June afternoon, she discovered a micro environment in a southern corner where the temperature was a few degrees cooler. I didn't give much thought about her selection or that this would be my final resting place too. To me, a casket was like a thousand washing machines I'd stuck my head into as a salesman; tight and claustrophobic.

But this morning, the love of my life would rip into me with gusto if she were alive. I stood over her grave unshaven and wearing a bright orange snorkel coat with dirty fur around the hood that must have belonged to some scrawny twelve-year-old kid because it barely covered my stomach. Jack wore one too but given his wasting condition it fit nicely. We rented the coats from M.B. for twenty bucks a day and they reeked of tobacco. We paid another hundred to borrow her "classic" black Ford Escort with no working turn signals and hardly any gas. Lucky for us we robbed a bank.

We no sooner pulled into the cemetery than Jack held onto his stomach and began laughing uncontrollably.

"What's so funny?" I asked, beginning to laugh myself and not knowing why.

Jack put down his sun visor even though it was a cloudy day. "I've worn some pretty ugly threads in my day, but I look like a carrot and you resemble a butternut squash." He flipped the fur-lined hood up and looked like he came from skid row. "Veggies aside, I'm afraid we may trigger a zombie apocalypse if we stay here too long."

"You always liked horror movies and at least that would take care of our legal issues. But look on the bright side. Orange is the new black and the primary color of my future wardrobe."

I got out of the car and minutes later studied the lifeless grass over my wife's grave as doubt crept into my soul again. Greater minds than mine had wrestled with the question of whether this is all there is. When I let it get the better of me, I imagined a day soon to come when a long line of worms lined up at the deli counter asking for "a quarter pound of Dennis, sliced thin please."

Merriam tried for years to make me open up and talk, but I never wanted to cause her any grief ever again, so I remained silent. My wife warned you could drown in a puddle if you set your mind to it. And she was right. No matter how many times I retreated to our bedroom to stare at Jean's memorial card sheathed in plastic and repeat the Lord's Prayer I remained face down in the water.

Thinking about the dead made me look over and check on Jack. He leaned against one of the old pine trees missing half its branches and I didn't know which looked sicker. Three fat blackbirds mulled around in front of him and I wondered if he caught the symbolism, which depending on the culture could represent eternal life or temptation.

I planned to stay with Merriam for a few more minutes and explain our circumstances and Jack's apology, when my ears rang with one of those high-pitched whistles that substituted as a homing device as a kid. As I quickly mouthed a final Hail Mary, Jack whistled again. If I hadn't been on sacred ground, I would have replied in kind.

"You really are going to wake the dead," I yelled over.

He didn't reply and pointed toward Main Street. Following his finger, I caught sight of a white feathered hat followed by two dozen more. In short order the small army marched up the driveway. They wore crisp crimson-colored uniforms with white-gloved hands holding brass instruments. I expected a hearse to bring up the rear, but none appeared.

"What's this all about?" I asked.

Jack didn't take his eyes off the parade. "His high school band from Meredith."

"Whose high school band?"

"My father's, of course."

I reasoned we stopped at the cemetery so Jack could follow up on his apology and show a little consideration to Merriam. That's why I thought he followed me over to her grave. I wondered now if the apology was part of some master plan, so I would be sufficiently motivated to get him here this morning.

"Please explain to me why you invited your father's high school band here," I managed to ask through clenched teeth.

"Dad is buried around the bend and I thought he would enjoy a few tunes. Before you ask, yes, I arranged this last week too. But this salute would have gone ahead whether I was here or not."

"Salute?" I repeated under my breath. Why do this now when he would be joining his father any moment? All that's left here is an empty vessel anyways. "Look, I promised to help check off your list, but do I get to ask why this stop?"

"That's why you went into sales," he replied. The funny guy back in the car was now MIA. "You always needed facts and figures and sadly missed the subtle things in life."

"Which of course you found in plywood and ten-penny nails, which requires such deep insight." I hesitated to let the comment sting a bit. "It took me a while, but I finally figured out why you were so intent on teaching in Salem instead of using your education degree to get a better paying job in Massachusetts. You wanted to be near Rockingham Race

Track so you could be at the betting window before the kids made it home on the bus. You're right, though. I was a pretty boring guy working days, nights, and weekends to support my family. Nothing very subtle about that."

We stood there in silence, both bleeding inside as two twenty-somethings approached. Both men were blond and wore jeans and nice ski jackets. The taller one carried a notebook, the other a camera.

The stringer took the lead. "Is one of you Jack? We're from the *Eagle-Tribune*."

My friend bent over, pulled out an inhaler, and took a puff. I didn't know how to answer, since we were fugitives.

Jack held up a finger, signaling he needed a moment to catch his breath. Given his color, I didn't know if he would.

The young gentlemen looked concerned.

"I'd like you to hold off printing this story until it makes the front page," Jack said in a hoarse voice.

"I'm afraid that's above our pay grade," the photographer laughed, fiddling with his camera.

My friend coughed and spit a fifty-cent piece of white foam on the matted yellow grass. I glanced at the adjoining marker and silently apologized to Nellie Gist. When I looked back, Jack handed the reporter an envelope.

"Please don't misinterpret this," he said. "I just want to thank you for coming out on such short notice and want to give you twenty bucks for lunch. If you can't accept it, please give it to your Santa Fund. I'm not asking you to color the story, mind you; write it as you see it. All I ask is it gets on the front page so it gets read. My friend Dennis here will treat you to dinner after it's published." He grabbed the writer's arm. "I hope I live long enough to read it."

They both looked at me and I smiled weakly. I hoped they didn't mind sharing a cheeseburger from some fast food joint.

"Okay, you boys go ahead of me," he said, taking off his hat and stashing it in his coat. "It'll take Dennis and me a few minutes to join everyone."

We started inching across the grass and I noticed Jack beginning his frozen shuffle again.

"C'mon, Jack, what's this all about?" I asked. "You buried your father twenty-five years ago and I remember the nice funeral you had."

We walked a few more feet in silence and I admired the clean asphalt which the cemetery did not salt or sand in the winter. He began panting and I knew this was my best chance to get my point across without being interrupted.

"Look. I can understand you want to be respectful to your father. But we both know who you should be spending your last hours with."

Suddenly, our progress stopped and two bony fingers drilled into my ribs. It did feel like a revolver.

"Enough out of you," he said sharply. "When it's your time you can do it your way, which will be easy since you'll be alone."

"What do you mean by that?"

"Don't play stupid, Denny. I might be half crazy thinking I know everyone, but I certainly know you. Since you lost Merriam, you've disappeared. I might not have been around, but I kept tabs on you by calling around to the old gang. Andy and Steve haven't heard from you in three years. When I'm gone you'll have no one because you've turned everyone else away."

I shoved Jack and he fell back two steps. "What a joke, getting a lecture from a man who got his family counseling from the other bozos playing keno at Ned's Variety. And how did that bet pay out for you, Jack? Wife gone, daughter estranged, and here you are visiting dead people you will be joining any minute."

"Dennis, if I wasn't fighting to get my butt around this corner for my father's sake I'd use my last breath to beat the stuffing out of you."

The band wrapped up "God Bless America" when we finally reached the grave. The way Jack and I pushed and shoved each other on the way over they should have been playing "Isn't It a Pity."

I couldn't imagine what these youngsters were thinking standing in formation and playing their instruments for some unknown dead guy. I didn't know much about Jack's father except that he was a decorated WWII war hero and left for work before the sun appeared and returned long after it set. What I did know was he wouldn't understand this strange scene.

The sky looked depressed and a cold breeze kicked up. The music director, a balding twenty-something in a tan double-breasted pea coat, looked annoyed trying to decide whether to begin another song. My mind turned, wondering how he got roped into this grand plan too. Jack didn't want to ask God for forgiveness thinking it would come off as premeditated, yet his exit strategy seemed meticulously prearranged.

Jack finally acknowledged the maestro and he signaled the band to stand at ease. Suddenly, an overeager drummer dropped a solemn beat. In this bizarre situation, my crazy impulse wanted to throw my handkerchief on the ground and penalize the band five yards for a false start. Instead, Jack released the death grip he had on my arm and shuffled unsteadily toward the headstone.

He raised one hand to get their attention and scanned their young faces. Suddenly his face lit up. "Hey, I know you!"

I wanted the wind to howl and blow his words away, but nature apparently wanted to listen too. I heard some giggles and stepped forward to whisper in my friend's ear.

"What are you saying? You don't know any of these kids."

Jack rubbed the back of his head and looked tense, as if trying to remember what to say. "Uh, my father was a patriot," he began then stopped. The silence lengthened and became awkward even for a cemetery.

The band began to fidget and the mumbling became contagious. "This is lame," one lanky kid with a trumpet griped. "So what if the old guy bought us new uniforms. I'd rather be in my stupid algebra class than freezing my butt off out here with some half-wit."

My eyes popped and I almost lost my gum. Anyone watching would have thought I was either choking or had a serious thyroid issue. Granted, the kid deserved a knock up the side of the head for insolence. But I couldn't stop staring at the fifty new band uniforms my bankrupt friend somehow financed along with the bus transportation from fifty miles away. Jack accused me of living my life by the numbers, but it didn't take much of a mathematician to calculate his largesse cost a few thousand dollars. And for what? A few tunes for a guy six feet under? I concluded my buddy had either made one last score at the track or found another money stream. I thought back to the bank robbery and how calmly he acted. I made a mental note to research all bank robberies in the Merrimack Valley for the last year.

A gagging cough filled the air and Jack bent over. The kids were suddenly mesmerized, thinking they might get to see someone actually drop dead right in front of them and give them something juicy to talk about on the bus ride back. I just hoped my friend wouldn't begin spitting again as there would be no way to restore order after being grossed out like that. I moved forward to steady Jack's arm, but he pushed me away.

"I hate March because everyone is waiting for spring," he said, starting again and surprisingly in a new strong voice. "Yet, I resemble winter this morning; starting and stopping and coughing all over the place." He looked at the trumpet section. "I'll try and pull myself together so you can get back to unlocking the mysteries of algebra."

Jack stood up very straight and his expression changed as if surveying a new class in September. "Thank you very much for coming out today. I know you're all standing there, hoping this old guy will hurry up so you can get back to class and your lives. I don't blame you one iota, because that was me too until a few weeks back."

Suddenly, he pointed at me. "Just ask my best friend, Dennis, over there; he can tell you all about me if you're curious. But I'm afraid Dennis would be too kind with the gritty details. So let me give you a quick summary. I was so self-absorbed playing the ponies that when his wife, Merriam, died last year, I stayed in Florida. I didn't call or send flowers and one of my drinking buddies mailed a sympathy card for me. I always thought there would be time someday to come back and set things right. But unfortunately, you can't find someday on a calendar."

Jack kicked at the dead lawn and his mouth quivered. "Time heals all wounds, they say. Greeting card companies make a killing on pithy sayings like that, but I'm here to tell you time and pain can open up a chasm so wide and deep, no words can bridge it. Merriam is buried just around the corner, and I had every intention to pay my overdue respects today. The problem is I'm too disgusted with myself to do it. I should have said goodbye while she could still hear me and that opportunity is gone forever. All I can do now is apologize to her husband and my best friend."

I felt all their eyes on me and watched Jack stumble forward a step. "Funny how dying brings clarity. At best, I have one sunrise left in me. I wish I could have seen things in the past like I do now. It would have made all the difference."

I looked at the kids and they were paying attention. Two saxophone players stepped forward to hear better.

The former shop teacher read his audience and let the dramatic pause lengthen. "What would you do with your last day?" he suddenly asked, pointing to a lanky boy cradling a flute. The kid blushed to match the color of his new uniform.

Jack reached up and patted him on the back. "Don't worry, son, I don't expect an answer. You think you're bulletproof, like we all do. And me? I don't know if I will find the courage to confront Merriam today," he said, walking slowly over to a tuba player and inspecting the large instrument. "But I wished I had back straps like you to carry my heavy load. Luckily, Dennis is here to help me shoulder the burden. That's the mark of a true friend. Even though I didn't deserve it, he is here for me until the end."

Jack moved on until he was in the middle of the assembly. "I invited you today because I won't be here in May to smell the lilacs, or buy a flag for my father's grave," he said, pointing back to the gravestone. "Every Memorial Day we have this proud tradition of putting flags on all the veteran graves. If you look around you can still see a few that survived the winter. It reminds me of how my father loved the saying 'these colors never run.'"

The wind suddenly kicked up as if on cue and the remaining skeleton of a maple leaf inched its way across the sleeping grass. Jack motioned for a couple of the band members to help him and no one moved for an awkward moment, but finally two trombone players did and he led them over to the gray granite gravestone. "My father is buried here," he said in a gentle tone, caressing the letters. "One of nine kids, he lost his mother at three years old. My grandfather had to break up the family and consequently, my dad spent his childhood bouncing from one relative to another. Life was tough and when the Second

World War broke out, he joined the Navy at seventeen. My father served his country in the Pacific and fought in the largest naval battle of the war—and possibly in history, in the Battle of Leyte Gulf. My father was aboard the USS *St. Lo*, the first warship to be sunk by a kamikaze attack. He may have only been a kid at the time, but he was one hell of a man that day and risked his life to save a dozen men from burning to death or drowning. He came home from the war and my mother bound up his wounds and filled in the hole in his heart."

Jack knelt down and remained silent for a long moment. "Growing up, my mother used to say I should be proud to become half the man he was and he never talked about any of it. When I think back on my service in Vietnam—" Jack stopped and grabbed the headstone with his right hand as if some invisible hurricane force wind worked to blow him away. "I didn't understand until then how big a standard he set," he continued. "He was awarded the Medal of Honor for his courage."

Jack leaned back and took a few big gulps of air. "The VA is good about putting flags on the graves for Memorial Day, but on my last day I want to salute him and all the other heroes who gave us the blessings we enjoy today."

The band director gave the order and a lone trumpet softly played Taps. When he finished, the director brought over a wreath of white carnations and Jack placed it against the base of the headstone to shelter it against the wind. Reaching into his rented jacket, he produced a small American flag. Jack struggled to drill it into the hard-packed earth, and a pretty flute player with braided red hair knelt beside him to assure the stars and stripes were sufficiently planted to withstand any March gale.

Jack stood up and held her hand for balance. He looked exhausted, but the tension in his face had disappeared.

"Some might think I bribed the system to get you here today. Maybe so, but it pains me to see the first thing that gets cut in the school budget is always music. So I hope you enjoy your new uniforms and they give you pride. Please say a prayer for me when you drive by here because I'm not sure my parents will be happy I'm moving back in with them."

I waited until the procession made its way back to Main Street and the waiting yellow school bus before I approached him again. Jack kept talking to the newspaper reporter and I hated to disturb him until I saw a police cruiser pull up alongside the bus. I waved frantically at Jack and pointed at the road.

My friend quickly dismissed the reporter and shuffled over to me.

"I should have known we'd attract company," Jack said, taking my arm and directing me up the same path we came. I waved my hand in front of my nose as a fresh breeze drove the tobacco smell out of our coats and up my nostrils.

"Well, at least we have M.B.'s car so we should be okay," I said, trying to be positive for a change.

"Let's wait for a few minutes until the bus leaves. Then we'll stop at Merriam's grave on the way out. I have some carnations for her too, if she doesn't strike me dead first."

"No fear. She's a forgiving soul. And given what you said back there, I should learn to be too."

Jack tugged on my arm. "But we can't stay too long as we have a lunch date."

I smiled and licked my lips. "I hoped that was on the itinerary."

CHAPTER TWENTY-SIX

The trek from Salem to Lawrence felt more like a covered wagon crawl as we shied away from the main thoroughfare of Route 28 and hugged pothole-infested side streets. My teeth rattled with every hard knock in the old jalopy as we weaved a tortuous path into Massachusetts. The cloudy day only added to the misery as most everything looked dingy from the winter shellacking. The receding snow also indicted more than a few homeowners of Christmas inflatable manslaughter as the flattened corpses of Rudolph, Santa, and Frosty populated many front lawns.

Jack sat low in the seat asleep but I couldn't wait any longer. I reached over and gently tried to rouse him. He opened one eye. "Are we there yet?"

"No, but I'm not a camel like you. I need to stop and go to the bathroom."

"You're like a little kid sometimes. Can't you wait until we get there?"

"Sorry, but when you were playing dead back at the apartment I drank a quart of water with my crackers and peanut butter glue."

I scanned the road ahead and noticed the sign for Stella's Bakery on the right. It was a small joint in a cement block stand-alone building and devoid of customers. I eased the Escort into an empty space by the front door.

"Okay, I'm going to run in and use the facilities. I'll be back in a second."

"You kill me with your use of language sometimes," Jack said with his eyes closed again. "The facilities? Why can't you just talk normal and say the men's room? Just leave the keys in the ignition."

"Why?"

"Because if you're not back in five minutes, I'm leaving without you."

I opened the car door and kept the keys. "Nice try."

The bakery smelled of fresh bread and my starving eyes danced along the glass shelves displaying multiple treasures of cupcakes, cookies, cakes, and rolls. My full bladder kicked me in the groin to remind me why we were here. I glanced around the small lobby and became anxious looking for a public bathroom and finding none. Suddenly, I heard my name and glanced in the corner where a small television hung high on the wall. My favorite television anchorman, Chuck Montgomery, always looked like he just modeled for *GQ* with his Don Draper haircut and Brooks Brothers suit and tie. The camera panned to a snapshot of me and Jack leaving the hospice arm in arm.

"Police caution that Sullivan and Nagle are to be considered armed and extremely dangerous. Let's go to our reporter Paul Lynch, who is standing outside police headquarters in Salem, New Hampshire."

I whipped my head around to make sure no one else heard. The bakery remained empty and I quickly commandeered a metal chair from one of two patron tables and put on the Weather Channel.

"Can I help you?" a stern voice asked before I could demount.

I turned around to find a stern-looking bald man about my age wiping flour off his hands onto a white apron. He gave me a quick once-over and I could tell he wasn't impressed with the snorkel hand-me-down or my fiddling with the television.

I went for broke and wore the most innocent smile I could muster. "Hope you don't mind, but I wanted to check the forecast and see when this purgatory of a winter will end."

The baker sniffed the air like a skunk had invaded the premises, and then glared at me, no doubt afraid the tobacco smell from my coat would overwhelm the bakery. "What can I get you?" he asked.

"Can I please use your restroom first?"

The baker shook his head no emphatically. "The library is a mile down the street. Anything else?"

My bladder kicked me in the groin again warning me it would blow any moment. I crossed my feet and put my hand on my stomach, afraid the baker would soon need a mop to clean up a yellow puddle on the ultra-white tiled floor.

"Please, I can't make it that far," I said with urgency. Suddenly, I remembered a small tidbit I read a while back in some magazine in the doctor's office. "I have a medical condition."

The baker snickered and turned his back. "Well, there's a fire hydrant across the street. Some of the neighborhood dogs relieve themselves there."

The pain in my groin transferred to my throat. "Wow, you're a real class act. I'll have to add that comment to my police report too."

"What do you mean police report?" he asked, spinning around.

"Because I'm employed by the Methuen Police to gauge compliance with the Restroom Access Act that passed a few years ago. The law requires you to allow customers access to your restroom if a customer suffers from a medical condition. You denied me access so now you'll suffer the consequences."

The baker put his fat hands on top of the glass case and by the ugly look on his face, I thought he might climb over and knead me like a big piece of dough.

"You gotta be kidding me!"

At this point I had to go for broke. "No. The unit I work for is made up of teenagers and some retired folks like me. The kids go out and try to buy a beer and see if they're carded and if the store fails they get fined and some lose their liquor license. For you, I'll push for a big fine and maybe shut you down for a day or two. I'll make sure the *Eagle-Tribune* does a story on you too." I looked out the window. "Maybe they can take a picture of me in front of that fire hydrant you recommended."

I watched the baker's face become as white as confectionary sugar. "I'm sorry... I don't...know what came over me," he said stuttering and quickly led me to a small bathroom next to a large refrigerator out back. It was a lovely little bathroom with green marble countertops and an ornate round mirror over the sink. I quickly closed the door and smirked to myself in the mirror before hurrying to the toilet.

The baker was waiting with a large white box when I made my way back to the front of the shop. "Please accept my signature chocolate cake with vanilla buttercream frosting as an apology for the way I treated you," he said more to the box than me. "Can we please forget this all happened?"

I worked to keep a serious face and nodded. "Let it happen again and I'll throw the book at you."

Jack was awake when I got back in the car. "What's in the box?" he asked.

I placed the heavy package on his lap and started the car, not wanting to brag how I excelled at improv.

My friend looked inside and started laughing. "The frosting looks supreme, but I have to ask why it says *Mazel Tov, David!*" He shot me a confused look. "Who the heck is David?"

I looked over at the ridiculous inscription and laughed hard enough to inflate all the abused Christmas characters. "I don't know," I managed to confess when I finally regained control. "Maybe little David came down with the flu this morning. Rosa will like it and we can always scrape off the name."

Jack nodded. "That's nice of you."

I remembered my mug shot on TV. "No, I think the scale will still tip towards infamous."

My friend adjusted himself in the seat.

"Maybe you're right and I should have gone to the bathroom too." Jack started to open the door.

I put the car in reverse fast. "You snooze, you lose."

***

The small one-story wooden building, which needed painting since the Eisenhower administration, was located at the entrance of a once bustling textile mill complex in Lawrence, Massachusetts. Old-timers remembered it colored fire engine red, but any remaining pigment had retreated long ago into its sun-parched shingles. The building began as the office for the mill watchman to greet visitors and chide any workers arriving late or attempting to sneak out before the whistle blew. After a union strike in the late 1940s, the building was transformed into a diner. Management hailed the restaurant as being attentive to labor, but the workers mocked its motivation. They knew it was simply more cost efficient to offer cheap eats on-site than having workers wander downtown for lunch and come back late.

When the textile and shoe factories moved south, the entire complex spoiled as fast as unrefrigerated milk. The campus looked dismal for years like sister sites throughout New England, until generous incentives attracted new owners. When a few light manufacturing companies moved into the old mill, the diner reopened as Sam's Bagels and More and served breakfast and lunch Monday through Friday.

When we finally arrived at lunch time I snagged the last parking spot in front.

Jack played with the glove compartment latch. "I don't know why she has to work here. She's smart and capable of doing so much more."

I'd heard this complaint so often I knew when to nod and did it again one last time. A sign in the window advertised two eggs, bacon, toast, and coffee for $2.99 and I began hallucinating about those little packages of marmalade jelly.

"Kate went to a good college," he droned on. "I'll admit, maybe my daughter wasn't cut out to be a teacher. Education has changed so much since I retired, I probably wouldn't become a teacher today. Now, you spend all your time prepping the kids for standardized tests and being a surrogate parent. Still, she's a smart girl and should have a professional position with one of the hi-tech companies around here. Then she would be recognized for her talent and make good money. But here she is wasting her life pouring coffee, washing dishes, and surviving on lousy tips to make rent."

"Well, we can sit here and replay it one more time, or you can go in and have a conversation with your daughter."

Jack didn't move and I couldn't tell if it was out of stubbornness or fear. The way he licked his poor chapped lips told me the latter, but he would never admit it. In a flash, I bolted out of the car and opened his door. My intentions were good, but also a bit self-serving. I planned to deposit him in a booth to talk with Kate and I would find a seat at the counter and happily inhale two breakfast specials in the hope of diluting the cracker and peanut butter sludge plugging my intestines.

Opening the diner door resembled entering a wind tunnel of chatter. We rashly made our assault at the height of the lunch hour. Tens of conversations combined to create a loud din and I quickly scanned the layout. All the booths were taken as well as the counter seats. Most of the patrons were between twenty and fifty years old, wore casual clothes, and seemed to know one another. Two men in dark suits sat at the bar and ate in silence. I forgot about the eggs and toast and almost drooled over the smell of the fried chicken.

A bell rang on a stainless steel counter as a young short order cook plated a cheeseburger with fries. Kate suddenly appeared out of nowhere and transferred the heart attack special to a heavy man at the counter. She looked like a ballerina on the worn red checkered floor: pouring coffee, clearing plates, dispensing a slice of apple pie with efficiency and grace. Kate had an infectious smile and a cute figure which she displayed in black jeans and thin green sweater. She was blonde like her mother and wore her hair in a ponytail. I hadn't seen her in many years and had a hard time believing she must be forty now.

"Hey, I know you!" Jack suddenly yelled loud enough to blow out all the conversations.

Turning, I expected to find him pointing to his daughter. Instead, he cornered a thin Asian man with a receding hairline by the unmanned cash register who looked mystified.

"I think you're mistaken, mister," he replied in broken English.

"Hey, Kate, can you tell this guy who I am?" Jack said with his arms open wide. I noticed his pleading eyes were terribly out of alignment with the broad smile and swagger.

If his daughter felt flustered, it lasted only for a split second and she quickly waved her hand as if slaying a fly. "Don't mind him none, Jian. He's just an old fool." She turned her back and continued to clear a table.

Jack hung his head in dramatic fashion. "C'mon, Kate," he said in a more subdued voice. "We've been through this routine too often." He took three steps forward. "We need to talk."

She never looked up as she repositioned the stubby glass salt and pepper shakers next to the stainless steel napkin dispenser. "Sir, we're at capacity so you'll have to leave so we don't get in trouble with the fire department. I'm sure your companion can float you a couple bucks so you can check out the lunch specials at the track. I'll call ahead and tell them to rustle up some yellow bellied snake."

Kate began walking away. "Now, if you'll excuse me, I have real fathers to feed."

The lost look from the cemetery returned and Jack stood silent in the center of the diner as the patrons looked embarrassed and went back to their lunches and conversations. I gently pulled him toward the door knowing two things: he would need another lifetime to make things right with his daughter, and I would have to sneak back somehow to order my lunch to go.

With our retreat completed, Jack leaned against the hood of the car to catch his breath.

"What made you think a big entrance like that would work?"

He took a pill bottle out of his pocket, but offered no explanation.

"Stop hiding behind the cancer, will you?" I said, fishing a stick of gum out of my stinky coat pocket for a ten-calorie lunch. "You never can do anything quietly and have to be the center of attention." I took a quick break to put the gum in my mouth and enjoy the jolt of sugar. "No wonder your daughter doesn't want to see you. You didn't listen when she told you again and again she wanted to open a small restaurant. If I remember right that's been her dream since Santa brought her an Easy-Bake Oven. But you brow beat her until she finally got a teaching degree, just to please you. Then when she got laid off, you still wouldn't listen."

I leaned against the car hood too and looked up at the five-story brick mill. Some of the windows were covered in old plywood. Rebirth is slow, painful work.

"I remember my grandfather talking about the Bread and Roses Strike here in 1912 when the legislature reduced the work week and the mill owners slashed wages. Honestly, Jack, think of all the dreams that died here when kids were working six days a week, spinning wool and sweeping floors."

When I looked over, Jack had tears running down both cheeks. I tried to rub his back but he pushed me away.

"What time does this place close?"

I glanced at my watch. "In a little over an hour from now. We can wait in the car if you like, but I don't see how it will help. Why don't you just write her a note? I promise to deliver it when you're gone."

"I have to make it right today," he said and began to wander off.

"Where are you going?"

"It's my turn to use the bathroom. Okay, boss?"

"That's why I stopped at the bakery." I pointed toward the diner. "Well, we'll have to go back in. There's no bathrooms where you're headed, just an empty lot."

Jack kept walking away unconvinced.

"Want me to come?" I asked out of habit.

He glanced back and his look said it all.

I kept watch when suddenly there was a bright flash in the diner and all the lights went out. In short order, all the worker bees and the two guys in the dark suits began to slowly spill out. They looked about as disappointed as Jack, with one exception. The patrons left empty-handed and my best friend came up the side driveway with a bunch of electrical wires in his hand.

CHAPTER TWENTY-SEVEN

"Have you lost your mind?" I asked, grabbing him by the shoulders and giving him a good shake.

Jack looked amused at my dismay. "Why? Are you afraid I would electrocute myself?" he laughed, throwing the tangled red, green, and black spaghetti on the pavement. "You should know by now the Good Lord won't call me home until He's done with me."

"Perhaps, but pride is one of the seven deadly sins. And since you've exhausted my patience, I can't imagine what you're doing to His."

He ignored my comment. "Besides, you watch too much television. I wasn't dismantling a bomb. There were a few sparks, that's all. Not too tough for a shop teacher."

Before I could think of another word for stupid, Kate appeared on the diner stairs. She wore the same expression as me, only a lot meaner.

"Get in here right now," she yelled.

No woman had spoken like that to me for some time, though I knew Mrs. Werner would pierce my ear drums sufficiently when she finally caught up with me. Even Jack seemed surprised by his daughter's bluster. We immediately obeyed and slogged back up the three wooden stairs like we were headed to the principal's office. This time the place was nearly empty, except for one table in the far corner where an older gentleman finished putting on his coat and then scurried past us like a rat off a sinking ship.

Kate ordered us to a table near the door where the daylight crept in through old plate glass windows. There would be no shadows for the coming interrogation. I became delighted with the seat selection as the table contained a dinner plate cradling three uneaten onion rings and a pickle spear. The situation required keen timing and I decided to wait for the father and daughter to begin mixing it up before making my move.

I no sooner made my plan than I noticed a bigger payload on the table next to us; half a ham sandwich on a bulky roll with what looked like a hint of spicy mustard. From my vantage point I didn't see any bite marks either, so I planned to trade up.

"This is between father and daughter," I said and slithered away to pilfer lunch.

Jack called after me. "No, please stay. After all we've been through, I have no secrets. Plus, you can vouch for what I have to say, so there isn't any misinterpretation later."

I decided on a classic boomerang move and accelerated forward, scooped up the half-eaten sandwich, and arced back to the table. Kate locked her baby blues with mine then looked in amazement at the treasure I cradled close to my chest. There was nothing left to do but shrug and take a bite. The deli ham had a wonderful flavor and the spicy mustard woke up my taste buds.

Jack watched and shook his head.

"Yeah, you two make quite a pair," Kate said, zeroing in on her father again. "Please tell me you didn't knock out the power to the restaurant."

Jack picked up one of the onion rings I had dibs on and stared at it intently before throwing it back on the plate. "I didn't cut power to a restaurant. All I did was unplug a sorry-looking shed."

The rest of the plate went airborne and hit Jack squarely in the chest. If it had been bullets or a knife, his troubles would have been over.

"How dare you! You have no right to show up after all these years and then barge into my life like this."

"Don't be like your mother and throw a fit before I can explain," he replied in a surprisingly soft voice, while placing the empty white plate back on the table and brushing crumbs off his orange snorkel coat. "I wish I had enough time left to make up for failing you, Kate. I really do." He surveyed all the abandoned tables. "I'd be willing to do dishes until the next millennium to earn your forgiveness."

Kate didn't say anything and stared at the empty plate. My eyes wandered to the three golden fried onion rings lying prostrate on the floor next to me and I wondered just how sick I would get if I ate them. They were already high in calories and fat so what were a few germs mixed in? I looked at the neighboring tables for a bottle of ketchup.

Jack suddenly elbowed me to pay attention. I didn't hear the bell, but my friend came charging out of his corner.

"Dennis is taking me around town so I can get my affairs in order. I don't have much time left, honey. Actually a stopwatch would suffice."

"A stopwatch?" she replied with a right hook. "When I was ten years old, I remember Mom buying you a gold pocket watch for your birthday. I hadn't turned eleven before you pawned it to bet on a trifecta at Suffolk Downs." She rubbed the back of her neck. "At least your gambling buddies would try to make things right after they screwed up and bring their wives flowers and some candy for the kids. You just got angry and told us to forget about it." Kate took a deep breath before attempting the TKO. "Why are you even here? You should be crying with your bookie, instead of wasting time with me." She looked around and groaned. "If I'm lucky Sam will only dock me for the electrician, instead of firing my butt."

"You look good, Kate," Jack said in his typical move of redirecting. He reached for her hand but she pulled away. "You're aging gracefully, like your mother."

"Why do you say that? Have you tried to contact her?" she asked, alarmed.

Jack held up his hands in defense as if expecting another flying plate. "Believe me when I tell you my intentions are good. We haven't talked in over ten years."

"She doesn't need to see you," she stammered. "And what's left to say anyways? Your silver tongue lost its luster a long time ago making promises you couldn't keep."

Jack looked defeated. I expected him to cough or gag to buy time and consider how best to proceed. Instead, he just leaned back in the chair looking exhausted.

"Did you hear what he's saying, Kate?" I asked. "Your father came to see you today because he's dying and wants to make things right with you. This can't come as a surprise. I know his brother called you."

"All I can say is my father died a long time ago to my mother and me," she replied and leaned toward me. I could smell her perfume of bacon and my mind began to wander back to Mrs. Werner's house. "It's easy for you to get soft because he's your best friend."

I put my arm around Jack. "It's hard not to be nostalgic. We lived four houses apart on the same street. We graduated from playing with Tonka trucks to using up the strategic reserve of Bondo to patch the rusted rear panels of junk cars and chase pretty girls who rarely noticed us. When we were young—"

"Enough ancient history," Kate said, screwing up her nose. "When you're driving my father around town, I think you should stop at the eye doctor and trade in your rose-colored glasses. You never had to live with the man, did you?"

I bit my lip because I had no defense for the coming assault.

"Look, you could hibernate when he was on a binge and being a jerk to everyone around him. You didn't have to watch him sell anything that wasn't nailed down in order to try and win it all back in the next race. My mother used to cry herself to sleep at night knowing we couldn't make the rent because he loved the track more than us. When I was a little girl, I used to imagine a stable full of ponies somewhere in upstate New York. I thought my daddy was saving up so he could bring one home for me," she said with her blue eyes becoming moist. "When I got older, I realized I had it backwards. The horses rode my father."

I remembered when the gambling first took hold. Jack had landed a terrific job teaching Industrial Arts at Salem High and everything seemed to be falling into place nicely for him and Sarah. Then a few months later, the phone started ringing in my department at Wayne's Appliance around the time school let out. Occasionally, Jack would be manic after winning a few bucks the day before and wanted to go out and celebrate. More often he seemed frantic to borrow some money until payday. At first, I would lend him a few dollars figuring he would put it toward bills, or maybe take his wife out to dinner. Soon, I learned he was doubling down and trying to dig himself out of a growing hole with some angry loan sharks. His new behavior went along with other changes I noticed since he came home from Vietnam. The guy I grew up with wagered on nothing and had a wash-and-wear smile. Jack 2.0 pursued risk aggressively and would turn moody without notice.

When Merriam got wind of his expanding line of credit with me, she laid down the law. Our marriage was still rocky from my meltdown and finances were tight. I tried dancing around the issue for a while but when I refused to lend any more money, he never asked again. I knew he understood the reasons why, but it drove a silent wedge between us. Down deep, I thought he blamed Merriam and that was the reason he didn't come to her funeral.

I locked eyes with Kate. "You won't hear me make any excuses for your father. Yes, we're friends for life but that doesn't blind me to his faults and we had many an argument over the gambling. All I can say is he's too proud to ever let the word addiction pass his lips, but he knows that sickness made him choose handsome animals over his wife and daughter."

"That's what I love about this diner," she replied. "People in here have a no malarkey rule. You of all people should understand. I remember you calling me after your wife died looking for your absent best friend."

I waved her off. "Please, Kate, don't make this about me. I hadn't talked to your father in years and only wanted to let him know Merriam passed," I said, fibbing badly. Six months before her death, I received a Christmas card postmarked from the Villages in Florida with one line: *"Having a ball down here; there's dancing and cocktails in the square every night. Bet you would be happy down here."* There was no return address or telephone number to let him know Merriam faced her final round of chemo and things didn't look good. After she died, I debated contacting Jack at all and decided to tell his daughter so he could do the right thing. Kate was about as warm as the ice cubes in the half finished soda on the next table.

"Well, I called him like I promised. He was on a winning streak down at Pompano Park. He got in good with a couple of jockeys and they were showing him a good ol' time."

Jack slowly stood up.

Kate followed and cut him off. "You gotta build your network, kid," she said, imitating him, "that way you get the inside scoop. Three weeks later the money ran out and a nurse from the emergency room called. His new buddies beat him up when he couldn't cover the bar tab. He ended up running back here faster than any horse he ever wagered on."

I thought back to the cemetery. I knew more now than I ever wanted to. "Your father apologized to me this morning. He's taking ownership."

She looked underwhelmed. "Words are cheap at this point, don't you think?"

Before I could explain how her father thought the same way, Jack broke into a gagging cough. I knew he heard enough. The trick worked because Kate turned away, eyes downcast, and retrieved a white apron from behind the cash register. In the dim light, I watched her clear off another table my hungry eyes missed. She scraped all the leftovers from three plates into one; half eaten burgers, fries, pickles. Strangely, the wide palette of colors turned my stomach and I grabbed a piece of gum from my pocket. What tastes so good going down eventually ends up as sewage.

My dying comrade began to sway and I feared one more cutting word from Kate would knock him down for good. His mouth moved, but no words were coming out. I thought maybe he was trying to string something together that would cut through so much hurt; so many broken promises, so many years. Another moment passed and he reached inside his dirty, smelly rented coat and took out a long white envelope. He took a half dozen steps forward and placed it beside a half-eaten piece of blueberry pie on a nearby table and slowly shuffled away.

Kate eyed the envelope and I thought she would throw it back at him along with the pie for good measure. Instead, she stopped and quickly undid the ponytail and raked her hands through long blonde hair and I saw a heartbroken teenage girl missing her wayward father. She quickly wiped one eye and continued piling up the refuse on a metal tray. Jack was almost to the door before she finally retrieved the envelope. I held back and watched her expression change from anger to surprise before settling on hurt.

"What is this?" she asked, confused.

Jack stopped and made a quarter turn. "A couple weeks ago it would have been money for graduate school," he said, glancing quickly at me then looking around the diner. "Like I said before, I see nothing here but a sorry-looking shed like the type I had the kids build in my remedial shop class. It's not your fault though, because that Sam fella is too cheap to care a hoot about the place. I never dealt with the likes of that man before. Maybe because I'm used to talking myself out of a jam, or trying to convince some hoodlum with brass knuckles to give me one more chance. But him?" he said, shaking his head. "He just named his price and said that's that; take it or leave it, gramps."

He leaned against the celery-green counter for support. "Now that this is your place, I'm sure you will take after your mother and make it a nice joint. And I hope you change the name to Kate's because you have more class than Sam ever could."

Jack became unbalanced and sat uneasily on the swivel stool. "It would be nice to see you with a husband in here someday, instead of giving all your love to these working stiffs. You're a beautiful woman, Kate. I'm sorry if I made you suspicious of all men. They're not all bums like me."

"You mean you bought her the diner?" I asked, trying to comprehend what I just heard.

He nodded slightly and I held my breath. Where was he getting all this money? I realized I had misinterpreted our conversation outside. He let me lambast him about not embracing his daughter's dreams, when in fact he secured them.

"You have no right," Kate yelled and tried to pick up the tray laden with garbage. I watched a glob of mashed potatoes roll off the plate and splatter on the floor. She stared at the mess and began bawling. "You can't make everything right this way." She ran to the back of the restaurant and into the ladies' room. The door slammed shut.

Jack stared ahead and his mouth began moving again. No words came out, but the tears said enough.

I felt frozen in place watching this drama play out and debating who to comfort first, Kate or Jack. Suddenly, the sound of braking tires filled the air and I knew in my gut what that meant for us. I bolted to the window expecting to find a SWAT team waiting outside and hoping they didn't expect lunch.

CHAPTER TWENTY-EIGHT

A silver Mercedes sat at the bottom of the stairs blocking our escape and I figured undercover cops around here got to ride in style. No doubt Jack's antics of pulling the plug on the diner triggered the alert. Up until now, we'd successfully eluded everything law enforcement had thrown at us and this ending felt so anticlimactic. Even though I felt bone tired and the promise of a hot meal sure beat lusting after refuse on the floor, I wanted to follow through on my promise to Jack.

The car door flew open and to my amazement instead of a detective, Stu came bolting up the three stairs. His cantaloupe-colored hair contrasted nicely with the perpetual mourning uniform of black turtleneck, dress pants, and leather coat. He was five years older than his brother and three inches shorter.

I turned around to warn Jack of the approaching tornado, but the door flew open.

"So this must be where cockroaches hide!" Stu said in a high-pitched voice.

I knew it would be impossible to negotiate a ceasefire between brothers, but I moved quickly to cut him off in the hope of making it a fair fight. Stu must have thought he was trying out for middle linebacker in the senior football league, and the scouts were peering in the windows, because he flung me aside like a rag doll. Luckily, I landed on top of a table and my lips kissed a soggy side dish of coleslaw. I wiped the mayonnaise off my nose and wished this confrontation had happened when we were sitting in the car, so Jack could coax Stu to stick his head through the window. That way I could decapitate him even though I read severed snake heads can still bite for up to an hour.

"Have you lost the rest of your mind? Tying up nurses, stealing drugs, car theft, bank robbery, and assaulting a cop!" Stu yelled.

Jack smiled and spun himself around on the swivel stool while his brother fumed. "No, the assault is all on Dennis. I was eating an orange I found inside some house I broke into. When I came out I saw him deck the cop." He glanced my way. "See, I told you that wasn't smart."

Stuart pivoted to look at me. I planted my feet expecting him to unleash his fury on me and I was ready this time.

"He may be crazy, but he's on his way out. You, they will string up like a fat sausage," he snarled.

Offended, I looked down at my stomach, which I kept boasting was minus five pounds. Although the more I learned about Mark and Linda's bland diet, bulking up might be the better strategy.

"Did you stop by to have lunch?" Jack asked. "Because you better be nice to your niece since she owns this diner now."

His brother's neck swiveled faster than the poor girl in *The Exorcist*. "What are you talking about?"

Jack started coughing again and pointed for me to answer.

"He bought her the place," I said with a big smile, hoping to watch him melt like the Wicked Witch of the West and leave a puddle on the floor. "She's so overwhelmed she's in the bathroom pulling herself together."

Stu's face turned almost as beet red as his brother's did when gagging, but at least Jack was trying to expel something.

"That's real nice," he said, pulling on the turtleneck which suddenly became too tight for his turkey neck. "Bleed me for the hospice, so you can play Santa Claus to a daughter who hates your guts. You're a real piece of work, bro."

Stuart did a slow loop around the diner. "And tell me, where did you get that type of money anyhow? Last year, the IRS wanted to throw your skinny butt in prison for back taxes. I know you've been too sick to go to the track, so how long have you been robbing banks?"

I took a couple steps back, not wanting any part of this.

Jack grabbed the bottom of the stool as if buckling himself in for the exciting Round Up ride at Canobie Lake Park.

"Believe me, I appreciate everything you have done for your insolent baby brother, Stu. I just hope you learn a few things from all my mistakes, so you have the courage to make some changes in your life. I had the same advice for Dennis."

Stu looked up at the white tiled ceiling and let out a long groan. "You think dying puts you on some sort of pulpit? Well, no one's listening because you've lost all credibility with people." He leaned in close to Jack so they were nose to nose. "You sit next to some lady at chemo and she fills your head with stories about St. Peter and you think tattooing an upside down cross on your arm is going to get his attention?" He slapped his brother hard across the face. "It's all a lie, sucker. No one's saved. The only thing waiting for us when the lights go out is the same nothingness we wandered out of. Any other explanation is just make-believe. End of story. Go ahead and throw your Hail Mary pass as the clock winds down, but know this, bro—no one's waiting to catch the ball on the other side. No one."

I rushed forward and pushed Stu out of the way and checked on Jack. He looked as worn as the red checkered floor.

"Get out of here, you jerk," I said. "You're standing in our end zone."

Stu glared at me and let out an angry grunt. "Ah, still trying to play hero, Dennis? Well, don't worry none about coming to the funeral since you'll be in jail by then. But you won't miss much because we could hold the services in a telephone booth and still have plenty of room. After the thousands I've put out, I wish they would let me bury him in a trash bag."

"Go to hell," I replied.

"Which I prefer to the make-believe world you and Jack inhabit." He looked toward the ladies' room. And where is my least favorite niece? Hiding just like her old man, I guess." He reached in his coat pocket and took out his white iPhone. "I'm going to see if there's a reward for turning you two losers in. I have to make up for the soaking I'm taking somehow."

"Stu," Jack called out. "I hope you don't have to experience something like cancer to realize what a self-centered, corrosive man you've become. If I don't see you again, I'm sorry for everything I've put you through."

His brother didn't pay any attention and began punching numbers.

"I only have one question," Jack said. "What's up with Sarah? Kate seemed upset when I mentioned wanting to visit her today."

Stu stopped tapping the screen. "You don't know?" He let out a short snicker. "Sometimes you can't make this stuff up. She was admitted to Restful Waters yesterday and if you really loved her you would have known that."

Jack closed his eyes and began spinning fast on the stool.

Stuart shoved his cell phone back in his coat. "I'd like to see you try and pay her a visit now, bro. They would shoot you if your shadow even graced their lobby, terminal illness or not. I think turning you in would be too easy. No, I'd rather let you simmer in limbo about Sarah. If you went along with my plan you could've walked down the hall and spent your final hours with her. But as Mainers say, 'you can't get there from here.'" Now you can spend the end with your delusional sidekick." He began to walk away and then turned back. "And by the way, you should change your stupid hat to read 'Loser.'"

Stuart opened the glass door and then hesitated. "I'm planning to go to the hospice in the morning and see if I can recover any of the money, I prepaid for you. After that, I think I'll swing by and visit your wife as I haven't seen her in years. I'll tell her I begged you to visit, but you were too busy placing your last bet on a long shot. Now that's what I call aces."

CHAPTER TWENTY-NINE

Rosa proved to be a life saver and found a new bottle of Pepto-Bismol in the pantry. I drained half of the pink contents and planned to chomp on a fresh piece of gum when the faint sound of music surprised me. I followed a familiar guitar riff into the living room and my mouth popped open in disbelief. It was a good thing I postponed the gum.

Jack stood in the middle of the room slow dancing with M.B. Rosa stood nearby holding up her mother's iPad, which ironically played "Stairway to Heaven." My eyes became fixed on M.B. and her sad expression. I watched her hips sway to the rhythm of the music and realized she hid a very nice figure under all those baggy clothes.

Rarely had I seen my friend look so serene. He wore his lucky corduroy hat backwards and his eyes were closed with a blissful smile that didn't change as the dancers made small circles on the orange shag. I used to watch my parents do the fox trot and admire their coordinated steps and journey around the dance floor. Now couples mostly danced in one place, but the magic remained the same. I missed holding Merriam close like that and getting lost as a couple. I missed taking her to the beach and spreading coconut suntan lotion all over her freckled back and shoulders while carefully avoiding her strawberry blonde hair. I wondered if she needed sunscreen anymore and if so who was applying it. Rob Nelson always had a hankering for her and he kicked the bucket last year. "Touch her and I'll rip your wings off when I get there," I whispered.

Suddenly, I felt like an intruder and slowly retreated to the kitchen until the music stopped. When I wandered back in, Jack occupied the couch and whispered something to M.B.

"Sisters of Notre Dame," she said then shut up when she noticed me.

M.B. was a fortress with a moat of alligators surrounding her. Yet, somehow Jack had become one of her knights. I thought the relationship purely transactional; she provided a safe house and other accessories which he paid exorbitant fees to access. But the more I watched the way he looked at her, the more I realized chances were M.B. figured into the plan too. Up until now everything had been so choreographed, I sensed there would be some big reveal soon and it frustrated me. Hadn't I pledged to see this adventure through to the end? How come I was always the last to know? I kept quiet and chewed on my gum.

"You look awful," Jack finally said. "Another couple days like these and you'll begin to look like me."

"Perhaps that's been your plan all along," I replied, rubbing my unshaven face and looking at his matching white stubble. "You decided since I've come this far, why not take me all the way with you?" I looked at my badly wrinkled and stained white shirt and wished I had deodorant. "Merriam would shake her head if she saw me now."

"Do you want a change of clothes?" M.B. asked then smiled. "My treat."

I hesitated for a moment, knowing beggars can't be choosers but afraid the outfit might be related to the smelly snorkel coats. Nevertheless, I craved good will from this woman. "Sure, that would be nice."

She nodded. "You can clean up and change before dinner."

Jack motioned to M.B. "Okay, fill him in."

His new best friend grabbed a tan woolen blanket at the end of the couch to cover him up. "Anyone else in your condition would say enough is enough," M.B. said, tucking the blanket around his thin frame. "But you're the most obstinate man I've ever met and I've met some real beauties." She finally glanced my way. "He wants to visit his wife tonight."

The Pepto-Bismol made it halfway up my throat before I managed to swallow it again, but this time it burnt going down. "Are you kidding me? We won't get within fifty feet of that place before we're arrested. And I can only imagine what Nurse Nancy would do with that syringe of hers, if she gets a chance." My chest tightened. Minutes ago, I wondered how I would stay awake if Jack needed me tonight. Now he wanted to go Hollywood on me again. "This is utter nonsense."

"Stop being a sissy and man up," M.B. said, standing up to take me on. "Restful Waters is the last place they would expect you to show up at."

"No, Republic Bank is," I replied before covering my mouth to burp. As usual, there was no reaction from Jack because it wasn't on his agenda. What spell did Jack cast on M.B.? "His brother knows we will try and visit Sarah. That's why he didn't call the police this afternoon."

"My brother is torturing me the same way he used to rip the wings off flies when we were kids. One by one. He doesn't think I have the guts to try."

M.B. studied me like she thought I was some gutless coward, regardless of how many dragons I slayed.

"Plus, it's not like you're going to strut in the front door and sign the registry. Jack and I came up with a plan to sneak you both in."

I opened my mouth to inquire about what crime we'd be committing next, when Rosa entered, proud to report the table was set for dinner.

M.B. smiled and headed for the kitchen. "Come with me, Dennis, and I'll get you that change of clothes."

***

From the hall, I listened as the chairs scraped on the kitchen floor and Rosa told Jack where to sit. I counted to ten, waiting for my invitation.

"Dennis, where are you?" Jack yelled. "I remember the girls used to call you Pidge in high school because you mulled around the cafeteria lunch ladies like a pigeon begging for bread heels."

The aroma of garlic bread filled the air and my stomach told me to hurry up and get this over with. I looked down at my lime green polyester bell bottom pants, matching jacket, and yellow silk flowered shirt. "I can do this," I whispered, determined to show M.B. she couldn't rattle me.

Rosa saw me first and started to giggle like someone was tickling her.

I strutted into the middle of the white linoleum floor and put one hand high in the air in a classic John Travolta *Saturday Night Fever* pose.

Jack hugged his stomach and alternated between laughing and crying. "I didn't know we had dinner and a show," he said before losing it again. Even M.B. smiled and nodded, impressed.

I found myself laughing too and couldn't remember the last time I let my hair down like this and it felt good. "Maybe M.B. can find a leisure suit for you too, Jack. After all, your theme song really is 'Stayin' Alive.'"

"Unfortunately, that suit is one of a kind," M.B. replied. "My ex wanted to make a grand entrance at a Halloween party a few years ago and ordered the ugliest leisure suit he could find online."

"Was the snorkel coat his too?" I asked, taking a seat across from Jack. "If he really wanted to turn heads, he should have arrived at the party wearing the neon orange over lime green."

Our hostess frowned and moved to the stove.

"Something sure smells delicious," Jack said.

"Mom said you have only been eating junk food and wanted to make you something special," Rosa said proudly. "So she made my favorite: chicken parm."

Jack leaned over and kissed the top of the little girl's head. "That's perfect, because that's my favorite too."

M.B. placed a large platter of chicken parmigiana in the center of the table followed by individual plates of green salads and sides of spaghetti. She had no sooner sat down than she jumped up again to retrieve the garlic bread out of the oven.

Jack studied the wonderfully breaded chicken cloaked in steaming tomato sauce and mozzarella and wafted the air toward his nose. "I always thought my last meal would resemble how I lived; fast food and no utensils. This is amazing." Jack bowed his head and folded his hands. "Dear God, thank you for the angels you have put in my life to see me through to the end. Please bless them as you have me and thank you for what is truly a Thanksgiving meal this evening. Amen."

He opened his eyes and rubbed M.B.'s arm and gave her a puppy look. "As much as I love water, it sure would be nice to have a beer with this wonderful dinner."

Rosa jumped up and went to the fridge and returned with two bottles of Bud. Grateful that the little angel remembered me, I gave her my last stick of Juicy Fruit gum, which quickly disappeared before her mother noticed.

I dug in and tried hard to remember my manners and not wolf down the home-cooked meal too fast. When I came up for air, I noticed Jack staring at the empty white plate in front of him like it was something from another world. Before I could reach over to help, M.B. put a healthy piece of chicken on his plate and sliced it into small pieces. Jack's hands began shaking and he managed one small bite. He chewed for so long, I wondered if he forgot how to swallow. When he finally succeeded, M.B. brought the bottle of beer to his lips. After a small sip, a hacking cough took hold for a long minute.

"Do you want a glass or a straw?" she asked.

He shook his head violently, too proud to have his final beer that way.

An uncomfortable silence followed as M.B. and I watched Jack out of the corners of our eyes, not wanting to embarrass him. Rosa lost interest and began playing with her food and making funny shapes on her plate with strands of spaghetti.

"Mom, can I go in the other room and watch my show?" she asked.

M.B. glanced at her half-eaten plate. "Not before you take two more bites of chicken. Then I want you to do your homework. I'll come in later and check, so no skipping."

Rosa looked at me. "Mom said when we have dessert later you would tell me why we have a cake for someone named David."

The comment brought a silly smile to Jack's face and then mine.

The little girl finished her dinner and quickly disappeared. With her daughter gone, M.B.'s face grew tense and she retreated back into her dinner. I studied her face again. The red mark from the morning was gone, hidden under a thick layer of mocha cover-up. She must have felt my eyes because she looked up and glanced my way. I decided to try one more time.

"A lot of kids would be better off if they had a mother like you."

She looked away; for once I had embarrassed her. I took another swig of beer. It tasted good and I could feel my nerves downshifting. A wise man would have enjoyed the rest of his dinner, but I couldn't help myself. "Rosa said you hope to move to Orlando?"

M.B. glanced at Jack quickly then stood up and began to clear the plates.

"You sure have trouble minding your own business. What else did you learn?"

I bit my lip and wondered what she thought I knew. "Rosa only said you would get a good job down there and take her to Disney on weekends."

"That's a big fairy tale, except the part about moving."

"Why?" I asked and reached for a second piece of garlic bread.

"Because your buddy here thought he could earn heaven points by paying my back rent. Unfortunately, his goodwill was misinterpreted. Now my landlord thinks Jack is subsidizing me, so he raised my rent another two hundred a month."

"Yikes," I said as the safest word to hide behind. My friend appeared to be attempting to buy his way into heaven.

"Worst part, it's retro to last summer," Jack whispered.

I caught Jack eyeing me. For a half dead man, he sure remained attentive to my every move.

"M.B. has been wonderful."

"You keep saying that and I agree," I said, hoping to fix my latest gaffe.

Jack pointed at my empty plate. "Sure you don't want seconds or thirds, Denny? You're going to need your strength tonight."

I inspected my silk shirt for tomato stains and felt conflicted whether I was happy to find none. I pushed back from the table and glanced at the clock. It was a little after seven. "So what's the plan?" I asked, trying to sound upbeat.

M.B. looked at the clock too and frowned. "We better start the prep work if you're going back to Restful Waters tonight. Meet me in the bathroom."

"Prep work?" I repeated.

"Don't worry none, Denny," Jack said as he picked up his beer and struggled to his feet. "You already demonstrated you can embrace being out of your comfort zone by wearing that hideous suit. It won't take much additional insanity to graduate to the next level."

I followed Jack down the narrow hall to the bathroom, wishing his legs would get stuck in neutral again, but of course they didn't.

M.B. waited in the old but clean bathroom only large enough for a small white vanity, toilet, and tub.

Jack stopped at the doorway so I could pass but I hesitated.

"Okay, what's this all about?" I asked.

M.B. draped a blue cotton towel over the toilet seat. "Hurry up and sit down. It will take an hour to get you both ready and I have a sink full of dishes and Rosa needs her homework checked."

Sometimes you go along to get along and I obeyed the woman. But then she opened a drawer and produced a big black electric razor that looked like my hedge trimmers.

I jumped up and knocked over an empty liquid soap container sitting on the side of the sink. Luckily it didn't break. "Whoa, what's going on here?"

M.B. threw the razor in the sink and motioned to Jack. "You deal with him. I don't have time for this." She picked up the soap container and left the room.

Jack came in and sat on the edge of the tub and motioned for me to sit back down. He took a tiny sip of his beer then offered it to me and I took a long guzzle before handing it back. "Look, Denny, we have to be creative if we're going to sneak back into that awful place. Thanks to M.B., we came up with the perfect disguise."

I stared at him, afraid to ask. "So you're planning to shave me so we go as skinheads?"

Jack rubbed the top of his balding head and smiled. "Wish it was that easy."

M.B. reappeared carrying a hanger which held a long black tunic. I thought we might be dressing up for the church choir until I noticed a headpiece in her other hand.

She gave me a once-over and looked at the tunic. "Extra-large should fit."

Suddenly I loved my lime green leisure suit and looked pleadingly at Jack. "We're going as nuns?"

"Not just any nun, my boy, but Sisters of Notre Dame," Jack said. "Pillars of the community."

"Are these Halloween costumes too?" I asked.

M.B. studied the headpiece. "No, these are real. They're from a retirement home in Ipswich. My aunt worked there."

I stared at the nun outfit, fondly remembering the Sisters of Notre Dame at St. Joseph grammar school in Salem and the transformation I watched after Vatican II. Before then, nuns hid their hair and wore long black dresses and veils. Then one spring, the sisters suddenly had bangs. By the end of the decade, they were wearing bright-colored sun dresses and strumming guitars at folk Masses. Now, we were turning back the clock.

"I don't know if I can pull this off," I said.

Jack slapped my knee. Remember what I told you, 'the man who thinks he can and the man who thinks he can't are both right.'"

"Yeah, but your dad and Henry Ford weren't talking about dressing up as a nun drag queen."

Jack stood up and moved to the hall so M.B. could take his place. "And it's not like you'll be alone. I'm getting dressed up too. Dynamic duo, right?"

I nodded slowly, not sure what I signed up for and worried the dear sisters who had educated me would feel insulted even if the cause was good. "I know I need a haircut but are you going to shave my head for the veil?"

M.B. grabbed the razor and started on the back of my neck. "No, I'll just trim the back real close. Then I want you to shave and get rid of your sideburns and I'll apply some makeup."

"I look really hot in bright red lipstick," I said, thinking back on my biker disguise.

The joke fell flat. "We can use bobby pins to secure the veil but we won't attempt that until you're ready to leave," M.B. said to herself.

I winced. "My shaving bag is in my suitcase at home."

"You can use my razor."

I closed my eyes, sorry I gave Rosa my last piece of gum. "But don't you use that razor to shave your legs?" I could only imagine how a razor burn would complement the hives.

She rapped the back of my head with her free hand. "Don't be stupid. I'll put in a new razor. Believe me, I don't want your cooties either."

Ten minutes later, she had me prepped and called Jack in to begin his transformation. I didn't want to look in the mirror when I finally stood, but it was similar to passing an accident on the road. You don't want to look but just have to.

"I'm afraid I'm going to have nightmares for quite some time," I said, wondering if I could really pass for a woman.

"I think you look fantastic," Jack said. "And I bet if we put you outside the mall for the weekend with a basket, people will feel so bad for such a sorry-looking nun you could fund the sisters' retirement home for a year."

"Maybe, but let's see how you turn out. We'll have Rosa be the beauty queen judge."

M.B. looked puzzled and studied her iPhone.

"What's wrong?" Jack asked.

"I'm trying to figure out how this headpiece goes together with something called a wimple."

"Leisure suits and wimples all in one evening. How can I ever top that?" I asked, thinking about Sarah's upcoming blind date.

CHAPTER THIRTY

When I first set eyes on Sarah with her long blonde hair and electric blue eyes, I knew she was destined to live in the parallel universe the jocks and in-crowd inhabited. But the down to earth way she carried herself led me to believe someone forgot to tell her, or maybe she refused to listen. When Jack showed up at a Christmas party with his arm around Sarah, he had a Steve McQueen smile and Joe Namath swagger.

They quickly fell in love and became inseparable. Jack loved Sarah, but she had to fit into his plans too. So in manic style, he proposed during the senior prom and she was swept away. As romantic as it seemed back then, his bride came to realize her husband's judgment could best be summarized by the old adage "fools rush in where angels fear to tread." Sarah embraced his spontaneity to a degree, but also wanted some stability. Jack preferred to swing for the fences, like when he put a down payment on a three-bedroom white ranch without telling his new bride. She dreamed of saving up to buy a colonial and became miffed to say the least.

Sadly, they should have flash frozen themselves on their wedding day as it was a bumpy downhill ride from there. Sure, there were periods of happiness, especially with Kate's birth. But usually the peace felt like a sixty-second commercial before the next drama aired.

After a brief honeymoon to Niagara Falls, Jack went off to war and Sarah worked at the new Kelley library in Salem, which opened in 1966 and had a first day circulation of 734 books. When her husband returned home two years later, he was a different man: exhausted and jumpy. He tackled his recovery with gusto by holding down a full-time production job in a textile factory and going to school nights at Merrimack College. Not surprisingly, he finished his education degree in three years but there were few jobs available and he campaigned hard for an Industrial Arts teaching job in Salem. Merriam and I both had a hard time imagining a man with no kill switch spending his days showing kids how to use power tools. When he signed on as the assistant varsity football coach, I knew he found the adrenaline he craved.

If football was a year round sport, it might have made a difference. Unfortunately, the short season and the insufferable long winters in New Hampshire gave Jack too much unstructured time. That's when he first hooked up with Paco, a young bookie with shoulder-length blond hair and no last name who made the rounds at the local watering holes. He introduced Jack to thoroughbred racing and the mystique of Rockingham Park, which was built in 1906 and proclaimed "the finest race course in the world."

I could put my hand on a Bible and testify Jack never had eyes for another female, except when he was checking out some new filly. Sadly, the end result proved the same. His infatuation with horses poisoned the marriage and eventually short-circuited his coaching career too.

For a while Sarah was annoyed but forgiving. But as the bills mounted so did the bitterness. Then the high school quietly dismissed him as coach when rumors of the horse betting surfaced. Jack barely held on to his teaching job. The ensuing cycle was always the same: Sarah would kick him out and he would buckle down to win her back. They would be together for a while until the peace got boring and Jack called Paco.

Sarah finally called it quits after fifteen years, which was probably closer to ten given their frequent separations. Sarah went back to school and became a nurse. However, when it came to making the break official, Sarah hesitated and never filed for divorce. Merriam and I debated for years the reason behind the procrastination: exhaustion, sentimentality, the hope for some miracle reunion? Whatever the reason, it certainly wasn't for financial support. Jack was always looking for money to make the next installment payment so his legs wouldn't be broken.

CHAPTER THIRTY-ONE

Jack and I sat side by side on the couch looking like a couple of menacing gargoyles from a Gothic gutter. Rosa peeked around the corner every few minutes to giggle and ask when we would put on our veils, which made my stomach ache in anticipation. After a half hour I wondered whether water or chicken parm would be spouting from my mouth soon.

When M.B. told Rosa it was time for bed, she came in the room to say goodnight. "Mom said you're going to a masquerade party," Rosa said.

Jack opened his arms and she gave him a big goodnight hug like she had known him for quite some time. Then she shook my hand. "Will you win a prize?"

I looked at Jack in mascara and lipstick and smiled. "Already have."

Rosa's face grew serious. "I think you're fibbing because you both look nervous. My mom tells me whenever I'm afraid to take a deep breath and stand up straight. Remember that."

Patting her head, I glanced over at Jack. "We'll fake it until we make it."

M.B. whisked her daughter off to bed and I concentrated on not scratching my face and smearing the thick layer of cover-up.

Time slowed and Jack suddenly began slipping in and out of consciousness. Whenever he did wake, his gaze would focus on the ceiling. The scene catapulted me back to my last night with Merriam. I held her hand and listened to her pant as if running a marathon she would never finish. Whenever she woke, I stroked her fevered forehead and offered ice chips and told her again and again how much I loved her, how proud I was of her gallant fight, that it was okay to let go. She would drink in my face then look past me, as if gazing at a new horizon. The next day I realized she was watching the window behind me, holding on for the daylight. Near the end, I asked if she saw anyone; her mother, father, one of her siblings, perhaps Jesus? I wanted to know for her sake and selfishly for me. Her eyes became big with the dawn, but the question never answered. It was the only day Jean Bradley left me alone.

Watching Jack reminded me again how dying is a natural process. His breathing became labored, face flushed, extremities cold. The air had a peculiar sour smell too, like he was exhaling the cancer. M.B. sensed it too. She kissed his forehead lightly before exiling herself to the kitchen for the final vigil. I knew she didn't want me to see her cry.

I considered taking off the black tunic, but was so tired I settled for slipping off my shoes. A half hour passed when he suddenly woke up, the faraway look miraculously gone.

"What are you doing sitting there?" he asked, licking very chapped lips. "You were supposed to get the car warmed up for us. He looked around. Where's M.B.? She has to get our veils just right."

"It's okay, Jack. You're already a legend given how hard you tried to set things right. God knows it too." I held his hand, surprised at its new warmth. "Kate knows you love her and I promise to visit Sarah," I whispered. "Just rest now. You've done enough."

Jack closed his eyes and must have let my words penetrate that big ego of his, because I saw an angry expression slowly spread across his face like it did back at the hospice. "Dennis, if you let me die on this couch tonight, I promise to come back and make your remaining days on earth a living hell." Opening one bloodshot eye, he struggled to sit up. "Now stop with the verbal diarrhea and let's get on with it. Neither of us is getting any younger."

M.B. heard the latest rally and put on all the lights in the living room and busied herself completing her twin Frankenstein creations. Jack and I took turns whimpering in pain as she magically used bobby pins and duct tape to put everything in place. When she finished she smiled and asked us to stand next to one another.

"Why?" I asked.

She took out her iPhone. "I just have to get a picture of this."

I groaned and looked at my best friend. "Now we look like two characters in the *Star Wars* bar scene too."

Jack smiled. "Yes, we've run the gamut of disguises, haven't we?" He took a deep breath and froze.

"Are you okay, Jack?" I asked, alarmed.

"It's Sister Bernadette to you, buddy," he whispered in obvious pain.

At 11:30 p.m. I loaded Sister Bernadette into the black Escort and began another trek to Salem.

Jack propped himself up in the seat with his chest heaving one big wave after another. The race was coming to an end and the hospice seemed as far away as San Fran. There was no time for back roads so I shot up Route 97, squinting into the oncoming traffic. They say laughter and tears are close cousins, and I let out a short laugh thinking how ridiculous we looked.

"What's the date?" Jack suddenly asked.

I had to think for a moment as this week felt like a dog year. "The nineteenth of March, although it's almost midnight."

"Born on the thirtieth of December and exiting on the nineteenth of March. I should have played those numbers," he said with a sigh. "Just my luck though. The biggest race of my life and I won't live to see it."

"Sure you will. We're only a few minutes away from the hospice."

He shook his head. "I'm talking about the track."

"Haven't you been heartbroken enough for ten lifetimes?" I asked in disbelief, surmising he must be hallucinating about the past. He'd taken the final dose of morphine before we left the apartment. From here on out there would be no relief.

"Have we passed Field of Dreams yet?"

"What?"

"You know, the place on Geremonty Drive next to the high school."

The community park was five miles away from the hospice and I figured he must be gauging the distance with tenacity like Merriam did in the end. If he died now, I wouldn't know what to do. The thought made me push the accelerator to the floor, wishing I was rushing a pregnant woman to the hospital and not a friend to the morgue. The front end of M.B.'s Ford shimmied. I missed my Caddy.

"When you get to the park pull in."

"Main Street is a straight shot and we don't have time for a detour," I managed to say calmly, despite my racing heart. Maybe he wanted me to stop so he could die under some trees.

Jack grabbed my arm. "Denny, please don't argue with me." The tone was firm; desperate.

Geremonty Drive appeared over a short hill and I banged a quick left and raced a quarter mile past the high school and almost missed the driveway for the park.

I could smell antifreeze and knew I pushed the old car too hard. "Okay, we're here, buddy," I said, close to panic.

Jack kept his eyes closed and smiled. "Good. Now follow the driveway to the picnic area next to the playground."

He even knew where he would give up his soul? "This isn't a good idea, buddy. The police station is just around the corner and there is only one way out."

Jack straightened the front of his tunic. "Let them come. All they will see are two nuns saying their evening prayers."

"But we don't have time for this if you want to see Sarah before it's too late."

"I didn't know you were the official timekeeper," he said in a stronger voice than I thought capable. "Just do what I say and have a little faith for once. Okay?"

I crawled forward on the narrowing path, certain if my son could see me in this nun's habit, he would have me committed.

"I'll do whatever you want, but this dress really slows me down," I said, hoping to dash his plans to carry him to the swing set. "And we don't have coats again and it's freezing out."

"That's my best friend, always the worry wart. You think I'm up for a five-mile hike? Stop with the lip and hurry up."

"Whatever you say, Sister Superior." I followed the driveway to a small parking lot. Jack pointed to where he wanted me to stop and I obeyed.

"Okay, now what?"

"Put on your high beams."

"Sure. Why don't I light a flare too?" When I flicked the switch, I shrieked in fright at a towering pine tree man standing twenty-five feet tall at the end of the grassed picnic area. Its legs were a good fifteen feet long and connected to a long slender torso that ran up to a massive head with Medusa-type hair. Two outstretched arms gave the impression he was tiptoeing through the park and I blinked twice to make sure he wasn't.

"I used to come here all the time with Merriam and walk the trails. When did they add this monster?"

"Ah, he's no monster, Denny. I named him Peter and besides you, he's my best friend," he said, pointing toward the hulk. "When I was first diagnosed with lung cancer last year, I drove around aimlessly until I met Peter. If I had the energy, we'd get out of the car and I would introduce you, but you can get a good sense of him from here; his impressive stature and how his head is bent in a pensive manner."

I glanced in the rearview mirror thinking this could not get much more bizarre. "Yeah, he's something, all right. Now, can we get out of here?"

Jack suddenly grabbed my arm. "You're always in such a rush you miss the message. Isn't he amazing?"

"Look, if we don't go now, I'm afraid the last thing you will see is Peter and not Sarah." I reached for the gear shift, happy it was an automatic.

My friend pushed my hand away. "I'll take the risk because you need to study him for what I'm about to tell you."

Ah, here comes another piece of the puzzle. "Okay. What is it?"

"Joseph Wheelwright is the artist who unearthed Peter and other tree sculptures like him. He searches through the woods to find a yellow birch, cherry, or pine tree with just the right configuration of branches and root ball," he explained. "When he harvests the tree, he turns it upside down. The root ball becomes the head, the split trunk his legs, the branches arms. You should Google his work. It's simply amazing. Peter is touring the northeast and will be here until June."

"Interesting." I stared into the rearview mirror again, expecting to see a police car at any moment making the rounds.

"Interesting?" he repeated. "Do you mean that in the American sense of the word?"

"What do you mean?"

"In other countries they use the word as it's defined. Here we use it to hide behind something we're not comfortable discussing or don't want to be bothered with."

"Okay, I'll be crystal clear. I don't care about your stick friend. Now can we go?"

"That's a mistake because I want to change your perspective. Why don't you get out of the car and take a good long look for yourself? I'm counting on you to come to the same conclusion I did. There's immense beauty when things get turned upside down. Peter is the embodiment of that."

The headlights were illuminating the woods behind the sculpture and a jogging trail that led to the high school. "Look, you've turned my life upside down this week, but beauty is not the first word that comes to mind."

Jack moaned and leaned back on the headrest. "You disappoint me, Denny, and I don't have the time or strength to steel you for what lies ahead. Just know my intentions are good and this will give you the courage to make the necessary changes in your own life. I wanted to bring you here to put you in the right frame of mind before I tell you something. I thought Peter would help."

"I hate to break the news, but Peter is nothing but an upside down tree and a dead one at that. Lucky for him he didn't end up as a telephone pole or a cord of cheap firewood. What do you want to tell me?"

Jack rolled his head and the old nun gave me a sad look. "I wondered if you figured it out by now but couldn't tell. I thought I could read you but not this time."

My veil was too tight and beginning to give me a headache. "What is it? Spit it out, man."

"Okay," he said, looking away. "I just wish I could live long enough to see you make peace with the knowledge." He rubbed his face hard, trying to stay awake, and when he pulled his hands away I noticed he'd smeared his makeup. "When the chemo didn't work, I came here to mull over what I wanted to do with my remaining days. It would have been so easy to pack a duffel bag, head down to Key West, and die a 'Parrot Head.' Talking it over with Peter, he convinced me to take a different path and really turn things upside down. Initially, I interpreted that to mean doing a bunch of crazy things like some desperate guy with a bucket list on steroids. Some would be fun; others—well, let's just say they weren't very nice. But sitting in the shadow of my new friend and admiring how the snow erased everything after a storm, I realized every day is a blank canvas and decided to make things right with my father, daughter, wife, and you."

"Which is why we have to get moving as Sarah is just up the street."

"Not before you let me tell you who M.B. really is."

I frowned. "Okay, I admit I was wrong to give you grief about her. I realize she's special to you. I understand now."

He nodded. "Yes, she is, and she's been a dear the last few days." He grabbed my wrist. Don't you want to know how I know her?"

The car felt hot and I rolled down the window. "Well, I watched you two slow dance and thought there must be some connection. At first, I wondered if she was your girlfriend. But she's almost half your age and I don't care how much money you throw around, she wouldn't put up with your shenanigans. Then I thought how you and Sarah broke up and how lonely you were." I hesitated. "Is she a daughter from some affair you had when you were on a binge?"

Jack let out hoarse laugh that breathed new life into him. "You're a real piece of work, Denny. Are you so thick you never wondered what M.B. stood for? I find it incredible you never even asked her last name."

I lost my breath.

"Suit yourself. But from the pictures, I would say Maggie Bradley is the spitting image of her mother, Jean Bradley. Wouldn't you?"

CHAPTER THIRTY-TWO

"Get out of the car right now so I can strap you to that dead tree," I screamed. "And when I get out on bail, I'm going to hold a raffle right here and the winner will get to light the match and we'll toast marshmallows and make s'mores over what the birds haven't pecked clean." I drew an imaginary map on the windshield. "I can see a line of people stretching back to Haverhill and fighting each other to buy a ticket. With all the money I'll be able to afford a new condo next to Mark."

"Well," he replied dryly with a wink. "That's so like you; always the sales guy using some crazy gimmick to get people aroused. At least you'll have something to live for."

"You have no right," I yelled again, and, my voice having nowhere to escape in the close quarters, pierced my eardrums and woke up all my hives, which felt like a million bee stings. "This is supposed to be your deathbed confession, not mine. Remember?"

He looked away.

I rolled the window up and down and then up again to do something with my left hand, which wanted to nail him almost as hard as the hives on my face, throat, and arms were pelting me. "You think you know everyone you meet nowadays, but have you forgotten who I am?"

"Look, the reason—"

I smacked the dashboard hard with my right hand and pain shot up my arm, reminding me how sore it was from punching the cop. "I loved you like a brother all my life and risked everything I hold dear to see you through this; my relationship with my son, my reputation, my freedom, and this is how you say goodbye to me?"

"Denny, you have to understand a few things."

I grabbed his veil and pulled him in close. "No, you do. You should be ashamed of yourself. Jean Bradley has been my secret shame and regret for forty years. Why in heaven's name would you think I'd want to face her orphaned daughter? You of all people should understand that after what you did."

He pulled away and broke my grip. "What are you talking about?"

"C'mon, Jack. Remember something important to me for once. I was lost and strung out on booze from the whole tragic affair. You came to visit me in the hospital after those two guys robbed and beat the stuffing out of me. We talked for a while and when I fell asleep, you left a beautiful poem you wrote me about courage. It provided a spark of hope."

Jack smirked as he clearly remembered. "Yeah, that surprised me because I always took you for a numbers guy." He paused for a long moment and stared out the windshield toward Peter. "I left the poem, but I didn't write it."

My mouth opened but no sound came out as I felt my mind seize like an engine suddenly without oil. The whole foundation I built my shaky recovery on was crumbing here in the dark. I felt like throwing up all over my nun getup and grabbed the steering wheel to stop the dizziness.

"I think Stu had you pinned right. You're rotten to the core," I said, my voice strained. "All these years I thought you were so distraught for me, inspiration moved a shop teacher to rescue my soul. And now I find out it's all a lie?"

Jack started to wheeze and fought it off. "Wait a minute, buddy. Before you add to my ever growing list of sins, did I ever tell you I wrote it?"

"No, but you left it so I assumed."

"Well, that's a horse of a different color, isn't it?" he said, trying to find my eyes. "That little piece of paper magically glued Humpty Dumpty back together, and yet you never thought to mention it to me? Never wanted to thank me?"

"I started to a hundred times, but you know guys like us don't talk about that sort of stuff; especially you."

"Yeah, and to say we were best buddies we didn't talk about a lot of things that really mattered, did we? And if you ever did ask, I would have reminded you how true beauty lived with you every day of your marriage."

"Don't try and change the topic by bringing up Merriam." I slapped the air. "So you lifted the poem from some dusty book in the library. I get it. I can see you now, typing it up and inserting my name. How touching."

"Ah, the man sees but is still blind. Merriam was scared to death and you were broken beyond repair. Your wife wrote the poem, not me."

I empathized with Peter now; the tenets of my life were being ripped out by the roots and turned upside down. "Merriam was a wonderful woman, but hardly a poet. The only writing she did was making out the grocery list."

My friend let out a low whistle. "I'm glad she's not alive to hear you right now, because she would slap your face good and hard and then drop-kick you over Peter. Don't you believe people can do some pretty amazing things when they love someone? You were her entire world! She saw you self-destructing and wanted to rescue you."

My head felt heavy, like a bucket of wet sand had found its way inside. "You can try and twist this like a pretzel so it's all about me. But you have no right to interfere with my life like this."

"Ah, Denny, interfere is a strange word to use after we've spent our entire lives together. Before you go ahead and make plans to plant crabgrass on my grave, know all the facts. I received a call from Merriam after you were fired from Henley's. She wanted me to help chase away your demons and the whiskey bottle you were determined to drown in. At first I laughed at her, because I had one devil on my own back and owed another fiend five hundred bucks. Merriam was furious and hung up on me. But when those thugs put you in the hospital, she showed up at my house with the poem. I told her I didn't understand its meaning because the poem sounded like you were doing better and that wasn't true. Merriam said that was the point. She knew you were too proud to ask for help, but she wanted to highlight the love which surrounded you. She asked me to get it to you and never say who wrote it. Now my promise is expiring with me."

My eyes blurred as I recalled the lines I'd assumed Jack wrote about my neighborhood fights.

But call on that persevering heart,
Which has always sustained you.
Recall the boy that did not run
From the neighborhood bullies,
But took them on one by one.

I forgot how much I had entertained Merriam with those tall tales from when Jack and I were young. Then I realized I missed the biggest clue of all.

So take a deep breath, my friend,
And move the plow forward one step;
Confident you will never be alone.
For I will remain by your side,
To ensure your rows are straight.

Shame washed over me. Now I understood my very best friend had always been my wife. She stood by when everyone else deserted me, including Jack. I clenched my jaw, wishing I could be alone.

Jack was still talking when I tuned him back in. "So I left it on the hospital tray when you fell asleep. I thought it was a nice gesture, but didn't believe it would accomplish much."

He rolled up his sleeve and rubbed the tattoo of the upside down cross and winced in pain. "Until last year I thought it nearly impossible to string a bunch of words together to make people change. To me, those pretty words on that white sheet of paper were like throwing fertilizer on grass long after the grubs finished devouring the roots. If anything, I feared it would move you to drown yourself in Seagram's after being discharged."

"No. It gave me the courage to pick myself up," I whispered.

"Okay, I was wrong. But you never really got over it, did you? You came back but it was never the same."

"What are you talking about? I never mentioned Jean, Maggie, or the accident again. And certainly never to Merriam because of what I put her through." I closed my eyes and felt that old desperate feeling rising up within me. I wished I was home with the laminated prayer card where I could whisper the Lord's Prayer until the panic attack subsided.

I opened my eyes and found Jack leaning in close as if reading me. I looked in the rearview mirror and saw Jean Bradley. She sat in the back seat crying and pulling her red wool hat lower over her ears.

"The thing is, even if I wanted to talk to someone—and mind you I didn't—you were always running for the gold at the end of your bookie's imaginary rainbow. No matter how much time we spent together, or how many beers we had, if the conversation wasn't about some big payday, you would tune me out."

"You just admitted we didn't talk about some things."

I cleared my throat. "I lied, okay? So I did the only thing a husband and father should do. I sucked it up, swallowed it, and never let it out."

"But Merriam knew."

I shook my head. "That's impossible and you need to drop it."

"Heaven doesn't make many women like your wife. Merriam knew how you suffered until the day she died."

"Liar!" I opened my car door. "Enough is enough. I can walk home and leave you here. This old Ford is better than any coffin you can afford anyways."

"Listen to me, Dennis, this is the last of it and then I'm through," he said, grabbing my chin and making me look at him. "Merriam called me last February, six weeks before she passed. I couldn't believe she tracked me down because I was lying low at the time. She told me how much the guilt had eaten at you. She knew all about the memorial card you kept of M.B.'s mother tucked inside an envelope with three hundred bucks and the spare key to the Polara stashed in your wallet."

I beat the steering wheel with both fists as Jean Bradley howled in my ears. "You don't understand. It's blood money, blood money, blood—"

Jack pulled me toward him and I stubbornly hung onto the steering wheel, not wanting to be embraced. "Your wife knew you lived your entire life trying to be noble and never wanting to worry her. She knew when your anxiety spiked and she would make you take her out for a ride to explore some deserted place to get your mind off it. But Merriam worried who would look after you when she was gone. No one would be around to break the cycle when you needed help. Your wife tried to get Mark involved, but he didn't understand. He never knew you any differently and he was building his own life. I know it pained her to have to ask me to look in on you."

I shut the door. The long train of lonely nights since she died ran across my mind. The bags under my eyes felt like heavy potato sacks and I shivered in cold sweat. "Wow, aren't you a special friend. Never mind you missed her funeral. It's been nearly a year and you never checked in on me once even though you were living ten minutes away. And the first time I hear from you is this week when you need me to rescue you."

"I'm truly sorry, Denny, and this selfish friend of yours is trying to keep a promise even if it's very late," he whispered with his voice breaking. "Maybe I was too enthusiastic in trying to fix too many things in the end. God forgive me if I hurt you. It wasn't my intention."

"Intentions take thought and you threw that to the wind ever since you came back from Vietnam."

The comment seemed to instantly melt my friend and he slumped back in the seat and closed his eyes. "Since we're so determined to give each other autopsies tonight, you might as well know why."

"What are you talking about?"

"You saw it at the cemetery. I thought I had the same DNA as my father and when the time came I would prove my mettle. If that meant I would die, so be it. I didn't want any bridges named after me, only to be remembered as a courageous soldier."

Jack played with the side mirror. "I had my chance during the Tet Offensive and the Battle of Huế. The street fighting was brutal and we had to retake the city block by block in stifling heat. On the second day in, we were making our way down a small dirt street hugging pockmarked cement buildings that smelled of gunpowder, mildew, and rotting flesh when we came under sniper fire. I hurled myself behind a couple of rusted barrels for cover. B.J.—a skinny kid from Charleston and the card shark in the platoon—took a nasty hit in the thigh and began screaming for help. Suddenly, a couple of grenades exploded nearby and everything went eerily quiet. Three of my platoon buddies lay dead on the other side of the street. Gunfire erupted again and guys started screaming all around me. B.J. lay exposed only fifteen feet away and I knew I had to get him out of that killing zone. I hesitated for only a few seconds at most as I saw my bride standing over my grave crying and saying I promised to come home. When I shook off the fear and began crawling toward him, B.J. took another round in the head."

I bit my lip. "I'm sorry, Jack. I know how you must have felt."

Jack punched my arm hard. "No you don't, and I'll use my remaining life to beat that into you if you try and compare it with trying to save turtles. They called me a hero the next day when I scaled a wall to take out an enemy machine gun. But that wasn't courage. I just didn't care anymore about risk after B.J. came home in a box. In the end, I'm not a tenth of my old man."

We sat silent for a long moment, both exhausted.

"I have one more confession," Jack whispered.

"Are you kidding me?"

"After Merriam called me last year I was curious and decided to track down M.B. I couldn't explain why at the time, but after this week I understand it was all part of His plan. She's an old soul and one of the best things I ever did, although it wasn't easy. I didn't have much to go on, but I met a guy who worked at the Social Security office in Haverhill who played terrible poker and owed me a couple hundred bucks. He gave me her address and I disconnected some wires on her car so I could play hero. We had coffee and struck up a friendship. I gave her a few bucks now and then."

"You gave someone money besides your bookie for the past year?"

"If I won at the track, I would send her a hundred bucks. Nothing special. And she has been such a blessing. She introduced me to some really good people like Ink. He's a cool dude with a soul."

I had heard enough and started the car. "So she knows who I am?"

"We're chasing mayflies, not hornets, remember?" he replied. "I think she's smart enough to know there's a reason why I wanted her to meet you. She asked a couple times, but I kept my mouth shut. Where it goes from here is up to you. If I've taught you anything in the last few days, I hope you see it's never too late to make a difference. Make it right with her, Denny. Even if she threatens you with a knife and tells you she hates your guts, it sure beats sweating over a prayer card every night."

I refused to look at him and hid behind my veil, trying to find air after being buried under an avalanche of secrets. My mind kept repeating that Jack and Merriam knew everything and my son didn't care.

"Oh, one other thing," he said. "No matter what you decide, I told M.B. to see you for what I owe her."

I snickered. "Let me get this straight. You've been bankrolling her for the past year and she's still charging you?"

"It's not like that. I made some promises and she has some real challenges with that boss of hers."

"So you decided to leave me with another bill. Do we owe her just for the chicken parm or is there a special fee for housing the man responsible for her mother's death?" I put the car in reverse. "Either way, she's already fleeced us enough on this junk car and these nun outfits. What do I have to do, rob another bank to pay her off?"

"Nothing like that and I have it all worked out. The saddest part is it's going to be the biggest payday of my life and I'll be dead."

I took a left on Geremonty and headed fast toward Main Street.

"Tell a drunken jockey you have stage four lung cancer and it's amazing what you find out. I hung around bars for a lifetime looking for a tip that would give me an edge. Maybe I should have used that ruse twenty years ago." He sighed. "Remember this park."

"How can I ever forget it?"

"Just know that Peter will become your new best buddy after I'm gone. Just be sure to stand far enough back so he's looking at you straight in the eyes when you return. It will make all the difference if you let him give you a hand."

"Whatever. Just be quiet and let me drive to the hospice and finish this mission before I lose my remaining sanity."

Jack slumped in the seat. I glanced at him in disbelief as his confession rang in my ears.

"By the way, you smudged your makeup and might want to fix your lipstick."

He rolled his head and stared at me. "You really scare me sometimes."

CHAPTER THIRTY-THREE

I was surprised to find my beautiful midnight blue Caddy still sitting alone in the same parking space at the hospice, patiently waiting like I just ran into the grocery store to pick up a few things for dinner. I thought my car would have been confiscated by now, along with all the contents of my house, and put through a battery of scientific experiments. I'd watched enough *CSI* episodes with their impressive army of investigators all sporting flashlights even in daylight, to imagine their criminal profile of me. *"Suspect is a senior citizen, widower, and neat freak and chews gum incessantly. He is also apparently obsessed with some woman who died in 1974."*

Suddenly, I sensed my beloved car might be used as bait and I looked around for an unmarked cruiser. Everything looked as desolate as it should be at one o'clock in the morning. If this was a stakeout, the police were well camouflaged in the tall pines. Not wanting to take any chances with my time-sensitive cargo, I headed to the opposite end of the parking lot, but took one last look. It would be a long time before I worried about the cost of gasoline again as my future mileage would be measured in laps around the prison yard.

The cold air amplified the stillness under the moonless sky. I opened the trunk and extracted the vintage wheelchair we rented from M.B. Before we left her apartment, she fixed a fat piece of duct tape across the back of the chair to hide the "Property of Bon Secours Hospital" label written in heavy black magic marker. A couple of days ago I would have peppered her with questions about how she came to possess the transport; now I knew better than to ask.

Loading Jack in the wheelchair became another trial. Our heated argument at the park took a heavy toll and he passed out before we reached the hospice. Try as I might, I could not rouse him and he continued breathing like a piece of heavy equipment without exhaust. Although only skin and bones, he remained dead weight, no pun intended. I fought the onset of a panic attack because there was no Plan B at this point. I had the sense we were down to the two-minute-warning mark, giving me extra motivation to risk a hernia. Grabbing him under his arms, I dragged Jack out of the car and plopped him into the chair. A whiff of the manly cologne caught my nose and made me worry how I might explain this men's fragrance on an old nun.

My rough handling succeeded in waking him up and he let out a guttural noise and I checked his breathing. An opaque film covered the irises of his eyes.

"Jack, we're here to see Sarah," I said with enthusiasm, hoping to rally his spirits for the last time. There would be plenty of time for me to replay the terrible fight we had minutes ago.

"Who would ever guess we'd end up being two nuns on the lam," I deadpanned, hoping for some sarcastic reply to indicate he was still present in this world.

My humor went unanswered. Jack tilted his head back and I hesitated for a moment to allow him one last look at the infinite crop of stars which filled the moonless sky as a nearby light pole hummed an electronic mantra. Unfortunately, it was a very short tour of the galaxies with no time to wait for a shooting star and quote some immortal verse. This was classic Jack. He considered twenty minutes late as on time. And when we used to argue about it, his reasoning was always "nothing begins on time." It would be a nice theory if it wasn't ulcer producing, especially as we were running late for his demise.

I checked my reflection in the car window quickly, making sure my dress and habit were still on straight, and after the fight I felt increasingly unsure I could pull this off. Sure, M.B. had applied rouge and light pink lipstick, but I still looked like a transvestite from a failed carnival side show. After all, how does one hide an Adam's apple? Jack, on the other hand, would probably pass. He looked so ghastly white you couldn't say for sure what sex he was. However, his bulbous white sneakers looked out of place, so I threw a blanket across his legs.

The sliding doors swished open automatically and I cleared my throat as we crossed the threshold. Some fast food restaurants might be open twenty-four hours a day, but after midnight you had to use the drive-through window. Not this place. The front lobby was lit up as if hosting a gala event and just waiting for the invitees to arrive and populate the burgundy leather couches and chairs.

The wheelchair greeted the white marble tiled floor and one wheel immediately made a terrible squeaking noise like a worn out shopping cart. At first, I thought the blanket might be stuck in the wheel, which would have been disastrous. Then I realized one of the brake levers was partially engaged.

"Give me a break," I said, thinking for a hundred bucks M.B. should have rented us a wheelchair manufactured after the Civil War.

We'd made it halfway across the lobby before a gray head popped up like a whack-a-mole from behind the white reception desk straight ahead. He was a short middle-aged man in his late fifties and my eyes were immediately drawn to the white logo on the arm of his navy blue shirt which read "Allied Security." I surveyed his bulging stomach and wondered what kept the buttons from popping. Calculating the odds, I determined with enough of a head start I might have a chance to outrun him if my long skirt didn't trip me. At that point, it would be every man for himself and Jack might have his Custer moment after all.

"Good evening. May I help you?" he asked in a cautious voice.

His laser-like focus and the two-way radio on the counter made my veil feel too tight across the forehead. I smiled as sweetly as I could without showing any teeth, and imagined myself back in high school making Jack howl when I imitated his brother.

"Yes," I replied and wondered if I'd shaved close enough. "My name is Sister Claire and we're here to visit Sarah Nagle. Can you please tell me what room she's in?"

"I'm sorry, Sister. Visiting hours are over."

I put on my best frown. "How long have you worked here, son?"

The confident expression turned defensive as his green eyes narrowed. "Why do you ask?"

"Because I want to remind you this isn't a hospital where people pop in to say hello during the day and talk about going home," I said firmly. "The last time we were here, the director assured us the mission at Restful Waters is to make the last hours memorable for the entire family."

"That is true, but you're not family."

"Rest assured, we are family. Sarah was a member of our parish family for over fifty years and we're here to pray and comfort her during the loneliest part of the night."

"I'm going to have to check and see if you are able to visit." He picked up the radio.

I looked up at the tray ceiling then pointed to a sitting area in the corner with two handsome Essex Manor high-back wing chairs. "I'm sure that is why so many grateful families remember this hospice after their loved ones pass away. Their donations not only assure comfort, but also for round the clock reception resources like you."

The man blushed, which contrasted nicely with his short white hair. "I'm sorry if I offended you, Sister. I'm just going by the book."

"No problem, dear. What's your name?"

"Patrick," he replied quickly, apparently afraid I would want his last name.

"And a saintly name nonetheless."

He pulled on the skin under his chin and pursed his lips. "I'm sure there's no harm in letting you in."

I pushed the wheelchair past the registry book where my regrettable interaction with Ruth began and hoped he wouldn't make me sign in. In order to identify the risks ahead, I stopped our caravan after ten feet and turned around. "Last time we were here we met Nurse Nancy. I heard on the news she was accosted the other day. A terrible occurrence and I do pray she has recovered?"

"Yes, that's why Restful Waters hired us for security. Seems the old rascals are still at bay. I understand the nurse is fine and will be in at seven o'clock. I can tell her to swing by if you're still here?"

"No, that won't be necessary as he—I mean we, will be gone by then," I stuttered and scratched my throat.

The receptionist looked puzzled.

Jack's phone rang with a loud buzz. I tried to ignore it, but after the third ring I decided to stick my hand down the front of his tunic and fish the phone out of his shirt pocket. It was slow going.

Clearly embarrassed, Patrick looked away.

The caller ID said it was Mark. I waited until the ringing stopped and counted to five just to make sure.

"Hello, Father. Yes, we're here at the hospice and about to go in and see Sarah now. Thank you for calling to make sure we got here safely."

"Hey, I know you," Jack suddenly whispered, pointing a trembling arm at Patrick. I froze, analyzing whether the security guard could tell a man's voice was coming out of the crippled nun.

The security guard hung over the desk, straining to get a better look. "What did she say?"

I mouthed, "She's not well," and quickly turned the wheelchair around. "That's the reason we're here to pay our respects so early this morning. Sister Bernadette won't be up for much later."

I pushed the wheelchair a few more feet then stopped and looked back with intensity. "Patrick, what's the room number?"

The security man scrambled to check his list. "Room twenty-three," he replied. "Would you like me to assist you?"

I flashed the universal stop signal with my right hand. "No, son, that won't be necessary. I would feel much more secure if you stay at your post." I hesitated then took a half-dozen steps toward Patrick. "On second thought, I do want to mention I am concerned Sister Bernadette will become quite excited if a Mr. Stuart Nagle arrives while we are here. Sarah is his sister-in-law and while I should be more Christian, Mr. Nagle is a horrible man. Sister Bernadette caught him trying to steal the raffle money at Bingo a few years ago and he threatened to beat her. I don't expect him here tonight, but he's such an odd fellow and carries concealed weapons. I just thought you should know."

Patrick's eyes opened wide like he expected a notorious criminal from *Goodfellas* to appear any second and I went in for the close. "You can't miss him. He has red hair, a funny voice, dresses in black, and is very arrogant. So don't be fooled if he tries to breeze right past you like he owns the place. If he does show up, please detain him and send someone down to tell me. We would like to leave by a side door before he's allowed in."

"Absolutely." He began writing the details down.

"Bless you, Patrick," I said, moving quickly to rendezvous with Jack. On the way back, I noticed a glass bowl full of fun-sized candy bars on a side table and thought it odd they were starving the inmates, but left all these treats out here. In one smooth movement I picked up the entire bowl and smiled back at Patrick.

"Our mission is hard work, my son, and Sister and I have to keep our strength up any way we can."

CHASING MAYFLIES

CHAPTER THIRTY-FOUR

We entered the dark room and I let out a small cough to announce us. I knew we must look like a frightful apparition: two hooded characters backlit from the light in the hall with Jack slumped low in the wheelchair and me grimacing trying to propel the ancient contraption forward. All we needed now was a couple of sickles to transform the room into a scene from a campy horror film.

Squinting, I could make out the small frame of a woman lying on her side sleeping.

"Hello, Sarah," I whispered and patted Jack on the shoulder to let him know we made it.

There was no movement from either of them. This didn't look like the reunion I risked my freedom and reputation for.

There was a small pewter lamp on the nightstand and I turned it on, casting the room in an amber glow. Ever so gently, I maneuvered the wheelchair alongside her bed careful not to crash into anything. It had been many years since I last saw Sarah, and whatever illness she suffered from broke my heart. Her stark white hair was combed over her ears and needed a good shampooing. The skin on her cheeks looked as if the embalmer had paid a visit before us. I could only guess what illness brought her here. Whatever the reason, it was a sad departure from the woman who'd turned the head of every boy in high school with a smile that made angels jealous.

My dying friend let out a low moan. I knelt down and got close to his face. "We made it, Jack. Sarah is here."

The name of his wife revived him somewhat and he reached for me. Suddenly, I heard movement in the hall and bolted for the door. If Nurse Nancy had clocked in early she would certainly see through our disguises after our previous close encounter. I didn't have the strength to take her on myself and lock her in the closet.

A young nurse about five feet tall came out of the adjoining room and I met her in the hall. She jumped back in fright.

"Hello, dear," I said softly. "Sorry to scare you."

The redhead gave me a quick once-over and I felt the full body scan. "Is everything okay?"

I nodded and lied. "Yes, thank you. I'm here to pray with Sarah and needed to stretch my legs for a minute." I took two steps back to lengthen the distance between us. "When Sarah first became ill, we talked for a long time and I promised to help her through the end. I know from personal experience nights are the hardest, the loneliness grows in the shadows until the dawn tames them again."

The frown remained and she looked past me into the dimly lit room and the back of the wheelchair beside the bed. If she went in now and found Jack in his condition, I would have some explaining to do. Our luck couldn't hold much longer, yet I hoped my nun outfit still held some leftover grace.

"Your promise must have been made some time ago given her condition," she said.

The minefield was right in front of me and I could see the path around it with a simple nod. I bit my lip, hating how Jack rubbed off on me. "Why do you say that?"

The young face suddenly melted as her mouth began to quiver. "You'll have to excuse me, Sister. My father was just diagnosed with early onset Alzheimer's too. I know Sarah fought its progression for several years. Working here breaks my heart knowing what his future holds."

"I'm so sorry."

"I met her daughter. She checked out the facility earlier this week."

I bit my tongue to keep myself from saying something a nun would never utter. Why didn't Kate visit her father or tell him about Sarah? It was my turn to look away and my eyes followed the yellow chair rail running the length of the hall.

The nurse touched my arm and brought me back. "If you need anything please don't hesitate to stop by our station at the end of the hall."

I nodded, recalling the skirmish with Nurse Nancy.

She scanned my face. "Are you okay? You have a terrible rash on your cheeks and forehead."

I caught a scent of jasmine perfume and wondered if Merriam hovered somewhere overhead. "Bless you. I'm sensitive to peanuts and unfortunately could not resist the temptation of a candy bar. I'll be fine by morning."

She smiled and I watched her disappear down the hall before I reentered the room and closed the heavy door behind me, wishing I could hang a *Do Not Disturb, Good Sisters at Work* sign on the handle. I made a beeline to the eyeball in the ceiling and without any gum to use, coated it with a thin layer of petroleum jelly from a tube on the nightstand. Hopefully, it would blur the picture just enough so the nurses or Patrick would not investigate.

Jack watched me and I bent down and removed his habit, which M.B. had to tape on as he didn't have enough hair to anchor the comb. His breathing was irregular and he winced in pain, rubbing his tattoo.

"Is there anything I can do?" I calculated whether to try and sneak into the pharmacy for morphine or troll the other patient rooms hoping to find some.

My friend didn't respond and gazed toward his wife.

Sarah suddenly made a gurgling noise and I moved quickly to her side. Her eyes were open but unfocused.

"Sarah, it's Dennis," I whispered. Her head moved toward the direction of my voice.

I leaned in close so my face filled her field of vision. "I know I look funny, but you would not believe what I've gone through to get your husband here." I pointed to the small figure below me. "Jack is really in bad shape and you're the last person he wants to see."

I stopped short and groaned. "No, I mean you *are* the last person he wants to see." Her small face looked up from the bed, confused by what I was trying to say while Jack tugged weakly on my arm. I couldn't imagine a crueler ending; Jack thinking he knew everyone and Sarah no one.

I maneuvered the wheelchair closer to the bed and guided his fingers through the railing to place his hand in hers.

Suddenly, I caught another faint scent of jasmine and sensed Merriam telling me what to do.

CHAPTER THIRTY-FIVE

Jack and Sarah were married on a brilliant but humid Sunday afternoon in July. Sweat ran down the sides of my face when I finally located Jack on the back stoop of the VFW hall, smoking a butt with a few of our high school friends. He acted like he didn't have a care in the world even though he was leaving for basic training in two weeks. I couldn't wait to show him all the gift envelopes and estimated the newlyweds would begin their life with four hundred dollars. Compared to my bank account they were beginning life very rich.

"Hey, your new missus is looking for you," I said in a serious tone.

Jack snickered and shot me a look like I really sucked eggs for announcing it.

The other three guys picked up on my gaffe. "Not married an hour and you have to report in already?" Jimmy teased.

"Man, you're going to be whipped if you don't put your foot down fast and tell her who's boss," Sparky the gear head said with a wink. "But maybe you should wait until tomorrow morning."

Tony reached in the vest pocket of his black tux and produced a nip of vodka. "I have something special here for my married friend to really rev up your engine."

I let out a nervous laugh. It was time for the toast and if Jack stayed out here much longer, Sarah would have both our heads.

My newly married buddy remained cocky, but signaled me with a quick wink. It was up to me to rescue him from embarrassment.

I swung low and grabbed him by the waist. "Sorry, guys, duty calls."

They called me a lot of names as I carried the groom back to the wedding reception. I had no sooner straightened his tie and white boutonniere than Sarah came out of nowhere and gave me a look which I instantly read: "I would like to kill you both right now, but I can't because I have to keep this smile plastered on my face for another two hours."

Truthfully, I didn't need the added drama because I was already a wreck, wanting to say something so profound in my toast that it would be remembered on their golden wedding anniversary. It took many more years to learn one of life's hardest lessons. The things you don't want remembered usually are. Unkind words uttered in haste when you're tired, cranky, or miserable will hibernate for ten, twenty, even forty years and be reanimated in an instant. But concentrate and try your best to string together a few words to convey love, hope, and courage and all you can do is pray a line or two will be remembered the next day. In truth, I really only wanted to impress Jack and Sarah as the rest of the audience would be too busy thinking about dinner or checking out the competition.

When the moment finally came, I raised my champagne flute and focused hard on the newlyweds to control my public speaking fright. Sarah was smiling naturally again, forgiving Jack for the first of many disappearing acts to follow. You couldn't script foreshadowing like that.

"To my best friend and his beautiful wife," I began strongly. "My sincere wish is the love you pledge to each other today continues to sustain and nurture you through the good times and the bad. May you live a long life and hold each other in the end."

Glasses clinked and Jack and Sarah kissed.

CHAPTER THIRTY-SIX

I knelt down and checked on Jack. He was bent over, panting and clinging to the bed rail with both hands.

I eased him back in chair. "You should be so proud," I said, recalling the same line I'd whispered to Merriam. "I don't know how you held it together these last few days, but you're the toughest man I've ever known and while it will be a good while before I think through everything you told me tonight, I'm glad you did. I only wish when my time comes, I could stand before the Good Lord with half the courage you showed in trying to set things right." I kissed his forehead. "No matter what I said back at the park, I love you, buddy."

Jack squeezed my hand. "Love you," he silently mouthed.

I lowered the stainless steel bed rail. Bending low, I grabbed him by the waist and he looked very frightened. "Don't worry, Jack. I call this move a nun deadlift." I gently laid him in the bed next to his wife.

Sarah watched me intently and I hoped she wouldn't scream.

"See, I promised to bring him back before the wedding toast," I whispered to her. Sarah didn't acknowledge my voice; she remained too interested in studying the dying stranger next to her. I said a silent prayer that somewhere in her brokenness she recognized her husband.

It was close to ten minutes before his face finally relaxed and he slowly reached for Sarah's hand. I recalled their first dance to "It Had to Be You." Looking back now, it should have been "Wild Horses."

If this was a Hollywood script, the camera would fade out for the perfect tear-jerk ending. But in real life, Jack was still breathing and I expected a raid any moment.

I tiptoed to the door and slowly opened it to survey the halls. They were empty and I stood like a sentry and kept watch for fifteen minutes which felt like an eternity. When I finally shut the door again, Jack was on his back asleep and breathing shallow. I noticed the long string of rosary beads he wore around his waist thanks to the Sisters of Notre Dame. I slipped the cross into Jack's right hand and he immediately grasped it and I knew like the good thief, his faith had saved him. I knelt down and whispered the Lord's Prayer as it was intended for the living and the dying. Not to beat myself for once, but in sincere supplication for my loving friends.

I stood up much too quickly and reached for the bed rail to steady myself and looked down at the sleeping couple. I suddenly felt like an intruder and believed Jack's final moments belonged alone with his wife.

A brown leather recliner beckoned across the room by the French doors and I decided to keep watch at a respectful distance and took the bowl of candy to keep me company.

The large black and white Seth Thomas clock on the wall moved slowly as I chewed through a half-dozen candy bars.

Jack's phone buzzed like an annoying fly and I woke with a start, knowing as you do when you've overslept. Seth confirmed my fears. It was 6:30 a.m.

I catapulted out of the recliner with candy wrappers flying everywhere like confetti and trying to muffle the phone, knowing Mark was calling again. Staggering over to the bed, I had to grab the cold stainless steel bedrail to keep from passing out.

Sarah was alone in the bed. I looked around the room, sniffing the air for any sign of his signature cologne. Nothing. I ran to the bathroom on the far side of the room and looked inside. Not there either. I look around again.

Jack had disappeared.

CHAPTER THIRTY-SEVEN

"Walk with purpose and few will impede your progress" was the slogan I coined after successfully sneaking into a sold out Rolling Stones concert at Carnegie Hall in 1964, and now I buzzed the empty halls and opened every closet door along the way. I tried to recall what room number Jack occupied before he broke out on Tuesday. "Thirty-one," I said aloud, hoping he got confused and went back there, although how he did it would be a question for the ages. Rounding the corner, I reached his former room and looked in. Six chairs surrounded the bed of an unconscious bald man who looked at least a hundred years old. I surveyed their backs; four men and two women. An older woman came out of the bathroom. She looked about twenty years younger with gray hair and tired hazel eyes. She looked at me with the same blank expression I saw too often in here.

"I'm sorry," I said and backed out.

I flew down an adjacent hall and spied the nurses' station, thinking Jack might have pleaded for morphine or in desperation attempt a repeat of Tuesday's fiasco. The young nurse I spoke with last night typed intently on a computer.

The clock on the wall read 6:45 a.m. Nurse Nancy would be arriving any minute.

I bolted for the lobby and on the way passed a male nurse in blue scrubs. He was about thirty years old with dark unruly hair and stood well over six feet tall with a muscular build. I hugged the wall and gave a polite smile as we passed. He seemed in such a hurry he didn't acknowledge me.

"Good morning, Sister Claire," Patrick called out with forced sincerity as I raced through the lobby.

I slowed my gait significantly and nodded, hoping my wild eyes wouldn't make him suspicious. Then again, not looking like a mess in a hospice looked more out of place.

"How is Sister Bernadette?" he asked.

"Didn't you see her leave an hour ago?" I replied.

The look on his face confirmed Jack didn't go out this way and also helped me gain three more steps toward freedom. "Just pulling your leg, Patrick. I know nothing gets by you." I caught sight of a small bowl of fruit sitting on a coffee table in front of a real leather couch. My feet scurried to take a short detour and snag a banana.

Patrick smiled. "Good to see you eating healthy this morning after the candy binge. How is your parishioner this morning?"

"Resting peacefully, I hope."

Patrick glanced at the digital clock on the credenza. "Nancy will be here any minute if you would like to say hello."

I smiled weakly, knowing if she caught up with Jack before I did, he would only need one shot to put him down. "Please excuse me, Patrick, as I have to get something from my car."

The doors slid open and a brisk breeze hit my face. I filled my lungs with the fresh air. The sun caressed a cloudless sky and made me wonder what it felt like to be looking down on all this madness.

I walked quickly along the sidewalk, trying to ignore the wind and cold without a coat, and scanned every nook and cranny; between cars, trash barrels, and evergreen trees. No sign of Jack.

As I looked ahead to plan another sweep of the grounds, my upper lip curled instinctively when I noticed a man in a black leather coat with a strange gait approaching. I remembered the threat Stu made yesterday to visit Sarah after he asked for a refund on his brother.

It was too late to leave the cement sidewalk without drawing attention so I bowed my head in contemplation.

If Stu saw my mouth moving as he drew near he probably figured I was whispering my morning prayers. Unfortunately for him, it was the opposite of seeking salvation for his soul.

"No coat, Sister?" he asked, smiling.

"God provides," I replied softly, afraid if I said it any louder he would hear me imitating him.

I counted to ten before I dared look back. In the next minute, Patrick would detain him, believing Sister Bernadette was still with Sarah. Most likely, a heated exchange would follow and if I were really lucky, the security guard would get all macho and frisk him for weapons. Being a Monday morning quarterback, I wished I had suggested his car contained drug paraphernalia too.

As sweet as it would be to sit and watch the coming fireworks, I didn't want any part of it and kept my focus on my black getaway car fifty yards away and blinked hard when it suddenly began to move. Who would steal a piece of junk? I tried to run but the tight skirt held me to a slow trot. The car made a quick turn toward the exit and I caught sight of rebellious Sister Bernadette.

"Jack!" I yelled, waving my arms furiously.

The car raced out of the parking lot with light blue smoke spewing from its tailpipe. I thought back to the parking garage and how I couldn't leave Jack alone in a foxhole, but apparently he didn't have an issue leaving me in enemy territory.

If the police later reviewed the security tapes, they would conclude I was a spastic nun at that moment as I checked all my pockets and slapped my forehead, realizing Jack stole my car keys while I slept.

Desperate, I looked across the parking lot and my Caddy was still patiently waiting for its owner's return.

I started for the car but stopped after three steps, as I remembered again I didn't have the keys to this car either.

Suddenly, I had a flashback remembering the time I drove Merriam into Boston for an oncologist appointment. After a long day, we discovered the keys were locked in the car. Merriam stood in the cold November rain with tears streaming down her face, exhausted. When we finally made it home, I went out and bought one of those magnet boxes you hide under the car with a spare key.

I looked up at the sky and thanked Merriam for being my guardian angel. And perhaps she was, because no sooner did I take three more steps than I noticed a police cruiser appear out of nowhere. I watched it glide slowly along and stop at my beloved car. The cop said something into his radio. They were trying to bait me after all. I watched as the cruiser slowly headed out to the main road.

I looked back; the front lobby still appeared quiet. My luck was holding, but havoc would ensue at any moment. I scanned the parking lot again and with no other options, hurried along the long driveway leading out to Route 28, hoping the cruiser would not return.

The cell phone rang and although history taught the perils of fighting a war on two fronts, sometimes it can't be avoided.

"Hey, Mark. It's the middle of the night for you. What's up?"

"Dad?" he asked, not waiting for confirmation. "I've tried and tried to reach you. Why won't you pick up? You and Jack are all over the news out here and my phone won't stop ringing."

"Listen, son, it's a long story and—"

"Stealing a car, robbing a bank, assaulting a nurse, punching a police officer, resisting arrest?"

I hesitated answering, because if Jack came back at this moment, attempted murder might be added to my growing rap sheet. "I know how it sounds, but things got complicated real fast."

"At this rate you'll be on the FBI's Most Wanted list by tomorrow. Where's Jack?"

I surveyed the dead Stella de Oro daylilies that lined the long driveway. How I longed to see those golden trumpet-shaped flowers. "To be honest, I really don't know. We dressed up as nuns and snuck back into the hospice so Jack could visit his dying wife. Okay, I know what you're thinking. What're the odds Sarah is on her way out too? I thought the same thing myself until I found out she's been sick for years. It's ironic she took ultra-good care of herself and the guy who burned a candle at both ends had the same shelf life as her." I turned around to look again. "Things were working out nicely until I fell asleep in a recliner. When I woke up he was gone," I said in one long breath.

The line remained silent for about five seconds. "Dad, this is all mumbo-jumbo to me. But now that Jack is dead, maybe you'll come to your senses."

I felt winded and took another deep breath, but still couldn't fill my lungs. "No, I said he's gone, not dead. Whatever is powering him is not of this earth. Somehow he managed to break out of the hospice for the second time this week and left me high and dry without a ride."

"What's with all this crazy talk? And why are you panting? This is what I'm talking about. You can't live alone," he said in machine gun fashion.

"Are we really going to start this again now?"

"Dad, tell me where you are so I can come pick you up."

"You're three thousand miles away, son. Now you're the one talking crazy."

"I'm taking the red-eye tonight and will be there first thing tomorrow morning."

"But I asked you to cancel your trip."

"Motion denied. Now tell me where you are. I'll call the police so they can pick you up and keep you safe."

"Yeah, safe in jail. We'll talk when you arrive. In the meantime, I need to find Jack so I can wring his neck."

"Dad, stop this nonsense right now tell me where you are." The tone was firm.

"I'm in New Hampshire. You know, the Live Free or Die state?" I hated my limited number of tricks with cell phones. "My cell phone battery is dying. Have a safe flight, son."

It was rush hour on Route 28. I peeled my banana to give me strength and began walking down the highway. Every tenth of a mile or so, I turned around to see if the posse trailed me in pursuit. The fresh March wind worked to tear away the bobby pins and duct tape holding my habit in place and I feared reliving an episode of the *Flying Nun*.

The closest strip mall appeared a few hundred yards ahead, but offered little protection when the search party arrived. I needed to get back to Haverhill and see M.B. Maybe Jack was headed back there too.

In desperation, I put out my thumb and attempted to hitch a ride. Meanwhile, I continued to peel and enjoy my banana. One car after another passed. To my dismay, none slowed down. In fact, many moved to the outside lane and one small boy in the back of a silver minivan stuck out his tongue at me. I threw the banana peel at him, but its wings never deployed and it slammed into the pavement before a Ford Mustang squished it good.

"I'm a hitchhiking, banana-toting, catch-me-if-you-can nun," I mumbled to myself. The absurdity of it all combined with exhaustion doubled me over in tears and laughter.

In the midst of my meltdown, a gray pickup truck stopped alongside me. Thinking it was an unmarked police car, I put my hands over my head ready to surrender.

"Why are you scaring folks on Route 28 at rush hour?" a familiar deep voice boomed.

I looked up and saw Mad Dawg. I might have jumped for joy if the tunic wasn't so tight. "Man, I'm sure glad to see you."

My new best friend squinted. That's when I realized I was still talking in a high-pitched woman's voice.

"I mean, it's really good you came back," I said in the deepest tone I could muster. "You have to help me. Jack took off in M.B.'s car and left me stranded here."

The big guy yawned, apparently not troubled with the madman in front of him.

I rubbed my eyes and looked down at my mascara-stained fingers. "Didn't you hear me? Jack's gone."

Mad Dawg remained unimpressed. You got bigger problems now."

I nodded my head in agreement and scanned the traffic. "Yeah, I'm wandering down the highway and Halloween is six months away."

Big Dawg finally laughed. "You talk funny and I don't need this from someone who's milking the system."

"Norman, after life kicks you around a few more years, then come back and talk to me about entitlements." I decided to walk to Haverhill if needed.

"Nobody calls me Norman except M.B. and she's earned it," he replied with a scowl. "I'd like nothing better than to leave you for your friends in blue, but Mr. Leonard sent me over to pick you up. He's concerned about Jack's sudden demise." He opened the door. "Now get your sorry butt in here fast, but keep the window open. I don't want you spreading your scabies."

"I keep telling you it's only a rash," I said, climbing in. "What does Leonard have to do with Jack?" I tore at the black veil to free my head.

"He owes him a lot of money."

"So why does he want to see me?"

He sighed. "Do I have to explain everything to you? Your buddy left you with the tab."

"But Jack isn't dead. That's why I'm out here trolling the highway."

"Whatever." He shot me a disgusted glance. "You might want to keep the veil on because my boss doesn't take kindly to people who owe him ten thousand dollars."

CHAPTER THIRTY-EIGHT

Working in sales, I met a lot of people from different walks of life. Still, with the exception of some strange characters who hung around with Jack, I didn't know any real gangsters. Nevertheless, I'd invested enough time watching television to recognize the stereotype. So it came as a bit of a surprise when Norman led me to a lone table for two next to the bar at the Dawg House to meet with Mr. Leonard. I sat down on the small pine chair and watched him inhale an all-American breakfast: two fried eggs, bacon, home fries, white toast. Steam rose from a large mug of black coffee. The aroma made me almost mad with hunger.

Leonard must not have been on the clock yet, because he didn't bother to look up or say hello. Naturally, I wondered if he had done a stint in sales too and was tapping the power of silence. No matter, I knew this game extremely well and took the time to size up this unimpressive thirty-something: slight build, wet-looking black hair combed straight back, designer rim glasses highlighting dark marble-sized eyes, and no jewelry whatsoever. This morning he wore business casual; tan khakis and a white button down shirt. Who was this imposter? He looked more like an accountant than a loan shark. It made me wonder why M.B. was so scared of this pipsqueak landlord and employer. The image of her red face flashed across my mind and I fought the urge to flip his plate over so he could wear breakfast. What was happening to me? The image of the white fan at the hospice with the worn ball bearing flashed across my mind. Maybe something had broken inside me too. Otherwise how could I explain this transformation? Up until this week I was the president of the local Milquetoast chapter and cowered when a car backfired. Now I looked forward to competing in *WrestleMania*.

Leonard finally raised his head and looked across the clean but worn pine top. "Good morning, Sister," he said even though I'd ditched the veil.

I knew my opening statement would set the tone for our meeting. "I'm pretty hungry, Lenny. Think you can have Norman rustle me up some breakfast too?"

In the next second, he stabbed my hand with a fork.

"Address me like that again and the next utensil I use won't be a spoon. Got it?"

I inspected the four puncture marks and kept my face blank. "Okay," I said, holding up my injured hand and smiling broadly. "You made your points."

Leonard wiped his hands slowly on a white paper napkin. His nails looked manicured.

"Although we haven't been properly introduced, I'm feeling you have no respect for your elders." I leaned forward with my elbows on the table to show he didn't intimidate me. "Didn't your mother teach you manners? The least you can do after dragging me down here so early is offer a cup of coffee."

Leonard chuckled and shook his head. "You're a piece of work, Sister, you really are. I would be happy to entertain you straight through lunch, but I'm afraid you're pressed for time. Although I do advise ditching the dress so it won't slow you down, unless you've come to like it." He scrunched the used napkin into a tight ball and threw it on the table. "But if you're agreeable after our discussion, maybe I'll send you off with a bagel to go."

I had the distinct feeling my remaining time on earth would include creative eating at every opportunity. "Agreeable to what?"

Lenny took a long sip of coffee and smacked his lips. "Wow, this is good java," he said with a grin before his face turned serious again. "Now, don't misinterpret me, Sister. I'm not saying you have a choice here as much as I'm highlighting the right attitude will be appreciated in this small business transaction."

I flashed a confident smile. "Well, your attitude so far speaks volumes."

"Hold onto that smile, Sister. You see, your good buddy went into the hospice before he settled his account with me."

"That's only half right. Jack went into the hospice twice this week, but I don't know where he is now. When you sent Norman over to pick me up he had just taken off in M.B.'s car. For all I know he might be dead in some ditch by now."

The man across the table yawned. "I don't care if he's in heaven, hell, or on his way to Tijuana. As far as I'm concerned, he's dead to me and that's all that matters."

"Look, I won't argue with you. What I would suggest is you discuss whatever issue you have with his brother as he'll be the executor of the estate." I grabbed the dirty napkin and unrolled it. "If you have a pen, I can give you his phone number."

Leonard snickered. "I never thought I would hear anyone use the word estate and Jack in the same sentence. Now that's funny," he said, clapping. "I know Stuart and with the exception of them sharing the same parents, they're complete strangers. You, on the other hand, were the one person Jack said always had his back."

"Sure, but I never co-signed any of his loans."

"Let me explain how this works," he replied and took the napkin from my hand and rolled it back into a tight ball. "In my business I survive by taking calculated risks. I knew Jack for a long time and we had our ups and downs over the years like all business associates do, and if we had the time I would share some whoppers."

"I don't care to hear them."

"I have to admit, Jack had a really good run a few years back. He got real close to a few jockeys down South and it paid off well and he didn't need my financial services for a while."

The loan shark pulled out a pack of Marlboro cigarettes. He lit one up, took a long drag, and tilted his head back before exhaling. The smoke hung like an expanding cloud over the table and I sat back in my chair to avoid it. "When Jack started losing again, some folks around here said he tempted fate too much, that he didn't know when to take his winnings and enjoy life. I disagreed. We all want one more bite of the red apple, don't we? Look at Wall Street if you want to see it play out on the big stage. They could drink the ocean through a straw and still be thirsty. No, Sister, my business plan works because no one is ever satisfied and eventually every Midas loses his touch. And so did your friend."

The last thing I needed was a diatribe on gambling and its comparison to Wall Street. I glanced at the closet Jack and I had shared for a couple hours on a bed of beer. It felt like a year had passed.

My eyes strayed too long, because I felt the prongs of the fork again. "Sister, stay focused."

"Hey, cut it out," I replied angrily before realizing it might prove unfortunate to reference cutting with a knife so close by. "I mean stop it, will ya? And where's your respect for senior citizens?" I hated to hide behind my age for the second time and usually reserved the senior tag when a discount was available.

Leonard's face softened. "I do respect my elders. That's why you're sitting here instead of treading water in the Merrimack out back. But if you don't pay attention, I may have to reconsider my values. What I'm trying to explain is Jack owes me ten grand."

I let out a low whistle and recalled how Jack tried to get a loan from the bank. "That's a lot of money."

"Good, I have your full attention now," he said, leaning in close. "Last month Jack asked me to loan him ten G's. At first, I refused because he wasn't worth the risk. Jack wouldn't take no for an answer and offered you up as the guarantor of the loan. I did my homework before agreeing and found out you are a pillar of the community. You own your home and from surveying your mail have a number of bank accounts and some healthy CDs. Though from reading your last car insurance bill, I think you can do better."

He leaned back in his chair. "So, unless you have a sack full of hundreds stuffed somewhere in that skirt of yours, you have an issue."

My head began spinning and I was surprised Mrs. Werner didn't catch them going through my mail. "You're trying to scam me," I said with my voice rising. "Jack would never do that to me."

"Hate to tarnish the memory of your dead buddy wherever he's rotting. Maybe you'll want to go cheap on the bouquet you send to the funeral home. That's your call. But you need to face the fact your friend left you with the tab. I guess he wanted to have a little fun on his way out and apparently thought you owed him big time."

"You're lying."

Leonard ground his half-smoked cigarette into the plate, upsetting what was left of one fried egg. The escaped yolk ran thick and puddled beside a lonely strip of bacon.

"I don't care what you think. I just want my money." He pushed the plate away as apparently even a slug gets disgusted on occasion.

"You have to understand I don't—"

The loan shark pounded on the table and it wobbled. "Stop with the lip right now. According to Norman, you're bleeding the system dry anyways, so you'll be whole after a few more social security checks."

"You're greatly mistaken. Sure I have some money but I put everything in a trust to my son. He's a lawyer and took care of everything." I hoped he didn't know it was a revocable trust.

Leonard studied me for a long moment. "Then I'm expecting your boy will do what's right for his old man." He reached over grabbed the top of my tunic. "Look, I don't care if you call your son, your banker, or your priest. Call all three if you like and take up a collection. Just know this: you have twenty-four hours to pay me in cash or I torch your house. Call the cops and you can split the hearse fee with Jack."

His tobacco breath made me want to gag and I blinked hard, hoping I would wake up in the leather recliner back at the hospice and find Jack asleep next to Sarah.

"Are you having an episode, Sister?" he asked, releasing me. "If so, it would explain whatever is going on with your face. I can't figure out if all those bumps are acne or your cheeks are embarrassed being seen in a tight black dress."

"I need more time. It's not like I can go to the bank around here given what's happened this week."

Leonard pointed to the door. "Like I said, you have no time for breakfast."

When I stood up static electricity caused my skirt to hug my legs. Even for an old nun, it was unsightly. Men had it so easy.

Leonard's belly laugh didn't restore my spirits any. "There's a convenience store nearby if you need to buy Static Guard," he said, standing up. "But I'm not totally heartless. If you like, Norman can drop you off at M.B.'s apartment to change. Be sure and hurry, though, because she's mad at you too."

"Huh?"

"It was a nice gesture by Jack to help M.B. catch up on the rent. Bless him for his generosity with other people's money. But he also raised my expectations on what apartments will fetch around here. Since she can't pay, I evicted her today."

"But she works for you."

"I'm her employer, not her father." He pointed a long skinny finger at me. "You misjudge me at your peril."

"We'll see about that," I whispered, turning to leave.

"Oh, by the way, Dennis."

His calling me by my real name made me turn around again.

"Do you like your name?"

"What do you mean by that?"

"I think it's the nun outfit that makes it so ironic. Do you know Dennis spelled backwards is *Sinned*? Should I call you Sinned or do you prefer Sister?"

Jean Bradley cried out from her cement liner six feet down and out of habit I searched my mouth for the Juicy Fruit gum which wasn't there. I quickly reached down and took the remaining piece of bacon encased in yolk and crammed it in my mouth. It tasted burnt but it would have to do.

"You really should have checked my references."

CHAPTER THIRTY-NINE

I doubted the existence of angels before I met M.B.'s daughter. When Rosa brought me a blueberry muffin and cup of coffee after I changed back into my ridiculous leisure suit, I knew she must be hiding her wings. Being back in the apartment again was jarring as everything seemed frozen in time. The coffee table was still covered with bobby pins, eyelash curlers, and bottles of makeup. Given what Mr. Leonard told me less than an hour ago, I figured M.B. would be half packed by now.

It felt odd taking the same chair I occupied nine hours ago. In my mind's eye, Jack was still lying on the couch, sipping the remainder of his beer when he could. The tan blanket M.B. used to wrap him up like a mummy sat in a ball on the floor next to Rosa, who concentrated on a small handheld computer game. Every few seconds the game beeped and the little girl smiled.

I took another small bite of my muffin to stay awake. It tasted doughier than it looked and like everything else this week not what I expected. "So where's your mother?"

"Looking for boxes. Where's your friend?"

"To tell you the truth, I don't know." Prison hospital or the morgue were my guesses if pushed.

"Did he go to Disney?"

I shook my head no, although who's to say? The MVP of the Super Bowl always manages to go there the day after the big game. And Jack surely brought his A game this week. If I had a say, his penance for deserting me would include getting stuck in "It's a Small World" and listening to the annoying soundtrack non-stop for a month.

"If he isn't at Disney, is he dead?"

Shame on me as I should have known this angel grew up fast. The only question was the fertilizer. Given M.B.'s lineage and Leonard's influence, it was probably a mixture of both.

I shrugged.

Rosa studied my face and I looked away at a lone bottle of Bud on the end table. It was the only beer I never saw Jack finish.

"All I can tell you, honey," I said, turning back to the little girl, "is Jack didn't want to leave for heaven until he took care of a few things. I am so thankful for how much you and your mother took care of him."

Rosa put her computer game down and began fiddling with her silver bracelet. I was suddenly transported back at Henley's, meeting her grandmother for the first time.

"And did he get to see everyone he wanted to?" she asked like a seasoned detective hoping the rapid questions would offer a clue.

I took a sip of the instant coffee and embraced the bitterness. "Yes, for the most part, although he left some unfinished business for me to take care of."

"Oh, you're back," M.B. suddenly announced from the doorway.

I somehow missed the heavy footsteps and noticed she wore the same clothes as yesterday. Did she sleep in them?

M.B. walked over to Rosa and whispered something quickly in her ear and I hoped she wasn't in trouble for letting me in. I was relieved when the little girl smiled and ran into the other room. I wished I could smile and run too.

Her mother watched her disappear and I scanned her face: no fresh bruises, but her eyes looked bloodshot.

"Any word from Jack?" I asked, not expecting any.

M.B. nodded. "Yeah, he dropped the car off about an hour ago and left in a white van. I don't know who was driving." Her voice sounded extra gravelly this morning.

I bolted out of the chair. "Are you kidding me? Did he say why he left me stranded back at the hospice?"

"He didn't say too much as he wore an oxygen mask, but said to tell you he was grateful for all your help. He said he had someone else he had to see."

I slumped back into the chair. "That's it? After everything we've been through he's leaving me like that?" I rubbed my temples. "Why wouldn't he ask me to take him?"

She shrugged. "Who knows? Maybe he went to see his brother."

"Not unless he knows the rapture is coming and wants to tell Stu to enjoy the coming tribulations."

She eyed me with a puzzled look. "You have a knack for saying the strangest things sometimes."

I retreated by looking down at the orange shag and imagined a chalk line outlining my body after my confession. But where to begin? Should I tell M.B. about the death threats from Mr. Leonard, or go thermonuclear and tell her I killed her mother? Without Jack as a bridge, beginning any conversation was awkward.

I stood back up and started tidying up the mess from our costume party.

"You don't have to do that." She moved to intervene.

I ignored her and attempted to fold the tan blanket.

She gently wrestled it away from me and I lost my end and it knocked over Jack's orphaned beer. It sat in a frothy puddle on the carpet.

M.B. quickly grabbed a roll of paper towels off the coffee table and knelt down to clean up the mess.

"Spilt beer is my lucky charm because that's how I met my wife," I said, looking over her shoulder. "Back in sixty-seven I watched the Red Sox pursue their Impossible Dream before leaving for boot camp." I chuckled. "Jack never stopped teasing me about that. He enlisted and ended up in the middle of hell. I signed up a year later and was stationed at a Navy supply depot in San Diego and enjoyed liberty on beautiful white sand beaches." I picked up the empty bottle of Bud next to M.B. and fingered the label. "Anyways, I was trying to flirt with the waitress—a beautiful strawberry blonde with eyes that matched the color of the sky in Eden, when she tripped and spilled sixteen ounces of Narragansett lager all over me. For the rest of her life, I teased her that beer was the most expensive one on the planet. The Sox had to wait another thirty-seven years for their ring, I only had to wait six. Neil Armstrong walked on the moon in 1969, but I strolled into heaven in 1973."

M.B. stood up with a handful of wet paper towels and forced a smile. "That's sweet. Now sit down before you collapse."

It was the first kind thing she ever said to me and I welcomed the opportunity to postpone the inevitable and collapsed on the couch. Jack whistled in my ear to seize the opportunity. *"Wait is a four letter word,"* he said over and over.

M.B. left the room and reappeared with a plastic storage container. In short order, she cleared all of last night's remnants and worked to sop up more of the beer with a blue terry cloth towel.

"Oh, I almost forgot," she said over her shoulder. "Jack also said it's very important you go see some guy named Peter today. He will help you settle all the bills." She crawled over to the couch and pulled out Jack's lucky hat and handed it to me. "He said you would need this."

I looked at the worn brown corduroy hat with its "Aces" logo and then at the hungry look on M.B.'s face. My good buddy promised her I would pay his tab and she made herself perfectly clear what would happen to me if I stiffed her. No doubt Mad Dawg told her too about my breakfast meeting with Leonard and knew I needed a lot of money fast.

"When I moved out of my friend's place last year, I went down to the liquor store and asked if I could take a few boxes out of the mountain they had sitting there," she said, standing up. "They said sure, as long as I bought enough wine to fill them." M.B. pointed to a bulging trash bag in the corner. "It's no problem moving clothes, but when it comes to everything else, they're pretty useless. Getting things squared today on what Jack owes would help."

The opening was about the size of a dime, but would have to suffice.

"I heard you have to move and I'm sorry about that," I said gently, hoping Leonard was lying and she wasn't blaming Jack and me on being evicted. "But I still don't understand why he's kicking you out. You're a loving mother, keep a tidy home, and even work for the jerk.

Isn't that worth more than a few extra bucks in rent and the chance some slob will move in? I mean, what else could he want?"

She put her hands in her pockets and shook her baggy dungarees once and I finally understood the reason for all the camouflage and my cheeks got hot. I'd been out of the real world so long I forgot the games men play. "Where will you go?"

She looked around the small apartment and shrugged. "I'm working on that."

"Do you have a good relationship with Rosa's father?"

She began tidying up a pile of newspapers next to the couch and I knew the alligators were hungry again in the moat. "I'm sorry. It's none of my business."

She ignored my apology. "We'll be down the hall for a while if you want to take a nap. Just promise me you'll go see Peter today. Jack drove me nuts making me promise you would go."

How could I tell her she was asking me to visit an upside down tree? "How much does Jack owe you?" I asked, sucking in my breath. All I could hear was a cash register ringing.

Now it was her turn to look embarrassed. "He paid some of it in advance and gave me some the other day when he woke up."

I wanted to say he owed the Republic Bank and Mr. Leonard a thank you card, but held my tongue.

"A couple more will cover it," M.B. replied.

"A couple what?" The decimal point made all the difference.

"Two hundred dollars and I need it by tomorrow."

I breathed a sigh of relief. "Tell you what I'll do," I said, taking a step toward her. I'll add another hundred if you let me borrow your car for a few hours today. That way, I can go see Peter." I looked down and frowned at my bell bottoms. "Do you have my old clothes? Maybe I can stop by the laundry on the way."

M.B. blushed for the first time. "Rosa threw them away in the dumpster."

"Oh my," I replied and looked down at Jack's lucky stained hat and frowned.

She handed me the keys. "I'm sorry."

"Did you hear Leonard is holding me responsible for what Jack owes him too?" I asked, thinking I might learn something about the loan shark.

She held up her index finger to stop me from continuing. "That doesn't concern me."

The tiny opening closed and Jack screamed in my ears to man up. Exhaustion, frustration, and guilt converged all at once and something inside finally snapped.

"Well, since we're being honest with each other, there's something I have to tell you." My heartbeat tried to blow out both eardrums.

She shook her head. "If it's about Leonard, I told you I don't want to hear it. I have a daughter to protect."

"No, it's about your mother."

M.B. looked like I just turned off the cooling water for the reactor core. "What about my mother?"

"I knew her," I stammered.

"In what way?" The bloodshot eyes were piercing.

"Not that way," I replied quickly, glancing at her oversized jeans. "A long time ago, I used to sell cars for a living. Your mother came to see me about a used car she wanted to buy and she brought you along. You were about four years old at the time and although Rosa is older, she's a dead ringer for you."

M.B.'s classic hands on the hips stance returned and her eyes drilled mine and she saw my guilt. "So what made that sale so different you remembered us after all these years? There must be something else you're leaving out. Jack was really high on me meeting you. So what gives?"

Jack gave the microphone to Leonard, who began singing in my ears. *"Spell Dennis backwards."* I wished I had the worn memorial card with me so I could show her daughter how much I regretted everything.

Forty-year-old tears began running down both cheeks. "I'm so very sorry, Maggie. She stole that car because I wouldn't let her buy it."

Her eyes got big and her mouth quivered. "I don't understand."

"I played around with the price and by the time I lowered it, she didn't have the money. She was desperate to run away with you and decided to steal the car. She paid me to leave the gate open so she could leave town in the middle of the night. I got cold feet and never showed up. I got drunk instead." I wiped my eyes. "You know the rest."

M.B. walked past me and opened the door. She didn't need to say a word. She kept staring at me like she might call the police any moment and report a home invasion, which was close to the truth.

I wanted to hear something loud enough to make my ears ache or have Big Dawg suddenly appear with a hot poker. Her silence was ten times worse, because it matched the same punishment I endured for so many years.

I avoided her eyes and sprinted to the car before she remembered I had her car keys.

CHAPTER FORTY

The things we fear in the dark often look tame in daylight, and it felt that way on my second trip to visit Peter. The parking lot remained empty but now looked depressing rather than frightful. The sun decided to only work half a day, which the clouds quickly announced with a brief snow shower of fat snowflakes. In another few weeks this sort of storm would be called poor man's fertilizer. But today, it was just another reminder no matter what the groundhog proclaimed, winter is a bully and leaves when it's good and ready to. And when spring finally did come this playground would be overrun by overactive kids thrilled at leaving the heavy equipment of boots, gloves, and winter coats in the closet.

Nearing the end of the parking lot, the Escort began to stall. The sudden engine cough made me wonder if the automobile had some strange symbiotic relationship with Jack so I didn't overshoot the target. Nothing would surprise me at this point, so I just went with it and let the car roll until it stopped.

Getting out of the car, I appreciated how easy it is to maneuver when you're not wearing a nun's skirt, but ironically preferred the conservative dress to my lime green suit, orange snorkel coat, and brown corduroy hat. But given my new assignment, looking unkempt matched my new persona of channeling dementia so I could converse with a tree. I made my way across the damp field thinking about possible headlines if the cops found me fighting with Peter. *Tree Drops Old Nut* was my favorite.

Peter seemed taller up close and though I would never admit it, I could see why Jack loved the sculpture. Studying the upside down tree made me think how long the artist must have wandered through the forest to find this one special specimen. It looked truly amazing.

I took a few steps backwards to get a better perspective. Even after finding the perfect body shape, how did the artist know the root ball would work? Last night, I got the sense of movement from this tree man. Now in the daylight, Peter seemed lost in contemplation with extended arms; one as if to balance itself against the sky, the other pointing down to the earth.

Peter was indeed an imposing figure and must have taken quite an effort to transport and jockey into position. There was a huge metal plate anchoring the giant to the ground, and I inspected it, looking for clues. Not finding anything more remarkable than a bit of rust, I walked around and around the sculpture. The only thing I accomplished was making a soggy ring around Jack's mute friend.

Frustrated, I opened my mouth and yelled; a good long one that hurt my throat and made my temples ache and should have brought the police. I really didn't care what Peter thought of my temper tantrum. If toddlers could get away with it on the nearby swings, why couldn't an old man at the end of his rope?

"Sure, he doted over you and shared his plans," I said, pointing up at his wooden friend. "I thought I might even find him here giving you a full report. And me? He kept it limited on a need-to-know basis and left me with a tab that would fund a winter in Florida instead of the jail cell I'll summer in." I looked up at the overcast sky perfectly matching my mood. "I'm amazed at what he accomplished this week, but why am I left with the dust pan and broom again?"

I pointed up at Peter and his hair waved back at me. "You know I should be home right now packing all my stuff to begin a new life out west. Instead, I'm out here in the cold carrying on with you, wishing Jack would show up so I could string him around your neck. And why did he name you Peter anyways? If it was up to me, I'd call you Frankentree."

Peter remained silent, which meant it shared the same stubbornness that defined my good friend. I pulled out Jack's cell phone and quickly dialed. Stuart picked up on the third ring.

"Who is this?" the whiny voice asked.

"It's me, Dennis. Have you heard from him?"

"Heard from who?"

"Your brother."

"Why would I?" Stuart asked.

"Okay, enough with the Abbott and Costello routine," I replied. "Jack took off this morning and I thought he might have stopped by your house." I kicked at the wet grass with my right foot and muddied the toe. I shook my head. My black dress shoes were a mess too.

"You're as delusional as him. I'm the last person he wants to see and I want to keep it that way. And I feel the same way about you."

"The feeling is mutual." I walked between Peter's legs and rubbed the back of my neck. It felt smooth from M.B.'s razor. "You said he had a woman friend at chemo. What's her name?"

There was a long silence and I expected him to hang up. "Barbara Collins, and she filled Jack's head with nonsense about religion and the afterlife. A bunch of hooey if you ask me."

"Does she live around here?"

"In Methuen unfortunately, though she might be six feet under by now so no one can hear her babbling anymore."

"Look, Jack left me with a mess. He owes a loan shark ten grand and he wants me to pay up by tomorrow or he'll torch my house. I thought you should know since he's your brother and you should cover this for him."

Laughter filled my ear before he hung up. I whipped off Jack's lucky hat and whacked Peter in the right leg as hard as I could and it made a slapping sound. He didn't move or say "Ouch!" so I kicked him hard in the shin and stubbed my toe and I was the one that cried out. "What am I doing here?" I said, looking up at the massive head. "At least in jail I'll have a roof over my head after Leonard burns down my house."

I shut my eyes for a moment and exhaustion washed over me again. Jack was sitting beside me in the car.

"Just be sure to stand far enough back so he's looking at you straight in the eyes when you return. It will make all the difference if you let him give you a hand."

I studied the sculpture again and walked fifty paces backwards before lining up with Peter's eyes if he had any. From this angle, Peter looked like he was being crucified. The new perspective would be amazing if I wasn't at the end of my rope.

"Okay, big guy, now what?" I yelled and waited, half expecting some magic to happen. After all, Jack always liked the big reveal. I glanced toward the parking lot, thinking maybe the answer would come by land.

Nothing.

I looked in the surrounding pine trees.

Nada.

I felt dizzy. Would that thug really burn down my house? I thought I might throw up and leaned over and put my hands on my knees and concentrated on breathing.

"It will make all the difference if you let him give you a hand."

I looked up and studied both of Peter's arms. Something in his right hand which pointed toward the ground caught my eye. I ran back and positioned myself under his arm and tried to get a better look at some type of square object nestled tightly in Peter's index finger about ten feet up.

I pulled on the brim of Jack's lucky hat wondering where to get a ladder when a crazy idea came to mind. Jogging back to the car, I almost tripped twice on my bell-bottomed pants. I threw the Escort into gear and drove slowly across the wet lawn, hoping for no mud. The grass felt squishy but held. With the car under the hand, I climbed on top of the roof and stood on tippy-toes to reach Peter's longest finger and tried to pull it toward me.

Peter turned stubborn, and we had a momentary tug of war until I lost my balance and flew backwards, hitting the roof of the car hard before rolling off and landing on my face in the wet grass.

Moaning, I rolled over and stared up at the overcast sky. Ink would love this blank canvas.

My butt began to feel wet and I struggled to get to my feet, afraid Leonard would think I wet my pants in fear. In the process, I noticed Peter's empty right hand and began searching the perimeter of the car. Next to the passenger door, I found a black paper hinged ring box with a snapping turtle painted on top.

My heart raced as I looked inside and found a rolled up note. I retrieved my reading glasses from my pocket and quickly inspected them to make sure they were still intact after the fall.

Dennis,

If you're reading this—congratulations for finally following my directions and saving a turtle!

Sorry, but I have to be a bit vague in case someone else stumbles across this note before you do—or you never show up. Apologies too for the IOU. Please don't be as upset as I know you are. You probably think I spent it at the track. Surprise! I didn't, but hope you will. If you're reading this after March 20th then it's too late and you can simply repay the crook I borrowed it from. If not, you have a chance of a lifetime to redeem yourself.

Let me explain. A few years back, I got in tight with some jockeys down in Florida then had a falling out. When I got sick, I took a trip down to set things straight with one of them. Suffice it to say, when I mentioned stage 4 lung cancer he thought I would be dead any minute and we drank a little too much tequila. He gave me two great tips. The first one bankrolled the diner I bought Kate.

The second tip is a whale of an opportunity on a horse everyone gave up on, except one dedicated trainer. That's where you come in. I left the $10k buried in Jean's front yard with the details on the race. You can close your mouth now before you get lockjaw. Yes, I'm talking about the only woman you fretted over more than your wife, and is now sleeping in the same neighborhood. Use the money to snag my big payday. Then you can pay off the loan and give the rest to M.B. Money can't buy happiness, but it sure can help finance a better life for her and Rosa.

I know you think I had a grand plan, and I did thanks to Peter. Studying him made me reflect on a good and simple man who denied his best friend three times out of fear. But he was forgiven and that gave him the courage to do some incredible things in his life and truly become the Rock. I learned when his time came he showed his love by being crucified upside down. I had an upside down cross tattooed on my arm to encourage me never to give up, no matter how difficult things became near the end.

I'll look up Merriam and get ready for the party when you join us. I hope you're very late.

I love you, buddy. Now make me proud!

Jack

CHAPTER FORTY-ONE

The picturesque New England cottage with weathered wood shingles sat a good two hundred feet back from the road, and if you ignored the utility lines feeding electricity and cable, you could easily imagine life two hundred years ago. Ten feet from the front door, a well-used bamboo rake with a few missing teeth leaned against an ornamental cherry tree that would turn stunning in another month.

The red front door opened as I approached and a cute black woman about forty stepped out wearing a Boston Red Sox cap and a Hollywood smile. "Hello, Dennis," she said like she'd known me since grade school.

I noticed she was as thin as Jack and watched her slowly descend three granite steps. "How do you know me?"

The smile never disappeared as she pointed to my head. "Because I dated that hat of yours for six months."

The image of Jack holding Sarah in the hospice flashed in my mind and I tried to hide my confusion by extending my hand. "Then you must be Barbara."

Her skin felt warm and soft. "Yes, and it's so nice to finally meet you."

I couldn't help myself. "You said you dated Jack?"

Barbara's brown eyes looked too big for the frail face and she giggled like a teenager and removed the baseball cap for a moment, revealing a purple bandana underneath. "No, I said I had a relationship with his hat, silly," she said, giving me a friendly push. "I met Jack in chemo. He was like a big brother and gave my poor husband a break.

Joe is out running errands or I would love for him to finally meet you. Jack used to park that hat of yours on my head and promise its good luck would be infused too." She looked down at my green pants and put her hand to her mouth. "Sorry, I used it all up."

I chuckled. "I'm still counting there's a few drops left. But that still doesn't explain how you knew it was me since Jack only left me his hat this morning."

Barbara hesitated like she'd said too much and knew it. "You get to know someone really well when you're tethered to an IV for hours. Jack told me so much about you I could pick you out of a police lineup." She touched my arm. "Not like some cartoon character, mind you, but someone who shared his adventures. He told me the story about you buying hot dogs at the butcher every week to make me laugh."

I blushed. "Yeah, I never lived that one down."

She touched my arm again. "Please let me hear your version so I can tell if he was exaggerating."

I tipped my hat back. "Well, after I got out of the service I was living alone and decided to buy some hot dogs for dinner so I drove over to Haverhill Beef. I took my place in line and studied a long row of refrigerated cases holding immense trophies of beef, chicken, and pork.

"Behind the cases, a team of butchers with blood-covered aprons were in constant motion as they proudly worked to fill every order. The line moved slowly as each customer seemed to want two pounds of everything in the case. Finally, my turn came.

"'Can I help you?' a young butcher inquired intently.

"'Yes, I'd like some Essem hot dogs,' I said.

"'Sure. How many, sir?' the butcher asked, sliding open a door and reaching into a massive box containing the national strategic reserve of Essem frankfurts.

"The butcher looked annoyed with my hesitation. 'How many dozen, sir?' he repeated,

"'Two, please,' I replied.

"The butcher looked disappointed. A puny order and no blood to smear on his apron. 'Okay, two dozen it is!'

"'No, no, no!' I said. 'I want *two* hot dogs.'

"The butcher studied me for a long second. 'Oh, I see, you're expecting company for dinner tonight,' he said sarcastically."

Barbara nodded and laughed with gusto, which made me understand why Jack told it.

I quickly glanced at the two small windows on either side of the front door.

"Jack's not here." She looked at the Escort. "If you had a faster car you might have caught him before he left an hour ago. I promised not to answer the door if you showed up, but couldn't resist meeting you." She giggled again. "I heard you're having a lively week."

I rubbed my forehead as another headache began. "How could Jack have the strength to visit you? He's at death's door."

"I guess he hasn't rung the bell yet or no one is answering, though he's in pretty tough shape and could hardly talk. He arrived in a white van and some big muscle guy wheeled him to the door."

"Who was he?"

She shrugged. "I don't know, though he acted like a male nurse that Jack hired. I didn't sense they knew one another."

"So why did he come here?" I asked then winced. "Sorry, I didn't mean it that way. I know you meant a lot to him."

Barbara walked over to the bamboo rake and picked up a manila envelope hiding behind its teeth. She let me peek in at dozen dark bulbs. "Allium are in the onion family and produce the most delicate flowers and are the stars of a spring garden. They're hardy enough to grow in any type of soil and are drought, deer, and rodent resistant." She cleared her throat. "These are called purple sensations and Jack said they remind him of me." She quickly wiped one eye with a long slender finger then beamed another courageous smile. "He made me promise I'd be here next spring to see them flower."

The bulbs looked as lifeless as rocks, but held the potential of a spectacular future. "All I've seen this week is one example after another of how fragile life is in every season," I said more to myself than her. "Where's Jack headed?"

"I think we both know where."

"No, I mean now? I don't understand why he left me alone like this. We have been through so much together and I promised to be with him until the end."

Barbara reached in the envelope and handed me one of the bulbs. "Some things in life are meant to be done alone. *For everything there is a season, and a time for every matter in heaven: a time to be born, and a time to die. A time to plant and a time to pluck up what is planted.*"

She stood there silent, looking at me. I shuffled my feet, wanting to ask how she got through to Jack when no one else could.

"Take a lesson from your good friend, Dennis. Embrace life and use the hands God gave you to make a difference."

CHAPTER FORTY-TWO

Facts sometimes don't tell the whole story. Jack knew my wife and Jean Bradley were both buried in Pine Grove Cemetery. However, in reality the poor lady I drove to madness might as well have been buried on the dark side of the moon because my shadow never fell on her grave. I had remained determined to keep it that way and specifically inquired about the location of her final resting place before Merriam chose our plot. Concrete liners or not, having those accusing eyes staring at me until the Second Coming gave me the heebie-jeebies even thinking about it.

The gruff groundskeeper in the cemetery office typed Jean Bradley's name into a laptop.

"She's buried in plot B27 over on Oak Terrace," he'd said, writing it down on a piece of scrap paper. "It's in a small cove about a quarter mile up the road. It just so happens I'm headed over there to prep for another burial tomorrow. If you want, I can show you her grave." He grabbed a tan jacket off a hook that matched his cargo pants.

"That won't be necessary," I'd replied so quickly it came out sounding like one word. The look he gave me was priceless. He must have thought Jean was my mistress and I was guilt ridden for eternity.

So here I was walking to a destination I vowed never to visit and with Jack still calling the shots. I considered stopping by Merriam's grave first, hoping my late wife would give me the courage to see this last mission through. This time I ignored the impulse, afraid she would lecture me and I wasn't in the mood to listen today. I knew there would be plenty of time behind bars to reflect on this week.

And it wouldn't only be Merriam who would rattle my ear drums. Soon, I faced a day of reckoning with Mark, Stu, Kate, Mrs. Werner, and a parade of police and lawyers, all eager to judge and blab on and on like I was a two-year-old. I was sure Linda would even get into the act and somehow work into the indictment that I bought her boxed wine and brought my son up sitting on imitation leather that exuded multiple carcinogens. There were no words this side of heaven to hold back the approaching verbal tsunami, and no life vest to prevent from drowning in it. All I wanted now was to surgically extract the ten grand from the gravesite and pay off Leonard so if I ever got out of jail, I would have a home to return to even if it came with an ankle bracelet.

The sky brightened and I noticed a few green clumps of grass where the sun played favorites. Spring would not be denied much longer no matter how many times winter pulled a hissy fit. I looked in the direction of my wife's grave and recalled the words which sustained me for so long:

Winter will no doubt come again,
Unannounced and uninvited,
As it does for each of us.
But with His help you will endure,
And rejoice in each new spring.

As I walked along, I realized it wouldn't be much longer before I joined her too. In reality, how many springs did I really have left? The thought snuck up on me from time to time, but didn't bother me like it did years ago. Actually, there were many lonely nights I longed for the end despite leaving my son behind with his stuck-up girlfriend.

"I miss you, honey," I whispered and the cool air made my eyes sting. It had been a while since I last choked up thinking about my wife and it surprised me today. You think you know a person after you live and love and work together as life lulls you into complacency. But Merriam's illness paraded into our lives without warning and shattered our routine. Then I noticed every subtle change. Our remaining time reminded me of flying. You think you're standing still, until you look out the window and see another plane flying by in the opposite direction. A moment later it's gone and so was Merriam.

I took a deep breath, knowing we did our best to appreciate those final months together. There were flashes when she would have a good day, or more likely when she applied enough makeup to hide how bad she felt. We would go out for a walk or a long ride in the country and pretend everything remained okay; there was no talk of chemo, chills, fever, hair loss, and shortness of breath. We turned off our cell phones too. As much we loved our son, family, and friends, we needed a timeout from the daily calls that always started with "How are you feeling?"

Truth be told, it was her good days that sometimes depressed me the most. We would be laughing and I would have flashbacks of our life together. There were so many good memories, but her cancer made me see many snapshots marred with a few missing pixels. They represented all the opportunities missed, when I could have added color and texture and chose not to. Each morning, I used to wake to the smell of jasmine with Merriam nestled in beside me. I was always too quick to jump up to go to work or run errands, instead of lying there to hold and love her.

Now there was no perfume, no partner and best friend; only a cold faceless pillow that could not love me back.

I stopped walking to rub my eyes because now I discovered Merriam had all this poetic beauty inside her that I was oblivious to. Her words touched a place inside me deeper than Jean's grave. They pulled me up from the darkness so I could go on, handicapped for sure, but still functioning. I suddenly realized why I didn't want to visit my wife's grave today. It wasn't the fear of her barking at my stupidity. No, quite the opposite. I was terrified I would collapse at her grave and never accomplish what I needed to do.

I quickened my pace and the cold sweat on my brow confirmed how much I dreaded the destination. Five minutes later, I was searching for Jean Bradley's grave, worried the groundskeeper gave me bum information. "B27 sounds more like a WWII bomber or a bingo number than a grave site," I mumbled, questioning my recall.

I prepared for another visit to the cemetery office, when I almost tripped over a small white marble marker that simply read "Bradley." While all the neighboring stones recorded the beginning and end dates—as if anybody outside family and friends really cared—Jean's marker simply confirmed she once graced earth.

I looked around at all the silent stone sentries encircling me, and I pulled the brim of Jack's hat down low, hoping not to be recognized. Seconds passed and heaven didn't strike me dead.

As I knelt, my hands shook badly and my mind replayed Jack's instructions.

"I am so sorry, Jean," I whispered, panting hard enough to penetrate the frost line. There were no signs M.B. ever planted flowers in front of the grave so in some sense winter resided here year round. My heart pounded in my ears as I felt along the front of the marker. Suddenly, my pinkie caught a small piece of loose rock. I took my car keys and worked at scraping away the hard topsoil in order to pry up one end. Underneath, I found a white Tyvek envelope.

I stood up much too quickly and bent over, hoping not to faint. Jean's sad eyes greeted me again as they did every night. "I am so sorry," I repeated softly. "You've been here for so long and I've spent all those years wandering in the desert knowing why."

Jean didn't reply to my pleas. She never did.

"And why has it always been about money with us?" I asked, stuffing the envelope in my jacket. "I promise to come back and make a respectful visit when I can."

A blue jay squawked loudly from a nearby maple tree like she didn't believe me.

I bit my lip. "Believe it or not, you taught me not to make promises I don't intend to keep." I took out my black bifold wallet and fished out the silver Polara key. It looked as worn as it did in 1974. I knelt down. "I should never have accepted this," I said, burying it where I extracted the envelope. I wiped my hands in the grass then touched the stone. "It's a shame no one brings you flowers."

Inside the car, I inspected a tight pack of hundred-dollar bills held together with a thick red rubber band.

"Enough is enough," I said, holding the ransom money to save my house. If I ever got hold of Jack on the other side, I planned to give him quite a shiner.

While I counted the bills, a green Post-it Note fell out.

Race: March 21, Dubai, $5M purse.
Go see Paco to make the transaction.
For the first time in your life, take a risk!
No matter how it pans out, you will find peace. Lean on Peter.
This is my final wish: so don't deny me or yourself.

Be Strong,

Jack

I looked around, feeling like I was being watched by the living and the dead. Glancing in the direction of Jean's grave, I remembered looking through the showroom window at a mother and child standing next to a lemon. I failed them both over money and fear and where did that get me other than feeding a laminated prayer card every night as penance? Maggie and Rosa deserved more.

Studying the instructions again in earnest made my heart race. I looked carefully through all the hundred-dollar bills for another note. When I came up empty-handed, I laughed so hard I lost my breath.

"Jack, you always accused me of being a numbers guy, but you never understood success depends on attention to details. This time you really messed up. You forgot to tell me what horse to bet on!"

CHAPTER FORTY-THREE

Paco had been conducting business from the same bar stool for as long as I could remember. Office hours commenced when the Grog opened at 6 a.m. with its infamous "hangover breakfast," until it transitioned to standard pub fare at noon. In similar fashion, Paco took the first bet of the day with coffee and the last with scotch. He ran a tight operation, recorded the wagers himself and only from people he knew. It was a sober strategy after an ambitious expansion plan in his earlier days came crashing down. Three years behind bars taught him it paid to control your appetite.

It was mid-afternoon when I finally made it to the restaurant and found the old bookie hunched over a coffee mug and sitting alone. Paco made quite a character with shaggy dyed blond hair which constantly surfed the collar of a blue silk shirt. He wore a signature tan sport coat, tattered around the edges. Whenever Paco strolled around town, heads would turn and whispers would follow in his wake. Others living on the edge of the law would shun this type of attention, or hide behind their surname. Not this guy. Paco had apparently decided long ago to develop his personal brand by dropping Francis in favor of a nickname. No one knew his last name and in border communities of New Hampshire and Massachusetts he didn't need one.

Some brands are timeless. Pushing seventy-five, Paco was still very active in the "retail business," and Jack boasted the old man had enough stashed away to buy a small island. Their relationship had survived all types of weather and some were as cold and windy as a night on Mount Washington. I intervened once in the early days, when

Paco exacted painful penalties if delinquent. Jack fell behind and I made one installment payment on his behalf, as Jack feared his knee caps would be whacked if he showed up himself. Over time they came to respect each other and appreciate the co-dependency.

Taking a deep breath, I sat down on a black leather stool beside him.

Paco must have been blessed with terrific peripheral vision because his eyes never ventured from the beige stoneware mug he studied.

"Nice hat," he said.

I took it off and put it on the glossy wooden bar with the logo facing him, hoping it would bathe us in whatever luck it still held.

"Jack and I made a bet last month whether you would show up. I thought the odds were in my favor, but your buddy always had a soft spot for the underdog. Now I owe him a fifth of Grey Goose," he said. "Funny I should end up owing him." He took a sip of coffee and rubbed a small crop of white whiskers under his lip he apparently missed shaving this morning. "We're both cut from the same cloth, but when all is said and done, he turned out different. He's sorry for his mistakes. I'm still waiting to feel anything but thirsty for an after dinner scotch."

"Well, up until an hour ago you would have won," I replied, biting my lip.

He finally turned and looked at me. The eyes were pale green and with the warmth of a shark.

"Has he called you today by any chance?"

Paco smirked. "I don't think they have phone service up there yet, do they?"

I shook my head. "No, that's not what I mean. I think he's dead, but I don't know for sure. It's a long story, but we were together at the hospice visiting Sarah and he was in really bad shape. I fell asleep and he vanished. I've called his brother and every hospital in the area but no one has seen him."

Paco squinted and pushed me hard enough that I almost fell off the stool. "You couldn't stay awake for one night to see him through?"

I nodded in shame.

"That man could be an unbelievable handful and he knew it. But Jack would flash that million-dollar smile of his and convince you into carrying him for another day. I know the two of you were best friends and that proves opposites do attract." He frowned and gave me a once-over before returning to his coffee. "According to Jack, you think too much," he said matter of fact. "If I learned one thing in life, that's the equivalent of kryptonite."

I nodded in agreement. "Not if you have a hoodlum chasing you."

Paco smiled, apparently in the know. "Leo has short man complex and tries to be a bully," he said in a long drawl to spray paint the insult sufficiently. "But if you were that scared, you'd be handing him an envelope instead of sitting here."

"How are you sure I didn't?" I asked, hating a know-it-all.

"Because you can't kid a kidder." He raised his hand and an attractive young brunette appeared out of nowhere and brought him a fresh mug of steaming coffee. The aroma was better than whatever bathroom cologne Paco showered himself in.

I raised my hand, hoping to order.

"You can have coffee in the other section when we're done. "Your seat is for transactions only and not idle chitchat."

I looked around. We were the only two at the bar and of the thirty or so tables, all but three were empty. "I never figured out why Jack liked you so much. You're nothing but a crook, and a rude one at that."

My words didn't penetrate the steel exterior and he took another sip of the black elixir.

"Be careful you don't burn yourself."

Paco let out a short laugh. "Glad to see you show some moxie. From the little Jack told me of his plan, I guess you deserve a little respect by now. Not a lot, mind you, but some." He waved to the waitress to get her attention. "Bring my new client an espresso," he said loudly then returned to his mug. "She makes a great one in less than a minute; just like this transaction."

I raked my hand through my dirty hair, which looked weird being ultra-short in the back and with no sideburns. How do I ask the next question without appearing stupid? I knew less about horse racing than almost anything else in life. The only insight I had was watching its manic-depressive effect on Jack.

"Okay, what's next?" I asked vaguely.

"How much are we talking about?"

"If you're asking me if I skimmed anything, the answer is no. Ten grand."

"What race?" he asked, taking out a small black notebook from his vest pocket.

My stomach knotted up as I hoped Jack had pre-communicated all the details. Either the bookie was playing with me or Jack didn't trust Paco as much as I always thought.

"Dubai," I said with confidence.

There was a heavy sigh. "Okay, let's speed this up. Which race?"

"The one with the five-million-dollar purse."

Paco nodded and looked at his gold watch. "They're nine hours ahead, so the race will be four in the morning our time." He made another quick note. "Jack did tell me you would be placing a straight bet. What horse are you riding?"

I hesitated and put on a stupid look, which wasn't hard. I held my breath, hoping Paco would shake his head and tell me.

Instead, the old bookie became aggravated. "C'mon, man, I don't have all day to coach you through this. I have a living to make."

The espresso arrived and I drank it down in one swallow, feeling the burn all the way down. "I don't know," I finally replied, staring at the dark oak counter. "Our good friend left out that one crucial detail."

Paco let out a low whistle and then grew silent for a long moment. "If it was anyone other than Jack, I would enjoy the biggest laugh of the day. Then I would tell you to go pay off that little runt Leonard because you're done."

I watched him mull over the options for an eternity and kept silent.

"Jack was a sly fox; he wouldn't leave you hanging like this."

"Unless he wanted me to rob a bank instead."

"Which you may have to if this gig doesn't work out." Paco reached slowly into his vest pocket and took out his iPhone.

"Let's see," he said, tapping on the screen then waiting for the app to load. "Okay, here we go. There are eighteen horses running." Paco showed me the screen. "Any names look familiar?"

I took the phone from him and squinted to read the list, feeling overwhelmed and trying to find meaning in "Man of War" and

"Saturday Silence." When I came to the last name on the page I sucked in my breath. "One-Eyed Jack," I said much too loud and the pretty waitress looked our way.

My excitement was lost on Paco. He leaned in close to study the program. "I don't give advice and no doubt you're sweet for that horse because of the name, but he's a dog and a slow one at that. He was scratched three times last year with leg issues. If you don't believe me, take a look for yourself." He pointed at the screen. "The odds are twenty-two to one. You'd be nuts to go with him." Then he glanced at my green bell bottoms. "Yeah, right."

I recalled the note from Jack: *The second tip is about a horse that everyone gave up on, except one dedicated trainer.* Scanning the roster one more time, I concluded this must be the horse. Knowing Jack, he probably had a hand in naming him too.

Putting on the most confident look I could muster, I slid the envelope in front of Paco. "Ten grand on One-Eyed Jack."

"Okay, it's your funeral," he replied, taking the envelope. "My take is still ten percent."

"Is that standard?"

Paco moaned. "Actually, it's fifteen percent but Jack and I go way back. Get out of here before I change my mind."

"How will I get hold of you if I win?"

"You should be more worried where I'll find you if you lose." Paco handed me my hat. "If I were you I'd rub the hat and hope there's a genie hiding somewhere inside the fabric." He glanced again at my green pants. "You better rub extra hard."

CHAPTER FORTY-FOUR

It was dark when I finally made it back to Haverhill after spending a couple hours driving around aimlessly on back roads and contemplating the risk I just took. At every stop sign along the way, I expected the passenger door to fly open and Jack would slide into the cockpit with a bag of seedless oranges he collected from some random house.

Knocking on M.B.'s door made me wish Jack was standing next to me so he could sell her on forgiving me. Hearing the heavy footsteps approach, I imagined her inviting me in to rest and share some chicken soup with Rosa. Irrational perhaps, but not outside the realm of possibility given the last few days. But when the door opened, it was clear my hasty confession had taken root in M.B.'s sour expression. The dark circles under her eyes reminded me of a raccoon.

"Any word from Jack?" I asked sheepishly.

She shook her head and avoided my eyes while holding out her hand so I could forfeit the car keys. I knew the second I surrendered them, the door would close for good.

"Maggie, I don't expect you to understand because I've never forgiven myself," I began quickly, before she could cement her ears shut. "I know the word sorry cannot span the gulf between the little mistakes we make each day and leaving you an orphan."

I looked down at my hands. Once they were smooth and strong, now they were peppered with age spots and trembling. "I know you think I must have been a selfish, stubborn, and insensitive jerk and I agree. However, after tormenting myself all these years over what happened, I realize my weakness was out of fear. It's one thing to be ruthless and rationalize everything away because you think you're some sort of rainmaker. It's more painful to know I acted like a coward to hold onto a stupid job my father arranged."

M.B.'s hand was still extended. "Spare me the psychoanalysis, Dennis. I've had enough deathbed confessions this week," she said flatly. "Although I do wish your buddy was still on my couch so I could chew him out about this grand intervention of his." She stuck a pointed finger in my face. "And where is the two hundred bucks Jack owes me and the hundred you promised for taking my car?"

"I promise I won't stiff you. Just give me a couple days and I'll make sure to get it to you with interest." I fingered the zipper on my ugly rented coat. "I'll throw in a bit extra for keeping the coat too," I said, handing her the keys. The door began to close then suddenly stopped.

"My father took off before I was born, just like Rosa's did. I was too young to remember much, except we were moving far enough south we would never be cold again. I promised my daughter a new beginning too." She hesitated and her dark eyes glistened. "I know that car represented a better life for us, though I don't know why she had to steal that junk instead of fleeing by bus or train."

I recalled Jean telling me how Hank the plumber promised her the car but decided to spare the details.

M.B.'s face hardened again and she backed away. "I have nothing left to say except get me my money."

The door closed in my face.

I walked slowly away, listening to my shoes scuff the sandpaper-like sidewalk heavy with grittiness from winter. The race was hours away and I only had thirty bucks left thanks to Jack and the Republic Bank.

"Okay, Merriam, where can I get some sleep?" I looked skyward then remembered my living room on wheels.

I cut across Essex Street and took a position in Lafayette's Square across the street from Haffner's gas station. I watched car after car gas up. Finally, a gawky teenager in a beat up Chevy truck with New Hampshire plates pulled up to the pump. He reached deep into his torn dungarees and counted out a handful of dollar bills to the cashier behind the glass. A minute later, after convincing him I was not a disco ghost and flashing twenty bucks, we headed back to Restful Waters. He let me out on Route 28 and I walked down the long driveway quickly, hoping my car hadn't been towed yet. To my relief, it was still sitting there like a faithful dog.

I slid behind a tall pine and pulled my hood up and waited.

A half hour later I was courting hypothermia and tired of debating if I should take the risk. With Jack probably in the morgue by now, I couldn't imagine the police using their limited resources to stake out my car.

Taking a deep breath, I made a run for it and found the hidden key under the rear fender. The Caddy crawled slowly out of the parking lot with no blue flashing lights in pursuit. Feeling the leather heated seats warm my bottom made me remember the normal life I used to lead and I missed it. However, no matter how much I blasted the heat, my teeth continued to chatter.

It was late and not wanting to attract attention with so few cars on the road, I threaded my way through a series of neighborhoods, feeling envious of the homes with two cars in the driveway and the warm glow of a living room light illuminating family life. When I reached Main Street, I pulled in behind St. Joseph's Church. Merriam loved the small fieldstone church her father helped build in 1929, and I wished they still honored the tradition of providing sanctuary for fugitives like they did in the middle ages. It would be better to wait out the rest of my days within the safety of the fieldstone church than risk the rack Leonard wanted to torture me on.

Luckily, the side door of the church was open and I rushed past St. Joseph's statue, averting my eyes from his judgmental stare. If he was disappointed in me as a husband and father, I shuddered to think what he thought of my activities this week.

The last pew in the church was as hard as all the others and far enough away from the tabernacle for a sinner like me. I genuflected then sat down and for a long minute closed my eyes and absorbed the silence, remembering the strength Merriam found here as the cancer spread.

When I opened my eyes, exhaustion washed over me. The church was dimly lit, with the exception of the red glow of a candle to the right of the tabernacle and a massive crucifix illuminated and hanging high above the altar. What daylight muted now stood out in sharp contrast. Even from a distance, the agony looked truly heartbreaking. I studied His outstretched arms, counted the five wounds, focused on the crown of thorns. It occurred to me how much Jesus suffered through each night alone.

My conscience asked why I decided to come here now. I could kid myself and count off a handful of reasons or face the truth and acknowledge it was to beg God to *deliver me from evil* by fixing the race in Dubai. Rubbing my face, I knew I had no right to think I could swing by the church in the middle of the night and cut a deal. And what would I offer in return? Attend church every Sunday, volunteer at the food pantry, or throw some coins in the poor box? A wave of shame swept over me as I realized I'd never visited this church to plead for my wife or Jack. Merriam went to her death, confident nothing but love waited on the other side. Jack found Peter and tattooed an upside down cross on his arm as a reminder it was never too late to overcome past failures and find the courage to make a difference in the time he had left. And me? I wouldn't let God forgive me because I never forgave myself.

I suddenly felt small and cowardly like I did at Henley's. A lifetime had passed over the last few days and I did feel a change. I looked up at the cross hoping He saw it too.

The minutes passed and my paralysis deepened; I didn't know what to say or do. I finally moved to the kneeler and bowed my head. "I'm sorry for the mess I made and even sorrier for what I didn't do," I whispered. Like my apology to Maggie, it was heartfelt, but felt so insignificant. Smashed turtles came to mind and I understood the reason for so many failed attempts. I always put myself first. Same was true tonight. "I'll accept whatever punishment comes my way, Lord. I pray Jack is with You and may perpetual light always shine upon him. Please give me the strength to see this through no matter how it turns out."

At 4:00 a.m. I arrived outside Paco's apartment. It was easy to find his headquarters, as he lived above the Grog. Not a bad commute, especially after a second scotch to top off a good day.

I waited another five minutes in case my watch wasn't aligned with Greenwich Mean Time. Walking to the small side door that led up to his apartment, I touched the brim of Jack's hat. I sniffed the air hoping to smell jasmine, but my nose began to run in the cold air. I hesitated waking up the old bookie, but the news outweighed any consideration of the time. I wondered why Jack chased this adrenaline rush his entire life as it only made me want to throw up.

Exhaling slowly, I watched the smoke escape my nostrils before pressing the button and hearing a nasty buzzer.

I looked up and the windows on the second floor remained dark. After three minutes I pressed the doorbell again. This time I held the button until my ears were ringing too.

A light came on in the upper front right window and I waited five minutes considering Paco's age and how stiff I was in the morning. When he still didn't come to the door, I lost my remaining patience and banged twice on the white metal door.

"Who is it?" a frightened voice yelled from the other side. Apparently, the old guy had been standing there listening for some time. Considering his line of work, I understood and feared he had a gun pointed at me.

"Paco, it's Dennis," I said in a friendly voice.

"Who?"

I took two steps back and to the right so he could see a piece of me through the peephole and in case he shot through the door he might miss. "It's Jack's friend Dennis."

The door opened an inch and the shark eye looked out from behind a thick gold chain.

"Have you lost your mind banging on my door and waking me up in the middle of the night?" he said hoarsely. "What do you want?"

I looked up and down the street. There was a dog barking somewhere in the neighborhood, but we were alone. "I'm so sorry to wake you, but I need to know how the race turned out."

"You're an inconsiderate idiot!" Paco yelled. "I could have your legs broken with one call. Come a little closer and I'll do it myself."

"I'm so sorry," I said, almost choking on the words. Too many apologies and none accepted.

"With twenty-two to one odds, I would have received ten calls by now if you won. You don't hear my phone ringing, do you?"

The door slammed shut then opened again just as quickly.

"And give that runt Leonard my regards, because he'll be doing me a favor when he knocks some sense into you."

CHAPTER FORTY-FIVE

Sitting in my car across the street from the Dawg House early Friday morning, I thought about another breakfast missed. While I had a passion for cereal and the multiple varieties of grain which highlighted the beginning of each day, eggs might well define my future. The only question was whether I would be scrambled, fried, or cracked open like a hardboiled idiot.

With that happy thought, I scanned the streets. It was early and only a random car or pedestrian passed and none checked out my fancy wheels. Jack thought I drove around in my living room, but my '93 Fleetwood was the ninetieth anniversary model from Cadillac. I bought it ten years ago from an old man who purchased it new then imprisoned it in his garage until he couldn't drive. Granted, it looked a bit dated compared with the new edgy models from GM, but I loved the ride.

A college-aged kid jogged by in a Merrimack College sweatshirt taking advantage of the temperature in the mid-forties and the beginning of spring. When I was a working stiff, I used to occasionally take a Friday off to play catch-up with chores around the yard. Now the pendulum swung to the opposite extreme and I spent my days stretching out the smallest project to fight boredom. I had my routine; do a little grocery shopping then enjoy some mid-morning coffee with a handful of other old bored guys hanging around Dunkin' Donuts. It was a far cry far from the retirement I imagined.

I found myself shivering even with the heater on high and it made me think back to Jack robbing the bank. At the time, I thought it was the cancer making him so cold. Now I knew otherwise. My teeth bounced off one another as if an electric current was running through the enamel. After a lifetime of watching Jack chase one loser after another, how did he make me bet everything on this long shot when I had so much at stake? I held the ten grand in my hand and all I had to do was pay off the crook and be free of him. No, I swung for the fences just like Jack always did and like him, lost everything. I thought about going to the police and begging for them to intervene. Would they listen to an old man after committing all those crimes? Maybe a better idea was to stop by the fire station and give them a heads-up to have an early lunch as they would have a busy afternoon.

I had one lifeline left and dialed his number.

The phone connected immediately. "Dad, I just landed at Logan and I'm on my way to get the rental car," Mark said in a rush.

"It's good to have you back home son. Listen, I'm sorry how our call went yesterday. The reason I'm—"

"Where are you?" he asked, interrupting me.

"Let's not start this again. I'm in my car," I replied quickly. "Look. Right now I need you to trust me. I got myself in a jam and need some money really quick."

"How much?"

"I'm disappointed you didn't ask about what type of trouble I'm in before focusing on the money. I need ten grand," I replied casually, like it was only ten bucks except for some extra zeros. "Since we have a joint account, I need you to cash out one of my certificate of deposits and meet me. And please don't lecture me about the penalty clause. I don't care."

"You really have me worried. Where are you?"

"What did I say? Don't use your lawyer tactics on me. Are you going to get me the money or what? I have a bill and it's due this morning and this guy doesn't take a check so get it in cash. I'd like to tick him off and pay him in dollar bills, but I just want to be done with him so take it out in hundreds." I turned the heater fan down so he could hear me more clearly. "And believe me, you don't want to hear about what happens if I don't pay him off."

There was a long pause.

"Mark, are you still there?"

"I'm here, Dad," he replied, sounding tired. "Let's wait and figure things out together."

"Wait? That's been my middle name and I'm dropping it. From now on wait is a four-letter word." I slapped the steering wheel.

"And how is being rash working out for you this week? That's a four-letter word too."

Evidently, I wasn't getting the money and didn't have the time or energy to persuade him. I busted my butt to raise a family and build a little nest egg, and here I was begging for an allowance.

"Forget it. But when this is all over, we're going to have a long talk, Mark. And yes, this time I am hanging up on you." I threw the phone on the floor. If part of his inheritance went up in flames, so be it.

Entering the club, I tried to repeat the strut I had back at M.B.'s apartment when I first put on the leisure suit, but my knees felt too wobbly and consequently I waddled like a duck. Big Dawg stood guard inside the door of the club wearing a Grateful Dead T-shirt like yesterday and this felt like a scene out of *Groundhog Day*. The big guy nodded with that sarcastic grin of his and pointed toward the table by the bar where Mr. Leonard enjoyed another hearty breakfast. Besides wanting to straighten out my son after this was over, I planned to commit one more crime. I would pay someone handsomely to hack into the social security database and delete Norman from the system to really mess with his head.

Mr. Leonard played his leading role flawlessly and continued enjoying the same breakfast as yesterday except substituting scrambled eggs instead of fried. He didn't look up, which I figured was designed to put me on edge, but the pause allowed me to catch my breath for the upcoming fight. I couldn't recall the last hearty breakfast I enjoyed and was beyond tired of watching other people stuff their mouths. Leonard was a punk and I decided my best shot of surviving the upcoming inquisition depended on taking the initiative.

In a flash, I reached down and grabbed a slice of bacon off his plate, careful to steal a whole piece as only heaven knew what germs he carried. I was in and out before he could react and my right hand remained free of stab marks.

Surprise spread across the loan shark's face, but only for an instant. He pushed the dish toward me and checked out my leisure suit.

"Times must be tough for Mister Saturday Night to pull a stunt like that. Especially if you want to keep all your fingers."

I sat across from him and nibbled slowly on the bacon. It tasted as burnt as yesterday. "It just upsets me to no end when I run across a youngster with no manners. I let it slip yesterday, but two days in a row?"

Leo adjusted his glasses. "You were here yesterday? I only recall meeting with an old, ugly nun." Then he smiled, showing off a mouthful of veneers. "Sinned is the name, right? Love the hat, although I think it clashes with the outfit."

His strong comeback meant I had to up the ante. I took a piece of toast off the plate and used his knife to spread some marmalade on it. He watched me intently and I worked hard to keep my hand from shaking. I took a good-sized bite and chewed slowly, all the time watching him watch me. He waited for me to swallow and I knew it would really spoil the drama if I started choking now. I imagined him spelling my last name for the ambulance personnel: S-I-N-N-E-D.

Leonard lit a cigarette and I knew I had five minutes max before my fate was sealed. "Well, have you come to seek penance?"

"Actually, I'm here to tell you I may be my brother's keeper but not his banker," I replied. "So you'll have to take it up with Jack when you see him next. Although I'm not sure you will." I glanced at the half-eaten breakfast. "But don't worry none. I'm sure they burn the bacon down there just the way you like it."

Suddenly, the plate flew toward my head and I ducked just in time as it continued on and landed on the dark floor. If I wasn't terrified, it would be funny telling him how he and Kate shared the same nasty habit when they got angry. I glanced at the devastation on the floor and noted the scrambled eggs sitting in little clumps. They looked extra dry and made me glad I sampled the toast and bacon instead.

"Old stray dogs sleep in the alley across the street and so will you when your house is torched today," he said barely above a whisper.

"Well, I can always go back to the convent and pray for you." I pulled my hat down tight.

Leo blew smoke in my face and snapped his fingers and Norman appeared. Leo's cigarette was only halfway done, but clearly I miscalculated the window of opportunity.

"Okay, I'll make a deal," I said minus the bravado.

"You're in no position to make a deal. I want my money and I don't see an envelope in front of me."

"If I could write you a check I would, but it would bounce and just get you more upset than you are now. My son lives out west and he won't lend me a dime and believe me when I tell you that's no lie. Even my house is in a trust." I rubbed my temple for dramatic effect. "I even thought about setting up an installment plan with you, but Jack got me in quite a jam with the law so I'm facing some hefty legal fees. The only thing I have left is my beautiful car," I said with real tears in my eyes. "And to put an end to all this madness, I'm willing to give my sweet ride to you," I added quickly, hoping to explain my offer before being pummeled.

For the first time in two days, Leonard looked interested. "What kind of car is it?"

"A Cadillac."

Big Dawg let out a good belly laugh. "Ask him what year it is."

"It's a ninety-three Fleetwood and they don't make rides like that anymore. It's their anniversary model," I said, realizing it was the first car I tried to sell in forty years and feared like last time the outcome would be tragic. My stomach churned at the thought of poetic justice.

Leo smiled broadly and I studied his false teeth, which looked too big for his small face.

"Tell you what I'm going to do," he said, standing up and looking down on me. "You have a garage, right?"

I nodded. "The original owner kept it garaged too and I have all the maintenance records."

"Well, Big Dawg will make sure to park your sweet ride in the garage with a tank full of gas so it can go boom when we light up your house. I'm thinking of stuffing you in the trunk too, but first I'm going to make you puke up the breakfast you stole from me."

I stood up to meet him. "I guess you're getting antsy to beat up an old man because you're tired of knocking women around."

Leonard snickered. "Ah, poor Mr. Sinned is an old blind knight too," he said sarcastically. "Apparently you can't see white trash."

I lunged at him before processing the thought he might have a gun. Too late, I was committed and learned from my father the best way to tackle a bully was below the knees. Luckily, not much changed from my last encounter with one sixty years ago and down he went. I scrambled to get on top of him to get in a few punches, but he moved too quickly to one side and my head butted his. My nose got momentarily lost in his black hair and I smelled the sweet gel he used. I grabbed his left ear and pulled hard. He let out a short yelp.

Suddenly Norman was lifting me up like a rag doll. It's funny the things that cross your mind in a panic. All I could think about was Houdini and how he challenged men to punch him in the stomach and died when someone hit him before he prepared. I tried to tense my stomach muscles, but they all retreated toward my spine.

"Hey, Leo," a new voice suddenly called out.

I looked around and saw Paco strutting into the room with two large henchmen with long dark hair and matching brown leather coats and blue jeans. It looked like my imminent death was a team sport now.

Mr. Leonard looked flushed and quickly finished rearranging his clothes. His left ear was bright red and he managed to shoot me a murderous look before turning toward the bookie.

"What are you doing here?" he asked.

"I should be asking you the same thing," Paco replied. "Do you have a beef with my associate?"

I wanted to pinch myself, sure I misheard.

"You mean this leftover from the disco era?" Leonard asked with a dismissive laugh. "Well, he owes me ten grand and we were just discussing the terms."

"Interesting dialogue," he chuckled. "From here it looked like the leprechaun was teaching you a thing or two."

"Jack owed him the money, not me," I said even though Paco knew I spent it.

"Loans don't have a past tense with me," Leonard yelled. "Jack made him the guarantor so it's on him."

Paco reached into the vest pocket of his legendary tan sports coat and took out a manila envelope and threw it on the table in front of my torturer. "This is done. Got it?"

Leo inspected the contents then nodded.

The old bookie picked up my hat off the floor, put it on my head, and began guiding me toward the door. We had only traveled a few feet when he stopped and turned around. "One more thing, Leo. Make any more trouble and I'll come back here and kick the rest of the stuffing out of you myself. You're such a sorry-looking punk."

He glared at Big Dawg. "And the same goes for you, Norman. Try anything and by the time I'm done, your new nickname will be Little Pug."

CHAPTER FORTY-SIX

Dazed, I stumbled out of the bar and followed Paco to his black sedan parked in front of my Caddy. I leaned against the hood, feeling the pain in my ribs from tackling Leonard. The bookie stood beside me checking his cell phone for messages.

"What's this all about?" I asked. "I thought I was dead to you."

"Call it a courtesy call for my newest client," Paco said with a smirk. He sniffed the air. "So, this is what morning smells like outside. Who knew?"

"I don't understand. I lost."

"One-Eyed Jack may have been a dog yesterday, but he ran like a possessed fiend today and pulled off the upset of the year. It caused such a ruckus, I didn't get the call until after I gave you grief for waking me up." Paco let out a low whistle. "Man, I'm sure there's quite a story on how Jack got that tip."

I looked up at the cloudless sky. He rescued me even though my name truly was Sinned. "Thank you," I whispered.

"No need to thank me," Paco said, thinking my prayer was meant for him. "I took my cut and figured you'd want me to settle the score with Leo from the proceeds." He reached in his baggy pants and produced a yellowed handkerchief and wiped his face. "Promise me something."

I looked at the old bookie and smiled for the first time in a while and it felt good. "Sure."

"Give up gambling because you don't have the stomach for it."

I laughed. "You don't have to worry about that."

The bookie shoved his handkerchief back in his pocket. "Now get your butt in my car," he said sternly.

"But I don't need a lift," I said, pointing to my car.

Paco's face flashed the same angry look he had at four this morning. One of the hulks that accompanied him opened the back door.

"But we're good, aren't we? You got your commission, Leonard has his ten thousand, and I intend to send Republic Bank a check."

The bookie pushed me forward. "Jack said you think too much, but I think it's all the yakking you do that gets on my nerves."

I held my tongue for fifteen minutes until we reached Geremonty Drive in Salem. I noticed a large white utility truck blocking the entrance to the Field of Dreams. Our car slowed down and the truck backed up so we could pass.

I turned around in my seat and looked out the back window. A man began putting down orange cones to block the entrance.

Saliva pooled in my mouth. "Why are we here?" I asked Paco, riding shotgun in the front seat.

He ignored my question and we continued toward the picnic area and stopped where we had a full view of Peter. I could still make out my tire tracks from yesterday.

"Good thing this park is free or I'd have to buy a season's pass," I said while trying to figure out why Paco would go to all this trouble to kill me off when Leonard would have done it for free. Then it hit me. One-Eyed Jack lost the race but out of respect to Jack he paid Leonard off and now wanted to punish me for being such an expensive pain in the butt. But why here? It was a tricky location too with the Salem Police Station just around the corner. My demise would have to be quiet.

"Get out," Paco said.

"Look, I appreciate all you have done and will repay you. My son just flew in this morning. I can call him and—"

The hulk sitting beside me reached over and opened my door. "You heard what the man said. Get your butt out of the car."

I stumbled out and looked up at Peter, wondering what he thought of this whole tragic affair and betting he didn't have this trouble at the other locations he visited. It seemed to me he should be hanging his head a little lower for steering me wrong and now witnessing my execution. Merriam taught me clothes make a man and if anything my neon green armor would certainly help me "rage against the dying of the light."

A different white utility van pulled into the lot and stopped twenty feet away.

Paco stood next to me with his fake blond hair wafting in the light morning breeze.

The driver of the van got out. He was another large man like all the rest in Paco's employ. However, this one wore blue hospital garb and had a big head of hair and I recognized him immediately as the man I passed in the hall at the hospice when I was searching for Jack. He disappeared around the back of the van and I heard the back doors opening. I watched enough TV to know he was carefully laying plastic sheathing so I wouldn't leave any blood after they dumped my body.

Another series of loud bangs followed and a moment later the man wheeled a long white wooden box next to the van and disappeared around back again.

Paco smiled at me. "Jack is here."

I stared at the white makeshift coffin. "How dare you steal Jack from the morgue," I yelled and punched Paco hard in the arm. "Do what you want with me, but enough is enough! You can't desecrate my friend like this. He deserves a proper burial."

Paco rubbed his arm and shot me a dirty look. "What are you talking about? Jack will have a nice funeral after he dies. It really grates on my nerves that you think you have the monopoly on him. Jack was my buddy too and helped me in ways you could never understand."

I heard a noise and saw a wheelchair appear from the back of the van and I almost fainted seeing Jack. He wore an oxygen mask and was wrapped in a thick red and green plaid blanket.

Jack waved and a tsunami of shock overwhelmed me. I started running toward him laughing, but stopped halfway when anger put on the brakes.

Exhausted, I walked the final few feet. Jack looked as jaundiced as a ripe turnip. He took off the oxygen mask and tried to whisper something.

I put my ear to his mouth. "So did my lucky hat help you win?"

Paco dabbed his eyes with his old yellow handkerchief.

I pulled the brim of the hat down tight. "Perhaps. But how can you lose when one-eyed jacks are always wild? I thought for sure you were the jockey."

Paco's men retrieved a large commercial propane patio heater from the long white box and set it up next to Peter. Two chairs followed and we sat there—three men around one saintly tree, drinking a six-pack of Bud in the sun and watching a half dozen robins hop around the grass looking for worms. Paco and I did all the talking and drinking as our friend drifted in and out of consciousness and his breathing became increasingly labored.

The afternoon remained cool, but we didn't mind because in these parts March sometimes comes in like a lion and goes out like a lamb. And so did my best friend as that frenetic heart of his began fading as the sun lengthened Peter's shadow.

At three o'clock the man from hospice came over and examined Jack with his stethoscope.

He looked at Paco and silently mouthed "It won't be long now." Leaning over, he took off the oxygen mask. "Let me get rid of this contraption," he said softly.

Paco buried his face again in the ancient handkerchief.

I knelt in front of Jack and held his head against mine, forehead to forehead. "Nine words secured paradise for the good thief. This week showed you have the same heart. Say hello to Merriam for me. I love you."

When I pulled away, his eyes were barely open and he began mouthing something. I strained to hear but my ears were too old. "It's okay, buddy," I said, hoping that would cover it.

Jack reached for me and I put my right ear closer to his mouth. "Run hard 'cause I'm betting on you."

His breathing became erratic and shallow then suddenly stopped. Babies enter this world with tight fists grasping onto life. I looked at Jack's hands now open wide in complete surrender. They felt warm and soft and I knew they were embracing God.

My eyes filled and the first gentle spring rain belonged to me.

CHAPTER FORTY-SEVEN

The friendly Russian cab driver pulled slowly up to the front of my house before I told him to stop. Thankfully, the white ranch wasn't decked out in yellow police tape and I handed the cabbie a twenty and got out. A new red Chevy Cruze sat alone in the driveway and I figured it must be Mark's rental car and hoped it didn't leak oil. I watched the picture window and caught sight of my son moving something across the living room.

Surprisingly, the back door was unlocked and I became perplexed by the missing kitchen table and chairs until I found my son building a mountain of furniture against one wall in the living room. The bonded leather couch and recliner along with the dark oak kitchen table formed the base of the mad structure. Four kitchen chairs were piled on top along with a hodgepodge of end tables, couch pillows, table lamps, and oddly, the three boxes of Cheerios I snagged at Market Basket last week for two bucks. Mark had perfect hearing, but kept his back to me and worked to find a slot for a brass wall clock he removed from the white wall. The screw left behind looked lonely.

"If you're trying to circle the wagons, I think you have the wrong wall," I said, pointing to the picture window and front door. "I can help you move it and then we can barricade the back door."

Mark stopped mid-motion but didn't turn around. His blue denim shirt and dungarees were neatly pressed and far from the kid I raised who thought the hamper was where you retrieved clothes in a pinch. I could tell he wasn't exaggerating about running; he looked trim and fit.

"I ordered a dumpster this afternoon and it'll be here in morning," he said. "I thought we could get away with a ten-yard container, but you're such a pack rat we'll need a twenty." He turned around and tried to contain his shock at my appearance.

"What on earth," Mark stuttered. "Did you trade in all your clothes at some freak secondhand store? And what is with that haircut?"

I laughed and spun around so my son could get the full effect. "I think I finally broke this suit in and given the action it's seen, we should auction it off."

Mark ignored me and pointed back at the pile of furniture. "All this stuff is trash. Linda can help you pick out new stuff when you finally move. Although with the jail time you're facing, you can bunk with your grandson." Mark looked at me and his face appeared flushed.

I jumped forward, grabbed his arm. "You talk in riddles sometimes. Is Linda pregnant?

He pulled away. "Don't be ridiculous, Dad. I don't leave anything up to chance."

I pulled on my lower lip and swallowed hard. "I see the apple doesn't fall far from the tree. I'm sorry."

Mark ignored the apology and his blue eyes narrowed. "So did you pay your bill?"

"Well, if I counted on you this place would be ashes now. Thankfully, I have other acquaintances that are more responsive than family." I glanced toward the hall. The paperwork for the certificates of deposit were in a fireproof safe in the bedroom closet. The banks were open until noon on Saturday if I wanted to take Mark's name off.

"And Jack?"

"He's gone."

"Please be more specific this time. Is he dead?"

I nodded and watched my son. It didn't feel that long ago when he was a four-year-old tyke riding a blue pedal Fisher-Price car across the hardwood floors. Merriam worried he would ruin the shine. I was so excited I didn't care; floors could be refinished.

Mark glanced at his white iPhone. "I have to make a call before we turn you in. A buddy of mine in Sacramento knows the best way to handle the process."

I walked over to inspect my pile of belongings; quite the menagerie and yet all related. "I'm not turning myself in until after Jack's funeral," I said firmly.

The worried look of a son disappeared. "That's impossible." The tone now a mix of anger and frustration.

"Why?"

"Because all this nonsense ends right now," he said and put his hands on his hips like M.B. did. "Now this is what's going to happen and I don't want any arguments. You're going to take a hot bath while I call in some food. I know takeout is crap around here compared to what we have in Novato, but I'll order us some Chinese. After we eat, I'll make my call and then we'll talk about the booking process. Then you're going to get a good night's sleep. Tomorrow morning, we'll have an early breakfast at McKinnon's and I'll take you down to the station." He looked around. "Linda and I will get the house cleaned out and put on the market in the next couple weeks."

My hands began to shake and I buried them in my pant pockets. "Wow, you have it all figured out. Can I do anything?"

Mark shook his head. "No, you've done enough to last a lifetime, never mind one week." He worked to rebalance the wall clock on a sofa cushion.

I looked over at my leather recliner acting like Atlas holding up what I once held precious. My eyes caught sight of a tear in the recliner seat where Mark had carelessly positioned an end table.

Taking a deep breath, I walked slowly to the front door and opened it wide.

"Get out of my house," I said, struggling not to yell. "Right now."

Both arms fell off my son's hips. "What?"

"You heard me. If I wasn't so tired, I'd make you put everything back in its place first, but my ears couldn't take your malarkey for that long."

My son pouted and folded his arms. "I'm not going anywhere."

"And neither will I, now or after I serve whatever sentence they throw at me. This is and will always be my house. The same house I bought with your mother when she was expecting you and the one in which you used to respect me. I see clearly now that I'll have more independence in jail than moving out west so you can babysit me and keep your conscience clear for moving so far away." I crossed the room and pulled him toward the door so hard he tripped over his feet. "I love you but I never abdicated being your father. There's no expiration date for that no matter how old I am."

Mark broke away and retrieved his wool coat from an oak rocking chair in the corner and stood in the door looking down at me. "You're tired and cranky, Dad. Get some sleep and I'll be back in the morning. You have a long journey ahead."

I smelled the expensive cedar cologne Linda went on and on about and pulled on my nose to stop a sneeze. "At least you got one thing right tonight," I said and pushed him past the threshold and slammed the door behind him.

I watched from the front window as the red Chevy Cruze drove down the street, fully expecting Mark to turn around and take another shot at reasoning with his old man. Instead, a flash of blue from the other direction caught my attention. A cruiser was barreling down the street, lights flashing but no siren.

I froze for a millisecond thinking it might be best to turn myself in now rather than put Mark through the hassle. After all, what was left to prove? Then I recalled our confrontation with Stu at the diner. *"Ah, still trying to play hero, Dennis? Well, don't worry none about coming to the funeral since you'll be in jail by then. But you won't miss much because we could hold the services in a telephone booth and still have plenty of room."*

My feet never hit the floor until I grabbed the white refrigerator door handle to brake. The back door faced the front of the street and I would be dead meat if I tried this escape route. I did a one-eighty and raced down the hall and almost overshot the bedroom. My small overnight suitcase was still sitting beside my cherry bureau along with the laminated prayer card sitting on top. Any other day for the past forty years, I would have risked a jail cell filled with starving zombies not to be separated from Jean Bradley, but no longer. In a flash, I threw the back window open, happy the screens were removed before winter.

In my mind I will forever remain seventeen and as spry as James Bond. In reality, gravity accelerated the escape and I fell out of the window into the wet grass. The sound of an approaching siren filled the air as the cruiser now had backup. I quickly closed the window and frantically searched my yard ready to play the adult version of hide and seek in the dark. My small white utility shed beckoned, but I knew unless I could shrink myself to fit under the lawnmower it provided no cover and would be an easy mark. Looking skyward, I could see two maple trees would provide a wonderful canopy to hide in a couple more months, but tonight they shivered naked. The lone pine tree between my house and Mrs. Werner's offered the only option to climb skyward undetected, but the lowest branch pointed at my neighbor's back deck as if to give advice.

I asked myself if I had the gumption to knock on her door after everything I put the poor woman through. "Any port in a storm," I said, hoping to generate the needed courage.

Running on the tip of my shoes hoping not to leave footsteps, I sprinted across the soggy lawn and up five stairs to a broad wooden deck stained redwood. The deck furniture hid underneath a big blue tarp in one corner and I threw myself down beside it. Peering back at my house, I could see hungry flashlights zigzagging along the evergreen bushes outlining my foundation. It would only be a few minutes before they expanded their search.

I crawled over to the glass slider and tried to open the door and naturally found it locked. Cupping my hands, I tried to look in, but could see nothing in the darkened kitchen. What did I expect to find anyhow? Mrs. Werner waiting with a candle and dinner?

Throwing caution to the wind, I rapped hard on the glass door two times, never expecting a response and planning a sprint to the Meissner house.

To my amazement, the kitchen light over the sink suddenly came to life and a ghostly figure of a woman wearing a white terry cloth robe appeared. She looked like Mrs. Werner except the platinum hair now stretched past her shoulders and a stark white mask enveloped her face. If she ever desired to be the Ghost of Christmas Past at the holiday festival, the role was hers. She walked cautiously toward me carrying a Louisville Slugger.

I waved my arms to get her attention and she froze like some hunted animal. When she finally came toward me with a batting stance reminiscent of mighty Yaz, I almost yelled for the cops.

The glass door opened a sliver. "You have quite the nerve," she whispered much too loud.

I ran out of fancy one-liners two days ago. "I know and if you ever loved Merriam please let me in."

She frowned and glanced over at my house glowing in blue, then back at me, and shut the door and shuffled away with the bat balanced on her right shoulder. When the kitchen light went out my heart sank and I began to crawl away, prepared to forage for dry and seedy oranges at the Meissners' house.

The slider suddenly reopened and she waved me into the dark kitchen. I took two steps toward her and the ghost stopped me.

"Take off your shoes. I just washed the floor."

I blushed in the dark and quickly kicked them off and put them by the door. The heel of my right foot felt the smooth linoleum floor and I wanted to apologize for my holey sock.

She motioned and I followed her down a short hall and into the same living room where I made up a story to steal her car. There were no Swedish jelly cookies on the coffee table for comfort. I'd have to do this cold-turkey.

"I can't believe what has become of you," she said, giving my badly wrinkled leisure suit a once-over. Deep lines creased the white facial mask. "Dennis, please tell me you have a terrible headache."

"Why?"

"Then at least I would know you are having a stroke like my husband did. He had a few mini warnings before the big one got him and acted funny too. Smile at me and let me see if one side droops."

I grabbed her hand. "Look. The fibbing stops right here and where it all began. I have been awful to you, Kirsten, and am sincerely sorry. I will gladly tell you the whole story once the cops leave."

Mrs. Werner double-checked the sash knot on her robe then looked me straight in the eye. "Answer me a question first. Did you lie about your car being in the shop the other day?"

"Yes," I replied and left it at that. No need to explain why.

"And what about News Year's Eve?"

"What about it? I loved the hot wine and the food." It was my turn to frown. "Okay, it gets lonely sometimes if you want to hear me say it. Merriam and I used to go out on New Year's Eve and—well, I appreciated the invite."

She continued to stare.

"Okay, I made it up about my son needing me too." I searched the white textured ceiling for comfort.

"Why?"

My cheeks got hot and the doorbell rang. Mrs. Werner waited.

I looked her straight in the eyes. "I was scared of the mistletoe, okay?"

"What?" she asked, looking puzzled.

There was another knock at the door

"Hide behind the love seat. Quick." She pointed.

I positioned myself behind the source of my fear and where I could peek at a rectangular gold mirror that hung on the wall reflecting the front door.

When the door opened, I sucked in my breath as the cop entered the room and I studied his features. He had short blond hair and the parentheses on either side of his mouth combined with the beginning lines in front of the ears indicated he was middle-aged. I also bet next month's social security check this macho guy lied about why he was sporting a butterfly bandage above the right eyebrow. Obviously, it was too high for a shaving accident. I guessed he bragged about chasing a linebacker-sized crook down and caught a boot in the face tackling the giant, although he would still have to explain the wrecked cruiser.

"Sorry to disturb you, ma'am. I'm Sergeant Mahoney and as you can probably tell from the news reports, we are trying to locate your neighbor Dennis Sullivan. We received a report he came back to his home tonight."

Mrs. Werner let out short nervous laugh and I knew she must be a terrible poker player. "Yes, I thought I saw him and called the station myself. But I just saw his son leave so I guess the nosy neighbor got it wrong this time."

My eyes popped. Mrs. Werner called the police?

The cop looked down and I knew he must be scanning the entry tiles looking for wet footsteps. "Nosy or not, we need your help. Your neighbor is wanted for grand larceny, accessory to robbery, assault with a dangerous weapon, and assault and battery on a police officer. And that's only page one," he said matter of fact then snickered. "Maybe when we catch him we'll charge him with capital mayhem to make the paperwork easier. It's too bad his Raisinet partner is dead or they could bunk together for the next century."

I made a fist and looked away because I wanted nothing more than to sucker-punch this cop again. Merriam might be six feet under, but I could still hear her lecturing me about turning the other cheek. Out of respect for her, I let my hand relax.

"Well, if he comes around here, I'll do you the favor and scare him to death," she said, pointing at her face. "But you need to watch your tongue about ragging on your elders because under this mask I'm the same age. You should show a little respect, Officer."

Mahoney nodded quickly in embarrassment and left.

Mrs. Werner stood in the door and watched the blue lights fade. When the coast was clear she headed my way and I jumped up to thank her and hoped she would offer me some leftovers. She did wonders with different types of cheese. My stomach proved much too anxious as something caught my foot and I tripped into Mrs. Werner waiting arms steeped in floral perfume.

I didn't dare turn my head and kept my eyes fixed on the blue velvet love seat three feet away.

CHAPTER FORTY-EIGHT

Lying low at Mrs. Werner's house for two days gave me sufficient time to plan my exit strategy at Jack's funeral and also explain the whole saga to my kind benefactor. I also thought maybe with a bit of luck as time passed, my fish story might become embellished and even make me look a bit macho. If that failed, I could always pen my memoir and entitle it *My Escapades as a Geriatric Fugitive.* Hopefully, I would garner a few laughs about the biker chick and nun disguises and sympathy for wearing the ugly disco suit.

Now my swashbuckling success looked risky, as I donned a blue hat with a tall white plume and hiked up my matching polyester pants, as we assembled across the street from St. Joseph's Church in the small rectory parking lot. The bright sun pushed the temps into the fifties this morning and kids would be running around the playground come recess time at the parochial grammar school behind the church. Trying to blend in with the high school band constituted a pretty lame last act, but Paco and Mrs. Werner argued it provided the best cloak of invisibility.

The Salem High band director approached carrying a beat-up trumpet and looking almost as uncomfortable as me. "Just so we're clear, no one in the band had any prior knowledge of this," he said as if trying to convince himself. "We're only fulfilling the last request of a retired Salem teacher and everything has been cleared with the family and the pastor. Of course they don't know you're marching too."

"Great. Do you have anything you would like me to sign so it's all on me if anything goes wrong?" I asked. "Even so, they may still wonder how I got my hands on a band uniform."

He thought about it for a moment then shook his head no and looked around to make sure no one was eavesdropping. "Like I said, we will make one attempt. If the police order us to stop, all bets are off. Got it?"

I nodded. "I know you're sticking your neck out, Ronnie. Jack said you were one of the good guys. Now I see why."

The band director blushed and handed me the trumpet. "Just hold this up to your mouth so you don't stick out. And promise me again, no matter what happens you will still carry through with your offer."

"Yes, I will fund a band scholarship in honor of Jack," I said for the tenth time since yesterday. A silver hearse pulled up in front of the church. Jack hadn't ridden in a limo since his wedding. "Starting next year, though, as my funds will be stressed for the foreseeable future."

The young blond reporter from the *Eagle-Tribune* appeared out of nowhere and recognized me, which didn't instill much confidence in my latest disguise.

"Sorry to hear about your friend."

I couldn't recall his name and didn't have time to care. "Thanks. I think he would get a kick out of the band. Did you print the story yet?" I asked, not having had an opportunity to read a newspaper in days.

The reporter laughed. "No, Jack called me back later the same day we met at the cemetery. He told me he still preferred page one, but asked me to wait until after he was gone." He shook his head in disbelief. "I thought he wanted me to rush the story, so he could take pride in the tribute to his father. Jack was vague about the reasons, but said he hoped the story would have more meaning when all the facts came out." He laughed quickly. "He also expected you to put the 'fun' in funeral, whatever that means. And please, don't even attempt to show me any additional appreciation like Jack promised."

I bit my lip, not knowing what else to say, but hoping all of Jack's known bills were settled. Hollywood couldn't have scripted this ending and I wondered how Jack had this much faith in me. Now I understood again why he played the ponies. "Well," I said, pointing at the band, "he was quite a character and wanted to go out his own way."

The reporter sighed. "And something tells me so will you." He pointed to two policemen fifty yards away. "At least I'll know where to find you tomorrow if I need some additional quotes," he said as his look grew serious. "You and Jack really stirred things up this week. Just be careful and don't do anything stupid."

"Verbally or physically?" I asked then grinned with my mouth closed so he couldn't see my teeth chattering. I watched a familiar car pull up to the curb. From the collection of junk piled high in the back seat of the tired-looking Escort, it looked like a natural ringer if they ever resurrected *The Beverly Hillbillies.*

I excused myself from the reporter and waited.

M.B. emerged from the car and must have shrunk her clothes in the wash because the black sweater and skirt fit very nicely. The boots were gone too, replaced by smart-looking shoes with a low heel.

I snuck up from behind as she finished putting on a black blazer. "Were you able to score some boxes to pack?" I asked much too happily.

M.B. twirled around and looked as cold as winter past. "What the hell do you want?" She turned away without waiting for an answer.

This was my last chance and I grabbed her by the shoulder. "I need one minute, Maggie."

She pulled away and her right hand moved to her hip so quickly I expected to be gunned down like a scene out of some old western movie. "Only my mother called me Maggie and you certainly don't have the right," she said, giving me the evil eye.

I hung my head and nodded. "Look. I'll be lucky to make it through the front doors of the church to pay my respects without being arrested and before that I need to tell you—" I stopped and took a deep breath, wishing I could ignite the air with eloquence to reach her. I looked over at Paco's shiny new black Cadillac Escalade sitting in the pastor's reserved parking space.

M.B. wasn't listening and studied the chaos of shoes, clothes hangers, and extension cords in the back seat of her car.

I widened my stance for balance. "Jack knew me better than I knew myself. I cursed him for that insight, but am eternally grateful now," I began. "He made me realize my wrong had a cascading effect, not just on you but Rosa too."

I rapped on the car roof to get M.B.'s attention and she looked up. "More importantly, Jack taught me redemption is impossible if you keep the guilt bottled up inside. The only relief I ever found since your mother died came in risking everything to make things right." I took a business card out of my pocket and handed it to her. "Forgiveness is earned, so here is my down payment."

She read the card and looked puzzled.

"That's the name and phone number of Paco. I'm sure Jack told you about him. Give him a call next week or stop by the Grog. The best time to talk with him is after breakfast. He can be a real grouch before he's had coffee. And don't ever, ever wake him up if you value your life."

"And why would I do that?" she asked sarcastically.

"Because you can tell him how you want to be paid. He can set up an account for you here with the winnings, or transfer it down to Florida if that's where you're headed. Just promise me you won't let him talk you into any gambling schemes."

"What winnings?" The confused look now mixed with anger.

"Jack left me the money he owed Leonard along with a tip on a big race. The horse came through. I had to pay off Leonard, cover Paco's commission, and mail a check to Republic Bank. Even so, you still made out great."

"All this nonsense for the two hundred bucks Jack owed me?" M.B. laughed. "And how about the other hundred you promised for renting my car, plus interest and some extra money for the winter coat?"

It was my turn to chuckle and it never felt so good. "No, I'm talking about roughly *two hundred thousand* dollars," I said slowly so I could watch the look of surprise dawn on her face. Whatever jail time I faced, that sunrise was worth every second.

"I don't want your money!" she said in a sharp raspy voice reminiscent of Janis Joplin. Tears welled up in her eyes.

The band director motioned urgently for me.

"Oh, I almost forgot." I pulled a tattered white envelope out of my back pocket. "Here's the three hundred dollars your mother gave me on a deal I should never have made. I debated a thousand times whether to donate it to charity or just burn it, but nothing felt right until now." A tickle in the back of my throat started and I turned and studied the old Ford to regain my composure. I suddenly remembered a little girl wiping the sad-looking headlights on a Dodge Polara with a checkered blue handkerchief.

"One more thing," I said, pointing to my Caddy parked behind the rectory. "Three hundred should be enough gas money to get you to Florida if you stay under sixty-five. Rosa will have plenty of room to stretch out in the back and sleep. I'll give Paco the keys and title for you."

I looked up at a crop of small white clouds making their away across the morning sky. "That Caddy is one sweet ride and please don't ever refer to it as a living room on wheels."

The band director waved again as the band lined up.

A minute later we began marching in formation.

One policeman kept the traffic stopped on Main Street while the other watched our advance, no doubt curious why the high school band would be performing at this venue. I slouched down a tad next to the other trumpet players and remained in perfect step with the line. When the procession crossed the street, we made a crisp left turn to line up with the front stairs of the church.

The doors of the church opened and the funeral procession began with two altar servers and Father McGowan in the lead. Ten feet behind, the walnut casket followed on a metal dolly accompanied by Stu and three retired teachers serving as pall bearers.

The band director gave the signal. The approved plan meant marching down the main aisle of the church in a two-by-two formation playing the "Funeral March." I knew Stu would have me arrested before we ever played the song Jack wanted so I had tipped off the drum section beforehand and they distributed the revised sheet music.

I waited until the lead flutist entered the foyer of the church. Okay, now!" I yelled.

Immediately, the band kicked into a lively rendition of "When the Saints Go Marching In" and Ronnie looked like he might have a stroke as he realized his band had been hijacked. I glanced at my partner—a beefy two-hundred-pound linebacker playing the tuba, and smiled. When the casket reached the front of the church it stopped and the pall bearers moved into a pew with the exception of Stu, who stood frozen in place next to his dead brother and seething.

The band director flew in from the side aisle with his face looking like an overripe tomato ready to burst and led the band around the casket and into the choir area on the right side of the altar.

I removed my feathered hat and stopped opposite Stu. Only Jack separated us and for as long as the good Lord lets me live, I will relish the look on Stu's face when he saw me. Lemons are sweet next to his ugly mug.

Father McGowan, a saintly-looking man in his mid-sixties who resembled Dick Clark with a thick mane of brown hair and a young face that never aged, watched from the altar wearing white vestments. He looked surprised but had a twinkle in his eye.

Back in grammar school, the music teacher used to tell me it was okay to just mouth the words, which I knew was code for being tone deaf. But today, no choir this side of heaven could keep me from belting out the final stanza.

"This is a travesty!" Stu said much too loudly in his funny soprano voice when the song ended. In the next instant, he bolted around the casket, determined to slay me.

Given the wild pace of this week, my pulse didn't quicken much and I waited until my nemesis was about three feet away before opening my mouth wide and pointing in horror at his crotch.

"Your fly's open!"

Stu put on the brakes as his eyes looked down, and I pounced and wrapped my right arm around his thick neck, putting him in a tight headlock. With my left hand I held on to his dark blue tie like I was riding a wild mechanical bull. "Come to your senses, man, we're in a church!" I pleaded and managed a quick glance up at Father McGowan. The pastor looked mesmerized like he was watching a train wreck.

Stu growled horribly and managed to punch me in the ribs twice and with his shock of red hair it must have looked like I was wrestling a runaway rocket. We spun around twice and I decided in the next revolution to quicken the dance then abruptly let go and jump out of the way. The timing proved perfect and I watched in amazement as Stu launched head first into the front of the Jack's casket with a terrible thud. He crumpled like a broken Mr. Potato Head on the tiled floor, but Jack had momentum now and began his escape down the aisle. I chased after the runaway casket and caught up with him after a half dozen pews.

The entire congregation held its breath as Stu moaned and his bleached-blond forty-something girlfriend with the orange tan shimmied out of the first pew in a tight-fitting black dress to help him. From what I could see, he wasn't bleeding any but I knew he must be hearing bells and was probably so embarrassed he wanted to jump in with Jack and hide.

Suddenly, everyone's eyes were on me as I struggled to roll the casket back up the aisle and the funeral director quickly appeared to help. "I didn't want any of this," I said in a conciliatory tone directed toward the pastor. I'm just here for Jack."

Father McGowan rushed to the edge of the altar and motioned for everyone to sit down. I slipped into the nearest pew and sat next to Kate and immediately caught a scent of some exotic perfume. She wore a navy blue skirt and white jacket and looked as beautiful as her mother. I smiled sheepishly and Jack's daughter returned a look mixed with dismay.

"I've been a priest for forty-two years and thought there were no surprises left in this life," Father McGowan boomed. He rubbed his forehead for a long moment then turned and smiled at the high school band. "I congratulate you on the lively rendition of 'When the Saints Go Marching In.' It's an appropriate song for a funeral and the fervent hope and prayers we have for our departed friend, father, and brother, Jack." He shifted his focus to Stu with furrowed brow. "I understand death triggers a range of emotions, but I need to remind you we are in God's house which requires reverence." The pastor turned and looked my way with the same scowl. "We are gathered here to celebrate Jack's life and earnestly pray perpetual light may shine upon his soul. I fear our petitions will be marred in the environment of discord we have seen this morning." The pastor hesitated and let his words sink in. "What we need now is a spirit of reconcilement. While we usually share the sign of peace with one another later in the Mass, I would ask Dennis and Stuart to lead by example and shake hands now."

"You've got to be kidding me," I mumbled, but the hard look on Father McGowan's face clearly indicated he wasn't. I looked over at Stu and he ignored the directive and kept his face buried in his hands while his girlfriend rubbed his back. I glanced up at the massive cross behind the altar and thought how He turned the other cheek no matter the wrong. I stood up and walked across the aisle and extended my hand.

Stu and his girlfriend ignored me but I remained steadfast.

"Stuart!" the priest called in a loud tone.

The hateful little man finally looked up and grabbed my hand and pumped it hard only once. "I'm going to sue you for everything you got," he whispered.

I looked at the tiny knot on his blue tie from our tussle and figured he would need a pair of scissors to cut it off. "Peace be with you," I replied.

The heavy wooden doors at the back of the church suddenly opened and the loud boom drew everyone's attention. Two policemen entered with weapons drawn. Maybe Stu had it right and travesty was the right word for this scene. To my relief, Paco raced toward them with his arms wide open. He whispered something quickly to the tall one and I was pretty sure I just made a handsome contribution to the Policemen's Association.

The funeral Mass continued and I forced myself to block out the chaos about to consume me and concentrate my thoughts and prayers for Jack. After Communion, Father McGowan walked to the head of the altar in a much more relaxed mood.

"Yesterday, Dennis called and asked if he could say a few words about Jack, who was his lifelong friend, and came to intimately witness his journey in faith." He turned to me and smiled for the first time today. "You are welcome to use the lectern, Dennis, or if you prefer stand in front of the casket as I'm sure everyone will be able to hear you."

I felt like the best man again but this time woefully unprepared without a script. I stood up and planned to make my way to the thick oak lectern for cover, but when I passed the casket I felt Jack tug on my arm and I turned around. My eyes surveyed the twenty or so people in the pews. Most I knew: a handful of retired teachers, Paco, Kate, M.B., Barbara, and Ink the tattoo artist wearing his best dress Bad to the Bones leather coat. I also spied Mark sitting next to the reporter from the *Eagle-Tribune* in the last pew. My son wore a dark suit with no tie. The little towhead boy had dark hair now, but kept the same cowlick he shared with Alfalfa.

Stu and his girl ignored me and looked down. I also noted the two policemen had strategically located themselves in front of the band where they had quick access to me.

The bulge in my throat grew.

"My wife loved this beautiful church," I said quickly and listened to my voice echo in this holy place. "Father said there is little that surprises him anymore and that was my life too until the last few days. Then I found out I didn't know my best friend, wife, son, or even myself. Thankfully, Jack believed my blindness didn't have to remain permanent." I blinked to hold back the tears. "The man who thinks he can and the man who thinks he can't are both right. I understand why now."

I touched the casket and couldn't help but wonder if it was empty and wanted to shake it to make sure. Jack had escaped everything up to now, why not death too?

"I'm not here to lie and say Jack was a saint; few of us really are and he would be mad if I fibbed about him now. No, we all have our faults and my buddy had some real whoppers." I scanned the church and locked eyes with Kate. "Jack might have been a shop teacher, but he knew and also feared the famous Shakespeare quote: 'The evil that men do lives after them; the good is oft interred with their bones.'"

I took an old Rockingham Park race program Paco gave me out of my back pants pocket and laid it on top of the casket. "Jack never shrunk from long odds, whether it was on a horse or a friend. He held on when others would have given up because he always believed in tomorrow's potential. An overused strength can also be a weakness and in Jack's case it brought him bankruptcy and heartbreak to his family. After spending the last few days with him, I can sincerely attest it also gave him the courage to overcome excruciating pain in the hope of making a real difference in the lives of those he loved." I glanced over at Father McGowan and smiled. "And Saint Peter showed him how to persevere in his quest to walk on water." I coughed to clear my throat. "After the tribute to his father in the cemetery, I'm sure his dad is telling him today how much it meant to him. In a similar fashion, I know how much he yearned to touch his daughter and wife and seek their forgiveness." I found Kate's eyes and smiled. "Only then was he prepared to meet his Maker and seek His."

The police began to stir and I knew it was time to close.

"I want to also thank the Salem High School marching band for coming to celebrate my friend's life today. Jack and I promised each other long ago after too many beers that the surviving friend would oversee 'When the Saints Go Marching In.' I wish I hadn't won that bet."

I looked at Jack's brother and nodded. "Stuart, I apologize for hurting you. The policemen have been extremely generous in allowing me to remain through the Mass, but I'll leave now so you can say your last goodbyes."

A few kids in the band moaned and I waved for them to be quiet. "That's okay, it really is. Jack and I already said our goodbyes many times over the past week. But for those of you that do go to the cemetery, I know Jack requested 'Amazing Grace' be sung at his burial. If you can listen to those lyrics without tearing up, then indeed that is a travesty."

An awkward silence followed. I had never sung a solo in my life and promised myself never to try, but my tongue would not be denied this one.

"Amazing Grace, how sweet the sound,
That saved a wretch like me,
I once was lost but now am found
Was blind, but now I see."

I leaned over and kissed the top of the casket. "You were right. Peter is quite an inspiration," I whispered. "Rest in peace, my friend."

CHAPTER FORTY-NINE

Ink put the stainless steel needle gun down and turned off the stereo blasting heavy metal music which had successfully swallowed most of my occasional wimpy moans caused by a sixteenth-of-an-inch needle.

A small amount of blood pooled at the tip of the three-inch upside down cross on the inside of my right forearm. The gray-haired tattoo artist noticed it too and wiped it away quickly with a clean cotton pad. Peeling off purple latex gloves, Ink smiled for the first time in an hour. "Normally, I don't do repeats, but I made an exception given the circumstances so you and Jack are now officially twins." He grabbed my arm and inspected it up close. "I have to be careful tattooing people your age because the skin can be as thin as parchment paper. Luckily, you have more fat than Jack did so you'll bruise less." He felt my wrist and screwed up his face. "Your pulse is racing."

I peered inside my white T-shirt. The pair of black flies with long fangs looked like they were settling into their new home on my left breast as the bleeding had stopped.

Ink got up from the low wooden stool and walked a few feet to a small coffee machine on a table in the corner next to two red plastic chairs reserved for clients or support buddies. The walls in the studio were covered with posters of rock concerts at the Boston Garden in the early 1970s: Led Zeppelin, The Rolling Stones, Moody Blues, Jimi Hendrix.

"How did you come up with the name 'Color My World' for the tattoo parlor?" I asked in an innocent voice, not wanting to let on I knew the soft rock tune by Chicago of the same name and that it was definitely much too mellow for a member of the Bad to the Bone gang.

The tattoo artist poured steaming coffee into two Styrofoam cups and let out a short snicker, like he'd been asked the same question a hundred times before. "My girlfriend talked me into it and she's a marketing pro. It turns out the name attracts new clients, especially girls who want to get their first tattoo." He pointed out a small window overlooking Route 28. "There's a bridal shop across the street and the owner is cool. A lot of stag parties begin or end here."

Ink handed me a cup of black coffee and made me wonder for the tenth time today where Rosa and M.B. were living now. "Guess I should have told the paper about my tattoos this morning so you could get some free press."

"Why are they doing another story?" he said into the cup. "I must admit you and Jack looked pretty good on page one last week, though I wish they had a picture when you were dressed up as biker chicks. I had the opportunity to take one with my iPhone too, but we were busy trying to get you past the cops." He snickered. "I would have framed that one on my wall." He sat down beside me and inspected the tattoo gun. "I think the 'Curtain Call' headline said it all. By the way, how long did the police interview you to get the full story?"

I took a sip of coffee and relished the strong taste without cream and sugar and it stood as a daily reminder of my new raw outlook. "Well, it took a legal pad and two cheap ballpoint pens for me to get it all down, but I had plenty of time during my twenty-one days of observation when I wasn't being poked and probed to review it all. I was also examined by a number of well-meaning doctors from competing camps. One group thought Jack kidnapped me and with his dominant personality, succeeded in brainwashing me. When I told one of the young therapists I was no Patty Hearst, she had to Google it to understand the reference."

I took another gulp of the strong coffee and got up and handed my new buddy a small wad of twenties for the two tattoos. Ink smiled and grabbed my left arm. "Still plenty of canvas here after your next adventure. Come back soon and we'll design something crazy bad." He winked. "Remember you get Jack's discount too."

The deliciously warm April sun hit my face as I opened the door and made my way down a long flight of wooden stairs. Walking to the small lot out front, I took a deep breath of the spring air which smelled of anticipation. To my surprise, I didn't need to call Kirsten for a ride home as Mark stood next to a white Prius dressed in blue jeans, a green windbreaker, and white and blue running shoes.

"Hey, I know you!" I said, smiling.

"Hello, Dad," Mark replied, looking up at the tattoo parlor. "I'm not going to ask what you're doing here because I'm too tired for another fight."

"So we'll have the big reveal later then." I read the worry in his eyes despite the polite smile and wrapped my arms around him and gave him a big hug. To my surprise, he wrapped his arms around me too. The last time we embraced like this was just after his mother died and we held on to each other just as long this time.

Mark pulled a fresh pack of Juicy Fruit gum from his jacket. "Hope you'll accept this as a peace offering, because it's about all I can afford at the moment." He let out a quick laugh and handed it to me. "I still can't believe that dear neighbor of yours lent me half the bail money. Yesterday I thought you'd be in jail until the trial."

I stared at the pavement and noticed a few determined sprigs of grass growing up through the cracks. "Mrs. Werner—I mean Kirsten—has been a good friend and I treated her atrociously. I intend to make it up to her, but it still bothers me you two had to finance my freedom. I have enough savings."

"Dad, you have a lot of legal fees coming up and if we're not careful you'll be learning to like cat food," he said, rubbing his chin. "I'm also afraid you did a Jack by giving your car to that woman."

I grabbed my son's right arm and looked him straight in the eye. "That is the crux of the matter, Mark. Jack is a verb and I'm sick of being a noun. Look, I'm done with going along to get along. We need to talk, and I mean really talk, and we haven't had a chance with me holed up in jail and you working your butt off to get me out." I glanced at a row of pear trees lining the parking lot. Their branches were full of buds and ready to pop with the next warm day. "I have my reasons regarding Maggie."

"What am I going to do with you, Dad?"

My son looked anxious and I recognized the traits he inherited. "Well, now that you bailed me out, I guess anything you want. Although I was hoping we could get a bite to eat first. I know this tiny diner in Lawrence that has a killer lunch and it's under new management. I've had a hankering for their onion rings for the past three weeks."

"I'm glad you're in such good spirits, but the road ahead has some big potholes. It took every legal trick I knew and some intense negotiation to get the battery and assault charges against Mahoney dropped."

"Yeah, I figured as much. Jack warned me about that."

"You're lucky Stu didn't press charges either."

I smiled. "Well, at least not yet. Knowing him, he's probably saving up his therapy bills so he has proof of the pain and anguish I caused. At least Father McGowan saw the whole thing go down."

"Well, I had a long talk with the prosecutor too. The good news is you'll probably escape serving any jail time, but the community service will be significant. My guess is at least two thousand hours."

"That's fine. At least it will jump-start my plan to do some good, plus it will get me out of the house."

"I intend to ask the judge if you can fly out west and spend a week with us first. Even if I can't talk you into selling the house again we still need to talk about the future. You're still three thousand miles away."

"I'm not the one that decided to move across the country. If you're so worried, why don't you move back here?"

"Maybe it's not too late to revoke your bail money," he said with half a smile, but the tone was serious.

I stroked his arm. "See, you like your independence too. Wonder where you picked up that up? Tell you what, I'll come out and visit if you make me a promise."

Mark studied me warily. "You used to be so predictable."

"That's the nicest compliment you've paid me in some time." I grabbed his arm. "When I visit, I want to take a hike over the Golden Gate Bridge and explain everything. I think it will help you understand your father a little more and why what I did for Maggie was not a handout. I read the hike is under two miles and if we need more time, we can always turn around and do it again." I opened the pack of Juicy Fruit gum and offered him a stick. "And if it's too much and you want to jump, there's crisis hotlines along the way."

"What about Linda?"

I frowned. "What about her?"

"I want you to make an honest effort to mend fences with her. You need to spend some time with her."

"Sure, as long as it's not over sushi. I have enough stomach problems without courting parasites. I'll take her out for a burger and a beer."

"C'mon, Dad. You know she's a vegetarian."

I shook my head. "Okay, then a big piece of fried dough with lots of cinnamon and powdered sugar and then some maple walnut ice cream. I want to see her eat something that requires a ton of napkins and a ten-mile run to burn the calories off." I chewed on my gum for a moment. "I have to find out for myself what you see besides the blonde hair and the California tan."

Mark frowned for a micro second. "That's not fair. She has a lot of substance."

I gave him a soft push and laughed. "Wow, that's a pretty poor sales job if you ask me," I said.

He stuck the stick of gum in his mouth. "I remember as a kid going through all your coat pockets when you were at work looking for Juicy Fruit like it was some sort of buried treasure. All these years later and I still don't know what flavor this is or why it's the only gum you chew."

"I can see we'll need more than one hike for you to understand all the secrets of your father."

He laughed and glanced at my head. "We can begin with that hat."

I pointed at my special brown corduroy hat. "This is Jack's lucky hat and I'm testing out the premise that life can be aces if you try. Treat me right and maybe I'll leave it to you when I'm gone."

Mark rolled his eyes. "Yeah, that and five bucks will get you a nice cappuccino."

"See what I mean? I hear Linda talking again."

"Let's agree to a ceasefire for the rest of the day, okay, Dad?"

I extended my hand and we shook on it. "Mind if I drive?" I asked, pointing at the Prius. "I'm in the market for a new car."

We both laughed nervously and I was surprised when he handed me the keys.

I'm not sure if Ink watched our departure, but if so, he would have been impressed with how carefully I obeyed all the rules of the road. This afternoon, I intended to borrow the car and visit the florist. I planned to buy a nice bouquet of daffodils for Kirsten and hand deliver them along with the promise to take her out for a nice Italian dinner in Boston's North End. Next, I would visit the cemetery and plant some heather in front of Jean's grave, since it flowers in the winter and would be a good reminder spring comes for all of us if you wait long enough. I also planned to bury her memorial card there alongside the spare Polara key. From now on, I would recite the Lord's Prayer as it was meant. Not to ease my guilt, but in thanksgiving to the One who made me realize even in the depths of despair, hope is still possible if you find the courage.

And who could leave the cemetery without visiting Merriam and Jack? I would brighten their day with yellow tulips too. And before I left, I planned to ask Jack to put a good word in for me with the gate keeper and our special patron saint. Maybe if I showed some real spunk down here and ran like a One-Eyed Jack being pursued by a swarm of mayflies, I would win by a nose when my time came. Jack and I were betting on it.

ACKNOWLEDGMENTS

Every book has a back story. The motivation for *Chasing Mayflies* came out of the experience of watching my father lose a courageous battle with lung cancer in 2009. He exemplified for his six children, two dozen grandchildren, and growing clan of great-grandchildren what a Christ-filled life looks like. Although my father was the polar opposite of Jack in the novel, I know he would have a good laugh at some of the antics in the story and also recognize some of its bittersweet content. And in full transparency, my mother, brothers, and sisters did break Dad out of hospice the day before he died—but legally. So, to Mom (Grace), Christine, Paul, Jude, Joe, and Mary: I never felt closer to you than in helping Dad to his heavenly home.

Chasing Mayflies experienced its own five-year saga on its journey to publication. The terrain proved exceedingly difficult at times and the weather fickle. But as Mark Twain once stated, "If you don't like the weather in New England now, just wait a few minutes," which I regularly did. Even so, the book and its characters grew more resilient with each passing season and new revision. While I would like to recognize a few extraordinary partners in this magnificent journey, first and foremost, I thank God. He shows mountains can indeed be moved if you have "faith as a grain of mustard seed."

I thank my wife and best friend, Robin, for her love, support, and eagle-eyed proofreading skills. I know how much she sacrificed when I had to travel extensively in my career. That she allowed her work-obsessed husband to regularly disappear into what John Gardner defined as a "fictional dream state," to write, edit, polish, and repeat "seventy times seven" is a testament to our forty-year marriage. Robin, I owe you all the nature hikes and kayaking you desire.

Heaven blessed Robin and I with daughters Heather and Taylor and grandsons Nolan and Wesley. I will never forget Heather barraging me when she was in high school to get back to writing and not abandon the muse who inspired my youth. Same holds true for Taylor, as she provided constant support and called me many a night on her way home from work to discuss next steps. Along with Heather, they shared the role of chief editors and marketing strategists for this and previous works. I also highly value the creative insight and support of Heather's husband, Michael Beaudoin, whom I love as a son. Together with Robin, they make an unbeatable marketing and street team.

I am also indebted to literary agent Kimberly Shumate for her early support of *CM* and two other novels and sharing with me the lessons of a tough and competitive industry. I appreciate the feedback received from the Amazon Breakthrough Novel Contest in 2014 when *Chasing Mayflies* reached quarterfinal placement. Lessons learned were then incorporated into the manuscript and propelled it to runner-up status for the Tuscany Prize. However, the true award proved to be the honor of working with award-winning editor Natalie Hanemann and bringing the novel to its full potential. Special thanks also to Peter Mongeau, founder of Tuscany Press, for his insights and Max Perkins-like editing style.

I am also grateful to Jesse Greever and Christopher Dixon at eLectio Publishing for their phenomenal support in first publishing the novel. I am very excited and privileged to join the Black Rose Writing family and owe a debt of gratitude to Reagan Rothe for re-releasing the work.

Lastly, I appreciate the kind wishes and encouragement from family and friends, including my extended global family at MilliporeSigma.

I sincerely hope you enjoyed this memorable "R.I.P" roaring, hilarious journey and take its message to heart. I look forward hearing from you on my author site at vincentdonovanbooks.com

NOTE FROM THE AUTHOR

Word-of-mouth is crucial for any author to succeed. If you enjoyed *Chasing Mayflies*, please leave a review online—anywhere you are able. Even if it's just a sentence or two. It would make all the difference and would be very much appreciated.

Thanks!
Vincent Donovan

Thank you so much for reading one of our **Humor** novels.
If you enjoyed our book, please check out our recommendation
for your next great read!

Parrot Talk by David B. Seaburn

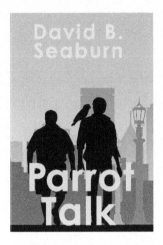

"...a story of abandonment, addiction, finding oneself—all mixed in with
tear-jerking chapters next to laugh-out-loud chapters."
—Tiff & Rich

Made in United States
North Haven, CT
11 February 2022

15988201R00178